D0193187

Also by Louise Shaffer

The Three Miss Margarets
The Ladies of Garrison Gardens

FAMILY ACTS

BALLANTINE BOOKS

NEW YORK

Family Acts

A NOVEL

Louise Shaffer

Family Acts is a work of fiction. Names, characters, places, and incidents are the products of the author's imagination or are used fictitiously. Any resemblance to actual events, locales, or persons, living or dead, is entirely coincidental.

Published in the United States by Ballantine Books, an imprint of The Random House Publishing Group, a division of Random House, Inc., New York.

BALLANTINE and colophon are registered trademarks of Random House, Inc.

LIBRARY OF CONGRESS CATALOGING-IN-PUBLICATION DATA

Shaffer, Louise.
Family acts: a novel/Louise Shaffer.
p.   cm.
ISBN: 978-1-4000-6063-4
1. Theaters—Conservation and restoration—Fiction.   2. Female friendship—Fiction.
3. Georgia—Fiction.   I. Title.
PS3569.H3112F36 2007   813'.54—dc22   2007015866

Printed in the United States of America on acid-free paper

www.ballantinebooks.com

2 4 6 8 9 7 5 3 1

FIRST EDITION

Book design by Dana Leigh Blanchette

For my mother, whose copy of the complete works of Shakespeare—compiled in 1936—has been my constant companion throughout the writing of this book. And for my husband, whose love of the theater inspired it.

Part One

CHAPTER 1

New York City 2006

Some genius at the Academy of Television Arts & Sciences decided that that they should do a tribute to Katie's mother at the daytime Emmy Awards ceremony that spring. At first, the timing was a mystery to Katie. Her mother, Rosalind Harder, had died four years earlier, and she'd retired three years before that. In the world of television, seven years was a lifetime. But when she thought about it, Katie understood. Daytime television was in trouble, audiences were shrinking, and two shows teetered on the brink of cancellation. There wasn't a hell of a lot for the academy to celebrate, so why not take a few minutes to remind everyone of the good old days when Rosalind Harder had over forty million loyal fans tuning in to watch her play Tess Jones on the massively popular soap opera *All Our Lives?*

They asked Katie, who worked as a writer for *All Our Lives,* to speak at the tribute. Katie dutifully penned a ten-minute speech that captured the charismatic woman who had been her mother, while not dwelling on the fact that the late Rosalind Harder could also be, in the words of one of her harried producers, "the diva from the dark side." When she finished writing the speech, even Katie realized it was one of her best efforts. Which meant it was damn good—her standards for her own work tended to be pretty brutal.

In honor of the great event, Katie had her nails done, renewed her prescription for her contact lenses so she wouldn't have to wear her glasses, and, in a moment of wild abandon, bought a new evening dress. The saleswoman admitted it was an "unusual" shade of green, but she assured Katie that the skirt was slenderizing. Shopping wasn't one of Katie's skills. Normally her ensemble for awards shows consisted of her trusty black chiffon palazzo pants paired with a loose-fitting tunic when she was feeling chunky, and a glittery chemise tucked in at the waist when she was feeling more svelte. But, carried away by the excitement of the moment, and the saleswoman's flattery, she forked over a small fortune for the gown and took it home, telling herself that it would look better on camera than it did in real life.

But two mornings before the Emmy Awards show, she woke up in the throes of a full-blown anxiety attack—something that had never happened to her before—and when she finally started breathing again, she knew there was no way she could face standing up in front of the entire daytime industry, plus whoever might be watching at home. So in spite of the new gown and the snazzy manicure, she conned Teddy Raider, her mother's longtime agent, who also represented Katie, into delivering the speech in her place. On the great night, Katie planned to sit in the audience with the rest of the *All Our Lives* writing staff and listen to someone else deliver her words. That was what she had been doing most of her adult life; Katie was one of five dialogue writers working for the show her mother had made famous.

Being a scriptwriter in daytime television wasn't exactly a glamorous gig. The writing stars in the wonderful world of soap opera were the head writers, who thought up the stories that played out for months—or sometimes years—on the shows. Those who turned out the daily scripts, like Katie, were the invisible drones. The only reason people in the industry knew the name Katie Harder was because of her high-profile mother. So, on Emmy night, when she took her place in the auditorium of Radio City Music Hall, Katie expected to be, as she always was, anonymous. She and her colleagues were relegated to the bad seats at the back of the auditorium because no one ever wanted a picture of the writers.

♫

The tribute to Rosalind Harder took place halfway through the show, at the moment when the highest number of viewers would be watching. The testimonial kicked off with the actor who had played her last husband trotting out onstage to inform everyone that they would now be treated to a montage of scenes from her oeuvre as the star of *All Our Lives*. The lights dimmed, a huge screen descended onto the Radio City Music Hall stage, and Katie waited in the darkness with the rest of the audience to watch her mother.

Suddenly, there was Rosalind on the screen in front of them, doing her first show; a lanky, eager girl with a mane of silver-blond hair, amazingly blue eyes—her press releases always claimed they were turquoise—legs designed for the era's short skirts, and a set of cheekbones the camera loved. She seemed to burst through the screen, bigger than life, and the familiar light, high voice filled the music hall.

For the next few minutes, as clips from one scene followed another, the audience watched the adorable youngster grow—God forbid anyone say Rosalind had aged—into an adored icon. Katie closed her eyes, knowing the sentimentalists around her would assume she was grieving for the loss of her mother.

The video finally ended, and as the entire house rose to its feet for the obligatory standing ovation, the screen showed a still shot of Rosalind's first entrance as Tess. When the audience sat down again, she was frozen in front of them in her heyday, forever young and beautiful, and oh so incredibly alive.

The final item in the festivities was Teddy reading Katie's speech. Without wanting to, Katie felt herself sit up straight, her manicured nails digging into the upholstered arms of her seat. There was a pause while a mic was set up in the center of the stage, and then Teddy walked out and stood in front of the image of Rosalind.

The speech was as good as Katie had thought it was, and by the time Teddy finished it, there wasn't a dry eye in the hall. Satisfied, Katie slouched down into the bustier that made up the top part of her green gown, and relaxed. She'd done her best and now the ordeal was over. She could sit in obscurity through the rest of the show. After it was over, Teddy would find her, and they'd go to the must-attend parties. She'd keep her head clear for the political schmoozing, and then drink champagne until she could get the hell out and go home.

As one of the two most successful agents working in daytime, Teddy had other clients he should have been sucking up to, but going to the Emmys with Katie was a tradition he'd started when she was twelve. She'd needed an adult to sit in the audience with her while she watched her mother win that year, and he had offered his services. The fact that he still kept the tradition going was one of the many reasons why Katie loved him mindlessly.

Teddy walked off the stage, and Katie looked up at the screen, waiting for her mother's picture to fade so daytime television could get on with the business of giving itself awards. But Rosalind's face didn't fade. Instead, the talk show host who was acting as master of ceremonies walked up to the microphone and said, "I know we've all been moved by this fabulous memorial for one of our great leading ladies. Before we move on, I'd like to ask someone special to come up here. Ladies and Gentlemen, Katie Harder, our beloved Rosalind's daughter." Then three handheld cameras appeared out of a nightmare and descended on Katie, who realized that someone somewhere had decided to go for an unscripted TV moment. At the same second, she realized just how hideous her dress was.

There was no way out. Grinning like cold death, she sucked herself up in the bustier so her little rolls of underarm fat smoothed out, and hoisted herself out of her seat. Grabbing a handful of her heavy satin skirt—what the hell had possessed her to deck herself out in fungus-green with a train, for God's sake?—she stumbled down the aisle which had suddenly become longer than the Bataan Death March, and somehow managed to get herself onto the stage and behind the mic. And there she was for all the world to see, a troll standing in front of, and in contrast to, her glorious mother.

According to Katie's last run-in with the scale, she was nine pounds overweight. Her dark brown hair had never been tamed by brush or man, and her brown eyes were blinking behind the glasses she'd worn because she wasn't going to be appearing on the stage that night. Only, now she was. There was applause—considerably less than there had been for Rosalind's montage, she noted—and then the place got quiet. Still hanging on to her death grin, she racked her brain to think of something to say. It had to be something charming and loving about her mother, and the industry that had been so good to both of them. And she had to do it now, on her feet, without her computer to hide behind.

The mic hadn't been adjusted to her height of 5'3". She reached up on tiptoe, risking leaving the bustier behind, leaned in, and said to the crowd in Radio City Music Hall and however many millions of her mother's fans watching at home, "Hi. I'm much prettier in person."

CHAPTER 2

New York City 2006

"Explain again why you're wearing that getup," Teddy said. The awards ceremony was over, and *All Our Lives* had lost in every category. Now Katie and Teddy were sitting in a coffee shop on Seventh Avenue catching their breath before beginning the ritual partying, and Teddy was eyeing her gown as if it had grown in a petri dish. Her agent was in his early sixties and tall, with a face that was still boyish, except for a pair of world-weary dark eyes. There wasn't much he hadn't seen, and it had been a long time since anything had surprised him. In spite of that, he was the kindest person Katie knew.

"The saleswoman said the cut gave me stature," Katie said.

"Hunt her down and shoot her," Teddy advised.

"I'm working on it. And speaking of hunting down and shooting, what sadistic son of a bitch decided to ambush me tonight?"

"You didn't know they were going to ask you to talk?"

"You did?"

"This afternoon. The show ran short at the dress rehearsal and they thought it would be touching if you did the unrehearsed-words-from-the-heart thing. Someone was supposed to call you so you could be ready to fake it. They didn't?"

"If they had, do you think I would have repeated the same speech I gave you, word for word?"

"I thought that was odd."

"I couldn't think of anything else. I was too busy watching my entire life flash past my eyes."

A man, probably a tourist, had noticed that she and Teddy were tricked out in fancy dress and was gaping at them. Katie favored him with a regal little wave, and he reddened and turned away. No doubt about it, he was a tourist.

"It was a terrific speech," Teddy said. "Rosalind would have been pleased."

"That's me, I live to please. Or is it 'appease'?"

"That sounded bitter. Want to tell Teddy about it?"

"It's just . . . I don't know . . . the night . . . humiliation in a public forum," she lied. Then she added more honestly, "Seeing Mother up there on the screen."

Softhearted Teddy's eyes filled. "I miss her too, Katie," he said softly. Which wasn't exactly what she'd meant, but she let it go.

"Did she ever tell you how much she hated it when people called me Katie?" she asked.

"But it's your name."

Katie drew in a breath and intoned, " 'Well have you heard, but something hard of hearing: They call me Katharina that do talk of me.' "

"Excuse me?"

"Don't get the reference? Act Two, Scene One, *The Taming of the Shrew* by William Shakespeare—and you call yourself a theatrical agent."

"I call myself a working stiff who makes his living representing people who can quote Shakespeare. I leave the artsy stuff to clients like you and your mom."

"Mother always wanted to play Katharina—she's the shrew. Mother had a thing for Shakespeare, but I think she was afraid she didn't have the acting chops for most of his roles. For some reason, Katharina was the one part she was sure she could pull off."

Teddy sighed. "She was on my case all the time to get her stage work. Back when she and I were kids, working live was still the gold standard. But you know how theater people are about soap actors. The only places that were interested in her were out in East Nowhere."

"And East Nowhere wanted her because she was a soap star. She must have been pissed."

"Hurt, was more like it," Teddy said reproachfully. "Rosalind had her dreams like everyone else."

"So she named me for the most famous ball breaker in English literature. Can we get out of here? We have bad parties to attend, and these sandals are turning my feet into hamburger."

"There's something I want to say to you first. Before I get too drunk." He hesitated. "It's time for us to re-sign your contract."

"Hand me a pen."

"No. I'm cutting you loose, Katie."

"What?" She was pretty sure she hadn't heard him right, but her stomach lurched anyway.

"Actually, I want you to cut me loose. I want you to fire me."

"Why the hell would I do that?" Katie tried to keep the panic out of her voice. She couldn't imagine her life without Teddy; he'd been a fixture in it since he was a struggling young agent and she was a baby. "Have they been bitching about me over at the show? If I did anything to make them mad . . ."

"Everybody loves you at the show."

"Then what did I do wrong?" She was going to start crying if she didn't watch it. She swallowed hard.

"It's not you, it's me."

"The classic break-up line. Damn it, I expect to get that from straight guys who aren't old enough to be my father."

"Uncle, please." Teddy patted her hand across the table, and Katie's tears threatened to spill. "Now listen carefully, because tomorrow I'll be kicking myself for letting one of my best cash cows go." He drew a deep breath. "Daytime television is circling the drain—"

"They've been saying that since Mother started in the business."

"When your mother started, there were twice as many shows on the air as there are now. By the time you started writing, we had eleven; now we're down to eight. And no one's developing new ones."

"People will always want to watch soaps."

"That's not what the ratings say. Did you see the numbers for *All Our Lives* last week?"

She hadn't, because when things got bad, the producers stopped letting the worker bees see the reports.

"*All Our Lives* is in the toilet, sweetie. I give it another year, maybe two, before they pull it."

Katie swallowed again and forced herself to smile. "I'll get another show."

"You could. But why?"

"There's this thing I have about eating regularly, and I have to pay your commissions." That was his cue to laugh—or at least chuckle. It didn't happen. "Teddy, lighten up. You're scaring me."

"You're too young to be stuck in daytime. Most of my clients have been doing it for so long, they can't go anywhere else. But you've got years ahead of you."

"Daytime is what I do."

"You hate it."

"When did I say that? I never said that." But then, in spite of all the swallowing and smiling, she was crying. Three tears had splattered down onto her fungus-green bust and were staining the satin.

"Sweetie, stop. You'll look like shit." Teddy leaned in and tried to blot her gown with a paper napkin. The stain spread. "Every time I talk to you, you're kvetching about how they've dumbed down the scripts. Remember how mad you got about the talking snake?"

"That was a dream sequence," she said, defending the story that had sent her into Vesuvius mode.

"You wrote dialogue for a reptile, cookie. And what about the new actors they've hung around your neck? They just hired a guy from that reality TV show."

"He's only playing a small part."

"In real life, he repairs refrigerators. He's going to make those models you've been writing for look like Sean Penn." Teddy made a try at drying her face. "The soaps never were great art, but there was a time when the suits running them had balls. Remember when Rosalind did the story about breast cancer? Nobody was talking about stuff like that on TV, daytime or prime time, and the sponsors were freaking, but—"

"But *All Our Lives* did the story anyway," Katie recited the tale by heart. "And they made history, and mother got her second Emmy nomination. Your point?"

"There's no way anyone in the industry would take a chance like that today. And you know it."

She *did* know it, but if she admitted that he was right, her whole world was up for grabs.

"Besides," Teddy went on gently, "it's time for you to stop taking Rosalind's hand-me-downs."

"I'm not! That is so not fair."

"You work for her show; it's the only job you've ever had. You inherited me. You don't even know what could be out there for you." Teddy made another swipe at her face. "Rosalind's been dead for four years, sweetie. It's time."

He really loved her. No one would ever care this much about her again. She took the paper napkin from him and blew her nose. "Okay, I'll work on a couple of spec scripts for a sitcom—"

"No."

"I can do it in my spare time—"

"You don't need another job. Not right now. You need to work on your own stuff."

And then she understood. "This is about that goddamn play, isn't it?" she demanded. He didn't answer, but he didn't have to.

The year she'd turned thirty, depressed by her upcoming birthday, and yeah, okay, by her not-exactly-skyrocketing career, she'd written a play. An actress who worked on the soap had wanted to do the lead, and they'd managed to put together an off-Broadway production that got good reviews. Katie was even nominated for an OBIE. That one tiny success had morphed her once hard-nosed agent into the stage father from hell.

"That play was good, Katie," he said now.

"There's no money in writing plays."

"There is if you have one done on Broadway. Or if someone picks it up for a feature."

"It wasn't commercial enough for Broadway. Everyone said so." She tried to sound firm, as if that ended the conversation.

"It was your first shot and you had a hit. You've got to keep trying."

"I don't want to," she said. It was a monster lie, but she couldn't tell him the truth.

"You're saying that because you're burned out. You need to clear the soap out of your head. I want you to take some time off."

"Okay, whoever you are, beam yourself up to the mother ship and send back my agent. He's the guy with the receding hairline who has a grasp on reality."

"Cute. Don't try to get around me. "

"This conversation is not working for me—okay?"

"No. Not okay. If you won't fire me, I'll fire you. "

"Jesus."

"You need to do your own thing, as we used to say when I was a kid back in the Paleolithic Age. And you need an agent who can help you."

"Teddy, stop this, please."

"I do daytime. That's where I have my contacts. I don't have juice anywhere else." He took her hands in his. "When we started talking about your mom, that's when I knew I had to say all this. Rosalind was an unhappy lady, sweetie. I don't want that for you."

She pulled her hands away. "If you fire me, I'll just find another agent who'll rep me in daytime."

"Okay, tell me this. Why did you write that play if you love what you're doing so much?"

He deserved at least a piece of the truth—if she could find a way to say it that didn't sound totally unbalanced. "Mother never talked about the past; my father, her family, all the little details a kid might want to know—those topics were the emotional third rail in our house. But one time when I was complaining because she'd named me after Katharina in *The Taming of the Shrew*, she told me she was called Rosalind after the character in *As You Like It*.

"Shakespeare again."

"Always. And she told me that giving the kids the names of Shakespearean characters was a tradition in my family." Katie shrugged so he wouldn't see how important the next part was to her. "I guess I figured if I wrote a play maybe that would be lucky for me. You know—calling on the spirits of my ancestors."

"And they came through for you," Teddy said gently.

"Once. For a very small off-Broadway production. Now can we please get going? If I'm going to be looking for a new job, we might as well start kissing ass now." She started to stand, but he grabbed her by the wrist.

"Katie, have I ever let you down?"

"No. But—"

"No buts. I want you to promise me you'll think about what I said." His eyes were so serious—there wasn't even a hint of a smile in them. "I'll think."

But it's not going to change anything, she told herself.

CHAPTER 3

New York City 2006

The next morning Katie woke up without her usual day-after-the-Emmys hangover. She'd been so determined to prove to Teddy—and herself—how happy she was that she'd stayed sober. When hammered at industry parties, she had been known to trash the life's work, and Teddy always remembered every word of her rants. She didn't want to give him any ammo until she was absolutely sure that he'd gotten over his I'm-firing-you-for-your-own-good thing. So she'd been on a mission to adore everyone—the writers she worked with, the network suits, even the idiot repairman/actor from the reality show. Instead of going for her usual early exit, she'd insisted on partying until the bitter end, and had fallen into bed at four in the morning.

When she finally emerged from her bedroom the next day, it was ten o'clock. She never stayed in bed that late. As the child of an actress who'd had to be at the studio at six AM, awake and functioning, Katie had learned young not to sleep in. Now, as she wandered into her kitchen for her first cup of coffee of the day, she looked at her co-op as if she were seeing it for the first time. The apartment, which she'd inherited from her mother—score one for Teddy—was in a prewar building on Riverside Drive on the Upper West Side. When Rosalind had purchased it in the seventies, it had cost a pricey-for-the-time thirty-seven thousand dollars. Today it was probably worth upwards of two million. Katie had never bothered to find out exactly how much, because she'd always assumed she'd live there until she died.

It was a big space for Manhattan, with an eat-in kitchen, a living room, a dining room, two bedrooms, and a bath and a half. The half bath had a partial view of the Hudson River. Rosalind had redecorated it every few years, but the basic color scheme had always remained the same: white, silver, and liberal splashes of the same shade of turquoise as her fabulous eyes. After her mother had died, Katie had purchased a comfy brown sofa with plans of redoing the place to suit her own taste. Somehow she'd never gotten around to it, so the drab little sofa crouched unhappily in the midst of Rosalind's glitz. However, the apartment was still Katie's home, and leaving it was out of the question. Or was it? Would she be better off in some trendy neighborhood in a building where the doormen hadn't known her all of her life? Where were the trendy neighborhoods, anyway?

"Damn Teddy," she said out loud as she turned on her coffeemaker—her purchase, not one of Rosalind's, thank you very much—but there was no point in blaming Teddy. The truth was, she *was* living with Rosalind's hand-me-downs. But why not? Rosalind's hand-me-downs were terrific. Her late mother had been one of those force-of-nature people.

In 1975, when Rosalind Harder waltzed into New York to become a star, she came armed with her well-documented beauty, a will of iron, and not much more. Her acting experience consisted of playing the lead in every show presented at her Alabama high school and working for one season as an apprentice in a professional summer stock company. She'd never told Katie the name of the theater. "It was a terrible old place," she said when asked. "It's been closed forever."

In addition to looks and determination, Rosalind brought a toddler to the city with her. The official, if somewhat hazy, story about little Katharina's father was that he'd been married to Rosalind for just a few months before he was killed in Vietnam. It had happened before his child was born, and his brave young widow was too pained to talk about it—or him. This gooey version of the facts had kept the press at bay—in the seventies, the soap opera magazines weren't exactly hotbeds of investigative reporting—but Katie had always had her doubts. For one thing, there were no pictures.

While Katie could imagine that her mother might find it a downer to keep photos of her dead husband lying around, there was no way that Rosalind wouldn't have hung on to at least one shot of herself on her wedding day. On top of that, she had always refused to tell Katie the man's name. The one time when Katie had pressed her about him, she had screamed, "Just be glad I never let myself get stuck with that pussy-whipped mama's boy!"

All of this secrecy made Katie think that perhaps her mother was being less than honest with her loving fans in TV land. It was Katie's take, never publicly aired, of course, that her father probably had been a soldier, and might even have bought it in the jungles of Vietnam, but that he and her mother had never actually done the for-richer-or-poorer ceremony. That would explain why Rosalind's grandmother—the woman who had raised Rosalind—had never met Katie. "Gran's the kind of good Christian who just makes you want to go out and start sinning, " Rosalind said once of the only relative she and Katie had.

After giving birth, Rosalind had scraped together enough money to come to New York. Katie was never sure exactly how she'd done it; that was another part of the story Rosalind left murky. The part that happened after Rosalind got to New York, though, had been well reported in the fan mags.

One week after arriving in the Big Apple, the intrepid Rosalind landed a job as a showroom model in the garment district, and found an apartment in a marginally safe neighborhood. She made an arrangement with the woman who lived across the hall to watch young Katharina while she was working—those were more innocent days when you could still trust your neighbors—and went to auditions on her lunch hour. That was how Teddy found her. He was working in a third-rate talent agency that held cattle calls to drum up the client list, when she marched in to do Ophelia's mad scene from *Hamlet*. Her matter-of-fact delivery and dazzling looks couldn't have been more wrong for Shakespeare's fragile ingénue, but Teddy thought she might be right for the lead on a new soap opera that was casting.

There was a tiny hitch: the low-end agency Teddy worked for handled actors who worked as extras, and day players who had less than five lines per show, while the part of Tess Jones on *All Our Lives* was a starring role. Teddy never should have been able to land an audition for Rosalind, but he was young and cute, and after making a couple of promises he had no intention of keeping, he got her in the door. Rosalind took care of the rest.

Some fashion magazine had dubbed the winter of 1975 the Season of the Thoroughbred Girl, and they might have been talking about Rosalind Harder. She "borrowed" an outfit from the showroom where she was modeling and strolled into her audition wearing a white suede shirtdress with pale hose that showcased her world-class legs, and a white silk scarf that set off her hair and eyes. The casting director dragged the producer out of a crucial meeting to watch her reading. When it was over, the Queen of Daytime—as they called Rosalind four years later when she posed for the first *TV Guide* cover ever given to a soap actress—was born.

Katie grew up on the set of *All Our Lives*. When she was small, the dressing room next to her mother's was made into a playroom for her. When she was old enough to attend high school, that same dressing room was where she did her homework. Each day, after she'd finished her math and social studies, she was allowed to go sit in the makeup room and watch the monitor above the mirrors as the show was being taped.

The makeup room was the heart of the studio; all of the actors congregated there to hang out, gossip, and to beg someone, anyone, to cue them on their lines. Soap actors were always desperate to run their lines. They were under-rehearsed, they were working way too fast, and every day they had to absorb wads of dialogue that sounded exactly like the dialogue they had memorized the day before. The cast of *All Our Lives* quickly discovered that the shy kid sitting in the corner of the makeup room was happy to help them, and they exploited her shamelessly. They also discovered that when a clunky phrase wouldn't stick in the brain, the kid could come up with a way to paraphrase it so that it did stick—and it sounded more like human speech. Members of the cast began asking Katie to smooth out their speeches. Naturally the show's writers started screaming. Some of these writers were clients of Teddy's—by that point he had his own agency and was handling writers, directors, and producers as well as actors—but his actors told him the girl was amazing.

Like any good agent, Teddy watched the show every day, and he began paying special attention to the scripts he knew Katie had altered. He realized immediately that the actors were right, Rosalind's little girl had real talent. So thanks to Teddy, Katie worked on the *All Our Lives* staff as an intern during all of her school vacations. Two days after she graduated from college, she had her first gig as a scriptwriter for the show.

All of this was done with Rosalind's blessing. Eventually. At first, the idea of her child working on her turf, and possibly grabbing some of her spotlight, had brought on a meltdown—it had happened in Teddy's office where no one else had seen it—but Katie had quickly disappeared into the ranks of the faceless writers who toiled in the background, and Rosalind had relaxed. In time, she came to see the advantages of having her own personal in-house writer to bitch at when the scripts weren't to her liking. Fortunately for everyone, the *All Our Lives* writing staff was never nominated for an Emmy on a year when Rosalind wasn't.

Katie poured herself a cup of black coffee—after years of drinking the day-old coffee on soap sets, she liked hers dark and mean—and walked quickly into the bedroom. *Enough with all the second-guessing and doubting*, she told herself. She was going to get dressed, go down to the lobby, get her mail, and do something useful with her day. Full of purpose, she started dressing. But the talk with Teddy just wouldn't go away.

"Okay, exactly what is your plan for the future?" she asked herself out loud as she pulled on her sweats. Talking to herself was a habit she'd picked up as a kid. Back then it had been a great way to clear space on a crowded New York street, but these days people just thought she had an invisible earpiece for her cell phone. "I'll re-sign with Teddy and re-up my contract with *All Our Lives*," she answered herself.

For as long as it's around, added an unpleasant little voice in the back of her head.

"And when it's not around, Teddy will find me a gig on another show." Katie pulled socks and sneakers over feet that were swollen from the killer sandals.

And then what? the voice in her mind persisted.

"Then . . . that's it. I'll hang on until the pensions kick in and I can retire."

For another thirty-five years? Really?

"So I'll try to get a job on the staff of a nighttime show."

Lots of luck, with a résumé that has nothing but daytime credits. Nighttime producers think daytime writers are something you scrape off the bottom of your shoe. Plus, you'd have to move to L.A.

"I'll do what I have to do—when the time comes. Not now." She finished dressing, dragged a brush through her hair, and looked at herself in the mirror. "I could always just slash my wrists," she said to her image. It was the kind of over-the-top line she'd have cut from any of her scripts, if she'd ever been demented enough to write it. "Hack," she said to the Katie in the mirror. And on that happy note, she walked out of her apartment, got into the elevator, and went down to the lobby.

The mail had arrived and it had already been sorted. There was an envelope in her mailbox for her. She reached for it, and then read the return address twice when she saw the unfamiliar writing and postmark. It was from somewhere in Georgia, from a lawyer she'd never heard of.

CHAPTER 4

Los Angeles 2006

The dog was so young it hadn't grown into its extremely large feet yet. It was also very dirty and, if the ribs poking through its patchy coat were any indication, it was starving. It sat on Randa's doorstep wearing a length of old rope around its skinny neck. Holding the rope was Randa's eleven-year-old daughter, Susan.

"Mom, he was tied to a parking meter outside the mall." Susie's voice throbbed with indignation. "He was out there in the hot sun, and he didn't even have a bowl of water. Just this note." She pulled a grimy piece of paper out of her school blazer pocket, and read, "*You want him, he's yours*. Who does something like that?" Her daughter demanded. Her blue eyes were blazing; her face—still little-girl round—was red, and damp from the heat. Randa considered telling her to tuck her blouse back into her skirt, but decided against it. Her fierce child had no time for trivialities when there was a wrong to be righted. Because, of course, what Susie expected her mother to do was save the dirty little mutt by taking it in.

Randa looked desperately to the curb in front of her house, where one of the new hybrid SUVs was idling. In the backseat were three of Susie's classmates from the pricey private school she attended in Westwood. Two of these girls loathed Susie almost as much as she loathed them; the third was her one lone friend at Cross Winds, a girl named Jennifer Porter who was as smart and unpopular as Susie was. Jennifer's mother was driving the SUV, because it was her week for car-pool duty. Randa waved frantically at the woman, who gave her a big fake smile and began to pull away from the curb.

"Wait!" Randa called out, but Jennifer's mother was already heading out of the cul-de-sac.

"Let her go, Mom. Mrs. Porter is *useless.*" Susie dripped scorn with every syllable. "Do you know what she wanted to do? She wanted to *leave him there.* If I hadn't said I'd take him home, he'd still be tied to that parking meter. She wasn't even going to try to help."

The dog's head was hanging. It didn't have the energy to pant. Randa didn't want a dog. And if she had wanted one, this dog, which was undoubtedly flea ridden, in addition to being one of the ugliest she'd ever seen, would not have been the one she'd have chosen. But as she looked down at the poor thing, she felt a knot in her stomach. The animal needed help. . . . She couldn't just turn her back on it. She leaned over and was about to touch it, when a mantra her former shrink had embedded in her brain came to her rescue. She'd finished her therapy with Dr. Alexander a decade earlier, but his words still came back to her in times of crisis. *You have a right to say no.*

"Susie, we can't . . . ," she began, but her daughter knelt down next to the dog and began petting it.

"He needs a drink, Mom," she said.

You don't have to be rigid. That was one of Dr. Alexander's maxims. *There's always a compromise.*

"You can give him a bowl of water in the garage. We'll keep him here tonight, and tomorrow morning we'll call the animal shelter."

"They kill them after three days at the shelter! Mom, look at him. He'll never get a home in three days!" Susie was almost crying, and crying was not her style. This was serious.

"We can't keep him, honey."

Susie was on her feet. "Why not?"

Randa could have pointed out that she was a single mother raising and supporting her child on her own. But she'd never, ever lay that guilt trip on her daughter.

"A dog needs attention and we're both busy. You know the hours I work. My clients—"

"They're a waste of space!"

That wasn't fair—not totally. Randa was a business manager in the entertainment industry. She worked out of her home with one assistant, and was successful because she offered a personal touch that the larger, more high-powered management agencies did not. When the veteran television writer with twelve hit shows under his belt had a meeting with an infant producer who didn't know his name, Randa was the one who convinced the distraught scribe that picking up his old cocaine habit wasn't the way to cope. When the Lindsay Lohan wannabe decided to blow six weeks of her sitcom salary on a Rodeo Drive shopping spree, Randa figured out how to pay the little brat's mortgage. Because Randa's office was in her home, her clients thought nothing of calling her at two in the morning. Her assistant, Andy, said she should have regular business hours and enforce them, but Randa knew being available was what gave her an edge.

Susie tried to blink back tears and lost the fight. "This dog is worth six of those losers, Mom. And I want him. He'll be there when I get home from school. I can play with him and teach him stuff—he'll be like a friend."

"Honey, you have friends."

"No, I don't! Not anymore. Jen's going to Carmel next year. Her mom got into Reiki after the divorce—it's like this healing religion thing—and now they have to move so Mrs. Porter can go to school to become a Reiki master."

Randa's heart sank. Losing Jen was huge. No wonder Susie was on the verge of tears. "Baby—" Randa began, but her child cut her off.

"And don't tell me I'll make more friends at school, because they all hate me."

"I'm sure they don't—" Randa tried again, but Susie was past listening.

"They hate me and I hate them! All they want to talk about is hot boys— like they even know any—and clothes and their dads' three-picture deals."

She's really unhappy there. How did I miss that? A hunt for another school was indicated. Randa sighed, remembering how many schools they'd looked at before Susie had settled on Cross Winds.

Meanwhile, the dog seemed to realize that it wasn't going to be moving—at least not for the moment—and lay down at Susie's feet with a little whimper. She bent down again to stroke him. "See? He already likes me."

"Honey—"

"I want to keep him!"

"He's probably not even housebroken. If we bring him inside, he'll . . ." Randa trailed off because her daughter had done one of her lightning switches from a child to a forty-year-old. Susie straightened up, and gave her mother a knowing look.

"This is because of the living room, isn't it?" she said. "You've just had it redecorated and you're afraid he'll mess it up."

"It's not only that," Randa protested weakly. Dr. Alexander would have told her to come in for a refresher course if he could have heard her.

"Mom, all that stuff in there, it's just . . . things," Susie steamrolled on. "This dog could die if we don't help him." Then she turned back into an eleven-year-old. "Besides, the new carpet already looks like someone puked on it."

"This is not about the carpet," Randa said. But it was. Randa didn't want the dog and its fleas anywhere near her living room.

"We don't have to have things, Mom," Susie said, picking up a fight that had been going on between them for over a year. "We don't have to have this big house that's screwing up the environment because we have to keep it air-conditioned, and I don't need to go to that crappy school—"

"Watch your language. And stop trying to change the subject."

"This *is* the subject! You won't let us keep this awesome dog because he might trash our carpet or take time away from your dumb clients—"

On cue, Randa's cell phone rang. Andy had gone home for the day, and this was her special number reserved for emergencies. When she didn't answer on the second ring, the call automatically transferred to her office answering machine, and since her office was right off the foyer, they could hear the Lindsay Lohan clone screeching, "Randa? Randa, are you there?" as they stood out on the front steps. Randa made herself ignore the voice.

"This dog *needs* us," Susie said, as if that were the clincher.

"We can't take care of the whole world—"

"We don't take care of anyone but ourselves," Susan broke in. "You're not, like, Angelina Jolie or someone, Mom."

"Randa!" the voice on the answering machine shrieked.

Susie was watching her, willing her not to answer. But answering and being available was how she made her living. "Honey, I have to . . . ," she started to say, but to her amazement, she felt her own eyes well up. And she couldn't let her little girl see that. "Put the dog in the garage for tonight, Susie," she said firmly. "I'll take it to the shelter tomorrow."

And her daughter, for whom she would have slain dragons, gave her a look full of loathing. Then Susie gently helped the dog to its feet and headed for the garage. Randa watched her, wanting to run after her. But what would she say?

"Randa, where the fuck are you?" The voice on the answering machine was now in early-stage hysteria. Randa went into her office.

By the time the Lindsay clone's latest emergency was disposed of, six more desperately urgent messages had collected on Randa's voice mail. She gritted her teeth and ignored them. And although she couldn't bring herself to turn her cell phone off, she put it on her desk, turned the volume on the answering machine down as low as she could, closed the office door behind her, and went to the garage to look for her child.

Susie wasn't there, but the mutt was settled in with a pillow for a bed, water, and a bowl full of rice and chicken, a concoction that Randa could almost guarantee was recommended on some website for starving dogs. Susie was a tireless Internet researcher. When Randa found her in her room a few minutes later, she announced tersely—without looking up—that she was online looking for no-kill shelters.

Feeling both relieved and guilty, Randa left her daughter, and started back to her office. But her newly decorated living room was right across the hall. She stopped at the doorway and looked in. She'd had the room painted in shades of taupe and cream, the kind of light, classy colors she'd dreamed of as a kid. Every stick of furniture was new. The silk curtains that billowed out from the top of the floor-to-ceiling windows filtered out the bright California sunshine, leaving a mellow glow. Usually, looking at the room made her feel good, but now she wanted to cry again.

We don't take care of anyone but ourselves.

Susie was disappointed in her, that was the hard part. Randa knew she had it backward. She was the mother, and her daughter was supposed to worry about disappointing *her,* but her Susie wasn't an ordinary little girl. This was not just the fond assessment of a devoted parent; her child was a bona fide genius with the IQ scores to prove it. Randa had suspected as much when Susie started reading billboards and traffic signs at the age of two, but, not wanting to put her baby under pressure, she'd refused to follow her pediatrician's advice and have her tested. A year later the child's preschool had insisted. By that point, Susie was sneaking the *Los Angeles Times* into her Barney backpack and working her way through the hard words during rest period.

It was clear that her baby was not going to be like the rest of her peer group, and Randa was determined that Susie would never feel bad about it. Randa started drilling her on the idea that being different was another way of saying you were special and terrific, and being like the crowd meant you were ordinary and boring. Susie had bought it. Maybe it was because from the second she was born, Randa had adored her with a passion she'd never felt for any other living thing. Maybe it was because Susie was hardwired to believe in herself.

But now it seemed that Randa's miracle girl wasn't happy. *He'll be like a friend,* she'd said about the mutt. Randa felt the tears sting her eyes again. Maybe she'd gone overboard on the march-to-your-own-drummer thing. But there was nothing she'd change about Susie. While her contemporaries were trying to dress like the latest pop diva, Susie's wardrobe consisted of natural fiber pants, T-shirts, regular shirts, and a couple of skirts for dress-up. She had never lobbied to bare her midriff, pierce her navel, or tattoo any portion of her anatomy. In a school where several classmates were already beginning to flirt with anorexia, Susie remained healthily and unfashionably solid.

The bulk of Susie's generous allowance was allotted to causes: relief efforts for disasters she'd read about on the Internet, and animal rights groups she assured Randa weren't doing property damage. Lately her daughter had been branching out into politics. During the last congressional campaign, she had supported the candidates of her choice with regular donations. She'd given Randa a furious lecture on civic responsibility when Randa had been too busy crunching the numbers for a client's pre-nup to vote. Remembering that moment, Randa sighed. Actually there *was* something she'd change about her kid—lately she'd been wishing that every once in a while Susie would try to understand where *she* was coming from. The mortgage on the house had to be paid. And even if her clients were a waste of space, Randa had no desire to live in an eco-friendly hut without electricity or running water.

Her cell phone had to be ringing by now. She hadn't heard it—the office door was probably muffling the sound—but she never went this long without a summons from someone. She should get the phone and return the calls on her voice mail. She should go back to work. Instead, she walked all the way into the living room, kicked off her shoes, and ran her perfectly pedicured toes over the rug Susie disliked so much. Randa had standing appointments—at her home so she wouldn't waste time on the freeway—for pedicures and manicures. She told herself it was a professional thing, that she had to look pulled together, but the truth was, knowing her toes were done boosted her self-confidence. Randa had never been very secure about her looks. Her hair was brown and too curly, so she had it straightened every six weeks and had highlights added that made it look tawny blond. Her blue eyes and creamy skin were her best features, and she could live with her generous mouth. The nose she'd had narrowed and the teeth she'd had fixed were the best she could buy. She kept herself slim by working out on the treadmill in her office, and wore the skirts of her business suits as short as she could without being inappropriate.

She looked around her living room. She could never explain to Susie what all this overpriced perfection meant to her. Susie couldn't imagine living in dingy hotel rooms with sheets that smelled, or sleeping on the sofa in a one-bedroom apartment in the scary part of downtown L.A. Randa could imagine it. In fact, she could remember it. Vividly.

CHAPTER 5

Los Angeles 2006

Randa's father had been an actor. His name had been Richard Jennings and he'd actually been pretty good at his chosen profession. He'd had a refined, WASPy quality that was very commercial when he arrived in New York in 1974. He'd moved well, his voice had carried to the back of any theater, and his diction had been superb. That diction, he once told his young daughter, was the result of listening to recordings of the great British actors when he was a boy. He'd wanted to be his generation's Laurence Olivier—he'd come closer to Ryan O'Neal.

Richard had come to the city in the days when a Broadway show could have a run without a TV or movie star playing the lead. He'd never opened a play on the Great White Way—he was the guy they'd tap to be the first re-placement after the original actor had gotten the rave reviews and the Tony nomination. Richard took over shows when they had been running long enough that the costumes were just a little frayed.

Sometimes he went on the road with a show after it closed on Broadway, traveling for a year or more with Randa by his side. She kept up her school-work long distance and learned how to adjust to cheap hotels, suitcases, and meals snatched on the run. Richard's career might not have been everything he'd dreamed of, but he had made a living. And the money would have been enough to keep him and his daughter out of those cheap hotels if he hadn't been, as he himself put it, a lush.

Randa had accepted his drinking as a part of their lives. She'd always known, even when she was a young girl, that her father was an angry man. The anger was buried under good manners and cheerful smiles, but it was there. Some of it came from frustration over his failure as an actor—or what he saw as failure—but Randa knew that wasn't all of it. Something else was always eating at him, and drinking was how he got away from it.

For the most part, Richard was a gregarious drunk; solo boozing was not his thing. He did his imbibing in bars, restaurants, dives, honky-tonks, and roadhouses—any place where there was a crowd. His paycheck melted as he bought rounds for friends he'd just made and would never see again. Sometimes, if one of the friends was female and relatively good-looking, he'd bring her home. Randa got used to the sound of strange women being sick in the bathroom while she got dressed in the morning.

Randa stood in the doorway of her living room. The cell phone really was ringing now, she could hear it. She should go answer it; her workday wasn't over.

But it never is, she thought. Her clients always wanted something. Defiantly, she moved farther into her living room and sat on her new sofa.

It had always amazed her—and her former shrink—how very little she knew about her own history. Her mother had died when Randa was still a baby.

"You never asked about her?" Dr. Alexander had wondered.

"My father made it pretty clear he didn't want me to," Randa had said. "I learned not to push him."

"What happened if you did? Did he get angry? Lose his temper?"

"Oh no, he wouldn't let himself do that," Randa had said. "He just . . . wasn't there anymore. One time, when I was very young, I asked him where he was born. He shut down for three days. Another time I asked him what his life was like before he moved to New York. That time he shut down for a week."

It had been hard to explain to Dr. Alexander why those times had been so bad, because in a way nothing in her life had changed. She had still made her own breakfast, had still gone to school on her own or studied by herself if they were on the road. She had still brushed her teeth, taken her bath, and gotten herself into bed in time for her own self-imposed curfew.

"So what exactly was missing when your father pulled away?" Dr. Alexander had asked.

"Talking to him," Randa had finally said. "Listening to him. He'd put *Eine kleine Nachtmusik* on the phonograph and tell me about Mozart at the age of six playing a concert for the empress of Austria. My father could describe the Sistine Chapel ceiling and the Last Supper so I felt like I'd actually seen them. We had a game we played: he'd quote a line from Shakespeare and I had to tell him what play it came from. I always got it right, by the way." She had paused. "The man never bought groceries for me to eat, or saw to it that my laundry was done, but he sure could talk."

"And when he was angry, you missed the talk," Dr. Alexander had said. *It was all I had.*

"He had a way of looking right through me," she'd replied. "It scared the hell out of me."

She'd seen that Dr. Alexander was studying her thoughtfully. "What?" she'd demanded.

"I'm just wondering if you still listen to *Eine kleine Nachtmusik.*"

"I like Beethoven and Bach better than Mozart these days."

She didn't have to see Dr. Alexander's expression to realize what a wimpy act of rebellion that was.

When she was a child, rebellion of any kind was not an option, so Randa tried not to have inconvenient questions. But sometimes in spite of all her efforts, curiosity got the better of her. Since she'd never met any of her relatives, when she was really young she fantasized about gray-haired grandparents producing huge Thanksgiving dinners, and children—cousins, perhaps—opening presents under large glittering Christmas trees. She borrowed these images from the TV commercials she'd seen—she spent a lot of time in front of the tube when they were traveling—and she wasn't sure she actually believed in them, although she wanted to with all her heart. Finally, after a particularly long stretch on the road, when her longing for a real home had gotten so intense that it had overcome her fear, she asked Richard about his family. Surprisingly, that time the results were not horrible.

"You never know. Maybe someday we'll run into some of my clan," he'd said.

It was a hope she hung on to, especially on the nights when Richard was out later than usual or the woman who appeared in the morning was hostile about the fact that he had a kid. Randa would go off to school daydreaming about the pretty grandparents who would rescue her.

Then when she was seven, The Bad Night happened. That was what she named it in her mind back then, with capital letters like the heading of an act in a play. And in spite of all her therapy, a childish part of her brain still thought of it that way. The Bad Night was when she learned that no one ever rescued anyone, and people could hurt each other so much it could change everything. It was after The Bad Night that things got really scary.

Randa leaned back on the sofa, and closed her eyes. Usually, she tried not to think too much about her childhood, but once the memories started, it was hard to stop them.

After The Bad Night, Richard began drinking in a new way that was more out of control. Getting work was harder for him. He missed auditions. When he finally had a job, he missed performances. That was new. There had been times in the past when he'd been hung over for a matinée, and he'd worked drunk two times that Randa knew about, but he'd always been in his dressing room for the half-hour call.

When he started his downward spiral, Randa panicked. She started nagging him, which he hated, and then she cried, which he hated even more. When he got fired the first time, she thought it was her fault because she'd made him mad. Years later, she realized he'd been branded unreliable because the drinking had taken its toll and he was having trouble remembering his lines. But when she was a kid, she promised God she'd never upset her father again if they could just have another gig.

God responded by handing them a seven-month spell when Richard was "between engagements," as the showbiz euphemism went. Finally, he broke the drought by moving them to Hollywood. He knew people out there who'd promised to help him, and camera work meant fewer lines to trip up his now permanently dicey memory.

Thanks to his gift for making friends, he did work in Los Angeles. The characters he played were too minor to merit names—in the closing credits he was listed as Thug #2 or Man Walking Dog—and his paychecks were small. Randa tried to grab them before he could cash them.

When Randa was sixteen, Richard tried to stop drinking. Randa drove him to his twelve-step meetings, cheered when he was on the wagon, and understood—wearily—when he inevitably fell off it. She cleaned up after him, got rid of the women whose names he couldn't remember, and covered for him when he was too shaky to keep appointments. She got a job waiting tables after school to help keep them afloat. By the time she was eighteen, Richard's body couldn't take the abuse anymore. There were three hospitalizations. The third time, he didn't come home.

The night before he died, he finally wanted to talk. His voice that had been heard in the back row of a fifteen-hundred-seat theater was so weak that Randa had to lean in to catch what he was saying.

"Your mother . . . ," he whispered. "She was crazy about you." He reached for her hand. "When you were born, she agreed . . . You're named for Miranda in *The Tempest*. . . . My family tradition." He closed his eyes, and started to quote, " 'How beauteous mankind is . . .'," but then his memory checked out on him. Or maybe he was just too tired to finish Miranda's line.

Randa did it for him." 'O brave new world,/ That has such people in't,' " she said. He nodded and started to drift off. She stayed still until her arm fell asleep and she tried to shift her hand in his—just a little. Richard opened his eyes. "Remember . . . 'brave new world,' Miranda," he said softly.

The next morning he was gone.

In the years that followed Richard's death, Randa took on her brave new world and whipped it into shape. She worked her way through college and became an accountant because numbers were reliable. She married the first boy she dated and had a baby who was the love of her life. She called the child Susan because it wasn't the name of any Shakespearean heroine that she could find. When she realized the boy she'd married would never stop sleeping around, she divorced him and began working with a shrink to make sure she never made such a bad choice again. By that point she understood that she'd been damaged, and that she couldn't trust her own instincts.

When Susie's father refused to pay child support and moved to Colorado, Randa was glad he was out of her daughter's life. She worked hard and gave Susie everything she herself had ever wanted. Their life was good. Or was it?

We don't take care of anyone but ourselves.

Susie just wanted to keep a poor stray, for God's sake. Why not let her? Why not be a heroine? Randa stood up and grabbed her shoes, picturing the look on Susie's face when she heard they were keeping the dog. But then she looked down at her perfect toes and the rug she'd lusted after for months, and she knew she couldn't do it. The dog would bring chaos into their lives. It wouldn't mean to, it just would. And she'd had enough chaos to last her a lifetime. She put on her shoes, and went back to work.

She was at her desk when Susie came racing into her office. "Jennifer's mom is going to let her keep the dog!" she shouted happily. "They have to call it Usui because that's the name of the guy who came up with Reiki, but who cares? I'm taking back every bad thing I ever said about Mrs. Porter!"

Jealousy stabbed Randa. "I thought she said no."

"Jen called her dad and told him about the dog, and he said he and her stepmom would take him. Jen's mom hates her stepmom. So Mrs. Porter said she'd keep the dog, which was what Jen wanted, because no way you'd let that airhead her dad married take care of anything."

For a brief, wild moment, Randa thought of telling her daughter—now that the dog's fate was safely settled—that she'd changed her mind and she had planned to take the stray herself. But she never lied to Susie.

"I'm glad it worked out," she said stiffly.

Susie gave her a look, and then she reached over to hug her. "It's okay, Mom," she said gently. "You do the best you can." She ran off to tell Usui the good news.

It wasn't until she was in bed that night and drifting off to sleep that Randa remembered she hadn't gotten the mail that afternoon. She never let that happen because her clients' checks and bills were sent directly to her. She thought about throwing on her robe and going to the mailbox. But the bedroom was cool and the bed was soft and she decided just this once she'd let it wait.

The next morning she ran out to get the mail before she was dressed. There was one letter in her mailbox. The postmark said it was from the state of Georgia. According to the return address, it was from some law office she'd never heard of.

CHAPTER 6

Georgia 2006

As a lifelong New Yorker, Katie thought she knew about muggy weather. But nothing had prepared her for the warm bath that passed for air outside the airport in Atlanta. It fogged up her glasses, and turned the long black skirt she was already sorry she'd worn into damp laundry. She could feel her hair tripling in volume, all of it frizz.

"A bit humid today," said her escort with a wink. Or it could have been a nervous twitch. Maybe it was a form of greeting, in this land down under. Katie contemplated winking—twitching?—back and decided it could be taken the wrong way. The escort's name was Raymond Moultire, Jr., and he was the reason she was sweltering in front of Hartsfield-Jackson Atlanta International Airport. Or, rather, his father was. Raymond Moultire, Sr., was the unknown lawyer who had sent her the letter from Georgia. In it, he had informed her that she was an heiress.

"An heiress of what?" asked her on-again off-again boyfriend, Jock, when she'd told him over dinner. Jock was an actor, ten years her junior, and way too handsome for her. Unfortunately, they both knew it. He was also unemployed and on the hustle, and he wouldn't have minded it if she could have swung a part for him on *All Our Lives*. They both knew that too.

"It's all very mysterious," she said. "This Mr. Moultire just says there's a piece of property involved. It's somewhere in Georgia. Not the Russian Georgia; we're talking *Steel Magnolias.*"

"Who left it to you?"

"Mr. Moultire doesn't say. But according to his letter, I'm one of two people who are inheriting." She paused. "There's going to be a reading of the will down in Georgia and I've decided to go."

"Why?"

"I've never inherited anything before." Which was true if you didn't count her entire hand-me-down life. *Thank you again for pointing it out, Teddy.*

"It's only for three days," Katie said out loud. And then she added, a touch too casually, "Want to come with?" It was a risky move. The invitation could have been construed as pressure, or even a push toward the forbidden commitment word—Jock defined their relationship as "friendship with benefits"—but the idea of getting him out of town and away from the endless supply of size-two bimbettes in his acting class was more than she could resist. "It might be fun in a Faulkneresque kind of way."

" 'Faulkneresque'? Gotta watch those cultural references, lady. They date you." He liked to remind her of the age gap between them, it seemed to make him feel better about the fact that she had a job and he didn't.

She sighed. "I take it that's a 'no'?"

He'd been planning to turn her down. She knew it, and he knew she knew it. Which was why he smiled sweetly and said, "I wouldn't miss it."

He waited until she bought their plane tickets to Atlanta before he announced that he couldn't go because he had an audition.

Raymond Moultire grabbed Katie's suitcase, put it in the trunk of the car, and settled her into the backseat. While she tried not to sweat on the upholstery, the lawyer—like his father, Mr. Moultire was a member of the Bar—slid into the front, and pulled away from the curb.

"We have to make a quick stop to collect your co-inheritress." Mr. Moultire winked annoyingly in the rearview mirror. He wasn't completely unattractive, Katie thought. She'd put him in his mid-thirties. He was tall and slim, his eyes were hazel, and although his face was on the thin side, he had a lot of nice brown hair. But everything about him screamed "nerd." And not a hip techno-nerd who would someday become a billionaire by creating the next YouTube. This was an old-fashioned type who harbored a secret passion for something esoteric and boring. Somewhere in his home, Katie knew, there was a collection of antique chess sets. Or comic books from a little-known series from the early fifties.

He was wearing a baggy seersucker jacket—she hadn't seen one like it since *Matlock* had gone off the air—and his navy-blue slacks were not quite long enough to hide his white socks. For reasons best known to him and his God, he had chosen to finish off this costume with a red bow tie. Katie had a quick flashback to the gorgeous Jock, who always wore his T-shirts tight enough to reveal his six-pack. The nerd broke into her reverie. "We'll be picking up the other lady at Terminal B—that's catty-corner to this side of the airport. I hope you don't mind," he said.

And what the hell would he do if she said "Sorry. I do mind"? Let the woman—he had said she was a lady—stew on the sidewalk in front of the baggage claim area? Katie told herself not to be bitchy. It wasn't Raymond Moultrie's fault that she was hot and damp and regretting her traveling ensemble. It wasn't his fault that her boyfriend had stood her up. And it certainly wasn't his fault that her post-Emmy chat with Teddy was haunting her. She'd had to look at her protected life in a new way, and she was finding she didn't like it or herself. The phrase "candy-ass" came to mind. But she wasn't going to think about that. Not now.

Katie wanted to be excited about this trip. She had a mystery inheritance, damn it! She'd wangled a week off from work by promising to write double scripts during the Christmas vacation, and now she was on her way to a small town in the South that she'd never heard of, for the reading of a will. If there was a God, that reading would be held in a mansion that was draped in Spanish moss. There would be magnolia bushes—or were they trees?—all over the place. But so far all she'd seen was this mammoth airport.

"I bet it's even bigger than JFK," she said to Raymond Moultrie as he neatly avoided a shuttle bus.

"I'm sorry?"

"Your airport. It's huge."

"Second largest in the country."

"Not exactly a Spanish moss kind of place," she muttered under her breath. She hadn't meant for the man in the front seat to hear her, but two intelligent hazel eyes caught hers in the rearview mirror. He was studying her in a speculative way that was a little unnerving.

"I've never been south of Pennsylvania before," she offered.

"I see."

"Coming here is kind of an adventure for me. I don't even go on vacations. I think it's the packing that stops me. . . ." She was oversharing, but it was hard to stop, with him looking at her like that. "I don't get out much," she added inanely. His mouth twitched. She was going to be seriously pissed if a guy who dressed like Andy Griffith started laughing at her. But he didn't. "I'm going to have fun," she told him firmly.

"I see," he said again, and then a van with a logo of a pig in a chef's hat almost sideswiped him and he went back to looking at the road.

The car pulled up in front of Terminal B, where a mob of sweating travelers was hauling luggage toward cars, and cabs. Out of the crowd stepped a goddess. Her business suit—light beige—was unwrinkled. Slim, long legs flashed out from under the sexy short skirt. In spite of the heat, her makeup was intact, and there wasn't a hint of shine on her too-perfect nose. Worst of all, her gorgeously streaked hair swung gently over her shoulders, frizz-free.

I wonder how many body parts are real, Katie thought. To hell with not being a bitch.

Raymond Moultire bounded out of the car, extending his hand to the newcomer, and Katie realized that there was a young girl with her. The kid was tall, but solid rather than elegant. She was carrying a laptop, and around her neck was a camera that looked frighteningly complicated to Katie, who was technologically challenged. The youngster's face was pink with the heat, and her curly hair looked like a portobello mushroom around her head. Clearly she was related to the mannequin, but they didn't seem to share basic features—or flaws.

While Raymond Moultire put their large pile of luggage into the car trunk—Katie was willing to bet the bulk of it belonged to Miss High Maintenance—the twosome settled themselves in the car. The kid hopped into the front seat, while the glossy one did a graceful little dance step that landed her in the back next to Katie. Her tiny skirt remained unwrinkled.

This could be a long three days, Katie thought.

The girl leaned over the front seat and cheerily introduced herself as Susie, adding that her adult companion was named Randa. They were mother and daughter and Randa was the one who would be sharing the mystery inheritance with Katie.

What else do we share? Katie wondered as she told them to call her Katie. *DNA, obviously. But whose? And why? How is she related to me?*

We don't even look alike, Randa thought. *How am I related to her?* She took a quick look at her co-inheritor and stifled a groan. Miss Basic Black was one of those tough New York chicks who always scared the hell out of Randa; the kind who was so confident that she wore an ugly skirt just because she didn't care what people thought. Randa just knew this Katie person would never ever do something as frivolous as get her hair done or have a manicure.

Okay, so the family holiday thing—probably not happening, Randa said to herself. *Even if we are cousins five times removed.*

She hadn't expected to make friends for life; they didn't have the time for that. She had three days to spend in this state, and then she was out of there. Still, Katie's I'm-a-serious-New-York-woman 'tude was going to get old fast.

This is going to be a long three days, Randa thought, and swallowed a yawn, because the jet lag was starting to hit.

She still couldn't believe she'd gotten on a plane and flown three thousand miles for what had to be a scam or the work of a nutball. As she'd told Susie when they were back in Northridge, million-dollar surprise bequests only happened in straight-to-DVD movies, and it was a sure bet that the "piece of property" mentioned in Mr. Moultire's letter was going to be something she didn't want. If it existed at all.

Originally, she'd planned to send Andy east with her power of attorney so he could sign whatever papers needed signing, and dispose of the swampland or toxic waste dump she'd been given. But then Susie had found out about the will and the reading. She'd begged to go, and after the dog fiasco, Randa couldn't fail her again. Plus, they never went anywhere and this was a good excuse to take off for a long weekend, just the two of them. So Randa had informed her clients that she would be away from her desk for three days, and she'd packed her suitcase. The upside was, she'd be able to get rid of her toxic waste dump herself. Or maybe that was the downside.

Voices broke into her thoughts. It seemed that her daughter had decided not to wait for Randa to begin the getting-to-know-you thing with New York Girl. Randa listened as Susie kicked off by giving Katie her mother's job history. Katie countered with her own résumé. Susie threw in Randa's status as a divorcée. Katie verified that she was single as well. The basics having been covered, a conversation could begin. With great aplomb, her daughter moved to Topic A.

"Do you know what this inheritance is all about?" she asked Katie.

In spite of her jet lag, Randa leaned forward. Hopefully the queen of no makeup had an answer or two.

Finally, Katie thought. Thanks to her really terrific child, L.A. Barbie was showing signs of life. "All I know about the inheritance is what I read in my letter," Katie said to Randa. "There was nothing about who, what, why, or how come. You too?"

Randa nodded her gleaming head; she seemed disappointed. "So I'm guessing you're as blown away as I am," she said.

"I've been going nuts trying to figure it out."

"So have we," Randa's kid broke in eagerly. "The thing is, we don't know a lot about our family. . . . Mom's father was kind of weird and—"

"Susie, too much info," her mother reproved.

"I'm just trying to explain why we're so clueless."

Randa turned to Katie. "I don't have any relatives in Georgia—at least, I don't think I do." She did a tentative little smile, as if talking about her family made her uneasy. That little chink in the armor was a surprise. Katie was used to toxic levels of confidence from women who looked like Randa. Even if they'd paid for the look. "I guess it does sound kind of strange that I don't know more about my family," Randa added.

If you only knew, Katie thought.

"My great-grandmother was from Alabama," Katie said. "She was the one who raised Mother, but they were way too poor to be handing out chunks of land now. I think." She looked at Randa's kid, who was watching her intently. "I don't know much about my family either," she admitted.

"Which would make us both perfect candidates for a scam." Randa had a soft voice, but she could summon up a tough edge. "I shouldn't have come here," she went on. "This is a busy time for me." As if to emphasize the point, her cell phone rang. She started to go for it and was stopped by her daughter's hand reaching over the back of the seat.

"Mom, you promised," said Susie.

Randa paused for a second, and then turned off the phone. "You win," she said, and unleashed another smile—a big, full one this time—at her kid. Katie looked at Susie and wondered what it did to your head to know you could cause that kind of reaction in another person. Particularly if that person was your mother.

"Not to butt in . . . The bequest isn't a scam," Mr. Moultire put in from the front seat. "I can vouch for that. Our firm wouldn't have touched the will if it was." He caught a glimpse of Randa in the rearview mirror and saw his testimonial wasn't inspiring confidence. "I realize you don't know us from Adam's house cat, but we've been in business for over seventy years. I can give you a whole bunch of references."

"Thank you," Randa said. "I'd like to take a look at them. And I'd like to meet the man in charge at your firm. "

Okay, so she's not dumb, Katie thought. It still didn't mitigate the Barbie factor.

"I'll be happy to introduce you," Mr. Moultire said. It looked like the idea tickled him. He was enjoying himself a little too much, Katie decided.

"Obviously you know more about all of this than we do, so fill us in," Katie said firmly.

"Your property was left to you in an inter vivos trust, " he said.

"Okay. Who is the grantor?" All three other occupants of the car flashed Katie a look of surprise. "I write scripts for a soap opera," she explained. "I know just enough legalspeak to be dangerous. The grantor is the person who leaves the other people the inheritance." She looked at Raymond Moultire. "So—who was it?"

"I'm afraid I can't tell you."

"Why?" Randa's kid demanded.

"The grantor wished to remain anonymous."

"Why?" Katie echoed the eleven-year-old.

"I'm afraid I can't help you there."

"But you do know who this grantor person is—right?" Randa cut to the chase.

"Not exactly. The reason the property was held in trust was to protect the grantor's privacy. We're working with a law firm from Atlanta that was contacted by another law firm from a town here in Georgia. That's all I know."

"It must say somewhere on some document who owned it," Randa powered on.

"Yes."

"So you can track it down—right?" The soft voice was really edgy now.

"Not without violating the intention of the instrument."

"And you couldn't just . . . ignore that?"

"It wouldn't be ethical."

There was a pause. Randa had several choice comments to make about ethics, Katie could tell. But she sat back and said politely, "Thank you." Clearly, when you were a business manager who dealt with a showbiz clientele, you learned restraint.

However, her child wasn't restrained. "What's the property?" Susie demanded. "Our letter said it was in a place called . . . Mase something." She stumbled over the pronunciation.

"Massonville," he said helpfully. "That's where we're headed right now."

"I tried to check it out, but the town's website was down," Susie informed him.

"Every chamber of commerce meeting we have, I keep saying we need to change our server, but that one's cheap, and we're on a budget." He smiled brightly. And winked.

Major nerd, thought Katie.

"It's okay," the kid reassured him. "I just thought we should know about the place. Your letter didn't say much. "

"It was my father who wrote the letter to you, and I'm afraid I can't tell you what the property is. You have to see it for yourselves. Didn't Daddy explain that in his letter?"

"No," Katie answered. He had called his father "Daddy." Or, more accurately, "Deddy." Katie knew she'd heard it, because there was no way she could have imagined that coming out of the mouth of a grown man.

"I'm sorry," said Deddy's boy, who not only didn't seem sorry, but who also grinned in a way that was downright annoying.

"How much longer to Massonville?" Katie asked, changing the subject. They had navigated the maze that was the airport, and they were heading south.

"It's about a two-hour ride."

"We have to wait that long to see what Mom got? That's mean," said Susie.

"I think it was meant to be . . . dramatic, " he said. His mouth was doing the twitching thing again. He really was enjoying all of this too much.

CHAPTER 7

Massonville 2006

Randa yawned and let her eyes close for just a second. There was no way they were getting any more out of Raymond Moultire—for all his Southern fried charm, the man could do a version of the lawyer's tap dance worthy of any big firm in L.A. Katie seemed to have realized it too, and she settled back to look out the window. Randa stifled another yawn, and opened her eyes. She never let herself fall asleep in front of people, not even on airplanes; there was always the danger that you'd make those disgusting little snorting noises. She forced herself to sit up and tried to think of something to say, but she came up empty. Raymond Moultire seemed to be happy just not being in the hot seat. The only sound in the car was made by Susie, who was busily taking pictures of the lush vegetation that grew along the sides of the highway. "It's so green, Mom!" cried her child of the Los Angeles desert. "And there are no sprinklers!"

"There's a deer up ahead," Raymond Moultire pointed out.

"Omigod! Mommy, look!"

Susie almost never called her Mommy anymore, and Randa missed that. Maybe this trip was going to be worth it after all.

☙

Randa woke up with a start. In spite of all her efforts, she'd dozed off. Now Raymond Moultire was turning off the highway. Almost immediately the landscape changed. Little low houses appeared on the side of the road. Some were tidy with neat porches and flower beds. Others were shacks with rusted tin roofs, and partially dismantled cars in the front yard. Occasionally there would be what looked like a tiny farm on a side lot. And along the side of the road there were large swatches of orange-colored earth showing through the bright green grass.

"Roll the opening credits," Katie murmured as she stared out the window. She seemed genuinely interested in her surroundings, which was a surprise. Randa had her pegged as the kind of New Yorker who had to have oxygen if she left Manhattan. And she was right about the scene they were passing. It was like the opening shot of every TV movie about civil rights that had ever been made. But seeing it in person was different.

"It's not very . . . picturesque," Katie said. Which was exactly what Randa had been thinking, but it was a dumb thing to say. She and Katie were going to need this lawyer's goodwill if they were going to finish their business and get the hell out. There was no point in insulting his state.

"L.A. is disappointing to people too, when they see it for the first time," she said, and shot the man a charming smile. Then she realized she'd just told him his home was a disappointment.

To make matters worse, Katie added with a big-city-dweller sigh, "Yeah, we have support groups for the tunnel people who are seeing Broadway for the first time. " Randa leaned back in her seat and closed her eyes.

"We're coming up on Cobetta, " Raymond Moultire announced forty-five minutes later. "That's where my family's office is."

"You said your father was the one who sent us those letters. Do you work for him?" Randa asked—just to say something.

"Actually, there's four of us: Mama, Daddy, me, and Georgeanna. She's my sister."

"You're all lawyers?" Randa asked.

"And you all work for your father?" Katie added. The idea seemed to have struck a nerve in her.

"It's more like we all work for Mama," Raymond Moultire said. "She's our big rainmaker. But she's very kind to us." He smiled and winked at them.

"Are we going to your office to read the will?" Randa asked.

"Eventually. But first I'm taking you to see your property. That's how your grantor wanted it. We were given instructions."

They swung into a little hamlet that was the size of a large L.A. grocery store. Susie took pictures of a minuscule main street.

"Welcome to downtown Cobetta," said their tour guide. "We are now fifteen minutes away from Massonville." He indicated an old house with a front porch and window boxes full of red geraniums. "That's our office building." The only hint that it wasn't a private home was the wooden sign on the front lawn that said MOULTIRE LAW.

The house sat on one side of a tiny square that featured a statue of the Revolutionary War hero the Marquis de Lafayette at its center. Various small businesses surrounded the square, including, Randa noted, one called Kara's Kuts and Kurls. On the side facing the front of the statue was a red brick courthouse that definitely qualified as picturesque.

"It's just like in *To Kill a Mockingbird*." Susie sighed.

Raymond Moultire gave her a wink. "Thank you, ma'am," he said. He was sweet, in a corny way, Randa decided. "By the way," he went on, "my friends call me R.B.; Bolton is my middle name, and since Daddy has always been Big Ray—Well, it's just less complicated."

How? Randa wondered.

Fifteen minutes later, as promised, they reached Massonville. Fast-food joints, car dealerships, and little shopping centers lined the sides of the road. In spite of herself, Randa felt let down. After Cobetta, she'd been expecting quaint.

"It looks like the valley back home," Susie said.

"There's a Wal-Mart," Katie said grimly. She'd been hoping for quaint too.

"There are a lot of towns that won't let Wal-Mart in," Susie informed them. The previous summer her allowance for July had gone toward defeating the building of one in Northern California.

"I wish we'd been that smart," R.B. said. "When it came here, we lost all the businesses downtown. They couldn't compete. Little family places that had been around for generations." He paused. "Now, Mama would tell you the big stores give people what they want—good stuff at a cheap price. She says that's progress."

As her child and Katie clucked their disapproval, Randa remembered the days when she had to shop in places a lot cheaper than Wal-Mart, and tried not to shiver.

A sign on the side of the road announced that they had reached historic downtown Massonville. R.B. smiled happily. "Massonville was built on the site of a Creek Indian village," he said. "We cover an area of about two hundred square miles. After the Civil War, we became a major center for shipping raw cotton, and we were one of the most productive mill towns in the state. We had seven railroads coming through here back then. The river was not only a means of transportation but a source of hydroelectric power." Katie was sitting up in her seat. She seemed fascinated by the quickie history lesson. "Right now we're heading into some of the old residential districts," R.B. said.

From what Randa could see, they were heading into a slum. Once, the houses had been gracious homes with deep wraparound porches. Now all you could see was peeling paint and rotting siding. Multiple mailboxes indicated that several families were crammed into what had been built for one.

"Massonville has gone through a rough time," R.B. said. "The last mill closed in 1996, and the shipping went years ago. But we're bringing this neighborhood back; we can't let these old places go."

"The past is never dead. In fact, it's not even past," Katie murmured. Then she looked embarrassed, as if she hadn't meant the rest of them to hear her quote William Faulkner.

That may actually be something we have in common, Randa thought. For a second she thought of telling Katie about her father and the Shakespeare quotes when she was a kid. Then she decided it would sound too strange.

They drove through a dilapidated business section with boarded-up buildings. A department store had been recycled as a thrift shop, and an old movie theater was now selling wigs and cheap lingerie.

"Damn," Katie said softly.

Susie put down her camera and sat quietly.

Randa rubbed her eyes, which were now burning from too little sleep. This inheritance was going to be even worse than she'd thought.

But then the car rounded a corner and they entered a new world.

"The river's on your right," R.B. said. The river had indeed appeared where he was pointing—it seemed as though it had come from out of nowhere—and they were driving on a turn-of-the-century boulevard that ran parallel to it. The road was paved with red brick, and a wide island planted with trees and flowers ran down the center of it. Fountains, stone benches, and old-fashioned streetlamps were scattered throughout. There were more big old houses here, facing the river and the boulevard. But these homes were immaculate, with trellises, gazebos, flower beds, and manicured lawns. On each front porch, a glossy bronze plaque announced the year in which the house had been built.

"This is the neighborhood we've restored," R.B. said. "Most of these houses were scheduled for demolition, but we have one of the most active preservation societies in the state." He pointed to a house that had once been painted a pale green. It seemed to be a work in progress. "That's mine," he added. "I'm renovating it."

Susie took a picture of R.B.'s home. For the past few minutes she'd been quiet, and Randa wondered what was going on in that busy mind. A silent Susie meant a thinking Susie.

As suddenly as it had appeared, the restored neighborhood seemed to vanish. The old brick boulevard turned into a modern paved road, and ahead of them was a jumble of large new buildings. With a noticeable lack of enthusiasm, R.B. pointed out a sports stadium, a convention center, a bright new hotel, and four complexes of modern town houses and apartment buildings with balconies overlooking the river.

"They're so . . ." Katie searched for the word. "You could find those condos in New Jersey," she finally said.

R.B. looked at her with approval in the rearview mirror. "Yes," he said. "Not a lot of Spanish moss hanging here." He paused. "Now, to be fair, Mama would tell you this is the kind of development we need in Massonville. Most of these units sell to poor freezing Yankees who are fixing to retire—and bring their disposable income down here with them."

Randa looked at the showy condos and thought about the restored street in the historic district and the crumbling mansions farther inland.

There was something a little schizophrenic about Massonville, she decided. In the front seat Susie put away her camera again.

At first, the string of flashy buildings seemed to be uninterrupted, but it was broken abruptly by a stretch of debris-strewn land that stood out like an empty gap in a mouthful of bright, shiny teeth. R.B. stopped the car, and Randa looked to her left. Way back from the road, a lone white building rose up from the bare dirt. It was old, it had probably been sitting in this spot across from the river for over a hundred years, and it had seen better days. A tattered canopy hung over the entrance, and a curved drive—once sweeping, now rutted and heavily endowed with holes—led up to it. R.B. turned the car and they began bumping their way up the drive. When they reached the halfway point, he stopped, which probably saved what was left of his shocks. "There it is," he said, gesturing in the direction of the building.

The front part of the canopy had torn away, but the words "Opera House" were still printed in gold across the front.

"It's a theater?" Katie asked.

"That's the Venable Opera House," R.B. said. "And it's all yours."

CHAPTER 8

Massonville 2006

A stunned silence reigned for several seconds. Katie heard herself break it. "That's our inheritance?" she croaked.

R.B. nodded. "It was built in 1876. What do you think?"

There was no way to answer. For one thing, thinking was beyond her at that point. Also, if she opened her mouth again, she was going to start laughing.

Then from Randa's ladylike lips came the words "Holy shit." She climbed out of the car and made her way across the front lawn, which looked like a war zone, to the entrance of the theater, where she stopped, looking dazed. After a moment Susie scrambled after her.

Katie stayed in the car and stared at the building that was half hers. The size of it was the first thing that hit her. It was taller than any of the surrounding condos, and it covered an area that would equal almost a city block. At one side of it, there was a gate and an overgrown path that seemed to lead to additional property in the back. A high brick wall enclosed the theater and the surrounding land on three sides—only the front entrance was open to the street.

The theater itself was boxy and square; the sides of it—what Katie could see of them—were brick that had once been painted white. Now there were large bald spots where the paint had worn away. The front of the structure looked like it was made of a different material, and unlike the plain brick side walls, it was ornate, loaded with curlicues, arches, pillars, and lacy balconies. It too had once been white, but now there were streaks of brownish red running down its snowy surface. It didn't take much imagination to think of blood.

"Okay, so this is what they mean by Southern Gothic," Katie said as R.B. came around to the side of the car and leaned in to offer her a hand.

"Well, you *are* down here in Faulkner country," he drawled. He'd recognized the quote she'd let slip. For a moment she thought how sad it was that he didn't have a better fashion sense. Then he winked at her again and she figured clothes were just the tip of the iceberg. She climbed out of the car, and she and R.B. began making their way to the others. The hem had ripped out on the back of her skirt, and it swept up a small pile of rubble behind her as she went.

They joined Susie and Randa in front of the opera house. Randa didn't seem to be able to take her eyes off it. "The façade on the building is cast iron," R.B. informed them. "It was bolted on so the front would look fancy. That was a uniquely American concept back in the 1870s. Sort of like a manufactured home today. This theater is one of the best examples in existence of that kind of work."

"What the hell are we supposed to do with it?" Randa said to no one in particular.

"It needs work," R.B. said, "but you have to look at the bones of the structure. Look at the potential."

"For what?" Randa asked again. She wasn't being sarcastic; she really wanted to know.

"Would you like to go inside?" R.B. changed tactics.

Katie nodded. Her brain still hadn't grasped the fact that she actually owned the old place—she had a feeling that was probably just as well—but she wanted to see it.

"Come on," R.B. said, barely able to contain his enthusiasm. He found a set of keys in a lockbox under a carving of the masks of comedy and tragedy on the side of the front door. "It may be a bit hot inside," he warned them as he opened the door, "but that's just because the windows have been

closed. There's a great breeze off the river when the place is opened up."
Clearly he wanted them to like it.

Actually, it was rather cool inside, but it was too dark to see much. Katie
narrowly escaped banging into a huge ottoman that loomed up out of the
murkiness in front of her.

"Hang on," R.B. said. He began pulling at heavy floor-length draperies
that covered the Palladian windows at the front of the lobby. Mechanically,
Randa went over to help him. She was the kind of person who would lend
a hand at her own funeral, Katie decided.

After producing clouds of dust, R.B. and Randa finally tied back a set
of draperies. A shaft of light from the window revealed a lobby that had
been white before water stains had turned the walls a mottled beige. There
was a line of marble arches, held up by a row of pillars that ran across
the front of the room. All of them were trimmed with badly chipped gold
leaf. The gold and white motif was repeated in the mosaic floor tiles, the
wall sconces, and a carved double staircase leading to a mezzanine. The
frayed draperies that hung over the windows were a faded crimson, as was
the carpet on the stairway.

"At the back, that's the entrance to the auditorium," R.B. said. They all
turned to the back wall of the lobby to look. There was a narrow hallway on
the left side of the auditorium. R.B. pointed to the doors on either side of
it. "That door leads to the stage," he said, "and the door across from it leads
to the owner's office. So the boss could sneak backstage to spy on his people without them knowing he was coming. The owners lived here on the
premises, you see."

"Who were the owners?" Susie asked.

"A man named Cecil Honeycutt built the opera house—the Honeycutts
were movers and shakers here in Massonville before the Civil War. But
Cecil's son sold it to the Venables in 1878. They were actors. It was a dynasty, really—like the one Drew Barrymore comes from. They kept the
opera house in their family for almost a hundred years."

"And then they sold it to our unknown benefactor," said Katie.

"Or it could have changed hands several times," Randa put in. "We don't
know. We don't know anything!" The situation was really getting to her.

R.B. quickly turned to a set of French doors with stained glass windows. "Over there, to your right, is the restaurant," he said.

"There's a restaurant?" Randa asked, a little desperately.

"With a full kitchen and a nineteenth-century bar. Across from the restaurant on the other side of the lobby is the elevator leading to the hotel rooms—"

"Hotel rooms? What do you mean, 'hotel rooms'?" Randa broke in again. Her voice was dangerously high. There was a black smudge across her short skirt, Katie noticed, and her shimmering hair was turning up at the ends.

"This was not only a theater; it was also a hotel. The theater, the restaurant, and the manager's office are all here on the ground floor. The second floor, which is on the mezzanine level, was divided in half. One side of it is the apartment where the owners of the theater lived. On the other side you'll find the dressing rooms for the actors working in the theater and the actors' lounge, or greenroom. The hotel rooms were on the third and fourth floors."

"A theater and a hotel all in one. Very Disney," Katie said.

"This was a happening place back in 1876." R.B.'s hazel eyes were shining. Katie had been right about him having an obsession. It was obvious that the passion of R.B. Moultire's life was old buildings. "Let's say you were taking a riverboat from south Georgia to Atlanta," R.B. went on, "and the boat stopped overnight in Massonville. The carriage from the Venable Opera House would pick you up across the road at the dock and bring you here. You'd have dinner, see a play, and go upstairs to spend the night on dry land." He did a slow turn around the dirty lobby, his arms outstretched as if he wanted to hold all of it. "Imagine the way it was back then, when it was all brand-new and state-of-the-art . . ." He trailed off because he was losing Randa. She was digging angrily at a section of broken floor tiles with the toe of her elegant sandal.

Okay, this has been a shock, I get that, Katie thought, *but why is she so pissed off?*

"There are about thirty hotel rooms in all, on the third and fourth floors." R.B. finished quickly, and he crossed the lobby. "If you'd like to come over here and see the elevator?"

Katie, Randa, and Susie trotted over and peered through the dirty stained glass window to see the inside of the elevator cab. It was paneled in some kind of dark wood and there was a wide mirror with a gilt frame on the back wall. The thing was huge.

"I've seen studio apartments smaller than this," Katie said.

"Legend has it, they had it enlarged when President Grant visited Massonville after the war, because he required an elevator big enough to accommodate his horse," R.B. said. "Personally, I refuse to believe Northerners slept with their livestock—no matter what anyone says." He waited for a laugh and reddened when he didn't get one. He was trying to make them love this old place—and he was trying way too hard. "My belief is, they had to make the elevator so large because of the ladies' hoop skirts," he said simply.

Suddenly Katie could see a whole scene in front of her. That always happened to her: when she was writing a script, there would be some detail, usually something stupid that no one else even thought about, that would bring the whole thing to life for her. Now it was the oversize elevator that did it. She could see the women in their silk gowns with their skirts swaying over the hoops, the men in black dinner coats with starched white shirts. She saw the rich Victorian colors—deep reds, blues, purples, and greens—she saw the lace ruffles and the fans. "The jewels would pick up the light from the gas lamps," she said softly. "The girls would be checking themselves out in the mirror in the elevator to make sure they were perfect."

Somehow, R.B. was at her side. "They had to walk in and out of the elevator single file," he said. He knelt down on the floor. "If you look down at the threshold, you can see the indentations in the wood from where they all stood before they got off it."

Katie got down on her knees. A part of her couldn't believe she was on the floor looking at shoe grooves with a man whose people skills gave new meaning to the word "goofy." Another part of her wanted the name and history of every human who had passed by this spot. Behind them Randa cleared her throat. R.B. quickly helped Katie to her feet.

"Well, shall we start the tour?" he asked brightly. "The opera house has been under lock and key all these years, so I've never seen all of it, myself. I think we should begin with the hotel rooms on the third and fourth floors."

"How safe is that elevator?" Randa demanded.

"Not to worry. This building has a caretaker. It's been kept up."

A cobweb had draped itself over Randa's shoulder. She picked it off and glared up at the water-stained walls.

"Of course, there is some work that needs to be done," R.B. admitted unhappily.

"How much?" Randa asked.

He paused, looking miserable. He wanted so much not to have to say anything negative about the theater. Katie heard herself saying, "Who cares? We're just looking around."

But R.B. was a mensch; a question had been asked and he was going to answer. "The electrical system isn't good," he said quietly. "The roof needs to be replaced, the outside brickwork has to be repointed, and the theater area—the auditorium and the stage—hasn't been upgraded in a very long time. But the elevator works and the floors are sound. You don't have to be afraid to walk anywhere."

He was goofy, but there was something so open and unguarded about the way he loved this old opera house. Once again Katie heard her own voice speaking. "What are we waiting for?" she demanded. "Let's take that tour."

CHAPTER 9

Massonville 2006

Randa was tired, dirty, and hot. The lobby of the opera house might have been cool, but the upstairs was an oven—no, actually, it was a steamer. Even the magic straightening potion her hairdresser swore by couldn't fight it. But neither the heat nor the humidity explained why she was dreading what was coming next.

They had traipsed through the fifteen bedrooms and the one lone bathroom on each of the upper floors. The bedrooms were full of mildewed furniture and they had found the skeleton of what had probably been a squirrel on one of the chair cushions. Eerily, all of the beds were made up as if the hotel were still in business.

Fortunately, the owner's apartment was locked and R.B. didn't have a key for it, so they couldn't go through it. But they had stumbled around in the darkened restaurant, while he'd pointed out the crystal chandelier overhead, the chairs stacked on the ten round tables as if ready for the evening, and the bar with the old glassware still on the shelves. They'd seen the pantry with the china and the silverware still in the cupboards, and the pots and pans still hanging over the stove in the kitchen.

"It's like the whole place is waiting for someone," Susie had said in a hushed tone.

"I wonder what the theater's like," Katie had added. That was when Randa had started shivering in the heat.

She'd tried to tell herself it was because the opera house was a money pit and she and Katie were going to have to dump this nightmare inheritance fast, and it was all too overwhelming. But she'd known that wasn't the reason.

The endless "tour" had brought them back to the lobby again. "We've saved the best part for last," R.B. said. "The theater and the stage!" He would have provided a drumroll if he could have. Suddenly Randa had to get out of there.

"Maybe we've seen enough for today," she said.

Her daughter looked at her as though she had an extra head.

"We can't stop now," Katie said.

"It was just a thought," Randa said, and shivered harder.

R.B. led them across the lobby to the little side door that opened to the back of the stage. There was no lock on it, so there was no hope of a lost key. They went inside.

At some point over the years, someone had raised the curtain, or perhaps it had never been lowered after the last performance—which according to R.B. had taken place in the early 1970s. As Randa walked out onto the stage, it seemed as if she could hear her footsteps echoing throughout the empty house. She took a deep breath. And there it was, the theater smell. It was impossible to describe, a musty mix of dried paint, dust, old grease-paint, and sweat. She'd grown up on that smell. When she was a kid waiting backstage for her father, it would get into her nostrils, and stay there, even after he had changed into his street clothes and they were outside walking home. She still smelled it long after her dad had stopped working onstage. She'd smelled it for a while after he'd died.

She realized she'd stopped shivering.

She turned around slowly, getting her bearings. R.B. had told them that the dressing rooms were on the same floor as the owner's apartment, which meant they were somewhere above where she was standing. There would be one or two big rooms for the stars—there always had to be at least one star dressing room—and the rest would be smaller. Since this was an old theater, there might be a couple of communal dressing rooms that were shared by the supporting actors—one room for the "boys" and one for the "girls." According to R.B., the greenroom was upstairs too—she wondered if it was actually painted the traditional lucky green. Sometimes in modern theaters it wasn't anymore, but in a house this age it might be. Someplace on the premises there had to be a shop for building sets and props. There was probably a wardrobe room too, although her dad had often played very old houses that didn't have one. In the early days the actors provided their own costumes and brought them along when they toured.

Randa continued looking around. In the wings, near the front wall, there would be the electric board for the stage lights. When the theater was built, they would have used gas, but the lights would have been converted to electric by the turn of the last century. She scanned the gloom and found the prompter's desk. Next to it was the old-fashioned monster lighting board—circa 1950, was her guess—right where she'd known it would be. She felt someone watching her and turned around to see that it was her daughter. Susie was smiling.

"I think there's supposed to be a light I can turn on," R.B. said. "That's what the caretaker told me." Randa nodded. There was always a bare electric bulb that hung down over the stage. It was called the work light and it was turned on for rehearsals when the rest of the theater was dark. While R.B. looked for it, Randa made her way over to the wings to check out the riggings used to fly in flats and backdrops that were suspended overhead. The theater still used the old system—it dated back to a time much earlier than the antiquated lighting board—of ropes and pulleys counterbalanced with sandbags, and was meant to be operated by hand. In a modern theater, the riggings would be mechanized. R.B. hadn't exaggerated when he'd said the stage of the Venable Opera House hadn't been updated in decades.

There was one more thing she wanted to find. Randa walked to the back of the stage and checked out the floor. It didn't take her more than a couple of seconds to locate the trapdoor. Most old theaters had one so that Macbeth's witches and Hamlet's ghost could appear and disappear in clouds of stage smoke. It was always the same, a door in the floor of the stage that opened downward, and under it was a platform called the elevator that went down to the cellar below. Usually there was some kind of lever that operated the whole thing from underneath the stage, but in this theater it looked like it had been hooked up to one of the rigging ropes. She realized she was standing on the trap and backed away. In every theater her father had played, there had been some old-timer on the crew who'd had a grisly story about the door opening by accident and someone falling down to the floor below. Randa moved to the middle of the stage, where Katie was standing, staring out, not moving.

"It's so different from a TV studio, " Katie said in the hushed voice people used in churches.

"I found it," R.B. shouted, as the work light went on. Now they could see it all, the bare wooden floor, worn smooth, under their feet; the fly rails above the stage, from which the set pieces were suspended; and the flimsy catwalk the crew crawled along to hang the flats and backdrops.

And in front of them was the vast darkness and silence of the empty house. "That stage is the loneliest place in the world, " her father had told Randa once. "But once you've been on it, you never feel alive anywhere else." One night while he was dressing after the show, she had waited until the theater had cleared, had sneaked out onto the stage, and had looked out at the rows of empty seats. And she'd understood what he meant.

"It never changes, does it?" Katie whispered at her side. "The theater is . . ."

"Magic," Randa finished for her. She turned around to see Susie standing behind her.

They looked at each other, and her child reached up and kissed her on the cheek. "I love you, Mommy," she whispered. Then she disappeared. Randa turned back to Katie.

"Kids," she said with a shrug. But if she closed her eyes, she could still picture the look on Susie's face.

From the back wall of the theater they heard the sound of a door opening, and outdoor light flooded in. "There's a way out of the theater back here, Mom," Susie called out. "I'm going outside for a while!"

"She'll be fine back there," R.B. said. "It's all closed in."

"Just for a few minutes, Susie," Randa called out. But the back door had already slammed shut.

CHAPTER 10

Massonville 2006

There was a stoop outside the back door of the theater. Susie sat on the edge of it. A few feet in front of her there was a high hedge of some kind. It looked like it was a border for a backyard behind the theater, and a gravel path ran alongside it.

She needed to be quiet so she could figure out how she felt. When she was younger, she used to make lists of her feelings on her computer so she'd have them catalogued in order of importance, but she had stopped doing that because she and Jen had seen a show on PBS about right-brain, creative people, and they'd decided that was what they wanted to be. List-making was a totally left-brain thing. Besides, her mom listed everything, including what shoes to wear with what outfit, and while Susie loved her mother, she definitely didn't want to be like her.

Susie crossed her legs up under her and closed her eyes. The images of everything she'd seen that morning crowded together. Massonville was so different from L.A. It was smaller, and quieter, and there wasn't even a quarter as much traffic. The river and the old houses people had fixed up were cool. Everything—the houses, the trees, and the people—all seemed to have roots, like they'd been growing in the same place for a while. That was way cool. Susie opened her eyes. She had to stop using the same expressions, like "cool," over and over. That was definitely not a creative use of language.

If she'd still been making lists, she would have made one of the new people she was meeting. So far there were R.B., who was dorky but nice, and Katie, who Susie had a feeling she was really going to like once she got to know her. But the most interesting new person wasn't actually new at all. It was her mom. When her mother had stood in the middle of the old stage, she'd become someone Susie had never seen before. Her face had gotten all kind of soft and shiny, and the little worry lines between her eyebrows had gone. Susie had thought about taking a picture of Randa standing there, but she'd been afraid her mother's new expression would go away. Mom always tried to look casual when her picture was taken, but she was still posing.

Susie stood up. There were three brick steps that went from the stoop to the ground, and they were a little uneven, so she was careful going down them. When she got to the bottom, she looked up at the opera house. "It's ours," she said softly, trying out the idea. It felt okay. . . . No, it felt better than okay; it felt real. More real than the house in Northridge—which she and Jen called the Puke Carpet Palace—or her school or her mom's stupid clients.

Susie backed up as far as she could, all the way into the hedge, so she could see up to the third floor. It had been weird when they were in all those hotel rooms with the beds still made up with the sheets and pillowcases on them. And it had been weird when they were downstairs in the kitchen with all the dishes and the pots and pans neatly stacked on the shelves and in the cabinets, like someone was going to use them. Susie had said it was like the place was waiting for someone. Now when she thought about that, she pictured her mother standing next to Katie on the stage. Her mom had said the theater was magic, and then the soft new look had come over her face.

All of a sudden, Susie knew she'd been right. The theater *was* waiting for someone. It had been sitting here in this awesome little town for all those years waiting for *them*! The whole thing was such a total no-brainer, she didn't know why she hadn't seen it right away. Now all she had to do was convince her left-brain, list-making, noncreative mother, who never did anything that wasn't practical, that they had to keep it.

The hedge was surrounding something that Susie couldn't see. She started walking along it, trying to find a way to get through. She wasn't quite sure why, she just knew she had to see what was on the other side. She began walking faster, so fast she was almost running. A piece of gravel got into one of her sandals, but she didn't stop to take it out. She kept on going until she found what she was looking for. On the right side of the rectangle was a wide break in the hedge. There was a gate in the empty place; it was all broken, and the hinges were rusted shut, but it had been some sort of an entrance once, with a kind of trellis thing over the top. It took Susie a couple of minutes to push in what was left of the gate, and to work her way through the high weeds that had grown up around it, but she finally made it.

She was in a garden. Once, when she was a little kid, she'd read *The Secret Garden*. She hadn't liked it at the time, but now as she looked around her, she could see how wrong she'd been. This garden was fancy, like one you'd find behind a big old-fashioned house—at least, it had been fancy once. Now it was all overgrown, but you could still tell what it had been like. The hedge that surrounded it was bushy in some places and ratty in others. The stone walkways that crisscrossed through it were broken, with grass growing up between the cracks, and there were no flowers in the flower beds, just weeds. There were stone benches all over, but most of them were broken too, and there was yucky green stuff on a lot of them.

Suddenly, Susie felt depressed. She needed something, just one thing, about this old place to be clean and not broken. Her mom didn't have any imagination and she'd be totally hung up on how much work it would take to fix everything and how much it would cost. There was no way she would see how great it all could be. Somehow Susie had to get her past that, but this garden wasn't going to be a help. She started to go, but then she stopped to look around one last time. That was when she saw three large gray human figures floating over the bushes and weeds.

CHAPTER 11

Massonville 2006

For a moment Susie wanted to run; she'd always hated creepy dead-people movies and TV shows. But she looked again and saw that the figures were actually statues made out of some kind of stone. They looked like they were floating because the underbrush was so high that the bases were hidden. There were two women and a man, each at a corner of the garden, staring out over the dirt and weeds with blind statue eyes. She looked over to the fourth corner, searching for a statue there. That corner was empty.

Susie made her way across the old garden to the statue that was farthest away from her. She had to tilt her head back to see the face because the base was so high. The figure was female—she looked like she was maybe nineteen or twenty years old—with curly hair that came down to her waist. She was wearing a dress that tied high under her boobs and fell to her feet in panels, and she was standing behind what looked like a railing, reaching out for something or someone. She should have been pretty, standing there in her fairy-tale dress with pointy sleeves like they wore in the Middle Ages, but her nose and her jaw were too big, and there was something about the way her fingers were curved that made her hands look like claws. The only girly things about her were her big eyes and her long hair. Susie tilted her head back even farther and tried to decide if she liked her or not.

"So you found the old girl," said a voice behind her. She jerked around to see R.B.

"Who is she?" she asked.

He began pushing down the weeds that had grown up around the base of the statue. "Help me get rid of this stuff," he said. They yanked away enough of it so that Susie could see the name that had been carved in raised letters under the statue's feet. It said JULIET VENABLE, and there was a date: 1881. Below that was a sentence in quotations that read, PARTING IS SUCH SWEET SORROW.

"Meet the first of the Venables to own the Venable Opera House," said R.B. "Juliet bought the place in 1878. Not being one to hide her light under a bushel, she had this statue of herself put in the garden three years later for the enjoyment of her theater patrons." He looked up at the statue. "She wasn't exactly what you'd expect Shakespeare's gentle Juliet to look like, was she? But that was her most famous part."

"She was an actress?"

"She and her brother both were. They traveled around the country in the 1870s with their own company; Shakespeare's *Romeo and Juliet* was their big draw. Then Juliet settled here and founded the Venable dynasty. During the 1910s and 1920s that family was our main claim to fame in Massonville."

"Did her brother settle here too?"

"No. The legend has it that when she bought the theater, Romeo Venable—that was his real name, by the way—took off. Actors were vagabonds in those days. I guess he just couldn't stand being tied down." He turned back to the statue. "She looks very . . . alone, doesn't she?"

Susie studied the strong jaw and the hands grabbing at the air. "I think she's the kind of person who always gets what she wants."

"Sounds like you don't approve of her."

"I think I don't."

"That's too bad, since you're probably kin."

"We're related to her?"

"I don't know for sure—but it makes sense, doesn't it?"

"But we live in California, and we've never even been in this part of the country before."

"There must be some connection between you and old Juliet up there. You inherited her theater."

He was right. Add another thing to the list of things she had to think about—if she'd still been making lists. "Would you mind if I took some pictures?" she asked.

"Go ahead. It's your mother's statue." He sat down on one of the crumbling benches to wait while Susie carefully aimed at every angle of the stone figure. The nice thing about him was that he didn't make her feel like he was getting impatient, so she was able to get all the shots she wanted. She was finishing up with several pictures of the writing at the base of the statue when something occurred to her. "Her name was Juliet and her brother's name was Romeo and those were the parts they played. Isn't that kind of strange?"

"Not really. The Venables always named their children after characters in Shakespeare's plays. It was a family thing. And since most of them were actors, unless they consciously avoided playing their namesakes, it was bound to happen sometimes. If you're through with Juliet, the next statue— chronologically speaking—is over in that corner."

Susie moved on to the second statue while R.B. got more comfortable on his bench. The second figure was of a man wearing a cape and a shirt with big floppy sleeves that was open halfway down his chest. His pants were really tight—they looked like the jeans one of her mom's clients wore when he was auditioning for women or gay casting directors—and they were stuffed into a pair of high boots. The figure was holding a sword up in the air. Except for a pointed beard that Susie thought was gross, he was handsome. But the expression on his face was kind of empty, so when you looked at it you didn't feel like you knew anything about him. It was clear he was an actor, though. You got that from the way he was standing with his feet apart and his head thrown back. He had that whole actor-y look-at-me thing going on.

R.B. explained that his name was Edward Rain, which meant he wasn't actually a Venable but had been married to one. His statue was made in

1935. The line under his feet said, THOU HAST MY LIFE; MY HONOR IS MINE OWN.

"That's not a speech from a play Shakespeare wrote, is it?" Susie asked.

"Lord love you, no! That's a quotation from *The Prince of Zanzona,* a piece of early-twentieth-century theater garbage that was Edward Rain's bread and butter. He earned enough money touring with that play to keep the opera house afloat for three decades, God bless him."

Susie took more pictures and then they moved on to the third statue, which was another woman. She was short and kind of stumpy and her face looked a lot like Juliet's. She was wearing a dress with a full skirt that came halfway between her knees and her ankles; it wasn't exactly an old-fashioned dress, but it wasn't like anything a person would wear in 2006. Her name was Olivia, and the date carved under her feet was 1952. But there was no line from a play.

"Why isn't something written on her pedestal?" Susie asked.

"Olivia wasn't an actress, so she didn't have a famous role," R.B. said. "There's a rumor that she was pretty upset when her husband stuck her statue in the garden, because she thought that honor should be reserved for the performers in the family." He looked up at Olivia, "But she deserved to be here. By the fifties there wasn't much call for live theater anymore, and the opera house hadn't done any real business for years. Olivia kept it going—Lord knows how—for another twenty years."

"Then what happened?"

"She lost her son—he was supposed to take over the theater when she retired—and after that, she just couldn't keep on fighting. At least that's what the old-timers say." R.B. paused. Then he added softly, "I guess it's always been a fight to keep this old place from going under." He looked kind of down, and for some reason Susie hated to see him like that.

"But it's still here," she said, to encourage him.

"Barely." He walked over to the corner of the garden that didn't have a statue and began pulling at some bushes. Susie thought about offering to help him, but decided not to. He seemed to need to do it himself. After a minute, when he'd cleared the spot, he stepped back, and she saw what had been underneath all the greenery. It was a base for a fourth statue—an empty base. There was no name written on it, and there weren't any lines from a play, just a date. It said 1973.

"The summer before her son died, Olivia bought this plinth for a statue she was planning to put here in this corner," R.B. said. "Then all of a sudden she canceled the thing."

"Why?" Susie asked.

"No one knows."

CHAPTER 12

Massonville 2006

R.B. checked his watch. "We should go back and find the others," he said. Susie still had a gazillion questions about the opera house and the statues and the Venables, but then he added, "Your mother will be wondering where you are, and I don't want her to get mad at me." He glanced up at the back of the opera house, which you could see above the hedge. "She already doesn't like this old place much—you know?" He was looking sad again. For a moment Susie thought about lying and saying he'd gotten it wrong and her mom really loved the theater, but he'd never go for it, he was too smart. Besides, he didn't need to hear stuff that would make him feel good if it wasn't true. He wanted her mom to keep the theater, and so did Susie. So they both had to face facts.

"My mother is afraid of her right brain," she told him. "She's a really great person, but she tries to be all about schedules and balancing the budget. And lists."

He nodded. "I know," he said. "Most people do." He smiled and gave her a little wink. The winking was definitely lame, but his smile was awesome because it went to his eyes. He really was nice. It was too bad he wasn't her mom's type. Her mother didn't date much, but when she did, the guys were very organized. And when you talked to them, they had a way of making you feel like they had something more important they should be doing. Her mother chose assholes, which was a word Susie didn't like to use, but sometimes it just fit. Nice R.B. Moultire wouldn't appeal to Mom. Susie sighed softly. And he probably wasn't going to be much help with making Mom see they had to hang on to the opera house either.

"Do you think a little lunch would sweeten her up?" R.B. asked, as if he could see what she was thinking. Susie sighed again and wished it could be that easy.

R.B. suggested a little barbeque place in Cobetta. It was across the town square from the Moultire office, so they could walk over and read the will after they finished eating. He said he wished he could introduce them to his parents and his sister but everyone was out of the office.

At first, when they were all sitting in R.B.'s office after lunch, Susie thought the reading of the will wasn't going to be very exciting. They already knew what they were getting, and R.B. had already said he didn't know who had given it to them or why.

But there was one surprise, after all. Whoever had given them the theater had also given them some money so they could run it. For a moment Susie got excited, because how could her mother say that the opera house was too expensive if everything was paid for?

"The money is to be spent on operating costs for the theater," R.B. told them. "You can't touch the principle, and at present rates it will generate about ten thousand a year."

Susie thought that sounded pretty good, but then Katie asked how far ten thousand would go toward covering the repairs, and R.B. looked really unhappy and said he was afraid it wouldn't go very far. And, it turned out, the money wouldn't even make a dent in the running expenses of the theater either. Mom said none of that was their problem, and she asked R.B. if the trust was tied to the building. He said yes, it was, and if they were to sell the property, the money would go to several different charities, and Mom said, well then, they wouldn't be splitting the ten thousand a year.

When they'd finished reading the will, R.B. said it would take a little time to clean up the paperwork, but since Mom and Katie weren't going to

be staying in Massonville, he could fax anything that needed their signa-
tures.

"How long before we can put the building on the market?" Mom asked.

"I'd say at least a month," R.B. said.

"And it will probably take forever to sell it," Mom added.

"I wouldn't count on a quick sale," R.B. agreed.

Or maybe no one will ever want to buy it! thought Susie. *Everyone says it's
so expensive and it's a mess . . . so, what if no one wants it?* Just the idea made
her want to jump up and down like a little kid.

That was when the Moultires' secretary—who had mega big hair and
acrylic nails painted bright pink—poked her head in the door. "R.B., while
you were out your mama called. She said to tell your clients she knows a
buyer for that old opera house."

Susie had never before hated someone she didn't know, but now she
wanted to close the door on the secretary's head so hard that her stupid hair
got squashed. But it wasn't the secretary's fault that her mother got all
happy and said, "All right! I guess we can stay an extra day or two for that."
That was just Mom being scared again.

There was a bed-and-breakfast in Cobetta that Susie had thought looked
awesome when they'd passed it earlier, but the Moultires' secretary had
booked them into the big hotel down by the new convention center in Massonville. Susie asked R.B. about the pretty place, but he said it didn't have
satellite TV or high-speed Internet, which would make her mother really
not like Georgia. Susie had a lot of stuff she wanted to do on the computer
herself, so she didn't say anything.

After they'd checked into their rooms, her mom laid down to take a nap.
Susie set up her printer and went to work transferring the pictures in her
camera to her laptop. She raced through most of the ones she'd taken before they'd arrived at the theater, but then she slowed down. She'd promised
Jen she'd send pictures of the new inheritance, and she e-mailed Jen tons
of shots of the lobby and the rooms with the beds still ready for someone to
sleep in them. Finally she came to the last pictures she'd taken—the ones
in the old garden with the three statues. She picked one of each statue to
send to Jen and typed, "My family. Can you believe?"

But then she didn't send them. There was something about those figures she didn't want even her best friend to see. Not yet. Not until she knew how they fit in with her and her mom. She clicked backward and started scrolling slowly through the statue pictures again. She had at least a dozen shots of Edward Rain with his sword and his blank face, and about as many of Olivia Venable. She hadn't taken as many of the empty pedestal because there was something so sad about it.

Finally she came to the statue she'd saved for last—the one of Juliet Venable. There were several pictures of Juliet's claw hands grabbing for something out of reach, and lots more of her face as she looked off at whatever it was that only she could see. Susie zoomed in as tight as she could on the image, and ran her finger over Juliet's features on the laptop screen; the jaw that was too wide, and the nose that made her look harsh. The face wasn't pretty, but Susie couldn't look away from it.

She's probably your kin, R.B. had said.

Are you? Susie wondered. *Are you my great-great-great-great-great-grandmother or something?* With her finger she traced two slow circles around Juliet Venable's big wide-set eyes.

Part Two

CHAPTER 13

Massonville 1878

In her dressing room in the Massonville Opera House, Juliet Venable drew a narrow black line at the edge of each of her eyelids, then stepped back to see her reflection in her looking glass. She'd placed her dressing table close to the wall lamps, to approximate the effect of the footlights onstage. Now she backed up and studied herself. A little more darkening on the lashes and brows, she decided, and she'd be done. The broad blue-black band so many actresses painted around their eyes was not for her. It made the eyes seem brilliant when seen up close, but from the house they looked like small black holes.

Juliet leaned in and brushed her lashes sparingly with black pomade. Papa always said she had true stage eyes, well opened and expressive. What was never said but was always understood was that she had to use them wisely; her eyes and her luxurious long hair were her only claims to beauty.

Her makeup now completed, she knocked on the wall that separated the two star dressing rooms, and waited for the answering knock that would tell her that her brother, Romie—his full name was Romeo—had finally arrived at the theater and was finishing his own preparations for the night's performance. But there was silence from his side. Where was he? She put on her wrapper, went out into the hallway, and rapped on his dressing room door, calling his name. Again, there was no response. From the far end of the hallway where the rest of the company dressed in two communal rooms, she could hear the sounds of actors getting ready for a first night. There was the joking and the chatting, the high-pitched laughter, and the singing that didn't quite cover jangled nerves. Someone began to whistle and was silenced by his colleagues. Whistling backstage brought bad luck.

Juliet moved quickly to the dressing room allotted to the men and leaned against the door so she could listen for Romie's voice. She preferred to stay alone before a performance, but sometimes he liked to have company. She waited until she was sure he wasn't there, then hurried back to her own room.

She wasn't sure what to do next. The stage manager had already called the half hour. Her costume hung on the wall, but she hadn't put it on yet. It was their custom when they played Romeo and Juliet for Romie to help her hook up the back of her gown, and she would hold his doublet so he could shrug into it. Then they would exchange two books, the Bible Maman had bestowed on Juliet at birth, and Romie's beloved copy of *Walker's Critical Pronouncing Dictionary,* which Papa had given him to ensure that he always pronounced the old-time names and words correctly. During the performance Romie's dictionary stayed in Juliet's dressing room and her Bible stayed in his. After the performance, the two volumes were returned to their rightful owners.

They had been performing this ritual since they'd first acted *Romeo and Juliet* in the theater Papa had run in Cincinnati. In those days they had played the balcony scene only. As a boy of six, and a girl of eight, they had recited words of undying love: "Good night, good night, / parting is such / sweet sorrow, / That I shall say good night till it be morrow." They were infant prodigies back then, a little novelty act Papa offered the audience after the adult company had finished.

Now Romeo and Juliet Venable, at eighteen and twenty, were the adults. Maman and Papa were gone and so was the theater Papa had managed for so many years. Now his son and daughter had begun their own touring company, and when they acted *Romeo and Juliet,* they performed not just one scene but the whole play. And by all accounts it was their best work. Juliet frowned, remembering that Romie hadn't wanted to include the play when they were planning their tour.

"We don't have to act those roles anymore," he'd said. They were standing on the stage of the playhouse that had been their home since they were born. Five weeks earlier Maman had died of cholera, and Papa had followed her three days later. Although the Venable family had come to think of the theater as theirs, it had not belonged to them—Papa had been hired by the theater's owner to manage it. After Papa's death, Romie had tried to persuade the man to let him take Papa's place, but he'd said Romie did not have enough experience. The owner had disbanded the company, leaving it's young leading man and woman without employment. Their situation had been desperate. Papa had had nothing to leave them. Even the home they'd lived in had been rented, and the landlord would expect to be paid by the first of the month. There was no time to mourn the loss of their parents; the young Venables had to find a way to support themselves. They'd decided to try their luck in the hinterlands with a theater troupe of their own. It was how their parents had begun years ago, barnstorming around the country until Papa was hired to take over the theater in Cincinnati.

The first order of business for the new touring company had been the choosing of the repertoire, and that was when the trouble with Romie had begun. "When Papa was alive we had to perform *Romeo and Juliet*," he'd said, "but Papa is gone now."

This was not the first time Romie had tried to shed himself of the play. When he'd celebrated his fifteenth birthday, he had told Papa that he was too old to play a romantic story with his sister. "I am not sure the public will accept it now that I am a grown man," he'd said.

"The great Fanny Kemble played Juliet to her father's Romeo," Papa had roared back. "The magnificent Charlotte Cushman played Romeo in breeches to her sister Susan's Juliet. The public accepts this convention, because it knows it is watching *acting*, and because brilliant actors make their own reality. My son will be no less than a brilliant actor."

And then later, more gently, Maman had said, "Your Papa has two children who are equally gifted. If you and Juliet do not act the leading roles together, he will have to favor one of you over the other. Which one of you would you have him choose, Romie?"

So Romie had gone on playing the role. But now Papa was gone and Romie had tried to set it aside again. Juliet hadn't let him.

"We must perform one Shakespearean play," she'd said reasonably, "and we don't have a big enough company for any of the historical dramas." More important, and they both knew it, none of those pieces suited their impetuous acting style half so well as the one for which Papa had named them. "We always have such a success with *Romeo and Juliet*," she'd added.

"But we're not children any more, Jule. Don't you want to make changes?"

She didn't. More than anything, she wanted things to go on as they always had. Besides, if they were to agree not to act opposite each other anymore, they would not be able to play any of the other great roles she had imagined for them: Hamlet and Ophelia, Othello and Desdemona, Macbeth and his lady; all would be lost to them if Romie insisted on "changes." She had drawn in a breath and said, "If you're tired of acting with me . . ."

"It's not that."

"You can go to New York and find a management to take you. You can strike out on your own." She hadn't meant a word of it. It had been merely a ploy to bring him to his senses. She had waited for him to put his arms around her and tell her that he would never, ever do that. Instead, he had stared at the stage floor and remained silent. Panic had started to overtake her. "If you do, it will be the end of us, because I will not find an engagement so quickly. I'm not a beauty. They will not want me."

"Jule, stop, please—"

But suddenly, the pain she'd been trying not to feel for so many days was overflowing. "First I lost Maman and Papa; now I will lose you!" The words had seemed to burst out of her, and then she had wept—for their parents who had died, and the theater that had been their home, and for the time when she had been happiest, when she and her brother had been Papa's infant prodigies. And Romie, who loved her and could never bear to see her hurt, had finally put his arms around her. There had been no more talk of dropping *Romeo and Juliet* from their repertoire.

But she could not act the play all by herself! Juliet pulled herself back to the present. Where the devil was Romie? He knew how important this engagement in Massonville was to them. It was only for three weeks, but the owner of the opera house had hinted that if all went well, they could be extended for the entire season. That would be a gift from heaven, because after three months of begging and banging on doors, this was the first engagement their fledgling company had managed to book—and it was the only one. If they did not please here in Massonville, they would be forced to disband their little troupe, and then . . .

We must have a success here! We must! Juliet thought.

But they would not have one if they weren't able to play on their very first night. Juliet's heart began to pound, and her head felt light. She sat down and forced herself to breathe, but she couldn't stop her mind from racing. Massonville was a river town, full of pleasure palaces, gaming houses, and taverns. Her brother had a taste for all three, but he couldn't. . . . He wouldn't. . . . *Please, dear Lord.*

It was time to dress. Thank goodness she never wore a wig. In her present state she would have stabbed herself with the pins. She stepped into her costume. Most actresses arrayed themselves in pale gauzes when playing Shakespeare's Juliet, but she did not believe the passionate daughter of the Capulets should be portrayed as a swooning namby-pamby. She wore a robe made of crimson muslin—she could not afford silk—with sateen panels she'd dyed to match and stitched on, so the costume shimmered in the light. The bright color had the added advantage of taking attention away from what one critic had unkindly referred to as her "unfortunate looks."

From the hallway outside her door she could hear the others starting to go down the stairs to take their places in the wings. She circled the dressing room, her skirt swishing. Damn Romie! What was she going to do? What would become of their actors if they lost this engagement? They had three in their company in addition to themselves: a Juvenile Man playing Mercutio, a Heavy Man playing Friar Laurence, and a Heavy Woman playing the Nurse. The rest of the roles were filled by the acting company connected with the opera house. Most of these local performers were amateurs. Juliet stopped her pacing and tried to imagine the humiliation of having to admit to this motley company that she and her brother had defaulted in their obligations.

The truth was, it would be mortifying to be dismissed by such a ramshackle operation as the Massonville Opera House. The building itself was beautiful. It had been built only two years earlier and the restaurant and the

hotel attached to the theater offered the traveler every modern conve-
nience, while the theater auditorium was elegantly appointed in the latest
style. Backstage, however, it was another story. The stage and the dressing
rooms were less than clean, and the "props" and what few stock costumes
the theater owned were stored in such a slipshod fashion that they were
filthy and virtually unusable. Worst of all, she'd been told that there would
be only one man working backstage during performances, an elderly stage
manager who, if his behavior during their rehearsals was any indication, was
given to sleeping on the job.

The sorry state of affairs might have been due to the fact that the man
who had originally built the opera house, one Cecil Honeycutt, had died a
year earlier. He had left the theater to his widow and his son, and, clearly,
they had not yet learned to manage it properly. So far Juliet had not met either of them. The son, whose name was James, had sent word that he was
busy, but he and the widow would grace the opening night with their presence.

The Venable company had been greeted by James's wife, Cornelia. Cornelia Morgan Honeycutt was not a pretty woman—*Why must I always notice
that?* Juliet asked herself. Cornelia's face was too pale, the mouse-brown
hair that framed it was unruly, and her mouth was too large. There was a
sadness in her large brown eyes that Juliet wondered about, but there was
great intelligence too, and an eagerness in her smile, and in her quick,
headlong way of speaking. Upon meeting the company, she had quickly dispensed with the formalities and demanded that all of the actors call her
Cornelia. She was charmed when she learned that the Venable siblings
were named after Shakespearean characters, and in a matter of days she
had picked up the actors' trick of quoting lines from the various plays they
were presenting. It was clear that Cornelia was severely stagestruck.

She attended rehearsals, provided refreshments for the company afterward, and even offered to help some of her local actors learn the parts they
did not yet know. In the two days it had taken the company to settle in,
her slim figure, usually clad in an unattractive gray gown—worn as half-
mourning for her late father-in-law, Juliet assumed—had become a familiar
presence to them.

Yet her involvement with the company made Juliet wary. Many things
could go wrong behind the scenes, and one did not want the theater's owner

knowing about all of one's mishaps and mistakes. But one also did not refuse the wife of the man who could extend—or end—the engagement. So Juliet smiled and expressed her gratitude for Cornelia's assistance—and remained guarded.

Juliet opened the watch she kept on her dressing table during performances. It was time for the play to begin. Knocking on Romie's door again would be futile; she would have heard him if he had come in. She would have to go downstairs and tell the stage manager to delay ringing up the curtain. The good Lord knew what excuse she would give. Or what she would do after that. Holding the back of her gown, she turned to leave, but was stopped by a knock on the door.

With a cry of relief she opened it. "Romie, where . . . ," she started to say, and then stopped as she found herself facing Cornelia.

CHAPTER 14

Massonville 1878

Cornelia was dressed for the opening night in another hideous gray gown. This one was trimmed with jet beading. Juliet suppressed an irrational desire to giggle. Her heart began to pound again.

As was her fashion, Cornelia came quickly to the point. "Juliet, I have not seen your brother come into the theater this evening," she said.

Lies ran through Juliet's head. *He is in the next room. He never left the opera house after the day's rehearsal.* Or perhaps, *My brother always dresses at home on first nights; he will be here.* But it would serve no purpose. Not now, with the house full, and James Honeycutt in the audience waiting for the curtain to rise.

As if reading her mind, Cornelia added, "My husband and his stepmother do not know I have come backstage. So far no one has noticed that anything is amiss."

Juliet's heart slowed back to normal. Cornelia wanted to help; that was obvious. Juliet made a quick decision. "I don't know where Romie is," she said.

"Would you allow me to send someone to look for him?"

"I'm afraid he may have gone to—"

"Our people know all the saloons on the waterfront." Cornelia began hooking up the back of Juliet's gown. "Unfortunately, they have to." She stopped her task, and sorrow showed in her large eyes. For a moment Juliet thought Cornelia was going to explain its source, but instead she went back to work on the hooks and eyes. "If you can think of some excuse to delay the curtain," she went on, "we will find your brother." A thought seemed to occur to her. "Unless you think he will not be able . . . ?" She trailed off.

"Romie can act even if he has been drinking liquor all day," Juliet said grimly.

"Unfair, Jule! He can act if he's been drinking liquor for a week," said a familiar voice from behind her. She whirled around to see Romie in the doorway.

He was leaning against the doorjamb with his arms crossed over his chest, looking impossibly handsome. Her brother was not very tall—no Venable was—but he had been born with Maman's perfect nose and mouth. From Papa he had gotten a head of Byronic black curls, and dark glowing eyes. Romie had all the charm and beauty of their family, and she had none. Acceptance of that reality had been the first painful lesson of her youth. And even now, as furious as she was at him, he could still take her breath away.

"I'll go down to the stage and tell them to wait," Cornelia said, and left Juliet alone with her brother.

They faced each other silently, and she was determined, for once, not to speak first. But Romie looked as if he would stay where he was all night, and the curtain was waiting for them.

"How dare you do this to me?" she demanded.

"I just had a couple of glasses for courage, Jule. That's all. Just a little for courage."

He had never been afraid of a performance in his life.

"You scared me to death." She was having trouble catching her breath. "I thought you were gone, and . . ." But she couldn't finish. Because that was what had frightened her more than all the rest, the fear that he had left. She was gasping now, and he saw it and came to her.

"Jule, breathe deep, " he said, and as always, she did as he told her. Then he said, "It's your own fault. I told you I didn't want to play Romeo and Juliet."

He had put her through all of it—the fear and the shame, in front of Cornelia—to punish her? He was teaching her a lesson? All her rage came back. She pulled back her hand to slap him. But Romie caught it in a grip made strong through years of stage fights and swordplay. "Oh no," he said softly. "Save that for the performance." And he went to change into his costume.

That night it was as if there was no one on the stage but the two of them. The early scenes in the play before Romeo and Juliet met barely existed for either of them; Juliet knew they were both waiting for the moment at the Capulets' ball when he would see her for the first time. And it came quickly, faster than it ever had. Suddenly, she was dancing at the party in her father's house with her crimson skirt swirling at her feet and her beautiful hair flying out behind her. And Romie was there watching her. She came to a stop in front of him, breathless, and looked up at him. He was supposed to be holding up his mask; he was supposed to lead her back into the dance. He was supposed to smile. But he didn't move. He held the mask at his side, and looked down at her. He did not smile. When he spoke, his voice was rough.

"If I profane with my unworthiest hand / This holy shrine, the gentle sin is this; / My lips, two blushing pilgrims, ready stand / To smooth that rough touch with a tender kiss."

She couldn't break his gaze. The truth was, she didn't want to. Around them she was aware of the other actors growing quiet, watching. She delivered her next lines, but she couldn't have said how, she was too lost in his eyes that glowed.

Now the moment arrived when the text called for the first kiss. Papa had staged it carefully, turning them upstage, blocking them from the view of the house so no one would see that it did not actually happen. "Convey the emotion," Papa had said. "The action is not important." But tonight she didn't move. Neither did Romie.

"Thus from my lips by thine my sin is purged," he said. His eyes were so dark they were black.

"Then have my lips the sin that they have took," she answered. They were so close now, only the tiniest sliver of air separated them. It would be nothing to reach up, and let her mouth find his. But that was when she heard it—the silence from the house that was more powerful than a roar. The audience was with them, watching every inch of them, waiting for something, it didn't know what. She saw Romie blink as if he were waking from a trance, and she knew he had heard the roar too. She moved back just enough to widen the sliver of air. There was a collective sigh, of relief or regret, from the house. When she left the stage a few seconds later, a wave of applause washed over the stage.

After that they could do no wrong. The public became the third character in their private play for two. They flirted and teased, and the house drove them on, every line, every move they made. The audience was cheering for them, aching for them, the star-crossed lovers, until finally she was saying the words of the scene they had been playing all of their lives.

"Good night, good night! parting is such sweet sorrow / That I shall say good night till it be morrow."

She was going to leave him now, because she had to, even though it felt so right to be with him. He climbed up to the platform just below her balcony and she leaned over the railing to give him her hand to kiss—the business Papa had rehearsed them in so long ago—but suddenly he pulled her down so she was on her knees and her hair was falling around them. He reached up for her face. *"Convey the emotion without the action,"* Papa had said. But now Romie was pulling her closer, and now they really were going to . . . and then Romie stopped. They stayed as they were, frozen in place, her hair a curtain around them, his hands holding her face. In his eyes she read something that could have been pain or fear. It was the same pain and fear she felt, that was making it hard for her to breathe. She pulled away from him and ran offstage.

As she stood in the wings, she knew they had come close to something . . . a line they could not, must not, cross. But they would go back to it, over and over again. Because that line was where their most brilliant acting took place.

She had a moment of doubt when she and Romie went in front of the curtain to accept the compliments of the house. His hand was shaking in hers and she thought she heard him murmur "Never again." But as she swept her curtsy to the sea of waving handkerchiefs, hats, fans, and walking sticks in front of her, and heard the applause that came from the heart, she knew she would never act as well with anyone else. And so whatever the cost, it was worth it.

CHAPTER 15

Massonville 1878

The morning after their triumphant performance, Juliet awakened feeling the most peace she had known since Maman and Papa died. There had been times in the past few months when she had worried that she was holding Romie back by keeping him with her, but after last night she knew she had been right. " 'The play's the thing,' " she quoted Hamlet from the depths of her bed. "The play-*ing* is the *only* thing," she added, mangling the words of the melancholy Dane. The fear she had felt the night before had vanished, never to return. Now, finally, Romie would understand why they must always work together. He could not deny that their performance last night had been as fine—no, as brilliant as any in the best theaters of New York. It had frightened him, but he would get over that. He liked to pretend he didn't care about their profession, but underneath his cavalier pose, he was as dedicated as she was. He could never leave her now, and she would not have to be alone. She got out of bed and dressed herself quickly. They would be acting a different play tonight—they had three in their repertoire—and she had called a rehearsal to put the local company through the stage business.

The walk from the boardinghouse where the company was staying to the opera house was not far, but Juliet had started early, wanting to get there before her cast. It was a beautiful morning; the air was still cool and there was mist on the river. She liked Massonville. It was, she thought, the perfect town for a resident theater.

The day of the small stock company like Papa's was almost over. In most cities that were big enough to support a theater, tours coming out of New York with star performers were becoming the fashion. But Massonville was unique. It wasn't large, but the riverboats and the train lines brought in a stream of visitors, and the river provided power for three cotton mills, which drew merchants, bankers, tradespeople, and professionals to the area. In addition, because of the money brought in by the commercial interests, the town was rich enough to support a female seminary and two colleges. Massonville had a ready-made audience waiting to be entertained, but it was still too small to attract the touring companies from New York.

She had reached the river. In front of her were the wharves; behind her were the homes of the wealthy who had flocked to Massonville after the war between the states. Juliet stopped and allowed herself to dream some more about the opera house. It was exactly the kind of haven she and Romie needed. If they had it, they would not have to troop around the country. They would not be at the mercy of gouging booking agents and lazy theater managers. They would be masters of their own fate, as Papa had been. Juliet began walking again. If she owned the opera house, she would offer a mixed season, she decided. There would be old-fashioned favorites like *Under the Gaslight* and *The Two Orphans* for the middle class, and more sophisticated fare like *Adrienne Lecouvreur* and *Diplomacy* for the wealthy. And, of course they would perform Shakespeare's works. Over the years she and Romie would act all the great roles together. They would build their following here, but if word spread, they might even become famous outside of Massonville. If they never did, they would still have a place they could call home.

The mist had risen from the river by the time she arrived at the theater. The building sat in front of her, large and dazzling white in the early morning sun. It seemed as if it had been there forever, as if it had taken root in the soil. *It will be here for generations to come,* she thought, and she felt herself dig her shoes into the ground as if she were trying to take root with it. She looked at the entrance—there was something missing. If the building were hers, she would put up a canopy over the front arcade. Written on it in gold lettering would be "The Venable Opera House." For the generations to come.

The front door opened and Cornelia hailed her. "I saw you through the windows," she said as she rushed up. "I was coming to find you. My husband and his stepmother wish to speak with you and your brother."

They had not yet met James Honeycutt or his stepmother. It had been rude of them not to have come backstage to congratulate the company after its triumph the night before, but Romie had been in such a black mood that Juliet had been grateful for the owner's bad manners. Now, with this summons, all was instantly forgiven.

They mean to extend the engagement! Juliet thought joyfully. But Cornelia was looking grave, not at all like the bearer of good news.

"Is something wrong?" Juliet asked.

Cornelia hesitated. "I'm not quite sure . . ." She looked up at the façade of the theater in front of them. "It is beautiful, isn't it?" she said.

"Yes," Juliet said. "It must be a great source of pride for your family."

Cornelia turned away. "It was Mr. Cecil—my late father-in-law—who loved the opera house. He wanted Massonville to be the London of the South." She paused, picking her words carefully. "Lavinia, his widow, is very young. And my husband, James, is . . ." She looked back at the theater. "I wish someone else owned it!" she said. Then she added quickly, "We should fetch your brother. They will want to speak with him as well."

They ran back to the boardinghouse to waken Romie.

CHAPTER 16

Massonville 1878

The owner's office was located on the left side of the lobby, a narrow hallway and a second door separating it from the backstage. The chamber itself was decorated in an older style: the woodwork was dark, and the wallpaper was covered with a green leaf and stem design that Juliet thought quite ugly. There were no windows, but a vent in the ceiling kept some air flowing through the room. One wall was given over to shelves full of books and bric-a-brac. The furnishings consisted of a large desk with an equally large desk chair upholstered in a green fabric, two smaller chairs—someone had thrown a handsomely worked afghan over one of them—and several small tables. Against the back wall was a carved circular stairway, which, Cornelia had confided, led to the family quarters above. Leaving Romie and Juliet in the office, she hurried up to the apartment to fetch her husband and his stepmother.

Not having been told to sit, Juliet stood in the middle of the room, but Romie sprawled out on a low step of the staircase. When she'd found her brother in the boardinghouse, he had not yet been to bed. She did not want to know the specifics of the night he had spent.

"Stand up," she hissed over her shoulder at him. Much would be for-given an actor who had made a big hit, but it would be better if he did not appear to be insolent. From behind her she heard the sound of her brother pulling himself to his feet. She resisted the temptation to look at him. When Romie was in one of his defiant moods, it was usually best to disre-gard him.

" 'I am the monarch of the sea, / The ruler of the Queen's Navee,' " he sang softly.

Gilbert and Sullivan were all the fashion in New York, and Romie had wanted to include *H.M.S. Pinafore* in their repertoire, even going so far as to obtain a pirated version of the work, since it had not yet been produced in the United States. Juliet had pointed out that neither of them were singers, and her brother now demonstrated that fact by warbling in an off-key baritone, " 'But when the breezes blow, / I generally go below.' " Then, having forgotten the lyric, he filled in with a series of "tum, ti tum"s until she could not bear it any longer. She whirled around to see him posed on the staircase as if singing to a large chorus, the afghan wrapped around him like a cape. He was grinning, but there was something horribly sad about him, and his expression caught at her heart. They had been victorious the night before; why couldn't he be as happy as she was? Why couldn't they share it? For a moment, she felt lost. Seeing how hurt she was, he quickly unwound himself from the afghan and went to her. "Poor Jule," he said softly. "Is it really so important to you that we impress these provincials?"

"It's important that we have an engagement for the rest of the season," she said tartly.

"And then what? Where do we go next?"

She didn't know. *If only we had a theater of our own. If only we could go back to the way it used to be.*

"Jule, we've failed. Our tour is a failure. They want stars on the road now."

"But if Mr. Honeycutt offers—"

"If he offers to extend our engagement, we will thank God and stay. But it will only be postponing the inevitable." He hesitated, and then he said the words she feared most. "We're going to have to go to New York, Jule."

"Is that what you want?" she asked in a choked voice.

He couldn't meet her eyes; he knew as well as she what a move to New York would mean. "I want to work," he said finally. "I want to act. Wherever I can."

"Papa used to say, '*Le bon Dieu* will provide for the future if we provide for the present.'"

He turned to her then, and stroked her cheek tenderly. "Papa is dead, Jule," he said.

Cornelia entered the room, followed by a man in his early thirties. This was the elusive owner of the opera house. "My husband, Mr. James Honeycutt," Cornelia announced. But as Juliet came forward to acknowledge the introduction, she thought she understood at last the source of the sorrow she'd seen in Cornelia's eyes.

Juliet had not led a sheltered life; like most actors, her brother and her father were not strangers to the tavern, and she and Maman had helped them both to bed on more than one occasion. But unless she misread the case, James Honeycutt was not an occasional imbiber. His reddened eyes, florid cheeks, and sour breath that no amount of peppermint lozenges could mask completely, told the tale of one who, if he was not yet a dipsomaniac, was on his way to being one. No wonder Cornelia's people knew all the saloons on the riverfront. Mr. Honeycutt barely acknowledged Romie and Juliet as he made his way into the room.

Behind him was what could only be described as a vision. She was young—it would have stunned Juliet to have learned that she was more than thirty—and so beautiful that she seemed unreal. Shiny golden curls cascaded from a pretty ribbon at the back of her head. Her delicate little nose and shapely mouth complemented her pink and white complexion, and her sky-blue eyes were partially hidden by thick lashes. She was slender, and short enough to flatter most men by having to look up at them. But the heavily draped mauve mourning gown—the color was lovely with her eyes—revealed a womanly figure. This, Juliet and Romie were told, was Lavinia Honeycutt, widow of the late Cecil Honeycutt and stepmother to James.

Juliet felt something twist inside her. *What I could do if I had that face!* she thought. *What an Ophelia I could play. And . . . what a Juliet!* And the worst of it was, the little innocent probably didn't even realize what a gift she had.

The widow floated into the room. At her side, Juliet heard Romie draw in a breath, and she felt another twist. " 'Nymph, in thy orisons / Be all my sins remember'd,' " Romie murmured. The widow heard him, but instead of blushing as one would have expected, she turned and examined him coolly from head to toe. Finally she rewarded him with a ravishing smile that displayed two rows of pearl-like teeth. So she wasn't an innocent, after all. And she was well aware of her gifts.

James was not impressed by Romie's charm or his ready use of Shakespeare—a misuse of it, under the circumstances, but let that pass. Juliet studied the man who held their fate in his hands. Looking past the bloodshot eyes and florid cheeks, she saw an anger in him, and an air of defeat that made her uneasy. How had Cornelia ever come to marry him? He seated himself carefully in the green chair behind the large desk, waved his wife and his stepmother to the other chairs, and left Juliet and Romie standing. Under his breath, Romie sang so softly only Juliet could hear him, " 'I am the monarch of the sea . . .' "

"I am sorry I have to inform you that I will be terminating your engagement at the opera house by the end of next week," James Honeycutt said.

The walls seemed to spin around Juliet. Romie ceased his sotto voce concert. "But—but last night . . . ," Juliet stammered. "But last night . . . we had a big success. Weren't you there? You must have seen—"

"Jule, don't," Romie said under his breath.

But she had to go on. "We have a fine company, and you will not find a more comprehensive repertoire. I promise you, we will bring in the public—"

"That is immaterial now. In a month's time the opera house will no longer be here," James Honeycutt cut in.

"Oh, James!" cried Cornelia. "You can't tear it down!"

He was going to tear down this theater? It was like hearing that he planned to slaughter a living being. It took all of Juliet's self-control to keep herself from shouting, "No!"

"Cornelia," said her husband, "this is hardly a discussion to be having in front of strangers."

"Ah, think of us as furniture," said Romie. He smiled at Lavinia, who giggled back, the little fool. Juliet longed to shake her until those blue eyes bulged. This beautiful theater was going to be rubble, and she was flirting with Romie. Not that it would do any good. Her brother limited his amours to females who could not by any stretch of the imagination be called respectable. And even though Juliet suspected that Lavinia Honeycutt had more than a little in common with such females, in the eyes of the world the widow was a respectable woman.

Meanwhile Cornelia continued to plead with her husband. Heedless of her audience, she moved to him, and tried to take his hand, but it was pulled back. "We do well with the hotel, James. And the theater could be profitable." She paused. "It was your father's dream."

James rubbed his head—his aching head, from the look of it—and turned away from her. "Father had nothing but dreams," he said.

"You think you can make more money with a mill, but you know nothing about manufacturing—"

"I am going to restore my family to its rightful place!" he said. His face turned red, his chin jutted forward, and his eyes were blazing with some deeply buried emotion Juliet could only guess at. "I cannot do that with the paltry sum I will earn from a damned playhouse!"

The curse hung in the air—James Honeycutt was not the kind of man to use such language in front of his womenfolk—but he did not apologize. All eyes turned to Cornelia for her response. Cornelia drew in a breath, and even in the midst of this collapse of all Juliet's hopes, the actor in her could not help appreciating the theatricality of the moment.

Cornelia decided not to challenge her husband. She returned to her seat, folded her hands in her lap and cast her eyes down. "Of course, my dear," she said.

James faced Romie. "As you will have gathered, it is my intention to demolish the opera house and build a cotton mill on this land. With such proximity to the river and the wharves, I am assured that it will be a successful venture. I regret that I must end your engagement earlier than you had anticipated, but it is only by a week, after all."

It may be only a week to you, but it is a lifetime to us! Juliet wanted to scream at him.

Romie seemed not to have heard the man. How could he be so calm? He turned to Lavinia. "And what of Mrs. Honeycutt?" he asked in his silkiest voice. "Do you not have some regrets for this poor theater that is about to give its life for a cotton mill?"

Juliet expected another simper or a giggle. But Romie had sensed something about the little ninny.

"I loved the days when my husband was alive and we would have great parties with all the actors," Lavinia said seriously. Her voice was insipid and childlike. "They were so charming," she continued, "and, as I was Cecil's wife, they were most gracious to me."

No, they toadied up to you, Juliet thought viciously. And little Mrs. Honeycutt had enjoyed playing the grande dame.

Lavinia was looking at Romie from under those heavy dark lashes. "Unfortunately, my husband had reverses during the war that we never knew about until after he died, and now there is nothing left of his fortune. I am to go back to live with Mama and Papa, at River's Edge—my old home." For the first time something like a real emotion crossed the perfect little face. "I do not wish to go."

"And why is that?" Romie asked.

"Papa is the only planter still living in the area. The war finished all of our neighbors." Lavinia's voice quivered. "It's terrible at home now. There are no picnics or balls—we don't even have visitors anymore. Nothing but Mama crying because we're poor and Papa ranting about the Yankees."

Juliet looked to her brother, expecting to see him rolling his eyes. To her surprise, Romie was gazing intently at Lavinia. "You are going to be very lonely there," he said softly.

"I can't bear the thought of it!" The lovely blue eyes were locked with his, and now they began welling up.

"Lavinia . . ." James attempted to intervene. But Lavinia was past all considerations of propriety. When Romie had a woman under his spell, he had that effect.

"I will be buried alive," Lavinia went on desperately. "And I will never find another husband because everyone who is left in the county is either poor like we are, or old. And I will not marry another sick, old—"

This time it was Cornelia who broke in. "I am sure you do not mean to say that, Lavvy!" she said sharply.

Cornelia's tone stopped Lavinia. She blinked, and wiped away her tears. But she did not turn from Romie's gaze. "James tells me the new mill will make us money," she said to him as if they were the only people in the room. "I need money! If I have enough . . . I might be able to bring Mama and Papa here to live."

"And what if the mill does not make enough money?" Romie prodded gently.

Her look of total despair was answer enough.

"I think we have nothing further to say." James Honeycutt cut off the tête-à-tête by standing up and looking pointedly at the door. The Venables were being dismissed. As they started to leave, Lavinia moved so close to Romie that he had to brush past her, and Juliet could smell the scent she wore. It was sickeningly sweet.

"Wait, I'll walk with you," Cornelia said to the two actors.

After the three left the office, Romie wandered back to the boardinghouse, but Cornelia and Juliet stayed behind in the opera house lobby. For a long time they were both silent, and it was as if they were trying to memorize the marble carvings and the gilt.

"I can't believe—" Juliet started to say, but she stopped herself. No matter what kind of attachment she felt for this theater, its fate was none of her business.

But of course, her companion knew what she had been about to say. Cornelia sat on the tufted ottoman in the center of the room, and motioned for Juliet to sit next to her. "Our 'peculiar institution'—that is to say, slavery—was a great evil," she said slowly. "It affected all of us—in so many terrible ways." She paused. "James was reared on his grandfather's plantation. On his birthday when he was ten years old, all the people on the place were gathered together and instructed to greet him as Master Jim. It was done because one day everything his grandfather owned would be his. His father was raised in the same way, but he was a very different kind of man. He hated farming and the plantation, and we now understand that he was in financial difficulties long before the war. That merely ended what had already been started. He built this opera house with the last money he had. The hotel makes a profit, and I have a little something my mother left to me, so James and I are not in distress. But my husband can't stop remembering when he was Master Jim. The memory of all that was lost . . . and the need to try to regain it . . . It is destroying him. And that little fool, Lavinia, is so money hungry that she goads him on—" Cornelia stopped herself and looked around the lobby again. "I agree with you," she said sadly. "I can't believe that all of this will be gone."

CHAPTER 17

Massonville 1878

For the next ten days, Juliet had no time to think about the fate of the opera house. She still had to rehearse her actors during the day and perform at night, and in her spare moments the same questions repeated themselves in her mind. *How can I keep Romie from going to New York? How can I see to it that we stay together?*

Later, when she looked back on that time, she realized that she should have known Romie was up to something. And after the scene he had played with Lavinia Honeycutt, she should have had some idea of what he was doing. But she couldn't let herself know. Because with all of her heart, she didn't want to. So she told herself he was staying away from rehearsals because he was feeling low about the termination of their engagement. She told herself the same thing when ten nights passed and he had not come into her dressing room for their special ritual before the performance. When she finally walked into his dressing room on the eleventh night—a night when they would be performing *Romeo and Juliet*—and found Lavinia Honeycutt in his arms, she was stunned. Romie stood as still as stone.

Not so Lavinia, who swept gracefully across the room to embrace her. Juliet forced herself not to recoil. "Wish us joy, Juliet," Lavinia said in her insipid voice. "Your brother has just asked for my hand in marriage and I have said yes."

Miraculously, Juliet's vocal cords were still functioning. "Romie?" she asked. His face was scarlet, and she knew he would never have chosen to tell her this way. But he didn't deny it. She couldn't breathe, and she was afraid she might faint, but Romie was looking at her, willing her to stay steady. There was some comfort in that, at least. Meanwhile the horrid little voice was going on. "We have it all arranged between us, Romie and I . . ."

She calls him by the family pet name? When did that start?

"I will keep the theater," Lavinia said. She seemed almost giddy at the prospect. And why not? Now she would not have to go back to her family home. And she would not be marrying a sick old man. "James cannot go forward with his plans for the cotton mill unless I acquiesce, as I own half of the property. This change will be a disappointment to him, but I believe I can bring him to my way of thinking. I will wait until tomorrow night after the performance is finished, when he is in his office alone, and I will speak to him." She smiled confidently. Ten days ago she had been desperate; tonight she was all smiles and confidence.

How did this happen so fast? Why did I not see it?

"Romie says when we are managing the theater as it should be done, there will be more than enough money to recompense James." She turned to Romie, who gave her a reassuring little smile and moved to her side. "We will hire a new company, we will present a season in stock . . ." Lavinia nattered on. Romie was standing next to her now, close enough to reach over, clamp a hand over her hateful mouth, and silence her. But he did not do it. "And of course, dear Juliet, there will always be a place for you," Lavinia finished triumphantly.

A place? The words broke through the fog that had surrounded Juliet's mind. What did that mean? *There will always be a place for you.* She looked into Lavinia's lovely blue eyes, and in them saw a glint of steel.

"May I speak alone with my brother?" she heard herself ask.

Lavinia didn't like the idea. She turned to Romie, who resorted to lovers' signals by making a funny face. It did the trick, Lavinia laughed, then kissed him on the cheek, and left them.

The door shut behind her with a bang that echoed around the dressing room. Juliet waited until the sound died before moving closer to her brother. But now that they were alone, Romie could not face her. He turned to his looking glass and began powdering his face with a hand that was shaking. Poor Romie; it was always his hands that gave him away.

"I am not sure what arrangement will be made to compensate James Honeycutt." he said, "Lavvy . . . Lavinia will discover his terms tomorrow night. Once they are set, we'll have a theater. And a much grander one than Papa's. That is what you wanted—isn't it, Jule? To have a theater again?"

You did this for me? So we could have a theater again? Pain turned to joy in an instant. But then she saw his face in the looking glass and she knew he was not telling her everything. It was true that they needed a home and a place where they could work. But Romie would never sacrifice himself for that alone. There was something else on his mind that he did not wish to tell her. She would have to wait to get it from him. Now she had more urgent business. She had to stop this engagement of his. She moved to him and put her arms around him.

"My poor, foolish darling," she said. "Of course I wanted us to have our own theater, but not like this! Not with you married to that . . . creature!" She laughed a little so he could join her and then they could both laugh again at how absurd he had been. But he was silent. She could feel him tensing in her embrace. "But never mind that now," she added quickly. "You can tell her you have made a mistake—"

"No," he said.

"We'll find another way, Romie."

He whirled around, breaking out of her arms. "There is no other way! At the end of the week, we won't have enough money to give our actors their fare home. We wouldn't have enough money for our own fare home—if we had a home."

Again she had the feeling that he wasn't telling her everything. But she put it aside. "We can work here and earn the money to leave—" she started to say.

"Work at what?" he broke in. "Will you take in washing? Shall I try my hand at the mill? We are actors; that's all we know. This is our only chance."

"No."

"Lavinia is not so bad as you think, Jule. She is intelligent, more than I realized at the beginning . . . and she has a sense of the absurd that . . ." He faltered for a moment, then looked directly at her. "I can laugh with her, and I . . . I think we will deal well together."

No! But she screamed it silently.

"We are very much alike."

No! Out loud, she said quietly, "What could you possible have in common?"

"I have worked as long as I can remember. Lavvy knew from the time she could understand such things that she must marry well. Neither of us had a childhood."

"You've talked about this?"

"Oh yes."

So fast? When did you find the time? How did I not know?

"She was a bride at fifteen, Jule. Think of it! That girl was married to a man old enough to be her father! All of his cares, all of his failures, fell on her. Then he was sick, and she did not leave his side."

Or, if she did, she will certainly not tell you.

But she couldn't say that. Because now she realized that Romie was trying to talk himself into loving the widow. The widow who was so very beautiful.

"Is it any wonder that Lavvy wants a different man now?" her brother demanded. "That she wants—" He stopped short. "The poor girl wants to have some fun, Jule."

"And she thinks managing a theater will serve the purpose? Thank heaven you can tell her otherwise."

"She is aware that there is a risk, but she is willing to try. She is offering both of us a chance to run it with her."

No, she said there would be "a place" for me. She looked at me with those steely blue eyes and said I will have "a place."

"She wants to be your friend," Romie said. "She has told me so. "

"And you believe her."

"Yes." He grinned his cocky grin, the one that had seduced Maman and every other female who'd crossed his path since he was in short pants. "She wishes to please me, you see."

"I could almost feel sorry for her." She turned and started to go.

"Juliet," he called out.

"We will talk about this later. Now we have a performance."

"Look at me," he commanded, and waited until she obeyed. "It had to happen, Jule. One of us had to . . . find someone. This had to happen."

And that was when she understood the reason why he had done all of this. It was her. He could not break from her any more than she could break from him, but what had happened during their performance of *Romeo and Juliet*—that feeling that had nearly overtaken them—had frightened him. He had sought out Lavinia to keep him safe.

Oh, my dear, don't you know that you and I will never be safe from each other? There will always be feelings that frighten us and we will always call on them, because we are actors, and when we are afraid, we are at our best.

She left his dressing room.

But they were not destined to be at their best that night. In fact, they had never acted so badly. After the performance was over, and everyone else had left the theater, Juliet stayed in her dressing room. She had taken off her costume and removed her greasepaint, but she felt too weary for the walk to the boardinghouse. She moved her chair away from her dressing table so she could avoid her reflection in the looking glass. She almost didn't hear the dressing room door open.

Lavinia entered. She'd dispensed with her mourning clothes and was dressed for an evening at the theater. There was no pale mauve for her now. She was magnificent in royal-blue silk. The diamonds in her ears looked expensive. Clearly, she'd decided this was her night of triumph.

"I waited for you at the stage door but when you didn't come out, I thought you might still be here," she said.

It didn't seem to Juliet that an answer was called for.

"I wanted to talk to you, sister to sister, as we soon will be." The words were said pleasantly, but the steel was back in the woman's eyes. "It is not going to be easy to repay James for his share of the theater. Romie tries not to worry me with these things, but I know what it will cost."

I am sure you do. To the penny.

"Naturally I want a good income from the opera house, as we all do." She circled the room. She had something she wanted to say, and she was trying to find a way to start. "The days are over when your father could eke out a living presenting old-fashioned, fusty plays."

How dare you presume you know about Papa—or the plays he presented!

"Yes, Romie has told me all about your family," Lavinia responded to the unasked question. "People today want entertainment; they want to see a bit of spectacle." She paused. Her diamonds sparkled in the half-light. She still could not come to her point. "I have heard there is a play called *Mazeppa*—"

"Yes, a tasteless melodrama in which the main appeal to the public is that the leading woman appears to be nearly nude."

"I am sure you exaggerate."

"Her costume consists of silk tights died the color of flesh, and a scanty tunic."

"One would not have to go that far."

"I assure you, one would. Without the flesh-colored tights the play has nothing to recommend it."

Lavinia let out a sigh of exasperation. This was not the sisterly spirit of cooperation she had called for. She dispensed with *Mazeppa*. "Juliet, let's not spar with each other. If I am to give up the revenue I might have from a mill, this opera house must earn money!" She drew in a deep breath.

Here it comes, Juliet thought.

"And that is why you must help me to convince Romie that he must make certain . . . adjustments."

Juliet felt a prickle down her spine. "Adjustments?" she repeated carefully.

Lavinia moved closer. Her pretty little teeth were so white. "I understand that you are naturally gifted as a theater manager. Romie says no one can rehearse a company better or tend to all the hundreds of little details—"

"I am an actress, " Juliet broke in. Thankfully, her voice did not shake.

"Yes, and Romie tells me there is a position in any company for what is called a Heavy Woman, who plays the older roles, often the evil ones, which are the most difficult—"

"I am a leading woman." Again, her voice did not betray her.

"You *have been* a leading woman. But perhaps now, for the good of this new enterprise, you would be willing to relinquish those roles to someone younger—"

"I'm only twenty!" Now her voice was shaking. So was her entire body.

Lavinia took a moment before delivering the blow. "But you are not very pretty—are you? And is that not what an audience wants to see? It's true that on the stage you have a presence, and you can be interesting to watch, but . . ." She left the thought hanging in the air.

There was no way to fight back. All Juliet could do was hate. "Have you spoken to Romie about this?" she managed to ask when her voice was steady again.

"Romie is such a good brother that he would never wish to hurt you. That is why I count on you to help me persuade him."

So he would require persuasion; that was something to hold on to. But what could he do to protect his sister? The theater would belong to his— but it was impossible to think of Lavinia as his wife. *Romie, what have you done?* she thought. But she knew what he had done. And she knew he was not capable of making it right.

The lovely woman standing in front of her was growing impatient. "Well?" she demanded. "Do we understand each other, Juliet?"

Oh yes, I understand that my brother has gotten us into a hornet's nest—a hellish one—and I must get us out of it. I've done it before and I will do it now.

"Lavinia," she said gently, "whatever you wish to do in the management of this opera house, I promise you, I will never stand in your way."

I will be miles away from here. And so will Romie.

Lavinia frowned. She knew there was something wrong with the answer, but she was not sure what it was. "I am glad you are so reasonable," she said uncertainly.

"I always am," Juliet assured her with a smile. "And thank you for being so frank with me. I will remember everything you have said." She opened the dressing room door. There was nothing for the widow to do but leave.

After she was gone, Juliet moved to her dressing table and looked at herself in the glass. It was all very well to tell herself she was going to get them out of this, but how? And when? Whatever she did, it would have to be soon. A trace of Lavinia's cloying perfume still lingered in the room. Juliet opened the window to let in some fresh air, and sounds of laughter and music rose from the restaurant below, where a late-night supper was being served. She

leaned over the sill to hear more of the cheerful noise, and saw a figure pacing in the shadows in front of the opera house. At first she could not recog-
nize the man, but when he moved into the light cast from the restaurant
windows, she saw that it was James Honeycutt. She closed her eyes and
murmured a quick prayer of thanksgiving. Now she knew what she was
going to do—or, at least, she knew how she must start.

CHAPTER 18

Massonville 1878

The following day, Juliet went through her chores distractedly. She had not yet formulated an entire plan, but she knew she had to get to James Honeycutt before Lavinia did. She knocked on the door of his office several times during the afternoon, but he was never inside. The rest of the company went home to have supper, but she lingered at the theater, continuing her watch.

The sun set, supper was served in the restaurant, and the other actors returned to get ready for the night's performance, but James's office was still empty. Juliet was becoming frantic. One worry crowded out all others: had Lavinia already spoken to her stepson? She had said she was going to wait until the evening's performance was finished, but she could have changed her mind. Juliet knocked on the office door and could have screamed in frustration when there was still no answer.

To add to her troubles, the elderly stage manager, who would be responsible for single-handedly running the evening's performance backstage, seemed to be unwell. She helped him with the setting of the drops and the gaslights—tasks that would have been done by carpenters and set-shifters in a properly staffed theater—and told him to take a walk outside to revive himself. Meanwhile she ran backstage to call the half hour herself. As she passed by the stage door, she looked into the narrow hallway just in time to see James finally going into his office. But it was too late to talk to him; she had to get into costume because she was on in the first act.

However, she was free for all of the second act. It started with Romie and the Heavy Woman in two long scenes, and then there was a duel with the Juvenile Man, followed by a five-page monologue for her poor brother. Romie always approached this speech with loathing, although it invariably went well with the house. The monologue brought down the second-act curtain. Since Juliet's character was offstage for all of this, she would have more than enough time to speak with James.

Under normal circumstances, once a play had started, Juliet liked to sit quietly when she was not onstage. Other actors whiled away their free time with gossip and card games in the greenroom, but that was not her way. The actor Tommaso Salvini once said that he walked into his characters before every performance and stayed in them until the end, and, while she would not have dreamed of comparing herself with that great man, she felt as he did.

But on this night, as soon as the curtain came down for the first entr'acte, she made her way to James's office. Her role in the play was that of a courtesan, a piece of incredible good luck as far as she was concerned. Her costume was made with an especially low décolletage, and she had applied her rouge with a deliberately heavy hand to further coarsen her appearance. If James Honeycutt was like most ordinary people, he had preconceived notions about the character and morality of theater folk. She intended to play on those prejudices.

She could not have said James was pleased to see her when she walked boldly into his office, but he greeted her with civility. Clearly, Lavinia had not yet spoken to him—another piece of good luck. He did not offer Juliet a seat, but she sat anyway, smiling genially and watching him as he settled himself in his large green chair. He had been drinking, that much was obvious from the careful way he moved, but in what condition was he? If certain inhibitions had been loosened, he might not respond with the righteous indignation she needed. However, there was nothing she could do but go ahead.

"I have here a list of requirements, " she said as she reached down into the front of her gown for the piece of paper she had put there. Had anyone done that bit of business off the stage since the Restoration?

"Requirements? Forgive me, but I don't understand . . ." In spite of himself James's eyes were on her hand and bodice. However, there was more than a little disgust in those eyes. Good, she would not be forced to call for help before she'd had a chance to put her scheme into effect.

"Requirements for when my brother and I take over the theater." She pulled out a heavily scented piece of notepaper on which she had scrawled the most extravagant requests she could think of, and laid it in front of him. The wealthiest theater manager in New York would have been scandalized by the cost implied. "We will want an orchestra for the incidental music in the theater, and one for the lobby in the front. I will need a maid to dress me, my brother will also have his own personal dresser, and I think two additional dressers for the rest of the company will suffice. Also, we must have at least five carpenters and set-shifters, as well as a gas man, and a property master."

James seemed incapable of speech.

"The lobby and the theater auditorium are quite hideous. We must redecorate them." It was actually hard to say that, given the beauty of the opera house. "And the backstage is unsafe. The riggings, for example, have been put in haphazardly." That last was true. The riggings had been reworked to accommodate some additional drops required by the last troupe that had performed in the theater, and the work had been done cheaply, without thought. The rope used for lowering and raising the curtain was located at the front of one side of the stage, while the rope that operated the trapdoor was at the front of the opposite side. The ropes used to fly in the drops were set on either side of the stage in no logical order, and none of the ropes were marked, which was an invitation for mishaps. It was only a question of time before a company of actors playing *Julius Caesar* would find themselves in front of a setting for *East Lynne*.

"It will cost dearly to straighten it out, I'm afraid," Juliet went on. This was not true. All that was needed to avoid a disaster was to tie differently colored flags to the rigging ropes to avoid confusion. But James's face had gone red in a most gratifying way. "I know the expenses will be high, but Romie and I are artists and—"

The man suddenly seemed to find his tongue. "What is . . . this non-sense? Did you not hear me say there will be no theater standing here in a month? And as for you and your brother taking it over . . ." His look suggested he smelled something rotting.

Now was her cue to play confusion, which she did extremely well. "Oh mercy. . . . Did Lavvy not tell you? But she said . . ." She looked around the room wildly, then snatched up the piece of notepaper. "There is no necessity for you to see this yet. " She paused with the paper in hand, looking at it as if thinking, and counted slowly to three. Then she favored him with a hapless smile and thrust it at him. "But the cat's out of the bag now, and perhaps that's not bad. Since we are going to be related."

"What?" James Honeycutt could roar almost as loudly as Papa.

"Why, Lavvy and my brother, you know. Surely you must have seen how it is with them. I must say I have never seen Romie manage so quickly to—Oh!" She stopped as if seeing his outrage for the first time.

"Are you telling me that your brother and my stepmother . . . ?"

Now was the time to play alarm. She got out of her chair and began sidling to the door in the hangdog manner of Charles Dickens's character Uriah Heep—if Heep had been female. "I think you should speak to Lavvy—Lavinia, that is."

"I am speaking to you!"

Babbling came next, which, she'd been told, was another of her better effects. "They are betrothed, and I assure you Romie is sincere. This is a very different case from that silly girl in Cincinnati, or those others who—but never mind that. And as for the mill you wanted, Lavvy says you will get over that. It is very exciting to manage a theater and I am sure you will enjoy it."

"Manage a theater? Me?"

"A theater company, I should have said. You already have the theater. It may not become profitable for a few years, but one learns to get by."

"Are you telling me that my stepmother has agreed to this?"

Juliet tittered. "She wishes to please my brother, you see. As she is to become his wife."

James looked as if he were about to have an apoplectic attack. It was time to make her exit. She picked up the piece of paper, which sat unread on his desk, and, making the gesture as vulgar as she could, she stuffed it down her bodice. "There will be time enough after the wedding to talk about our new theater," she said. "And the expenses."

On that nearly perfect line, she let herself out of the office.

Out in the lobby, Juliet couldn't decide if she wanted to get as far away from the opera house as her feet would take her, or dash into the restaurant and order champagne to toast herself. But she could do neither. She had to go up to her dressing room and wait for Act Two to end. She still didn't have a final plan for saving Romie—and herself—from his madness, but *le bon Dieu* provided for tomorrow if one provided for today. And today she had made a good beginning.

She was starting for the backstage when the restaurant door opened and Lavinia came into the lobby. She was dressed in her decorous half-mourning mauve gown again, and from the way she paused to brace herself before walking toward James's office, it seemed that she had decided not to wait until after the play ended to speak with him. Abandoning all thoughts of her dressing room, Juliet hid in the shadows behind a pillar to watch what would unfold.

At the office door Lavinia hesitated again. She was nervous—that was clear. She smoothed her dress over her waist, dabbed at her face with a cambric handkerchief, and patted at her already perfect hair. Finally, she pulled back her shoulders, fixed a bright smile on her lovely lips, and walked into the lion's den.

Juliet ran over to eavesdrop. The door was too thick for her to hear words, but soon there was the satisfying sound of angry voices shouting. Lavinia would not be bringing her stepson to her way of thinking anytime soon. Pleased with her handiwork, Juliet moved away from the office door, just as it flew open—barely giving her time to retreat behind her pillar again.

"I will tell Romie!" Lavinia shouted over her shoulder as she ran out of the office. "We will find a way!" The office door slammed behind her as she raced across the hallway, opened the stage door, and went in. Juliet followed quickly behind her.

The backstage was empty. The end of the act was approaching and, anticipating Romie's monologue, the rest of the cast had retired upstairs to their dressing rooms or the greenroom. On the stage, the first drop had been flown in, and Romie was standing in front of it staring off into space, gathering himself for his long speech and giving the audience a chance to catch their breath—the calm before the storm. Behind the drop, a rustle of silk indicated that Lavinia was at the back of the stage waiting for him to come off. From the sound of it, she was pacing back and forth. Romie moved downstage center and launched into his speech. Suddenly, across the stage, Juliet saw potential disaster. The stage manager was seated near the curtain rope. But either he had not heeded her about taking a restorative walk outside, or it had had a different effect from the one she'd intended, for he had dozed off. From his open mouth and heaving chest, she could see it was only a matter of time before he started snoring. More important, unless he awakened in time to ring down the curtain at the end of the act, it would stay up after Romie had ended his monologue and thrown himself onto the stage floor in a prostration of grief. Leaving her brother with the proverbial egg on his face.

Moving carefully, Juliet inched her way around the gas jets of the lights that were set in the front wing, until she was as far onstage as she dared go. She tried to signal Romie, but his back was to her. She was so absorbed by the imminent disaster that she did not hear the side stage door open and close. Nor did she hear, at first, that someone was behind her, tugging on the rigging. When she finally turned, she saw that James Honeycutt had grasped the rope that operated the trapdoor, and was pulling it. What possessed the man? She tried to move closer to him but she was blocked by the wing lights between them. For a moment James straightened up and glared at her brother on the stage, who was still facing away from them. She could barely make out the words James muttered under his breath, ". . . be damned . . . if you . . . act on my stage." James was trying to bring down the curtain so Romie couldn't complete the act. But he had the wrong rope! He pulled it again, but the counterweight held it in place. Onstage, Romie heard the sound, and hesitated for a second, but then he went on. Juliet mouthed the word "trapdoor" to James, but he was not looking at her, and began loosening the counterweight. Once the rope was free he could trigger the trap by mistake. Juliet started working her way around the wing lights to reach him. That was when she heard a rustle of silk behind the drop, the sound indicating that someone was back there, pacing back and forth. Where the trapdoor was.

Afterward, Juliet told herself it took her so long to get to James because her skirt was too big to get around the gas jets easily. She told herself she hadn't shouted out because a lifetime of training had taught her never to do so during a performance. She told herself she was not sure she had heard that telltale rustle.

James triggered the trapdoor.

Lavinia's scream filled the entire opera house as she fell. Onstage, Romie froze. The stage manager woke with a start. In the house, whispered rumblings began. James was still holding the rope as if in a trance. Juliet reached him and grabbed it from him. She could smell the liquor on his breath. Obviously he'd had another glass or two in the time since she had played her little farce with him. Would he have done this if his judgment had not been so impaired? It didn't matter; he sobered up quickly.

"I meant to ring down the curtain," he said, his eyes big and wild. "I did not intend that your brother . . ." Then, as the realization came to him in all its horror, he gasped, "My God, what have I done?"

"Don't think about that now," Juliet whispered as she pushed him away from the riggings, against the side wall of the theater.

"Lavinia?" he managed to get out.

"I'll see to her. Don't move," she said.

A portion of the cellar under the stage was used to store the few set pieces owned by the opera house, and there was a table against one wall where the props were kept. But most of the area was an empty space with a concrete floor. The distance from the stage to that floor was about fifteen feet, with nothing to break a fall. However, there was a ladder under the trapdoor that Juliet quickly climbed down. As she went, she heard the sounds of the audience getting to its feet. The stage manager was bringing down the curtain. Soon the backstage would be crowded with people. They would want to know what had happened.

Lavinia lay at the foot of the ladder. Her perfume seemed to fill the cellar. Juliet stood over the broken body for what felt like a very long time. Above her she could hear the sound of people running. Soon someone would discover that James was backstage. They would find a man who was in a state of shock, incapable of defending himself . . . a man who would need her help. And suddenly, with a bright and fearful clarity, she had the rest of her plan.

Le bon Dieu will provide.

Juliet looked down at Lavinia and knew what she must do.

CHAPTER 19

Massonville 1878

The first person she saw when she climbed back through the trapdoor was Romie. He must have run to the back of the stage after the stage manager brought down the curtain. "Jule," he whispered, horrified. "Jule, what—"

"There's been an accident," she said. She couldn't look at him yet.

"But—"

"Don't ask questions. Just remember it was an accident." She left him and rushed to James.

Most of the cast had run downstairs to the stage and were milling around. Cornelia came in through the backstage door with a group of friends from the audience. James was still standing near the side wall. So far he was too dazed to say anything, thank God. Juliet moved quickly to the center of the stage. She never knew how she found the words, and after it was over, she could not even remember what words she had used, but somehow she managed to tell the assembled group that Lavinia Honeycutt was dead. Cornelia began to cry and held James for comfort, as everyone surrounded them. Only Romie stood back. Juliet could feel him watching her.

It was the terrified stage manager who gave her her next opening. "Mr.

Honeycutt," the man said, "I know I had that rope secured before the performance."

"Indeed you did," Juliet said loudly so everyone could hear. "I saw you do
it." Her life and Romie's depended on what happened next, but the words
came out clearly and distinctly. Papa would have been proud.

The stage manager was looking at her as though she were an angel sent
from heaven. "That's right, Miss Venable, you can vouch for me. You know
it was not my fault. But how . . ." His eye fell once again, as Juliet had
known it would, on James.

"Mr. Honeycutt, sir, did you touch that rope?"

This was her moment. She let her voice catch as if she were overcome—
an easy thing, under the circumstances. "Mr. Honeycutt and I came backstage as quickly as we could after we heard the scream," she said, and she
closed her eyes as if struggling with hysteria—again, not difficult—then
opened them and forced herself to look at James. "We had been in his office, discussing a business proposition. Mr. Honeycutt wishes to sell the
opera house to my brother and me."

Over the crowd, James locked his eyes with hers. She held her breath.
If he accepted her lie now, while fear and the horror were fresh in his mind,
she would win her gamble. If he waited until he was thinking more clearly,
it would occur to him that he simply had to say he had been nowhere near
the rope and that would be an end to it. No one would question Mr. James
Honeycutt's integrity. Even if Juliet were to tell them what he had done,
who would take her word against his?

Fear and horror won the day. "Yes, " he said. "Miss Venable and I were
discussing the sale of the opera house."

Le bon Dieu will provide.

Thank you, she prayed silently.

From the shadows, Romie watched her.

CHAPTER 20

Massonville 1878

Neither Juliet nor Romie were invited to Lavinia's funeral. Lavinia had not had the time before her death to divulge her marital plans to anyone but James, and it seemed that James was choosing to ignore what he'd been told—and the encounter he'd had with Juliet. Juliet herself was happy to stay away from the service. She was even happier that Romie would not be attending. Something had happened to her brother. He looked at her now as if he had never seen her before. When he wasn't avoiding her altogether.

He hates me because he thinks I am profiting from Lavinia's death. But when we are able to perform in our own theater, without any interference from anyone, then he will thank me. He will get over all his fears and he will see that I did it for the best. Still, Romie's eyes made her uneasy. The sooner they went back to work, the better.

There were no questions asked about the incident. Accidents happened frequently in theaters, and no one wanted to intrude on the grief of the Honeycutt family. To Juliet's surprise, James did not delay the sale of the opera house. She waited fearfully for him to come to his senses and call it off, but his only interest seemed to be in getting as far away from Massonville as he could. Almost before Juliet knew it, the terms were set. It would take many years to pay off the purchase price, but, even so, the Venables had gotten the theater for far less than it was worth. When it came time to sign the papers, Juliet was afraid that Romie might refuse, but he did it without a murmur.

He will thank me.

The day before the Honeycutts left Massonville, Cornelia came to the boardinghouse to say good-bye. Romie had made himself absent as usual, so Juliet had tea with her alone.

"I am glad you and your brother own the theater now," Cornelia said. "It should be in the hands of those who know how to use it."

"But I'm sorry you are leaving," Juliet said, and realized to her surprise that it was true. She had never had a woman friend and it suddenly struck her that she might like one.

Cornelia shook her head. "This is best for all of us." Her eyes reddened. "Poor Lavvy's death has had one good outcome. James has needed a fresh beginning for years, and now he will have it. In our new home no one will remember that he was Master Jim." She rose and smiled. "I will miss you and your brother. Romeo and Juliet. I still think that is such a charming idea—to name one's children for characters written by Shakespeare."

"Our papa would be pleased to hear you say so. Over the years, Romie and I have had our doubts. "

"But you see, every time I read or watch the play, I will think of Romeo and Juliet Venable. Your papa made you unforgettable. "

The morning after the Honeycutts left Massonville, Juliet waited for her brother to wake up so they could move their few belongings into the family quarters in the opera house. When she finally went into his room at the boardinghouse, it was empty. Romie was gone. He left behind his costumes, and the worn, dog-eared copy of *Walker's Critical Pronouncing Dictionary.* He had taken his street clothing with him.

Juliet stayed in the boardinghouse for two weeks, and waited for him. She did not go outside her room, and she directed that all of her meals be brought to her, so that she would be where he could find her. But she knew he was not coming back. She had risked everything to keep him with her, but he had left anyway. Now she was alone—just as she had always been afraid she would be. As she sat in her room for those agonizing two weeks, she knew she would never love anyone again as she had loved him.

Juliet sold Romie's costumes to the ragman, but she couldn't bring herself to part with the dictionary. She packed it into her theater trunk with her Bible to take with her when she moved alone into the family apartment in the opera house.

She had a canopy stitched with the words "The Venable Opera House" in large gold lettering, and put it up in front of the arcade. She had the backstage rigging ropes rearranged and tagged with colored flags so that no one would pull the wrong one by mistake. She had the ugly wallpaper removed from the owner's office.

From the beginning, she managed her theater well. She seemed to have a nose for talent, as the saying went, and the small company of actors she hired quickly gained a reputation for the high quality of the performances they gave. She didn't intend to stop acting herself, but somehow with her duties at the hotel and the restaurant, as well as running the theater, she didn't have the time to rehearse and perform. She never missed a payment to James Honeycutt.

Her theater grew with Massonville and gave it a cachet that set it apart from other booming towns in the area. In 1881, the grateful town commissioned a statue in her honor. They chose to immortalize her as she was when she played Juliet in the balcony scene from Romeo and Juliet. On the base of her statue they engraved the words she had first said when she was eight years old in her father's theater in Cincinnati, PARTING IS SUCH SWEET SORROW.

Juliet had the statue placed in the garden behind the opera house, where it become a point of interest for patrons strolling among the flower beds during intermissions. She never told anyone that she had decided not to put it in the lobby of the theater—which had been its original destination—because she did not want to see it every day and be reminded of the time when she and Romie had acted together and her life had been wonderful.

After her business was established, Juliet hired an actor to be her company's leading man. He had Byronic curls and beautiful eyes, although there was no fire and not much intellect in them. She married him and bore him a daughter and two sons, after which she stopped pretending to have any respect for him. Eventually he grew tired of her endless criticisms and left her. But he had served his purpose; she had Ophelia, Horatio, and Antonio Venable. The children would always be Venables. Her husband's last name was soon forgotten by everyone.

Antonio did not live past his third year, and Horatio, she soon realized, was as useless as his father had been. Her daughter, Ophelia, however, was different. The child was Romie to the life—a feminine version. She had the glowing eyes, the hair, and the perfect features, and her mother prayed that she had the talent.

When she was still small, Ophelia began following Juliet on her never-ending rounds of chores and duties. By the time she was ten years old, the little girl could hold the book for a rehearsal or set all the tables in the restaurant. Juliet soon found herself confiding in her small daughter; as the curtain was ringing up on the evening's performance, she would take Ophelia into the office with her for a late supper, and recount the day's trials and triumphs.

And always Juliet ended each of these sessions by saying, "We must keep the opera house running and we must keep it in the family. For the sake of all the Venables who will come after us. Nothing else matters; this is our legacy."

And beautiful little Ophelia would nod solemnly as if she understood what a legacy was. Perhaps she did; she was very intelligent.

As she approached the age of forty, Juliet found her energy was waning. The occasional shortness of breath that had plagued her when she was younger progressed to a racing heart, dizziness, and pain. One day, when the feeling in her chest was very bad, she unearthed Maman's Bible and Romie's pronouncing dictionary from the trunk where she had kept them for so many years. She placed the volumes on the desk in her office. But, as with her statue, she soon found that the memories the old books stirred up were too distracting. She directed one of the stage carpenters to build a shelf at the top of the office wall, near the ceiling. When it was done, she battled the light-headedness that was by then her regular companion, climbed a ladder, and placed her family treasures on the new shelf. While she did not want them in front of her every day, every once in a while she found it comforting to pull out the ladder, climb up, and touch them. That was what she was doing when she died.

She was only forty-two when it happened, and the doctor said the cause was heart failure. Ophelia, who had inherited the theater, left the office as it was. The books remained on their shelf high up on the wall.

CHAPTER 21

Massonville 2006

Katie looked up at the rows of shelves that reached to the ceiling of the old office in the opera house. "You know that old saying? The one that goes 'If these walls could talk'?" she asked.

"It smells moldy in here." Randa wrinkled her nose.

It was the second day of their stay in Massonville, and after lunch they had gotten the lockbox combination over the phone from the Moultire law office, walked over to the theater, and headed straight for the office. They hadn't talked about what they were doing. It was almost as if they were channeling each other.

Next we'll be having sleepovers to talk about boys and paint our toenails, Katie thought. Or maybe it wasn't a girlfriend thing, maybe it was DNA. If they shared any. *Mother and her damn secrets,* Katie thought—not for the first time.

Still, she was glad she and Randa had come to the opera house together. Randa was the only other person around who knew what it felt like to wake up one morning and discover that you had inherited an ancient theater you'd never known existed—and possibly a family tree to go along with it—in a town you'd never heard of.

Katie checked out the room again. The décor was seriously Victorian: heavy on wood paneling, swagged draperies, wall sconces, and large, stiffly upholstered furniture. The spiral wooden staircase leading upstairs to the family apartment added a nice period touch. "Sherlock Holmes would love this," she said.

"Sherlock would have to hire a cleaning service, " Randa said. She'd traded her business suit with the sexy skirt for a slacks-and-blouse combo in a pale shade of pink that was perfect for her. Katie had put on a ruffled beige sundress with daisies on it. It did nothing for her, but at least it hadn't been purchased during one of her super-thin periods, so it fit well.

Randa sat on a thronelike green chair behind a desk that was so huge it took up most of one wall. The regal thing worked for her, Katie decided. In spite of her glossy look, Randa had gravitas. Now she sighed and leaned back so she could see the shelves that were crammed with papers, books, old playbills, pictures, and what looked like hundreds of scripts. "It would take months to go through all of that stuff," she said.

"It might be fascinating, though," Katie said.

"If you want it, after we sell the place, we can have it boxed up and sent to you. If you find anything interesting, you can let me know." Randa seemed to brighten at the thought.

For a moment Katie brightened too. It would be a way to keep a little piece of the opera house with her, like a souvenir. Then she pictured the boxes, sitting in her apartment, calling to her when she should be working. And she thought about her career that needed a jump start and the decisions she didn't want to make, and how she always took the easy way out.

"I write a script a week; I wouldn't have the time," she said.

"Right." Was Randa disappointed or was it her imagination? "What soap do you work for again?"

"*All Our Lives.* You know it?"

"I think one of my clients was the head writer on it for a while."

"Who was it? If they worked for the show, I know them."

Randa paused. "Steve Dickerson."

"The Dick was your client?" Randa nodded.

"This was a voluntary thing? No one held a gun to your head?"

"I was going through a dry spell and I wanted a pool for my house. Don't look at me like that. I got rid of him after three months."

"We were stuck with him for a year."

"I'm sorry. If it's any consolation, I think that was the longest gig he ever had."

"How did we get so lucky?"

"He was working long distance from L.A. so he teleconferenced his meetings. Usually his breath was enough to clear a room."

"Nasty?"

"As evil as his soul," Randa said.

"Please say bad things have happened to him since he got fired from my show."

"I've heard he works in reality TV now."

"Thank you." They looked at each other and started to laugh.

Are we bonding? Katie wondered. Then Randa pulled a tissue out of her shirt pocket and began wiping dust off the top of the desk. *Okay, probably not.*

Randa seemed to be avoiding making eye contact. Either that, or the desk was dirtier than it looked. "There's something I . . ." She stopped, then started again. "Susie had a talk with R.B.," she said. She wasn't having an easy time with this. "It seems that the Venable family always named their children after Shakespearean characters. It was something they were famous for." Randa studied the desk, then gave it another swipe. "I'm named for Miranda in *The Tempest.*"

Katie felt a dozen small needles land on the back of her neck. "I'm Katharina in *The Taming of the Shrew*. My mother was Rosalind in *As You Like It.*"

"My father was Richard."

"Richard the Third."

"Or the Second."

"Okay, I don't know about you, but I've just had my quotient of bizarre for this week."

"But this is a link—maybe," Randa said. "There's got to be one. We know that—that's why we're sitting here." Then after a moment she added, "Damn it."

"What?"

"All the times I wanted to ask my father about his family . . ."

"What happened when you tried?"

"Deep freeze. You?"

"Screaming, yelling, small objects flying into walls."

"My father had a lot of memories he couldn't handle. He wasn't much good at emotions."

My mother's favorite word for my father was "pussy-whipped." She was also partial to "ball-less wonder," Katie thought about confiding. *I always thought that blew a hole in the press releases she gave out about her hero husband, who died in Vietnam.* Then she looked at Randa's perfectly coordinated slacks and blouse and decided to keep quiet.

"I went on the Internet this morning," Katie offered as a change of subject. "I tried a couple of genealogy websites, but I'm not very handy with a computer. I'm still scared I'm going to make the gremlins inside it mad, and then they won't e-mail my scripts to the studio." She waited for a sneer from the oh-so-competent Miranda, but it didn't come.

"My kid is back in our hotel room doing research as we speak," she said. "She's already sent for one of those CDs that show you how to build a family tree. Of course, we'll all be back home by the time she gets it done."

"Maybe she could send me a copy."

"I'm sure she'd be glad to."

They both looked around the old room.

"You think this buyer will make an offer right away?" Katie asked.

"I hope." Randa got up, pulled a Handi Wipe out of her purse, and cleaned off her fingers. Katie tried to remember the last time she had packed a tissue or a Handi Wipe, and came up empty. "I have clients having major panic attacks because I'm out of my zip code," Randa went on. "They don't really need me, but I've trained them to think they do."

"That sounds powerful."

"Actually, it's more like being under house arrest." Then she added quickly, "Not that I mind. " She smiled brightly.

"I wrote a play," Katie said, and wondered where the hell that had come from. "It was a one-time thing, though; I'll never do it again. I like working for television. It's great." She did her version of a bright smile for Randa, who quickly upped her own wattage. If they kept it up much longer, Katie's lips were going to be stuck to her gums. Finally they both looked away.

"It would cost a fortune to restore this place," Randa said after a long silence.

"And trying to do it from L.A. and New York would be insane," Katie added.

"We have lives."

"Jobs."

"Besides, they don't need a theater in this town. If a road show ever did come through here, they've already built that awful convention center."

"You've seen it?"

"Susie and I walked over to look at it last night after dinner."

"Me too."

"It's ugly."

"Ghastly."

So the bonding thing—it's not dead yet, Katie thought. "Maybe we could look into some other options . . . for the opera house . . . just to see if there's anything we could do." For a moment she thought Randa looked wistful, but then she closed off.

Okay, bonding not happening.

"There's someone who wants to take this place off our hands," Randa said firmly. "As far as I'm concerned, we listen to the offer, and if we're not getting totally ripped off, we take the money and run. And I intend to interpret the phrase 'ripped off' liberally."

What she was saying was mature and rational, and the mature, rational part of Katie agreed with her. But the immature, irrational part of her said, "This theater has been here for so long. Now we're the ones who are going to trash it."

"Maybe it won't be trashed. You don't know what will happen to it."

"Come on, you've seen what they're building here; the glitzy hotel we're staying at, and that convention center that looks like an egg crate. There's no way they won't tear down this old theater."

"You're right. I will tear it down," said a voice from behind them. Kate whipped around. Behind her, Randa jumped out of her throne chair. Standing in the doorway was a man. He wasn't the handsomest Katie had ever seen, but then she worked in daytime television, otherwise known as the Handsome-Guy Center of the Universe. The specimen in front of them definitely ranked in the Top Twenty of the Over Thirty Division. Randa inched around the desk to get a better look.

"Hi, I'm Mike Killian," he said. "MK Construction. I'm the guy who wants to buy this place from you." He paused for a couple of beats. "The glitzy hotel and the egg crate are mine."

Without meaning to, Katie backed up until she and Randa were standing side by side. Not for protection, she told herself, but they did form a kind of wall.

CHAPTER 22

Massonville 2006

Mr. Killian wore a black T-shirt and jeans—a look that didn't seem very Southern to Katie—but his three-syllable spin on the word "Hi" said local talent. The black ensemble, which he filled out quite nicely, was the perfect choice for his impressive tan, killer blue eyes, and head of thick black hair that was just starting to gray around the edges. His jaw and cheekbones did not have a bad angle, his mouth was television-full, and he was tall enough to be imposing. He also sucked up most of the oxygen in the room as he strode in and repeated his elongated "Hi." He stuck out his hand at Katie. "Are you New York or Los Angeles?" he asked.

"I'm Katie Harder," she said. For a second she thought she saw something flicker in his gorgeous eyes. It wasn't hostility, but it wasn't friendliness either. "Look, I'm sorry about what I said. I didn't know anyone was listening," she stumbled.

"You probably forgot you'd left the office door open, and that lobby is like an echo chamber," he said.

"I didn't mean to be insulting. I mean, I'm sure there are people who just love new construction, who . . ." She was drowning fast.

"But your taste runs more to our antebellum charm."

"You see, this building is so unique . . . so special . . ." Katie felt herself going into ditz mode again—it seemed to be happening a lot in the past two days. "People do manage to work around old architecture. They incorporate the façade or build in the air space above it. . . . Well, look at Grand Central Terminal. . . ." Next to her, she could hear Randa doing a little clicking thing with her tongue that sounded like disapproval. "It would be such a pity to lose this place, " she concluded weakly.

He studied Katie for a moment. "This is the first time you've been in a red state when you weren't changing planes, isn't it?"

"What does that have to do with—"

"Just a little game I like to play." He treated Randa and Katie to a big grin. "Now, since we're all together, I was thinking I'd like to take you out for something to eat and lay out my proposal for you." He patted a sleek leather briefcase he was carrying. "I have the contracts right here."

"C-contracts?" Katie stammered. "You've already got contracts written out for the sale?"

He nodded. "This way, you can look over my offer and I can answer any questions you have."

"But we're not supposed to have a meeting until Monday. We have the whole weekend." Suddenly she realized how much she'd been counting on that extra time. Three days when the theater was still theirs, and still safe.

"Well, of course you could wait," Mike Killian said. "I just thought this would give us a head start."

"Shouldn't we have our lawyers present?" Katie asked.

"If you want to, but—"

"But one of our lawyers has already ratted us out. " Randa's soft voice broke in.

"Ma'am?" the gorgeous eyes turned to gaze at Randa. Katie was pretty sure they were liking what they saw.

"You can call me Randa, aka Los Angeles. And I'm guessing that Mother Moultire told you the clueless chicks from the blue states were going to be here today. So you hustled your people skills over to nail down this deal now."

His eyes glinted appreciatively—he was definitely liking what he saw. "Los Angeles, a word of advice? Around here R.B.'s mother is known as Ms. Moultire, and I wouldn't let her hear me calling her Mother if I were you."

"There's some reason why you want this sale to go through fast." Randa rode over his lesson in local customs. "Either we have another offer—"

"You don't."

"We probably won't be taking your word on that. But let's say you're right. Then I'm thinking you had to do some fancy financing, and there's a clock ticking on your construction loan."

She may not have bonded with me, but I have definitely just bonded with her, Katie decided.

Meanwhile Mike Killian had stopped looking appreciative. "I'm not partial to fancy financing, so I don't have a loan. I have a loan guarantee. What that means to you is, sure, I'd like to make a deal, but I'm not hurting. And I'm not in a hurry."

"We're not in any hurry either," Randa said. "We just found out we inherited this place."

"And you're not even positive you want to sell it, right?" His drawl was tinged with sarcasm.

"Oh, I'd never try to tell you that, Mr. Killian. You may have thought I was stupid, but believe me, I'm not making the same mistake about you."

"Okay, here's why you want to sell to me," he said quickly. "I'm the only contractor around here who wants to tackle this piece of property. Because the zoning laws for the riverfront are so strict, your profit margin is very small."

"But it's not too small for you?" Randa asked. "That doesn't sound like good business to me. Unless there's something you haven't told us."

The appreciation was back in the man's eyes—along with a glimmer of amusement. Katie glanced at Randa to see if she'd picked up on it, but Randa's face was blank.

Mike Killian got back to the negotiations "I'm offering you one point two million dollars for your property. It's a good price, which you'll find out after you have an appraisal done."

"Try three appraisals."

"Get ten of them. It won't make any difference. The price is fair and I'm your only buyer."

"However, I'm sure you'll understand if we decide to wait for a while and see what else turns up."

"You could do that. But while you're waiting, this old white elephant is going to start falling down in chunks. Even though it's been maintained, it needs some major structural work. And they've got laws in Massonville about letting prime riverfront property deteriorate. So you're going to be spending a bunch of time flying out here to explain yourself to the city officials. And then you're going to be spending a lot of cash complying with the local standards after you haven't been able to explain yourself. Meanwhile, I'll be working on one of the other deals I've got going, and I won't be interested in buying your property anymore."

"Now you're back to thinking I'm stupid."

"Okay, I'll be interested, but I may just be pissed off."

"But you'll get over that."

He laughed, which made him even more handsome. "Los Angeles, when this is over, you've got to let me take you out for that lunch." He took his business card out of a leather case and held it out to Randa. "It shouldn't take you more than a couple of days to schedule those appraisals if you let Ms. Moultire arrange them for you."

"Nice talking with you," Randa said. But she took the card.

Mike turned to Katie. "And in case you think I'm just a grabby hillbilly who doesn't get the finer points, let me tell you about Massonville. It's a poor town right now, but it doesn't have to be. What the people here need are jobs and a tax base, and that's what they'll get when I build my condos. What they don't need is an old building that's outlived its usefulness—if it ever had any." He turned to Randa. "Nice talking with you too," he said, and he walked out.

CHAPTER 23

Massonville 2006

"Okay, can you tell me what that was about?" demanded Randa.

"You mean the warm, fuzzy moment when he tried to say he has a social conscience?" Katie asked.

"That. And why does he have such a case against this opera house?"

"You got that too?"

"It was hard to miss."

"Do we care what he's thinking?"

"It never hurts to know who you're doing business with." Randa wandered over to the staircase. There was a faded old afghan folded over the railing, which had probably been lovely a million years ago. Randa picked it up.

"Are we doing business with him?" Katie asked. "It didn't sound that way."

"You mean what I said to Biceps Man about waiting? That was just poker. When I get back to the hotel room, I'll call him and set up a meeting for Monday to go over the contracts."

"You think he was for real about the million dollars?"

"A million point two, and he meant it. I don't think the South's version of Donald Trump kids around when it comes to numbers."

"So we each get . . ." Katie had to stop for a second, because math was involved.

"That's six hundred thousand apiece," said Randa, who crunched numbers for a living. She sat on the bottom step of the staircase and began absentmindedly stroking the afghan. "It's a nice piece of change."

"Yes."

"I make good money, but I'm still in show business. Every one of my clients could get fired, or they could all fire me. Six hundred thousand dollars would be a nice addition to the safety net." Katie watched her rub a darned spot in the afghan with her finger. "And Susie's so smart. I've always wanted her to go to someplace like Yale or Harvard. Even if you allow for estate taxes and inflation, that money would cover it. Her tuition would be safe, no matter what happened to me. " She trailed off, looking at something in space that only she could see. She was probably envisioning her daughter's graduation from Harvard, Katie thought. Randa pulled herself back to reality. "What about you?"

"Everyone says the soaps are dying out, and that's all I've ever written. I've got to find a prime-time job, but you know how the industry feels about people who work in daytime. I'm going to have to do a lot of spec scripts, and a lot of freelancing."

Randa nodded. "Six hundred thousand would cover you."

"I could take the time to wait for a gig I really liked." *If there is one out there.*

"You'll have freedom and I'll be safe, " Randa said softly. "Not bad." She fingered the fringe on the old afghan.

"So you wouldn't want to turn down The Donald and wait."

"For?"

"To see if someone else wants to buy the opera house."

Randa gave her a knowing look. "Someone who will fix it up and love it? And do what with it?"

When Katie was seven, a mean kid actor named Johhny Martin who was working on *All Our Lives* had informed her that there was no Santa Claus. She'd done her best to make him eat his words, but in her gut she'd known it was a lost cause. She felt the same way now. "Randa, the condos Mike Killian's going to build will look like that frigging convention center."

"That's not our problem." Randa was hugging the afghan to herself now. "No one's going to want to buy this place and save it. No one with money. Maybe R.B. could find us a group that would take it for free and spend the next thirty years restoring it as a museum or something, but I wouldn't even count on that. And until the preservation geeks came along, you and I would be responsible."

Santa had died for Katie all those years ago when Johhny Martin had gotten her in a headlock. Now that she was a grown-up, all it took was irrefutable logic to kill a fantasy. She nodded sadly.

"This is a good thing, Katie," Randa said. "We just won the lottery."

So why do I feel like crying? And why are you holding that afghan like it's your last link to life?

As if she'd read Katie's mind, Randa stood up and began folding the old relic. "I'm not going upstairs to the apartment. I don't want to see any more." She placed the afghan back on the staircase railing where she'd found it. The sunshine fell on it and you could see how beautiful it must have been back when the threads were new and the colors were bright. "What's the point in getting to know this old place any better?" Randa asked.

There wasn't one. Since they were just going to turn it over to Mike Killian's bulldozers, why fall in love with it?

They closed up the opera house, put the key back in the lockbox, and walked out to the wasteland that had once been the front lawn. They stood together looking at the rusted white façade and the torn canopy.

"We should celebrate," Randa said.

"Yes."

But neither of them moved.

"Maybe later," Randa said.

"Sounds good," Katie said.

"I should go back to the hotel and check my e-mails."

"You go ahead. I'll be right behind you."

A few seconds later, Katie heard Randa picking her way along the old driveway. Instead of following her, Katie continued to stare at the building that—for the moment—still belonged to her. But she wasn't really seeing it. R.B.'s face as he stood in the lobby came back to her. The man was so . . . open. How did anyone live past puberty and not develop at least one or two defenses? She flashed back to another memory—a much older one.

Katie was eight years old, and Rosalind was throwing her annual Halloween party. The routine for this event was set in granite. Every year before the festivities began, Katie went out with the maid to trick-or-treat in their apartment building. She always wore an outfit whipped up by the *All Our Lives* costume designer—an acolyte who knew Rosalind expected her daughter to be attired in appropriately childlike Cinderella and Snow White costumes. After Katie had finished begging for Hershey's bars, she would retire to her room with whatever meager loot she'd managed to accumulate in their not-so-kid-friendly co-op and a tray of canapés courtesy of her mother's caterer. It was a ritual she had never questioned. But this year the producer of *All Our Lives* had hired a new costume designer. The new guy, inspired by Bette Midler's turn as a mermaid in her last concert—this was before Disney's Ariel—had created a glittery sequin-covered mermaid costume for Katie. It had been a bit of a squeeze getting her round little body into the thing—she still had most of her puppy fat when she was eight—but once she had, the sheer gorgeousness of it had swept her away. It had seemed a crime to let so much glamour go to waste. So after Theresa had deposited her in her bedroom, she hadn't changed into her flannel pajamas. She had waited until her mother's party was under way, and then she had made a surprise entrance in the turquoise and silver living room.

Years later, Katie would wonder if her mother had reacted the way she had because she had been surprised—she never checked Katie's Halloween ensembles. Or maybe Katie as a mermaid had been too much of a show-stopper for Rosalind. Or maybe it was just that Katie had given her an opportunity to do a little Shakespeare in front of an audience. Whatever the reason, once Katie had stopped all conversation by teetering into the room on her spangled shoes that were designed to look like a fish's tail, Rosalind had sung out, "There she is! My little Kate!" She had gone down on one knee and had begun to quote from *The Taming of the Shrew*:

"'. . . for you are call'd plain Kate, / And bonny Kate and sometimes Kate the curst; / But Kate, the prettiest Kate in Christendom.'"

Her mother meant to be funny, Katie knew. But no one was getting it. They were just bewildered by the strangeness of it. Rosalind never was good at telling jokes—she didn't have much of a sense of humor. Katie knew that too.

The silence in the room was awful. But Rosalind never stopped a scene, no matter how badly she was doing. So she stretched her mouth into a smile, and went on.

" 'Kate of Kate Hall,' " she quoted, " 'my super-dainty Kate, / For dainties are all Kates, and therefore, Kate—' "

Before she could finish the line, someone laughed. It was actually more of a nervous little giggle, but it was a response. And it was more than enough for Rosalind. She finally stopped her performance and eyed Katie in all her chubby splendor. Even though she was only eight years old, Katie knew she was in for it. "Although perhaps 'dainty' isn't the right word," her mother drawled. She raised an eyebrow. This time several people laughed. Probably the empty bottles of booze behind the bar and the diminishing pile of joints on the coffee table had something to do with it.

"No, that word doesn't begin to cover my little Kate." Katie saw that her mother's eyes were red. Rosalind wasn't exactly sober herself. "In fact, that costume doesn't cover you, honey bunch . . ." Suddenly, Teddy was at Rosalind's side, practically picking her up and setting her on her feet.

"Okay, " he said loudly. "It's time for Katie to go back to bed now."

It was the wrong thing to do, Katie could have told him that. Rosalind jerked away from him and drew in a breath to start yelling. But then she remembered her audience. She turned to Katie. "Don't be shy, my dainty one. Now that you've crashed the party, take a bow." When she said "dainty" she might as well have been saying "fatso."

Katie knew better than to run, but she started to back away, her sequined tail-feet making a funny dragging sound on the floor. Her mother's hand caught her arm in a grip she could still remember as an adult.

. "Bow, darlin'." Rosalind smiled at her with glittering eyes. Katie managed a smile and a bow before her arm was released and she could get the hell out of there.

The next morning she woke up to see Rosalind sitting on the foot of her bed.

"You almost made a fool of yourself last night," said her loving mommy.

No, you did, Katie thought but didn't say.

"Never let anyone see that they've gotten to you—not even me." Her mother started for the door, then turned back. "You think what happened last night was so bad. Well, you'll go through worse. And you'll get over it. I did."

The next day she signed Katie up for ballet class. "You need the exercise," she said.

Standing in front of the opera house, Katie wondered if everyone had childhood memories that could still make them cringe twenty-four years later. It was a question she'd asked herself often. As usual, she didn't have an answer. But once again, a vision of R.B., with his open face and his unguarded smile, came back to her. She turned away from the opera house and started walking fast toward the historic district.

CHAPTER 24

Massonville 2006

After leaving the opera house, Randa had walked into her hotel room to find her daughter waiting for her—and it had been obvious that Susie was ready to burst. However, the kid had managed to contain herself while Randa arranged for an appraisal of the opera house and set up a meeting with Mike Killian for Monday morning. It was only after she was sure Randa had finished all of her business that Susie pounced. "I went online and I found that website about Massonville that R.B. was telling us about, Mom," she announced triumphantly. "They have a history of the Venable family on it. I downloaded it and I made a copy for you!"

"Susie, I'm not interested."

"You will be. Just listen." She whipped out a sheaf of papers—presumably the Venable family saga—and began to read. "*In 1878 the brilliant actress Juliet Venable charmed James Honeycutt into selling the opera house in Massonville to her. Honeycutt was distraught over the death of his stepmother, who had perished in an accident in the theater, and there is even some research to indicate that he was thinking of having the building torn down. But through sheer force of her magnetic personality, Juliet saved it for posterity, and for generations of Venables to come."* Susie looked up to smile happily at her. "Isn't this great, Mom?"

That was when Randa understood. *She's fallen for the opera house and now she wants us to keep it. Damn!*

There was another pile of papers neatly stacked on the desk next to the computer. Susie had been collecting facts and figures to back up whatever verbal pitch she'd been planning. Randa's baby had learned her negotiating skills at home.

Suddenly Randa felt tired. And vulnerable. She slumped onto a squishy chair that some hotel decorator had thought was chic. Going back to the theater today had been a mistake. Because, okay, she could admit it, being there brought up memories of the old days. As Katie had said, *The past is never dead. It's not even past.*

Randa sat up. Her past *was* dead, and she didn't give in to sentimental bull. As soon as she was sure Mike Killian was playing fair with them, she was going back to the life she'd set up for Susie and herself. This would all be a blip on her radar screen.

Meanwhile, Susie was burbling happily. "Doesn't Juliet Venable sound amazing?" she demanded. "And there's a guy called Edward Rain—he was an in-law—who earned all the money that supported the theater for years. It's all in that history I copied for you."

Randa fought her way out of the chair. Time for a reality check. "Susie—" she began, but her child was on a roll.

"There's a garden in the back of the opera house with these statues in it," Susie rushed on. "R.B. showed it to me. There's one of Juliet. I didn't like her, but now that I've read about what she did, I want to see her again. And there's one of Edward Rain. I didn't really look at him before. We could go over to the garden right now." She looked at Randa. "Or tomorrow," she amended.

"Honey, I know this has been exciting, coming down here and finding out we'd inherited that opera house. But we live thousands of miles away from here, and—"

"I think we should move here!" said her child.

That was the thing about being a parent; just when you thought you had everything under control, your kid could come up with something that threw it all sky-high.

"Susie—" But before Randa could begin explaining why the idea was insane, Susie was moving on.

"Let's look at it logically," she said in a reasonable voice Randa recognized as her own when she was working the phone. "What's keeping us in L.A.? The Puke Carpet Palace? We should sell it before California real estate totally tanks. Your job? You told Andrew last week that your clients are dumber than hair. My school? It sucks. And Jen won't even be there anymore." She grabbed the pile of papers off the desk. "I've looked up some stuff. There's a really good magnet school here. It was listed in that article *Newsweek* did about the hundred best public schools in the country. I can take the test for it this summer, and I can always take extra courses on the Internet like I do now. They also have a museum, and there are three libraries if you count the two outside of Massonville—"

"Susie—"

"They have a TV station."

"Honey, even if I wanted to throw away everything and start my entire life over, I wouldn't move you here. You think you'd have anything in common with the kids in that school? You come from a different world. You'd be a complete outsider."

"What do you think I am now? Massonville has got to be better than L.A. Anything is better than L.A.!"

Susie's eager face was flushed, her eyes were begging. *When did I become the one who always fails her?* Randa thought furiously.

"All I need are two friends," Susie went on. "I can make two friends. And what about when I hit puberty? I could go crazy. I'm going to do my best not to, but you never know. Would you rather have me hung up on some boy here or a total loser like Jeremy Tate?"

Randa flashed briefly on the smirking twice-rehabbed-before-he-was-seventeen son of her most successful client. "Not all the kids in L.A. are Jeremy Tate."

"A lot of the kids in my school are. Everyone here won't be an angel, I know that. But don't you think I'll have a better chance with a boy who has to bag groceries to pay for his car insurance, instead of one whose father gives him a new Mercedes every time he wrecks the one he's got?"

She's so smart! Randa thought. "Susie, you've haven't thought this through—"

"And it's not just about me, Mom. It's about you too. You need a life."

"I have a life!"

"You have work. And me. And I'm going to grow up and go away some-day. You don't have any friends, you don't have a family. I was your date at the Golden Globes last year."

"That was because I wanted you to have the experience."

"That was because you didn't have anyone to go with."

Okay, sometimes she's too damn smart. "Susan, you feel very strongly about this right now, I get that. But I'm not leaving L.A., and if I were, I would never move to a little town in the deep South. Forget the fact that I'd go out of my mind, how could I support us? There's not a big market for the-atrical business managers here."

"We'd have our opera house."

"If you're thinking we could open a bed and breakfast or something like that—"

"No, a theater. Like Juliet Venable and Edward Rain."

"Oh God." But what had she expected? Susie was smart, but she was only eleven. "Baby, no one ever, *ever* makes money with a theater."

"We could do it. You always say a person can do anything if they really want it bad enough."

"Not this, Susie. This is like trying to make a living by winning the lot-tery. . . ."

"Remember when I wanted to give my oral book report on *Anna Karen-ina* and the teacher said it was too advanced for me?"

"That isn't even close to—"

"You said I could do it. We bought a map and a Russian history book and you hired that actress to teach me how to pronounce the names. It took us weeks."

"It's not the same thing!"

"Why not, Mommy? Why isn't it?"

Susie was crying now. And, damn it, so was Randa. Because how do you say to your little girl, whom you've raised not to be afraid, that there are times when she should be? How do you tell her that the world really is a scary place, and you lied when you said anyone can do anything? One thing you didn't do was keep on crying in front of her. Randa pulled herself to-gether.

"Susie, you know about my father. I've told you—"

"He was an actor, and he never made it, and you had to move around all the time and live in terrible places. But we won't be like that."

"We would be, if I let you talk me into this. Honey, it's okay for you to fantasize about having a theater, or joining the circus or walking on Mars. But I'm the grown-up. I have to be responsible."

Susie stopped crying and looked at her for a long moment. Finally she asked, "Are you happy, Mom?"

Oh shit.

How the hell do you tell your child you've never tried to be happy, that for you survival was always the goal? The only thing Randa could think of to say was, "You don't know what it's like to be broke."

That was when her kid's face got bright. "I never will, Mom, because you won't let that happen. You'll always make things work; it's who you are." Susie picked up the history of the Venables she'd copied off the Internet. "I'm not happy in L.A. I never have been and neither have you." She stopped for second. Then she said something she'd obviously been thinking about for a while. "We don't belong there." She handed Randa the sheaf of papers. "These people were so great; the way they kept handing down that theater, the parents saving it for the kids. You really should read about them. They could be our family." She went into her connecting bedroom and closed the door quietly behind her.

Randa looked down at the papers in her hand. *Just what I need,* she thought. *A goddamn theater and a goddamn family.* She hadn't wanted a family for years. Not since she'd gottten smart enough to know better.

She put Susie's "history" out of sight on a bureau and booted up her laptop. She had fifty-three e-mails and without even reading them she knew they were all going to be dumber than hair. She closed up her laptop and picked up a magazine, but concentrating on fourteen different ways to cook asparagus was impossible. She lay down on the bed and let the memories of family—and The Bad Night—flood in.

CHAPTER 25

Indianapolis 1982

The Bad Night happened during the summer when Randa was seven years old. Her father was working a dinner theater circuit in the South and Midwest, playing the lead in *Barefoot in the Park,* and Randa was trouping with him. She still thought her dad was the handsomest man in the world in those days, and if you looked at his publicity shots from the period, she wasn't too far off base. The drinking hadn't blurred his jawline yet or rounded his face, and he still had his waistline. But it was the light in his eyes in those pictures that made it impossible for Randa to look at the photographs when she was an adult. She remembered how the light had died.

But that summer when she was seven, everything seemed perfect to her. Her daddy was happy about the show and his role. Light comedy was Richard Jennings's natural forte, and in every town they played, his review in the local fish wrapper was a rave—only her father wasn't saying they were fish wrappers the way he usually did; he was calling them newspapers, and he was clipping the reviews.

Even more revolutionary, and wonderful from Randa's point of view, Richard was dating his leading lady. That meant he wasn't leaving Randa alone in the motel after the show every night while he went out with the crew to "unwind." Instead he and Sandy were in the room next to hers and Randa could hear the sound of their television as she drifted off to sleep. Sandy was a huge improvement over the women her father usually brought home. Not only did she remember Randa's name, she took her out for "girls' days" on Mondays when the show was dark. They'd have lunch at whatever chain restaurant in town had a soup-and-salad special, and then Sandy would find a place where they could get their nails done. Life didn't get much better than that, Randa felt, and she spent a lot of time praying that Sandy would stay around forever.

But when they got to Indianapolis, it seemed that life could get even better than it already was.

"You're going to meet my sister," her father announced. "She's bringing her husband and her kids to see me in the show."

Randa was thrilled. "I've never met Dad's sister," she confided to Sandy during their manicure-and-lunch outing. She thought about telling Sandy that they never talked about Richard's family, but she decided not to. Sandy had never seen her father get angry—she didn't know about the silence that could go on for days and the eyes that didn't see you. "Dad told me one time that I have an aunt, but that's all I know," Randa went on. Richard had been very drunk when he'd mentioned his sister, but Randa decided not to tell Sandy about that either. Her father had stopped drinking since he'd started dating Sandy.

Richard was happy about his sister coming to the show—happier than Randa had ever seen him. He reserved a table for four at the dinner theater. It was right in the first row, in front of the spot onstage where he played his best scene in the last act—the one that all the reviewers mentioned. He paid for four prime rib dinners for his sister's family, even though that was the most expensive meal on the menu; he and Randa and Sandy always ate the fried chicken because the help got it for free. Then to top it all off, two nights before their relatives were coming to dinner, he handed Randa a large flat box and said, "Here, try it on."

Surprises didn't usually come her way, and new clothes were even more of a rarity. Her standard summer outfit consisted of blue jeans and T-shirts because they were cheap and easy for her to wash in the motel Laundro-mats. But there were layers of tissue in the box, so she knew the gift was from someplace expensive. Her heart was beating fast as she reached in and carefully pulled out a dress. It was yellow, with a big fluffy skirt, a satin ribbon around the waist, and ruffles on the collar and the hem. You'd put it on a baby or maybe a doll—not a grown-up girl of seven who hated yellow. She wanted to throw the stupid dress back into the box. Then she looked up and saw her father's face.

"Oh, I love it!" she breathed. He wasn't the only actor in the family.

Sandy bought her a pair of shoes and socks to go with the doll dress because her father had forgotten to do that, and on the big night Sandy helped Randa set her hair. The plan was, Randa would watch the show from backstage, and after it was over, she would meet her kinfolk. As they left the motel, her father said she looked like a princess, which made wearing the Yuck Dress worth it. She and Sandy and Richard walked over to the theater together.

Like a family, Randa thought. And, as if she could read Randa's mind, Sandy gave her hand a squeeze.

Her father was so nervous that Sandy had to help him with his makeup, and she sat with him in the dressing room, holding his hands until the stage manager called places. Randa went with them down to the stage so she could stand in the wings and watch her father play his best part ever in front of his family.

Sandy's character was on at the top of the show, so she gave Richard a kiss and went onstage. Richard had to wait behind the set for his cue to go on. When the lights came up, Randa saw Sandy sneak a peek out at the house. She was facing away from Randa, but Randa could tell right away that something was wrong. Randa leaned out so she could see the front row of the audience and the table her father had reserved. All four chairs were empty.

Richard didn't realize it until he had made his entrance and was onstage. He was supposed to take a pause—that was in the script—but he stared at the empty table for so long that the stage manager was getting ready to prompt him. Finally, he said his opening line.

Sandy was off all night, but Richard had never been better. He didn't miss one laugh, his timing was perfect, and he played his big scene directly in front of the empty table. When they came offstage after the final scene, there were tears sparkling in Sandy's eyes, but when she reached out to Richard, he pushed her away. He didn't speak to anyone backstage, and everyone in the company left him alone. They'd all heard about his family coming to see him, and they'd all seen the empty table.

He didn't take his curtain call. He walked out of the theater without saying a word to anyone. Sandy and Randa stayed at the theater waiting for him until the stage doorman closed up for the night; then they went back to the motel to wait. At four in the morning, Sandy got a call from the company's stage manager. Richard was at the hospital in the emergency room. He'd gone back to the theater, and when he'd realized it was locked, he'd tried to break in by putting his arm through a window. He said he'd wanted to get his makeup kit out of the dressing room. He said he was quitting the show. When the police found him he was bleeding badly and he was very, very drunk.

He'd almost severed a nerve in his right hand, and the doctor said he'd have scars on his arm for the rest of his life. Sandy's face was as white as the hospital sheets when she signed him out of the emergency room. The theater didn't press charges, but the company fired him. Richard didn't say a word to anyone.

Sandy decided to finish the tour instead of going back to New York with Richard and Randa. She said it was because there was no way she'd get another summer gig that late in the season, but Randa knew that wasn't the reason. Sandy had seen how bad things could get with Richard. She cried at the bus station when she said good-bye to them, because she felt guilty—she really was a very nice person—but Randa knew they wouldn't see her again. Randa and Richard were on their own once more.

Randa assumed that everything would go back to the way it had been before. But it didn't. Richard's hand didn't heal properly and it hurt him all the time, which gave him an excuse to drink even more. Not that he needed an excuse. After The Bad Night in Indianapolis he seemed to give up.

When she was older, Randa tried not to blame too much on that one event. As her shrink pointed out, her father had always been self-destructive. "We all have disappointments," Dr. Alexander had said, "but responsible adults don't use that as an excuse to act out." And of course Randa had agreed. But the seven-year-old inside her always knew things would have been different if her father's sister had shown up for the goddamn prime rib dinner and Richard's performance in *Barefoot in the Park.*

Randa got off the bed, grabbed the Venable history off the bureau, and threw it against the wall. Her little girl, who had never known sibling rivalry or a parental guilt trip, thought families were all about Thanksgiving dinners and greeting card moments. *Well, I did too, once. But here's the truth, no one can hurt you like the people who are supposed to love you the most.*

Of course, she'd never say that to Susie. Because then her little girl would feel as old as Randa had felt when she was eleven. Besides, what she really wanted to say to her kid was, *I love you, and I've made a world for you where you're safe. Isn't that enough?* But there was no point in asking. Her daughter was already saying she wanted more. Randa looked at the papers scattered all over the floor and lay back on the bed.

CHAPTER 26

Massonville 2006

The hike from the opera house to the historic district was longer than Katie had thought it was going to be. She'd forgotten she'd have to pass the tacky condos and the awful convention center as well as the gaudy hotel where she was staying. And for some reason she kept picking up speed. By the time she reached the wide boulevard with the picturesque old streetlamps, she was breathing hard.

"Very attractive," she told herself between gasps. "What the hell are you running for? You don't even know if the man is going to be there." She slowed down to a trot. "And stop talking to yourself," she added sternly.

R.B. was in his front yard. He hadn't been kidding about restoring his house himself. There were two sawhorses set up on the grass and he was cutting a piece of wood with some kind of saw that featured a nasty-looking blade. Katie stopped abruptly at the edge of his lawn—and not just because her recent sprint had left her panting. R.B. had changed out of his nerd outfit, into a pair of cutoff jeans. He'd also taken off his shirt. He wasn't going to give Mike Killian a run for his money in a beauty contest, but he could place second or third in a cute butt competition, and as for the abs . . . Katie told herself she must stop being so shallow when it came to men.

R.B. saw her. He turned off his power tool, put on his shirt, and strode over to her. "Hey," he said. "Great to see you!" He smiled and winked at her. The spell was broken.

"Do you really like working for your family?" she blurted out.

It took him a second. Then he said, "You do have a way with small talk, don't you?"

"I'm sorry. That was so none of my business."

"Yes." But he didn't look annoyed. Maybe he liked the clumsy type. "Would you like something cold to drink?" he asked.

He had a cooler next to his sawhorse, and produced a Coke for her and the ubiquitous iced tea for him. They sat side by side on the stoop of his unfinished front porch and let the drinks cool them off.

"I write scripts for a soap opera," Katie blurted out again. There was something about him that seemed to encourage blurting.

"Yes, you said that."

"The show is called *All Our Lives*. My mother was Rosalind Harder. She played Tess Jones—that was the lead character—"

"You're kidding! My gran used to watch that show every day. She loved Tess Jones! She even wrote in for a picture of her and your mother signed it."

"Actually, the studio always hired someone to handle Mother's fan mail. I did it for a couple of summers when I was in high school. It was my first job—working for my mother." She paused. "Then I started writing scripts for the show. Which was like working for her in another way."

It wasn't exactly a blurt, but she certainly hadn't planned to say that to him; she never talked about her hand-me-down life to anyone. But she watched R.B. connect the dots and she knew that he understood. He stood up and went to the cooler for more drinks.

"Right after I got out of law school I went to Atlanta," he said. "I thought I wanted to get away from Massonville, and being Mama and Daddy's son, and Georgie's brother." He shrugged. "But this is home. I didn't want to live in Atlanta and try to be some hotshot. And our firm is the best in town, so it would have been stupid to go somewhere else. Not that we don't get into fights sometimes—you don't leave all that parent-and-kid stuff at the door. And Georgie never will forget I was her baby brother, and that she had to beat up Wally Johnson to keep him from giving me swirlies in the boys' bathroom when I was in the second grade. But if I want to work pro bono for some crazy cause they don't believe in, they'll help me, and if anything ever goes bad for me—they've got my back. You know?"

Katie nodded as if she did know, but she was remembering Rosalind Harder on the soap set holding one of her daughter's scripts, demanding to know how she was expected to say lines that were so bad it was obvious they'd originally been written in Chinese and had been translated by the deaf. The fact that the scriptwriter's names were never listed on their work, so Rosalind didn't know she was blasting Katie, had only made the humiliation a little bit easier.

"No one ever told me I had to write for my mother's show," she said slowly. "But I was good at it. It was an easy slot to slip into. . . . And if I wrote for her, I'd never . . ." But she trailed off, because she couldn't tell him that if she stayed behind the scenes and wrote dialogue for her mother, she'd never outshine her. And she certainly wasn't going to tell him that every year when the major soap fan mag did its annual spread of Rosalind Harder celebrating Christmas at home, the entire cast of *All Our Lives* was in the pictures but her daughter, Katharina, was missing. Instead she heard herself say, "After my mother died, I wrote a play. It was about a mother and a daughter."

Why do I keep talking about that? She waited for R.B.'s eyes to glaze over the way Jock's did whenever she tried to talk about her work.

"Was it good?" he asked.

"People said it was."

"That must feel great."

"Great" didn't come close. She could still remember watching Teddy's face as he read the final page. She could remember the first reading with the actors, when they all laughed at the jokes, and every rehearsal, and the opening night, and the reviews. She remembered sitting in her apartment and being happier than she'd ever been in her life because she'd written something that was her own. Because she'd finally had something to say.

"What happened to it?" R.B. broke into her thoughts. "Your play, I mean."

"It was produced off-Broadway. It was up for a couple of awards. And every once in a while a theater somewhere does it."

"When do you write the next one?"

"I don't."

"Because?"

She'd wanted him to ask that, she'd set him up for it, but now she couldn't tell him. Because it hurt too much and she would come off as needy. Guys hated needy.

"It's a long story," she said briskly. A brisk attitude was good for counteracting the needy thing—it meant you were efficient and not in need of rescue. "I just came over here to tell you that Randa and I met Mike Killian. I thought you should know that we're going to be selling the opera house to him."

"Why aren't you going to write another play?"

Maybe he hadn't gotten the needy memo. Maybe he was into rescuing. Whatever. He looked so genuinely interested that she started to spill again. "I tried to write another one. I tried to write a novel. I tried to write short stories. I tried for two years." Her voice had gotten quavery so she drew in a deep breath. "I just don't have any more stories to tell. That play was it." She drew in another breath. "It's not a tragedy. I'm just not . . . original. I'm the kind of writer who will always have to work for someone else. I'm okay with that. "

"Bullshit."

"I am." But her voice was quavering again. She jumped to her feet. "I'm glad we're going to be wrapping things up here. I need to get back to New York."

"But we've got a lot of stories."

"So?"

"Maybe you need to borrow a couple of ours."

"That's not how it works. You write what you know."

"Get to know us. Spend some time down here. The stories are the reason you don't want to sell the opera house."

"I never said I didn't want to."

"No, but you don't always say what you mean. You want to know how you're connected to that old opera house. You want to know about all the people who loved it, and took care of it and passed it down. Just the idea of losing all those stories makes you crazy."

That was the trouble with blurting out personal information to virtual strangers—even if they did seem to be incredibly sympathetic—the next you knew, they were making huge assumptions. "You don't know how I feel," she said. "You don't know anything about me."

"I was there when you saw that elevator. Most people, when you take them through an old building, check out the crown moldings and the carvings on the stair rails, and it's like they're studying for a test. But you look at a big old elevator and you see women in their hoop skirts. That's special."

He has an agenda, she told herself. *He's trying to save the opera house.*

"I can't hang around an old theater—no matter how beautiful it is—waiting for my muse to hit," she said. "Do you know how many careers die because writers with jobs decide to dump it all for their art?"

"There's a garden in the back of the opera house," R.B. said. "Let me take you to see it."

"I don't need to see any more. We're selling that old place as fast as we can."

"Just take a look at that garden. There are three statues there. One of them is a guy you need to see. He was as torn up as you are about making money."

"I never said I was torn up!"

"Neither did Edward Rain. That was his name. He was married to Ophelia Venable."

He's working you! Katie reminded herself. But she sat down next to him again.

"Edward traveled all around the country acting in this terrible play called *The Prince of Zanzona.* We have a copy of it in the library and I slogged through it when I was a kid. After all these years it's still the worst thing I've ever read. Poor old Edward supported the opera house by playing the prince for thirty years. If you see pictures of him, he looks like he's been ridden hard and put up wet—Edward, I mean. Not the prince. The prince was noble, brave, and really, really stupid."

In his nerdy way he was charming. But then he pushed too hard. "You'll see Edward in his prince costume when you check out the statue," he said.

"I don't think I'll be doing that." She stood up. "Thanks for the Coke." She started off across his small lawn in the direction of her hotel.

"If you change your mind, there's a side path that leads to the back of the theater," he called after her. "The gate is locked, but the key is in the lockbox. It's the big iron one with the curlicues on it."

When Katie got back to the hotel, there was a sheaf of papers stuffed under her bedroom door. At the top of the first page in capital letters was written "THE HISTORY OF THE VENABLE FAMILY." An attached note said that it had come from Randa's daughter, Susie.

CHAPTER 27

Massonville 2006

It was about an hour before sunset by the time Katie finished reading the story of the Venable family. When she left the hotel, the sky was still light, but it was starting to get a little cooler. The bugs weren't out yet.

She made good time walking to the front door of the opera house— she'd already gotten to know where all the potholes were in the driveway— and she opened the lockbox quickly. The key for the opera house was there, right where she and Randa had left it, but the fancy iron one R.B. had described was missing. It seemed she wasn't going to be visiting his mythical garden after all.

She wasn't disappointed—not really. She started to walk up the path to the riverfront. But then she turned back. The white façade of the theater was bathed in the deep golden light of the sun that would soon be setting. It gave off a glow that Mike Killian's egg crate convention center could never match.

The stories are the reason you don't want to sell the opera house, R.B. had said. *You look at a big old elevator and you see women in their hoop skirts.*

She let her eyes run over the front of the theater, and imagined it as it would have been in the 1870s. She saw the black canopy over the front door with the words "The Venable Opera House" proudly displayed. There were carriages parked under it, and a servant helping the ladies up the steps to the door. She saw formal gardens, a velvet lawn, and flowers planted in window boxes under the restaurant windows. Her gaze continued roaming to the far end of the theater. That was when she saw that the side gate was open. And it was not her imagination. She hurried over to it.

The path went down the side of the theater to the garden behind it, just the way R.B. had said it would. There was a high hedge surrounding the garden, and Katie could hear voices on the other side. She followed the sound and found the remains of a trellis and a gate that had been the entrance to the garden. She went through it.

Three gray-white statues rose up over the garden at three corners. In the fourth corner was an empty pedestal. Randa and Susie were standing in front of a statue of a man wearing a cape and holding a sword up to the sky.

"Juliet Venable is over there, Mom," Susie was saying. "She's wearing her costume for *Romeo and Juliet*. And that's Olivia Venable in the corner opposite her. She's wearing everyday clothes because she wasn't an actress." Susie turned to the statue in front of them. "And this is the guy who kept the opera house going, even during the Depression."

As she moved closer to them, Katie stepped on something, or maybe they just sensed that she was there, because they both turned. Randa laughed.

"You too?" Randa said. "Well, come meet Edward Rain. Our ancestor. Or not."

All three of them turned to study the statue of Edward Rain, which, according to the date carved under his feet, had been put in the garden in 1935.

Part Three

CHAPTER 28

Massonville 1935

If the old dictum stated that "Horses sweat, gentlemen perspire, and ladies glow," then at this moment Ophelia Venable resembled a horse. Sweat collected unpleasantly in the crevices under her chin, the corset holding up the jutting shelf of her bosom was as damp as new wash on the line, and she knew without looking that her face was the color of a tomato. For the tenth time she asked herself why she had chosen to hold this dedication ceremony outdoors in the high heat of a Georgia afternoon. But she knew the answer. She hadn't considered how hot it would be sitting on the platform she'd had the stagehands build in the garden behind the Venable Opera House. She hadn't taken into account the hours of speeches she and her two hundred invited guests would have to endure, or the endless number of Sousa tunes the high school band would play. Ophelia had been thinking about the moment when the statue of Edward Rain would be unveiled, white and sparkling, in the bright sunshine. As usual, she'd chosen theatrical effect over comfort, and, as usual, she was paying for it.

She shifted in her chair as applause from the audience indicated that the speech she should have been attending to had just ended. She clapped enthusiastically and smiled at the crowd seated in lawn chairs in front of her. So far they'd heard from the mayor, the ministers of both the Baptist and the Methodist churches, and the county ordinary. Now it was time for the family to say a few words. From the farthest end of the row of seats on the platform, her niece Olivia rose and began making her way to the lectern. Ophelia frowned; was that a written speech clutched in the girl's hand? Surely she didn't intend to read it. A Venable never *read* public remarks—even the most casual of addresses was always carefully memorized and delivered with charming little hesitations scattered throughout to give an illusion of spontaneity. But Olivia, who had now reached the lectern, shaded her eyes from the sun's glare and began to read. "This is a proud day for the Venables," she said in a dreary monotone. Ophelia sighed. This was going to be worse than the Sousa songs.

Of course Olivia was not the one who should have been speaking—even if the poor thing had possessed a speck of charm or grace. The person who should have risen from his chair and walked proudly to the lectern to thank the good people of Massonville was the honoree of the day, her husband, Edward Rain. But Edward had refused. Truth be told, she'd been fortunate that he'd agreed to attend the ceremony at all.

As Olivia droned on, Ophelia snuck a quick sidewise glance at the man to whom she was married. He wasn't paying attention to Olivia's carefully crafted speech, which was not a surprise—no one was. But he certainly wasn't smiling at the crowd that had come to sit under the baking sun on his behalf, although that shouldn't have been a surprise either. Edward's face was always sour now, the charming dimples that used to accompany his smile were now deep, angry lines, and his mouth was drawn down in a perpetual frown. He'd lost weight over the years—he and Ophelia were a regular Jack Sprat and his wife in that regard. His once-muscular arms and legs were slack ropes draped over bones. His fine, broad chest was sunken, and she hadn't noticed until this moment that he had forgotten to comb his hair. The contrast between this creature sagging in the sunshine and the glorious statue of male pulchritude about to be revealed—the man Edward had once been—couldn't have been more cruel. And the transformation was all her fault. Or was it? In spite of the audience staring at them, she shifted in her seat to face him. For thirty-eight years she had been his wife—and his jailer. What she had never realized until that moment was, he had been hers too.

"And so I give you my beloved uncle." Olivia concluded her remarks bleakly. "The man of the hour, Edward Rain."

The least he could have done was stand to acknowledge the applause. Fool that she was, Ophelia let herself hope for one second that he would. If only he would smile and make some gesture—no matter how small—to indicate that he appreciated this testimonial she had arranged for him. But of course he did not. Quickly, to cover his lack of response, she pushed herself off her chair, grimacing and overdoing the effort required to lift her bulk, for comic effect. She'd been getting laughs by making a fool of herself in this way onstage for years, and now she got one more from the sleepy audience in her garden. She started across the platform with the little skipping step that was her signature movement when she played her best-loved role, Mrs. Malaprop. The crowd recognized it immediately—the good Lord knew they'd seen her do it often enough—and gave her a round of applause. Ophelia threw a quick glance at Edward. His hands were in his lap, of course. Suddenly, through no will of her own, her feet stopped moving. Pain washed over her. Not a physical pain; she could have overcome that. This was something far deeper that made her bite her lip to keep from weeping. Because if she started, she would never stop.

Just once, she thought, *I don't want to be alone.* She always had been and she had thought she didn't care, but now it seemed to her that she couldn't stand it for another minute. Loneliness was going to crush her.

There were snickers from the audience. Their funny fat woman was making faces in front of them, and they were waiting for the comic bit that must inevitably follow.

Don't disappoint them, a voice inside her head said, coming to her rescue. *A Venable never disappoints the crowd.*

Brought back to her senses, she tugged at her corset slowly and deliberately. The massive bosom/shelf followed it, first to the left and then to the right, while she bugged out her eyes and watched it as if it had a life of its own. Then she yanked one last time and with a mighty heave continued on her dainty way to the podium as the audience gave her another hand. And as they did, her moment of weakness passed. There would be no tears from Ophelia Venable today.

Ophelia stood at the lectern—milking the moment—before giving the signal for the stagehands to drop the curtain surrounding the statue. There, in front of them, was Edward Rain as they all wanted to remember him. She turned back to the man who was too wrapped in his own misery to care that the crowd had come to its feet, and thought back to the day when she'd met him for the first time. It had been on April 15, 1897—she would never forget the date—when he'd been still full of hope and she'd been still slender and graceful.

I'm sorry, she said silently to her husband. *I'm sorry for both of us.*

But, as the applause swelled around her, she knew she'd do it all again. Because she had saved the Venable Opera House. It was the legacy her mother, Juliet Venable, had built. And Ophelia had kept it safe for all the Venables to come. If she had sacrificed herself and Edward in the process, so be it.

CHAPTER 29

Massonville 1897

Ophelia tucked the hem of her skirt up into her waistband and leaned out over the staircase railing to reach the chandelier. She managed four wide sweeps at the crystals with her feather duster, then stopped so she wouldn't fall. The crystals were clean enough, and she had no desire to crack her head open on the lobby floor below. If the truth were told, she had little patience for domesticity. However, times were hard for the Venable Opera House, and Mama had been forced to let three of the maids go. The one remaining girl had her hands full cleaning the restaurant and the theater. It had been Juliet's intention to keep up the hotel herself, but lately she had been experiencing a shortness of breath that her daughter found frightening, so every morning Ophelia dispensed with her corset and stockings, dressed in her oldest skirt and shirtwaist, and sallied forth with dust rags, a mop, and a broom. When he first saw her attired that way, her brother Horatio said she was a hoyden. He'd meant to be funny, but Ophelia had not been in a frame of mind to be amused. A week earlier Mama had had to settle more of his gaming debts, and the sum had brought on another attack of breathlessness for Juliet. Instead of laughing, Ophelia had handed her brother a broom and told him to make himself useful. This had resulted in

Horatio slamming out of the opera house and not returning for three days, leaving the company without a Friar Francis for *Much Ado About Nothing.* Fortunately, the stage manager was up on the lines, since Horatio had missed performances before.

Mama had been upset about Ophelia's self-imposed role as a house-maid. "If it were Horatio working like a hired hand, it wouldn't matter," she'd protested. "He only plays bit parts. But you are our leading ingénue. What if one of the hotel guests sees you scrubbing floors?"

But as Juliet spoke, her face was pale, and even the exertion of protest-ing seemed to tire her. For once in her life, Ophelia had ignored her. The best Juliet had been able to get from her daughter was a promise that Ophe-lia would try to avoid being seen as she did her chores.

Not that their current guests would have cared. Their hotel was not the fashionable place it had been when Juliet bought the opera house nineteen years earlier. Massonville's riverfront was now lined with cotton factories and warehouses, and, these days, the well-heeled travelers who had once enjoyed their hospitality stayed at the new hostelries in the center of town.

For several years Juliet had been running what was in essence a board-inghouse for traveling salesmen and minor businessmen who couldn't af-ford the more expensive establishments. A newly instituted breakfast at the restaurant had replaced the elegant theater suppers of yesterday, and the hotel rooms were often let out for a month or longer. The hardworking men who lodged in them rarely had the inclination or the money to see a play, and probably wouldn't have known that the girl sweeping the halls had re-ceived an enthusiastic hand on her third-act exit the night before. Still, a promise was a promise, and for Mama's sake Ophelia waited to begin her labors in the lobby until breakfast was finished.

This morning, she had to work even more quickly than usual. In a cou-ple of hours the company's new leading man would arrive at the railroad sta-tion. The carriage had already been ordered to collect him and bring him to the opera house, where he was to board in the hotel upstairs—free of charge. This was unheard-of generosity on Mama's part. She had always ex-pected her actors to pay their own way; even Sarah Bernhardt, who had filled the opera house to capacity during her run in 1881, had been presented with a bill on her departure. It was said that the notoriously tight-fisted Madame had vowed that she would never return to Massonville.

"It didn't matter to us," Mama had sniffed when she'd told Ophelia the story some years later. "We are a stock company. We have never depended on the caprice of stars."

But these days, even in out-of-the-way Massonville, the public wanted to know it was watching nationally acclaimed actors. The Venable Opera House had resisted this trend, but the audiences—and the badly needed box office revenues—had fallen off as a result.

Ever resourceful, Mama had come up with a scheme. "Our company will perform here at home for six months, and for the rest of the year we'll send out our own tour with our own actors," she'd declared.

It was not an impossible notion; the travel would increase the reputation of the Venable Opera House and give it some much-needed luster. And there was money to be made on the road. It was Mama's plan to stick to the hinterlands, where there would be little competition from the big productions coming out of New York. What she needed was an actor who was a draw. Or who could be groomed to become one. And that was why she was giving Mr. Edward Rain the valuable hotel room.

Without even seeing him! Ophelia thought. *Mama is pinning all her hopes on this man and he isn't even an actor. Not a professional one, at any rate.* Ophelia swept the carpeted stairs viciously, raising more dirt than she was collecting. She took a breath and forced herself to sweep more gently as she reviewed the few facts they knew about Mama's new leading man.

Edward Rain had been born in New Hampshire, of all places, and his father was a minister, of all things. After finishing his schooling, Edward had made his way to Boston, where he had eked out a living by planning social events for the wealthy and hiring himself out to give dramatic recitations at dinner parties. In his spare time he had participated in amateur theatricals. Mama had heard about him from an old friend who had seen him perform in one such production in Boston, and had written to Mama about his potential.

Mr. Rain, wrote the besotted friend, *has had no acting training, save for a few months of elocution lessons.* (That explained the recitations.) *But believe me when I tell you, my dear Juliet, that he has a natural talent that more than overcomes that deficiency. In addition, he is extraordinarily handsome and is one of those rare men who manage to charm both the ladies and the gentlemen. He has already built a small but devoted following for himself here in Boston, and I understand it is his intention to go to New York to try his luck as a professional actor as soon as he has sufficient funds. He is bound to make a success for himself there, but as one of his many well-wishers, it is my hope that he might have a few years of seasoning before he does so. And so I have thought of you. If you have need of a leading man, allow me to recommend Mr. Rain to you.*

On the strength of that letter Mama had engaged the man. And she had given him a free hotel room. And she was talking about mounting a production of *Othello* to tour the tank towns of the South and Midwest. For an actor she had never seen! Ophelia saw the clouds of dust flying around her and realized she was attacking the hapless carpet again.

Normally, Mama was a careful businesswoman, fair but stern, and tight with a penny. But every once in a while she would get what she called one of her "feelings" and would take a risk that stunned her daughter. The unknown Mr. Rain had inspired a "feeling." Or maybe it was just that Mama was desperate.

The brass wall sconces hadn't been touched in weeks and were in need of polishing. Ophelia looked at the clock above the elevator. Mr. Rain's train wouldn't be arriving at the railroad station for another hour, so she had plenty of time before she and Mama had to greet him in the office. She pushed an ottoman against the wall next to the elevator, pulled off her shoes so she would not ruin the expensive upholstery, and set to work. When the front door of the lobby opened three minutes later, she was barefoot and dirty, wearing her oldest, most heavily darned shirtwaist with her skirt pulled up well above the dictates of propriety.

"Hello," said a masculine voice that echoed gloriously around the room. Ophelia turned to see a young man framed against the open door in a shaft of sunlight. He looked like a vision in the bright light. Or a saint. Or an actor. "I'm Edward Rain," he said.

CHAPTER 30

Massonville 1897

Edward Rain was a man blessed with height and a perfectly proportioned figure. He had thick blond hair that curled onto his forehead, a well-molded mouth, eyes that seemed to be green although they could have been golden brown, and when he smiled—even nervously, as he did at that moment— two dimples formed. He was, quite simply, the most beautiful person, male or female, Ophelia had ever seen.

"You aren't expected for another hour," she said, mustering as much dignity as she could with her bare knees exposed.

"I took an earlier train." He didn't seem to notice her knees. Or perhaps he was being polite. She tugged discretely at her skirt and felt around the floor for her shoes with her toes, all the while keeping her eyes on his splendid face.

"But there isn't an early train this morning." She had found her shoes, but getting them on her feet without drawing attention would be impossible. Finally she gave up, sat on the ottoman, and put them on. "I know the railroad schedule."

His face reddened—was he blushing? "I arrived last night," he said, "and slept in the station. I didn't want to be late, and I thought if the train were delayed . . ." He stopped himself. For all of his zeal, he did have dignity. "I'm afraid I've made a mistake. My appointment with Mrs. Venable is not until noon. If you will tell me where I can go to wait—"

"How did you get here?" Ophelia broke in, feeling more in command with her shoes on.

"I walked."

"All the way from the railroad station?"

"It can't be more than a few miles."

"Four. Where is your trunk?"

"This is all I have." He indicated the lone suitcase he was carrying. "And there are some books that my mother will be sending to me from home."

The actors Ophelia knew didn't read books. Their mothers didn't send their possessions from home, and they owned theater trunks full of the costumes and paraphernalia they had accumulated over their years of working. Edward Rain had none of this.

He has none of an actor's showmanship either. And he's much too shy. Still, there is that face, and that voice. And there's something in the way he carries himself.

"You must be hungry, after walking all that way," she said. "We've finished serving breakfast in our restaurant, but I am sure I can find something for you to eat in the kitchen."

"You're very kind, but I don't think I should—"

"Perhaps I should tell you that I'm Ophelia Venable, and Mrs. Venable is my mother."

"Oh. I thought you were . . ." He reddened again.

"Yes, I'm sure you did. My mother says I bring shame on our illustrious house in this costume." Then she added in a hammy Irish brogue, "But it suits meeself for the washing up—don't you see." He laughed, and she thought that perhaps he wasn't so shy after all. She stuck out her hand. "I won't tell mother you slept all night in the train station if you won't tell her you caught me dressed like the scullery maid," she said.

"I'll go along with that!" He shook her hand and favored her with another smile—and the dimples. "And now that I know you won't be let go for being kind to me—did you mean that? About the breakfast?"

She led him into the kitchen, where he finished three portions of leftover grits and a plate of bacon.

"I only had enough money for my train ticket from Boston," he explained cheerfully as he attacked his cold grits. "I haven't eaten in two days."

Although she didn't know it at the time, that moment was probably when she fell in love with him.

The next morning Edward joined the cast for the first rehearsal of their new season. The theater was offering three plays that year: *The Rivals, Camille,* and an old barnstormer's delight called *The Prince of Zanzona,* which had been popular in the forties but was never performed anymore—a great mercy, in Ophelia's opinion. The play's leading character was a noble prince who, for three acts, faced down his enemies with manly fortitude, and then, having won all his battles, suddenly went mad in a soliloquy that lasted for most of the fourth act. After which, he capped off the evening by throwing himself off a parapet. It was in this piece of old-fashioned claptrap that Mama intended to introduce her new leading man. Even before Ophelia had met Edward Rain and realized she wanted to protect him from any harm life might have for him, she'd tried to persuade her mother not to produce *The Prince of Zanzona.*

"I'm sure it went over when you were a girl, Mama," she'd said. "Audiences loved all that 'sound and fury' back in those days. But this is 1897."

"Given the right actor, it will play," Mama had said.

Before the first rehearsal, Ophelia had tried again. "Mama, now you've seen Edward Rain for yourself," she had pleaded. "He's handsome, but there's nothing bravura about him. He doesn't have the temperament for the prince, and he certainly doesn't have the skill."

For a moment it seemed as if Mama's confidence had been shaken, but then she'd said, "I have a feeling."

The rehearsal was held on the stage of the theater. There were three new actors joining the company in addition to Edward Rain, so for the first few minutes everyone was busily greeting and sizing each other up. Ophelia saw Edward draw Juliet aside.

"I believe the prince in *The Prince of Zanzona* was your father's signature role, wasn't it, Mrs. Venable?" he asked. Not only was the information a complete surprise to Ophelia, it explained Mama's insistence on the play.

Mama's hard eyes lit up. "How did you know that?"

"My former elocution teacher used to save the newspaper reviews of the actors he thought were the best of his generation. When I told him about my engagement here, he showed me the pages in his scrapbook dedicated to your father. "

Ophelia had never seen her mother look so young. Edward Rain had found a clever way to ingratiate himself with his new employer.

And there is no reason why you should be disappointed about that, Ophelia told herself. But she was. Until he spoke again.

"I only mentioned this because . . ." He stumbled, blushing but determined to have his say. "Because I have an idea of my own about the part that may be different from what you are expecting."

The soft look was gone from Mama's eyes in an instant. "Do you indeed?" she asked in a freezing tone. Edward Rain seemed not to notice.

"Yes." He nodded enthusiastically. "The play is an old piece, but I think it can take a modern interpretation."

Ophelia closed her eyes and waited for the slaughter that was going to come. Mama hated modern interpretations. And there was no actor living who could outshine her memories of her beloved Papa. But there was no explosion.

"Well, we'll see what you have in mind, won't we?" Juliet said to her new leading man.

CHAPTER 31

Massonville 1897

Edward Rain revealed what he had in mind as soon as they began work. Before she put her actors through their paces in a new play, Mama always seated them in a circle and had them speak the lines all the way through. It was an unorthodox way to go about the business of rehearsing, but Mama said it gave her an idea of the pitfalls that awaited her. All of the actors in *The Prince of Zanzona* had already learned their parts, of course, but most of them were still stumbling a little. Not Edward Rain. He began his first scene with a full characterization, portraying a young man full of high spirits and joy. His long speeches were delivered simply but quickly, so that they seemed to be a product of youthful enthusiasm, not stale playwriting. In the first courting scene, Ophelia, who was playing his princess, was hard-pressed to keep up with him. It seemed Mama was correct; the right actor could give the old play a new life. Then, suddenly, he faltered.

He's stuck for his words, Ophelia thought, *and he doesn't know he should call for a cue.* She was about to signal the stage manager, who was holding the book to assist him, when Edward made a fidgety little movement with his hands, and a look of fear crossed his face.

It's a part of his performance, she realized. *He's setting up the madness at the beginning of the play.*

Edward repeated the little moments of mania with greater and greater intensity throughout the first three acts. Each time, the prince had more difficulty recovering from them, and each time it was harder for him to control his hands and his fear. He was fighting for his sanity. It was horrible—and mesmerizing—to watch.

Finally the fatal last scene with the treacherous speech was upon them. Mama cut in. "Mr. Rain, please feel free to move about," she said. Edward nodded and stood. He started calmly, almost as if the last two hours—and the battle he'd been enacting in front of them—had never taken place. Then the horrid hand gestures began taking over. He started speaking his words in a singsong, his eyes growing more and more mindless with sheer animal terror.

Then, abruptly, he stopped. It was as if he were having a moment of clarity. A dazzling smile broke over his face. Slowly and deliberately, he walked to the back of the stage. He climbed up onto the platform that would become the parapet when the set was finished, and with a little gesture of victory, ended his existence by jumping.

There was a long silence. Everyone knew they had just witnessed theatrical alchemy, Edward Rain had transformed an antiquated piece of bunkum into a study of insanity worthy of the most modern work of Mr. Ibsen. Edward came out from behind the platform and stood in the middle of the stage, dazed. No one moved. At her side, Ophelia heard Mama mutter under her breath, "He's one of those who are made of glass. You can see through to his heart." Ophelia turned to see her smiling, with tears streaming down her face.

"Mama . . . ," Ophelia started to say, but Juliet dashed the tears away.

"Ladies and Gentlemen," she called out to the company, "we will now stop for our midday meal."

The food was always served on the stage by the restaurant staff. As the company ate, they recovered from the spell Edward had cast over them. Ophelia could see that she was not the only one who had realized she would be working hard to hold her own against their new leading man. But in the air was the happy buzz of a cast that knew it was going to have a hit.

Edward seemed oblivious to all of it: the rivalries, the admiration, and the optimism. He sat apart, picking at his food. Ophelia moved next to him.

"How did you do that?" she demanded.

Of course he knew what she was talking about. "We are so much more enlightened about insanity today than they were in the forties when your grandfather was playing the prince," he replied. "Now we understand that it's an illness, and the seeds of it are often there from the earliest days of childhood." Edward paused, and she knew he was seeing something far away. He'd forgotten her. "They know something's wrong—those that are born afflicted—and they fight against it. They fight so hard . . ." Suddenly he remembered that she was beside him. "I went to the Boston Lunatic Asylum," he went on. "The doctors there were very kind to me. When I explained my situation, they allowed me to observe the inmates for several days."

"You went to a madhouse?"

"The buildings and the grounds are quite beautiful; they were planned by Olmsted."

"You know what I meant to say."

"I needed to understand the patients."

"But it must have been terrible."

The faraway look was back in his eyes. "In the beginning it was shocking. But one of the doctors said something that helped me. . . . He said he thought the sick do find a certain peace, if they can stop fighting their fate. I like to think that's true." He remembered her again. "After that, all I could see were . . . human beings. And that's what we do, as actors, isn't it? We try to show what it means to be human?"

The question took her by surprise. "I don't know. Is that what we do?"

Actor-style, he had lines ready to quote. " 'the purpose of playing, whose end,' " he recited softly, " 'both at the first and now, was and is, to hold, as 'twere, the mirror up to nature, to show virtue her own feature, scorn her own image, and the very age and body of the time his form and pressure.' "

"Hamlet to the players."

"The first time I heard that speech, Booth was playing the role—that was when I knew I wanted to be an actor."

"I've been acting all my life, but I've never thought about the reasons why we do it."

For a second he looked as if he couldn't believe her. Then he smiled. "Sometimes I think too much," he said.

But she couldn't let it rest. "It's always been the family business, you see. My mother and I worry about filling the house, and not paying too much for the scenery, and if the box office will fall off. I haven't had the time to . . ." She searched for the right words.

He found them for her. "Worry about yourself."

All of a sudden, she was aware of their roles reversing. Since he'd walked into the lobby of the opera house looking like a country bumpkin, she had been the knowledgeable one who had taken him under her wing. But now she saw that in his own way he knew more than she.

Mama says he's twenty-six . . . and I'm only seventeen.

She had to fight the feeling that she had lost something precious. "I must seem stupid to you," she said.

He gave a little shout of laughter. "You? Stupid?" Then he looked at her, and saw that she was in earnest. "I think you are probably the bravest person I've ever met."

And, at that interesting moment, Mama called them all back to work. As he stood up, Edward asked quietly, "Do you think your mother was pleased with my interpretation of the prince?"

From any other actor it would have been a bid for praise, but he was too modest for that kind of vanity. He looked genuinely worried.

"Mama was delighted," she assured him.

"That's good. Because I couldn't change it. You see, I know I'm right."

So much for modesty, she thought.

Of course, Mama did have adjustments for him. Edward Rain had a natural grace, and thanks to the elocution lessons, he had a command of his voice, but there were certain tricks of the trade that he didn't know. Mama set about teaching him, and he used every nugget of wisdom she gave him. Mama was impressed.

The first performance of *The Prince of Zanzona* was the roaring success they had all known it would be. After the last curtain call, when the applause had finally faded away, patrons of the opera house who for years had not bothered to come backstage after an opening night were suddenly swarming around Edward Rain's dressing room. Ophelia had to push her way through a crowd to get to him. And if she had hoped he might feel a little overwhelmed and need her at his side as he faced his admirers, she was to be disappointed. Edward Rain was shy, but he was also an actor, and he had no trouble accepting adulation. Later, at the party Mama always held after every opening night, Ophelia watched him down numerous glasses of champagne while several of Massonville's more prominent belles fluttered around him.

He is twenty-six and I am only seventeen. She left the festivities early and went to bed.

The next morning, Ophelia woke up feeling out of sorts and cross. The other actors were still luxuriating in their beds, dreaming of last night's triumph, while she, dressed in her scullery maid's clothes, was making her way to the fourth floor to clean the rooms of the salesmen who rented by the month. The only comforting thought she could find was that Edward was also living on the fourth floor, and since he would undoubtedly be asleep, she wouldn't have to clean his room as well.

It will be dirty for the rest of the week, and it will serve him right! she thought as she collected her mop and bucket. In a burst of defiance, she rode up to the fourth floor in the elevator instead of hiding herself by climbing up the back stairs.

Edward was waiting for her when the elevator door opened. Somehow he had managed to acquire clothes that were even more disreputable than her own, and his eyes were red from lack of sleep. But he said cheerfully, "I was certain you wouldn't let a little thing like a first night keep you in bed."

"Where did you get those trousers?" she demanded.

"The stage manager had worn them out and I persuaded him to sell them to me rather than cut them up for cleaning rags. Appalling, aren't they?"

"Why are you wearing them?"

"So I won't ruin my own clothes when I mop the floors."

"What?"

"I assure you I'm very experienced. I was the oldest of ten, and my mother couldn't afford to hire domestic help on a parson's salary."

"You can't mop floors. You are an actor with the company—"

"As are you."

There was no reason why she should want to cry, but she did and he saw it. She was beginning to realize he saw everything.

"If it disturbs you, I won't press my services on you. But the work would go more quickly with two of us. And I would like to help you."

It was the first time she could remember anyone saying those words to her. So even though Mama would be furious if she found out, she said, "Thank you."

The work did go faster that morning. Or maybe it only seemed that way because she had someone to talk to. She told him about her acting debut when she played the Duke of York in *The Tragedy of King Richard the Third* at the age of three. He told her about his large, loud family: his father, who sounded kind, and his mother, who had read the works of Shakespeare to him when he was a child. After two hours with Edward, Ophelia felt as if she had been his friend all of her life.

She never could remember whose idea it was to tie rags to their feet so they could dry the clean but wet hallway floor by skating up and down; she only knew how much they both laughed. And she would always remember how handsome he was in the old clothes he'd purchased so he could help her. So somehow, when all the mopping and sweeping and dusting was finally done, and they were waiting for the elevator to take them downstairs, it seemed the most natural thing in the world that she should look up into his eyes. And it was possible that she moved closer to him, although she wasn't aware of doing it. The only thing that was certain was that they were so close that it was almost impossible for them not to kiss.

I am not only a hoyden but a hussy! she thought in despair. But to her surprise, Edward did not pull away. After a moment he said softly, "Thank you."

She thought they might kiss again, but the elevator arrived.

CHAPTER 32

Massonville 1897

The weeks that followed what Ophelia named the Morning of the Kiss were some of the happiest she had ever known. As a child of the theater, she was not as innocent as other girls of seventeen—although if her brother Horatio were to be believed, many of the demure maidens of Massonville's prominent families were not exactly virtuous. However, those members of the public who delighted in believing that all actors led lives of depravity would have found Ophelia Venable a grave disappointment. True, she had been enacting love scenes onstage for several years and declaring her undying devotion to men many years her senior. But her understanding of the words she spoke was vague. And she would never have done anything to distress her mother, as her brother Horatio did. It was Juliet's credo that the Venable family must never give offense to the good, churchgoing citizens of Massonville. The opera house depended on the town's goodwill.

But now Ophelia had been kissed. In some ways it felt as if nothing had changed. She and Edward still played silly little games when he helped her with her chores. He listened to everything she said, and he always laughed when she told a joke. As for the fateful kiss, sometimes it was repeated when they were alone, and sometimes it was not.

What do you expect? she asked herself. *You are the daughter of his employer. He has to be cautious.*

Of course, such a mundane factor would not have stopped the starry-eyed lovers in plays written by Shakespeare, Dumas fils, and Sardou, but Ophelia had always felt those characters were chuckleheads. Edward might not dash around ranting about love, but he woke up every morning, no matter how late he had gone to bed the night before, to carry her bucket full of soapy water. And sometimes the kiss was repeated.

At first, she and Edward had tried to conceal their new relationship. But a theatrical company is like a family, where keeping a secret is all but impossible. For a few days, Ophelia knew that she and Edward were the subject of fervent gossip, but the interest lessened quickly. It didn't die out completely—there was still speculation—but mercifully it didn't seem to have reached Juliet's ears. Until it did, Ophelia intended to keep on kissing Edward whenever the occasion presented itself. And talking to him. And listening to him.

Listening to Edward was better than going to school. He had a far-ranging mind, and he was a voracious reader; everything interested him, particularly new philosophies such as Darwin's theory of evolution and the recently discovered science of the mind known as psychology. But what he loved to talk about most was acting. He said he thought Ophelia was a natural comedienne.

"It's in your timing," he explained one morning when they had finished cleaning the hotel and had wandered outside onto the lawn. "I once saw Georgiana Barrymore—you have the same lightness of touch."

Being compared to a member of the theater's royal family was heady stuff indeed, but Ophelia was not one to get carried away. "I'm a good journeyman actor. Nothing more," she told him.

"Oh, in the roles you play now, with all that high emotion, you are only adequate," he agreed. "And there are times when you are barely that."

Stung, she made a little face and dropped him a curtsy. *"Merci du compliment,"* she said.

"There!" he said eagerly. "That is what I'm talking about! You resort to irony when you are hurt, not tears. That is how a comedian—"

"I was not hurt!"

"Of course you were. You have talent that is not being well used, and it hurt you when I said so."

"Perhaps you're wrong. . . . Has that occurred to you?"

She watched him consider it. "I'm not wrong," he said finally. "Not about acting." Then he seemed to hear himself, or perhaps he saw the expression on her face. Either way, he blushed and grinned. "I know I sound like a pompous fool, but . . . for people like us, to be the best we can is everything . . . and, you see, I've watched you."

Again, it wasn't a passionate declaration worthy of a great love scene, but Ophelia's heart leapt. He had watched her—that meant he cared.

"Be honest," he went on. "Do you really enjoy all that weeping and swooning you are called upon to do in *The Prince of Zanzona*?"

"You mean, do I like languishing on my sofa like an imbecile while you have all the good lines? Who would?"

"You know as well as I do that there are any number of dramatic actresses who would relish the role of the imbecilic princess. You're miscast."

He might be right about her acting, but he didn't understand her family business. "We run a stock company here—I fill in as I'm needed."

"Your talent is being wasted and that is a sin."

So intent had Ophelia been on their conversation that she had not noticed how far they had walked, until she saw the old dock in front of them and realized they had reached the riverfront. She looked around to see if anyone might have witnessed Juliet Venable's daughter brazenly walking alone in the company of a young man. The good people of Massonville must have known she was not always chaperoned when she worked with the actors in her mother's company, but those transgressions took place within the confines of the theater, where they could be ignored. Strolling along the banks of the river with Edward was definitely an activity that Mama would consider offensive.

"We should go back," she said.

As they were walking up the front lawn, she glanced up to the windows of the family quarters on the second floor and saw her mother looking down at them. Ophelia could have sworn that Juliet was smiling.

Mama might not have been so sanguine if she had known what Edward was suggesting as they walked.

"Do you think your mother could be persuaded to mount a production of *Twelfth Night* for you?" he asked.

Shakespeare's comedies never brought in the public as well as the tragedies did, and *Twelfth Night* had only recently begun to gain in popularity. Still, Ophelia was entranced by the thought of starring in a production, and even more entranced by the fact that Edward thought she could. So even though she didn't think it would ever happen, she said, "It would have to be done next season. We already have our repertoire for this year."

"I was thinking of the tour your mother is sending out next month. It would be the ideal vehicle for you."

Mama risk her all-important tour on me? You don't know her.

"I've seen *Twelfth Night* done with the lead actress playing both Viola and her brother, Sebastian," Edward went on.

Since Viola spent most of the play disguised as the page Cesario, that meant playing two breeches roles. It would be a difficult challenge for any actress. But one of Mama's biggest complaints about Ophelia had always been that she was tomboyish, and with her long lean legs there was no denying that she would wear the costumes well.

As usual, Edward was reading her thoughts. "Playing two boys would be a real tour de force," he said. "But you could do it; you have the intellect and the spirit, and you have the wit. There would be some rewriting required toward the last act, but I could do that. And if I played your Duke Orsino, only think what a good time we could have."

The plot had the duke becoming increasingly fond of Viola. He didn't realize he was in love with her until the end of the play when he found out she was a girl, but still it was a romantic involvement. Edward wanted to play a love story with her.

"Do you think your mother could be convinced?" he asked eagerly.

She was almost positive her mother could not be, but the double dream of touring with him and playing a lead in a production mounted especially for her was so seductive that she didn't stop him from talking to Mama.

"And if you would allow me to, I would play Duke Orsino," Edward said when he proposed the scheme to Juliet the next day. "He is—"

"I know the play," Mama broke in tartly, "and Orsino is one of the few id-
iots Shakespeare ever wrote."

"I'd say rather that he's very young and in love with love—" Edward
began, but Mama interrupted again.

"He's stupid. And while I'm impressed by your willingness to sacrifice
yourself for my daughter's sake, I have other plans for you. What would you
say to Othello?"

"You want me to play Othello for the opera house?"

"For one month here to finish our season, and then for an additional six
on the road. If you are as good as I think you will be, we'll make it a permanent part of our repertoire."

Ophelia watched Edward go to war with himself. She watched the side
of his soul that cared for her battle with the actor side. It wasn't an even
match. Mama's company might be small, but she had an excellent reputation, and playing Othello for her was an unheard-of opportunity for a per-
former who was just beginning his professional career. Edward would be a
fool to do anything but say yes and offer up a prayer of thanksgiving. But
miracle of miracles—and oh, how she loved him at that moment—he hesitated. Then Mama said, "I have hired Jonathan Tyrell to play Iago."

Jonathan Tyrell was a cut above the caliber of actor that Mama usually
hired. In fact, he was several cuts above. He'd made a name for himself
touring the country with such star managers as Madame Modjeska and Edward's idol, Edwin Booth. Ophelia might have won against Othello in Edward's battle with himself, but Edwin Booth was too much to ask. Edward
made one more plea to Mama for *Twelfth Night*, but Ophelia knew his heart
wasn't in it. And when Mama, suddenly looking pale and weary, said, "I'm
afraid I couldn't do without Ophelia to help here at the hotel while the company tours," Ophelia's heart wasn't in the fight either.

She laid her dreams aside, and began cuing Edward on the lines of his
new role. And when Jonathan Tyrell arrived in Massonville, she was waiting
at the train station to welcome him to the Venable Opera House.

CHAPTER 33

Massonville 1897

When rehearsals began, Ophelia told herself it was only natural that Edward seemed to become distant. The entire weight of *Othello* rested on his shoulders, and of necessity he was preoccupied with his performance. Furthermore, Mama had set aside an unprecedented two weeks for rehearsing the play, and since Ophelia was not going to be a part of the tour, she and Edward were no longer sharing the camaraderie of actors working together on a new production. Every new cast always developed its own jokes based on favorite lines and the "guying" or prank-playing that was a constant in any theater. So when she heard the laughter coming from the stage where the *Othello* rehearsals were taking place, Ophelia tried hard not to feel left out.

Edward still woke up every morning to help her with the cleaning, but as the rehearsals progressed he grew increasingly distracted. The little games they had played to pass the time stopped; they did not chatter anymore. She tried to engage him in gossip about the *Othello* rehearsals but that only served to make him irritable. Finally, unable to bear the change she felt in him, Ophelia said boldly, "Your Moor takes up so much of your attention, if I were in love with you, I think I'd be jealous."

She'd never flirted in quite that way with him before, but his response was a surprise. "Don't be ridiculous," he snapped.

If he had hit her, she could not have been more hurt. He saw it, and for the first time in a week she had his undivided attention. "Oh my dear, I'm sorry," he said. "You're right, the play takes all my mind these days, and I'm being horrid. Please forgive me."

"Perhaps you'd rather not help me in the mornings for a while," she said.

If she thought his anger had hurt her, now his smile of relief cut far worse. "Would you mind if I didn't?" he asked quickly. "Just until the opening night? Jonathan and I have some new ideas, and we have been working on our scenes privately before the rehearsals."

"How industrious of you."

"He knows so much; I learn from him all the time. "

"Then by all means you do not want to waste your time with me and my mops."

He didn't even notice as he dashed off that she was being ironic.

From the rumors Ophelia heard flying through the opera house, it seemed that Edward's dedication was worth the cost. The other actors in the cast said he and his older costar might well rival the great Iago and Othello partnerships of the past—the names of Booth and Forrest were bandied about. And everyone in the theater seemed to be fascinated by Jonathan Tyrell.

He was an attractive man, tall and lithe, with sardonic dark eyes, an olive complexion, and just enough snow in his hair to be interesting. In Ophelia's opinion he was a little too florid and too much of a dandy, but even she had to admit that he was gifted as a raconteur.

After the evening's performance—the company was still performing the regular repertoire at night while *Othello* was being readied—Jonathan would often meet the company for a late supper and regale them all with tales of the great actors he had known. He was a great mimic, and his impersonation of Helena Modjeska bringing an audience to tears by reciting the alphabet in Polish was sheer genius. And Edward was not the only

one who sat in worshipful silence when Jonathan described the reaction of
the great Edwin Booth when he heard that it was his younger brother, John
Wilkes Booth, who had assassinated President Lincoln.

"Booth went down into the cellar of the theater he owned and burned
all of his brother's costumes in the furnace," Jonathan told them, and then
proceeded to describe the scene so vividly that Ophelia thought he probably was as brilliant on the stage as everyone said he was. Of course, she
could have watched a rehearsal of *Othello* and judged for herself. But for
some reason she never had.

So the opening night was a shock for her. Edward and Jonathan gave
what was quite simply the best performance she had ever seen in the opera
house. The whole play was well done—one did not expect less from a production staged by Juliet Venable—but when Othello and Iago were together, the stage became brilliantly, almost brutally, alive. Edward with his
transparent openness was all passion, and heart, while Jonathan was especially dangerous because a strange tenderness underlay his malice. This
was obviously the "new idea" Edward and Jonathan had been rehearsing,
and it was effective in a way Ophelia found almost disturbing.

When Jonathan spoke the words "O, beware, my lord, of jealousy! / It is
the green-eyed monster which doth mock / The meat it feeds on . . . ," there
was a caressing note in his voice, and when he touched Othello's shoulder,
the gesture sent a shiver through the entire audience. Edward's agonized response of "O misery!" brought them to the edge of their seats, where they
stayed breathlessly until the final curtain.

The two leading men took all of their curtain calls together, in spite of
repeated pleas from the house for separate ones. The applause lasted for
twenty minutes. Mama stood next to Ophelia backstage and for once she
did not look weary. Ophelia found herself thinking back to the sunny mornings not so long ago when she and Edward had dreamed of doing *Twelfth
Night* together and wished she could turn back the clock.

However, clocks go forward, not backward, and no matter how one feels,
there is always work to be done. The morning after the triumphal opening
of *Othello* saw Ophelia in the office making last-minute arrangements for
the tour. But she was too restless to concentrate, and she decided to take a
quick turn around the garden to clear her head. When Ophelia reached the

garden gate she found that it was stuck. If it hadn't been, she would have walked right through. She wouldn't have stopped and seen the two figures facing each other as they sat on the bench under her mother's statue, sharing a stolen moment. There was so much longing in the way they leaned toward each other, it was as if they were lovers coming together for an embrace. She recognized them instantly; one was Jonathan Tyrell—and the other was Edward.

CHAPTER 34

Massonville 1897

The ground seemed to fall from under Ophelia's feet. She stepped back behind the hedge, not wanting to be seen. Or perhaps she did not want to see. Words and phrases half remembered and dimly understood raced into her mind: "Greek Love," "Charlotte Anne," and "Sister Boy." She remembered hearing about an actor who always traveled with the same dresser—a younger man—and she could see in her mind the raised eyebrows and knowing smiles that accompanied both names.

But none of that has anything to do with Edward! It can't!

Everyone knew those words and looks were reserved for effeminate, womanish men, and he was not that.

Yet she knew what she had seen. Or did she? Had she mistaken it? She forced herself to step out from behind the hedge and look again at the bench. The two men were closer together now. Jonathan reached out his hand to touch Edward, and Ophelia could sense how much Edward—her Edward—wanted that hand to caress him. She remembered the way Edward had distanced himself from her in the last few weeks, and she remembered the look on his face when he listened to Jonathan tell his stories. She remembered the connection between Edward and Jonathan when they acted together on the stage. She watched with an aching heart as Edward's face came within inches of Jonathan's hand.

Then, abruptly, Edward pulled back. Jonathan began talking. Ophelia couldn't hear his words, but she could see the intensity between the men as Edward began to shake his head harder and harder. Jonathan reached out again, and this time Edward jumped to his feet and started running away from the bench. Now she could hear Jonathan calling after him. She ducked back behind the hedge as Edward approached the gate. It wasn't a good hiding place, and under normal circumstances he would have seen her, but as he raced past her, Ophelia saw the same blind fear in his eyes that was in them when he played the last act of *The Prince of Zanzona*.

Ophelia was not one given to hysteria. When you owned a repertory theater, you learned not to give in to such emotions in the face of calamity. So she didn't run after Edward. She waited until he was safely out of the way, looked back into the garden to see that Jonathan was still there, and then she went back to the office in the opera house. She continued working, and she did not weep all day long. Her tears didn't start until the moment after the evening's performance, when Edward asked her to marry him.

Ophelia cried because she knew how happy she would have been if he had proposed the day before, or that morning, or anytime before she'd watched him sitting on the bench in the garden with Jonathan. She didn't sob out loud, but she couldn't stop the tears. Edward, who always saw everything, didn't seem to notice. He looked down at his hands and said, "If you would marry me, you would make me so very happy."

What he is really saying is, "Please save me."

But then she began to doubt again, as she had when she'd stood at the garden gate. She was young, and there were many things she didn't understand. And what if she was right and he was asking her to save him? Why not? She loved him—at least she could finally admit that—so why not save him from a life of disgrace and depravity? Why not keep him from being a man whose name brought raised eyebrows and sniggers? He was still her dearest Edward, who was brilliant and kind, and he cared for her more than anyone ever had. But *did* he care? She had felt that he did, but she had no basis for comparison. She wanted to curse her own innocence.

There was no one she could talk to. Horatio probably could have an-

swered her questions, but she couldn't betray Edward in that way. Horatio
had watched her blossoming romance with his usual cynicism. "Your Edward is a bit too perfect for my taste," he'd said one night when he and
Ophelia were alone in the apartment. "Never trust a man who seems to
have no vices, my dear. He will always have at least one secret one. And it
will be vile." No, she could never discuss any of this with Horatio.

Edward was still looking down at his hands. Her silence was becoming
insulting. Wasn't there some kind of socially acceptable phrase she was
supposed to recite in this situation? Something about being aware of the
great compliment he had bestowed upon her? No, that was a line from a
play she had appeared in once. And she didn't know whether she wanted to
accept or reject him.

"I'm sorry," she finally said. "I need some time."

He nodded without looking up at her. "I understand," he said. Then he
turned and walked away.

CHAPTER 35

Massonville 1897

After a night of very little sleep, Ophelia got out of bed with heavy eyes. She still hadn't made a decision. She wanted to marry Edward, but only if he was going to be the old Edward who was her best friend. She couldn't forget that the man who had asked her to be his wife hadn't been able to look up from his hands to face her.

Eating breakfast was out of the question, but there was still some unfinished office work awaiting her. As she made her way down the inner staircase that connected the family quarters to the office, she heard the sound of someone gasping for breath. She raced down the last few steps to find her mother on the highest rung of the ladder they kept in the office. Juliet's face was white, and she was holding on to the top bookshelves for dear life.

"Help me!" she choked out. She swayed, her hands loosened their grip, and she began to fall. Ophelia caught her before she tumbled to the floor. That was when she realized how easy it was to hold her; Mama didn't weigh more than a child.

How could I not have noticed? I have been so busy with my own affairs that I didn't see her dwindling to skin and bones.

"What were you doing, Mama?" Ophelia scolded, guilt making her voice harsh.

"I just wanted . . . to hold Romie's dictionary," Mama gasped.

"Romie" was her brother Romeo, who had deserted her many years ago. His dictionary was a beaten-up old thing that Mama kept on the top shelf for sentimental reasons. It was of no use to anyone, and for Mama to climb up to the office ceiling on a rickety ladder to get it was stupid and foolhardy. Ophelia was about to say as much when Juliet leaned against the wall and closed her eyes.

"I don't think I can do it anymore," she said. "All I wanted was a theater for us, for my family. I wanted the name to last. For Papa and Maman." She opened her eyes. "But . . . I can't do it anymore."

Ophelia was accustomed to her mother being tired, but she'd never seen Juliet defeated. Ophelia tried to push away her terror. "I'm going to send for a doctor," she said.

But Juliet grasped her hand. "No doctor, " she said. Then she mumbled so softly that Ophelia could barely hear her. "It's my punishment."

There was no way to push away the fear now. "Mama, I don't know what you're talking about. We haven't had such a successful season in years. The theater earned even more than the hotel, and—"

"The season was a success because of Edward Rain," her mother interrupted in a whisper.

"And now we have the *Othello* tour. That will bring in more money—"

"We need Edward," the soft, hoarse voice persisted. "Everything depends on him. And we are going to lose him."

No. We can't.

But she knew they could.

Mama roused herself and walked painfully to her big desk. From a pile of papers, she picked up a telegram. "We received an offer this morning to extend our tour to Trenton, New Jersey. It seems that Jonathan Tyrell has some friends who manage a theater there."

Ophelia saw the danger immediately. New Jersey was near New York, and if any important New York managers were to see Edward in *Othello,* he would get offers far better than any they could give him.

And if he and Jonathan were to get an offer at the same theater . . . The thought came unwanted into her head.

Mama was right, the future of their company did depend on Edward. It was he who brought in the audiences. Without him what would happen? Would they be forced to sell the opera house? Would some new name appear on the canopy over the front door?

"We won't take the booking in New Jersey, Mama," she said.

Juliet shook her head. "Even if we don't, word will get out. Edward is a brilliant actor. Sooner or later we will lose him."

Ophelia thought about seeing a new name printed in gold on the canopy over the front door of the opera house. She thought about never again having the joy of watching Edward act on her stage. And she thought about Edward, her best friend, who had taken away her loneliness and made her happy.

"No, Mama," she said, "we will not lose Edward. Not ever."

Before noon she told Edward she would be his wife.

CHAPTER 36

Massonville 1897

The morning after their wedding night, Edward woke before Ophelia and filled their bedroom in the family quarters with bouquets of roses. He said he was the happiest man in the world and he loved her with all his heart. In the days that followed, he was the old Edward who listened when she talked and laughed at her jokes. Mama was happy too. The smudges of weariness under her eyes disappeared, and she didn't say anything more about not being able to run the theater.

Jonathan didn't seem to be spending much time at the opera house now. He appeared in the evenings to play Iago when *Othello* was on the bill, but he left right after the curtain came down. He no longer regaled the company with his theater stories at their late suppers. Ophelia could almost believe she had imagined the scene in the garden. She told herself it was a coincidence that she never saw another performance of *Othello*. She just seemed to be so busy on those nights.

Remembering how distracted Edward had been when he'd been learning the role of Othello, Ophelia argued that he should keep his old room on the fourth floor so he would have a place of his own when he needed to get away. At first he refused her offer, but in the end, he accepted it. Her husband was her superior in talent and education, but she was starting to suspect that she had the greater strength of will.

The last month of their season at the opera house seemed to fly by, and before Ophelia knew it, Edward and the company had gone on tour. The first portion of the trip was to last two months, and then the company was to return for two weeks because they didn't have any bookings. After that break, the actors would set out again for three and a half months more. They would play small towns in the West and the South. The flattering offer from the theater in New Jersey had been withdrawn.

After he was gone, Ophelia missed Edward, but she had expected that and she had prepared herself for it. She had not anticipated how much she would miss the theater company. She was used to the life of a stock company actress—performing in three plays a season, learning a new one during the day while the old one was being performed at night. Now, for the first time in her life, there were no performances in the opera house. There were no rehearsals, no lines to learn, no backstage guying, and no actors strutting around with their temperaments, their peccadilloes, their big egos, and their bigger hearts. She and her mother were landladies now, running their hotel that had become a boardinghouse.

Her unhappiness was especially bad in the evenings. By habit, her blood would begin to race as the time approached when the callboy should be making his rounds announcing the half hour. Then she would remember that the callboy was on the road, and there was no half hour to be announced. Even worse was the lobby, where there was no buzz of excited theatergoers. The only sound was that of the tired salesmen trudging upstairs to their rooms on the third and fourth floors. There were no late-night suppers now; she, Mama, and Horatio ate early in the restaurant. "Like farmers," Horatio huffed. He disappeared for days at a time and Mama didn't bother to try to find out where he went.

One night, she and Mama sat in the living room of their apartment. Mama was reading a novel and Ophelia was trying to embroider a handkerchief—she'd been reduced to a boring task like that. The threads tangled and the little rosebud she'd been diligently stitching for an hour be-

came a snarled knot. In her frustration she cried out, "Damnation," and
then braced herself for a lecture from Mama—the Venable women did not
curse—but to her surprise, the lecture was not forthcoming. Instead Mama
closed her book and led Ophelia downstairs to the stage.

The curtain was up. Mama made her way to the side of the proscenium
where there was a lightbulb on a stand—electricity having been installed
two years previously at great expense. This was the "working light." Mama
turned it on, and there was just enough illumination to see the house.

"Oh, I've missed it," Ophelia breathed.

Her mother nodded. "We're not like other people. We'll do anything for
this. No price is too high." She walked to the middle of the stage and, in a
low voice, as if she were saying it to herself, she began Puck's farewell to the
audience from *A Midsummer Night's Dream*.

" 'If we shadows have offended,' " she began so softly she could not have
been heard past the first row, " 'Think but this, and all is mended— / That
you have but slumb'red here / While these visions did appear.' " Her voice
was picking up strength now, and Ophelia watched the years slip away from
her.

" 'And this weak and idle theme,' " her mother continued, " 'No more
yielding but a dream, / Gentles, do not reprehend. / If you pardon, we will
mend.' "

Mama's voice was as full and clear as a young girl's. There was power in
it, but sweetness too, and sadness for an actor's work that was so hard, and
done with so much love, but it never lasted longer than the memory of the
audience that witnessed it.

" 'So, good night unto you all. / Give me your hands, if we be friends, /
And Robin shall restore amends.' "

Her mother held for the applause that Ophelia knew they were both
hearing in their minds.

"I wish I'd seen you act!" Ophelia whispered.

That brought Mama back to reality. She turned her back on the empty
house and said, "Get a broom, Ophelia. While we're down here, we might
as well sweep the stage."

They came down to the theater every night after that. Sometimes they
swept away the red clay dust that collected in the cracks of the stage floor;

sometimes they turned on the work light and dreamed of the productions Mama could stage now that Edward was their permanent leading man. And Ophelia would stand on the stage that would one day be hers, and think, *I'm still Ophelia Venable of the Venable Opera House. Mama and I still have the only life we can live. And it's all because of Edward. I will always love him.*

And then he came home.

CHAPTER 37

Massonville 1897

When Ophelia saw Edward and Jonathan descending from the train together, she told herself nothing was wrong. There was nothing in the quick
look Edward threw back over his shoulder at Jonathan, and when Edward
greeted her there was no tension in his embrace. It was only her imagination at work, she told herself.

But her imagination kept on working. When Edward came to their bed
that night, he did all the things that had made him so happy only two
months earlier, but somehow it was different. After it was over, he did not
put his arm around her. He did not talk to her. And she knew when she
woke in the morning that he had not slept.

It does not mean anything. It cannot mean anything.

The next night he avoided her, staying awake to read until after she finally pretended to be asleep.

*I will not say anything to him. As long as I don't say anything, there is noth-
ing wrong. There are only two weeks to keep silent. I can last for two weeks.*

But Edward—her honest Edward—couldn't keep silent. "I must talk to
you about something," he said on the third morning of his homecoming. His
beautiful face was tired, but he was resolute.

He has decided to tell me the truth. No, don't think that. There is no truth to tell.

"I have some work to do for Mama," she said quickly.

"Later, then."

"Yes."

Now it was she who avoided him. She managed it for the rest of the day, and that evening she saw to it that Mama had supper with them in the restaurant. Ophelia dragged out the meal as long as she could, but eventually the last forkful of cake had been consumed and it was time to retire to the family apartment. To the bedroom she shared with Edward.

But then there was an unexpected reprieve. Mama rose from the table and said, "Edward, will you excuse us? I need Ophelia for a moment."

He wasn't happy about it.

He wants to tell me. But there is nothing to tell.

He didn't argue, and went upstairs alone. After he was safely out of the way, Mama led the way through the restaurant, out into the lobby, and to the stage.

Once again, Ophelia and Juliet stood on the stage with only the work light turned on. "We had another offer to book *Othello* into that theater today," Mama said. Then she added carefully, "The one in New Jersey that is managed by Jonathan Tyrell's friend. "

You didn't have to tell me; I knew which theater you meant.

In the semidarkness Mama grasped Ophelia's arm so hard that she thought she would cry out. "There cannot be any scandal connected with this opera house," Mama whispered. "Massonville is a small town. People here will not accept what might be overlooked in New York."

You needn't have bothered to tell me that either.

"Do not allow us to be disgraced," Mama said, and she began to walk away.

"Mama," Ophelia called out. Juliet turned. "I'm not . . . I don't know what to do," Ophelia stammered.

Her mother stood still for what seemed like a long time. Finally she spoke. "Edward is an honorable man," she said slowly and deliberately.

The shadows cast by the work light played on Juliet's face. Even in this dire situation, Ophelia couldn't help thinking, *What a Lady Macbeth she would have been!*

"If you were carrying Edward's child," Mama went on in the same mea-sured tone, "I am sure he would never think of leaving you."

"But I'm not carrying his—"

"Not yet," Mama broke in. "But things happen. And you are his wife." She turned off the work light. "My father always used to say, if we take care of the present, God will take care of the future," she said. "There is always something we can do, Ophelia. We are never helpless." She walked out, leaving Ophelia alone on the stage in the dark.

In the plays in which Ophelia had appeared, when the heroine encountered difficulties in her marriage, she tried to arouse her husband's passion. But Edward's passion was not hers to command.

Not anymore. If it ever was.

Yet she was his wife.

Edward was waiting for her in their bedroom. She wished she had time to brush her hair and tie a ribbon in it. She wished she had time to put on her prettiest nightgown. But he was waiting right now.

"Ophelia, I—" he started to say, but she rushed to him and took his hands in hers.

God will take care of the future if I take care of the present.

"Have I told you how much I missed you while you were gone?" she asked. "I'm afraid you married a bride who needs you very much." As she heard herself say the words, she knew they were true. Her voice began to waver. "You are the only person who has ever really seen me, Edward. You helped me clean the hotel. You said I have talent." With each word she found it harder not to cry. "You are the only one who cared what happened to me."

He didn't pull his hands away, but she knew he wanted to. As they faced each other, the misery was almost like a presence in the room. She searched frantically for something to say to make it go away, but in the end all she could think of was, "I think I loved you from that morning when I first saw you."

If it had been a line in a play, she would have said it was banal—worthy of bad melodrama. But it was honest, and that moved Edward. He leaned down and kissed her hands, which had grown cold in his. And she knew that for one more night, she had escaped; that the words he had wanted to say to her would not be said.

When she got into bed, so did he. He held her tenderly throughout the night, like one would hold something small and fragile. But there was no kissing. Edward did not do the things he had done before.

The next morning, Edward was gone before she was awake. For a second, Ophelia panicked. Then she remembered that at least she had managed to avoid Edward's fatal "talk" one more time. For the moment she would have to be content with that. She dressed in her scullery attire and headed for the fourth floor to do her usual morning cleaning.

Once, when he was still her best friend, Edward had told her about Dr. Sigmund Freud, who believed that there were no accidents in human behavior. When people tried to hide certain aspects of themselves, said the good doctor, there was an uncontrollable portion of the mind called the subconscious that would force a "mistake" that would reveal the truth. This mistake could happen even if the conscious portion of the mind wished to suppress that truth. The theory was as good an explanation as any for the reason why Edward, who knew her morning schedule so well, would choose his room on the fourth floor for a rendezvous with Jonathan.

When she recognized the voices through the thin door, Ophelia wanted to run. But then she heard her husband say, "You know I can't stay here, John. I have to tell her." There was not a doubt in Ophelia's mind who "she" was. Her impulse to run faded immediately. She leaned against the door to listen.

"Your leaving is not in dispute," said Jonathan. "But I fail to see why she must be told anything."

"I have to be honest with her; she deserves that much from me." Edward's voice was low and troubled. She could picture the way his brow was furrowed. "I want her to understand."

"You are proposing to tell your wife that you wish to end your marriage to her for reasons that she will find repellent and enraging. I assure you that she will never understand."

There was a sound. Was it bed springs?

I don't want to think of that.

Now it sounded as if Edward were moving about the room. "It was my fault. I should not have married her."

Jonathan's voice came back clearly. "You're not the first man to marry because he hoped it would cure him. Or help him escape from who he is. We are told we are degenerate, we are made to—but you don't need to hear a speech." There was a silence. Neither of them was moving now. "Have you thought of the danger?" Jonathan asked. "If you tell her, have you thought of what she could do to you?"

"She wouldn't," Edward said. As if she were in the room with them, Ophelia could see Jonathan's cynical smile. "I do care for her," said her husband.

"Eddie, you wanted to believe you were something you were not, and you made a mistake. Don't punish yourself for it. And don't punish her."

"I want to free her."

"For what? So she can suffer the disgrace of being a divorced woman?" She hadn't thought of that. *Oh dear God.*

"She's young, she can still find—" Edward started to say, but Jonathan broke in.

"A good man? Who will love her in spite of her past? Really?"

Edward, no! You can't do that to me.

"It doesn't have to be so histrionic, Eddie." Jonathan's voice was gentle. "After our booking in Trenton, you will have work in New York, I promise you. It will be an easy thing to tell her that you must stay there for a few months, and the months will extend. Then, when she has had time to grow accustomed to your absence, you can discuss divorce proceedings, without the need for confession. If you still wish for that."

I hate him.

"Or perhaps by then you will see that to have a wife in the background would not be the worst thing for you. In your circumstances."

"My circumstances?" Edward asked.

"Not all of your . . . friendships will be as discreet as ours. Don't look at me that way. You won't stop with me. Be grateful that I know it."

"And while I am building my career and having my affairs," Edward said so quietly that Ophelia could barely hear him, "Ophelia will become—what exactly? The duped wife? Like the pathetic creature who is married to Oscar Wilde?"

"I don't think she will remain duped for long. She's no fool. But she will accept what she must. She would not be the first."

Oh, how I hate him.

"Eddie, I agree it's a bad business," Jonathan continued. "But don't make it worse. For everyone."

"So I'm to turn her into a liar?"

"Call her your partner, if that's easier to say. Or your conspirator. And remember, she'll do it because it will be in her own best interests."

"I will not use her."

"What do you think she and her mother wish to do to you? Their theater was on its last legs when you walked through their doors to revive it. The old girl must have thought you were manna from heaven! And before you start bleating that Ophelia is not her mother, let me tell you, my love, that your little wife is cut from the same cloth. They will both bury you in the provinces for the rest of your days to save their precious opera house."

I would like to kill him.

"And that would be a tragedy, Eddie. You have such a gift. You don't even realize—"

"Oh yes, I do realize," Edward broke in. "This tour has shown me what I could be. That's why I have to go to New York with you." Through the door Ophelia heard Jonathan laugh. "What's so amusing?" her husband asked.

"Does it occur to you that, for my sake, it might be more . . . tactful to pretend that I am the main attraction in New York?" There was a pause. Ophelia could picture Edward's face reddening. Then suddenly he laughed. The dimple would be showing now.

"Oh, John, I'm such a selfish dog! Run while you have a chance."

"And miss watching you cut your swath through New York City? No, thank you. And you are not selfish, my child, you are greedy."

"Yes! I know!" There was a joy in Edward's voice that Ophelia had never heard before.

He feels free to be himself with Jonathan in ways that he could never be with me. And that was when Ophelia knew that Edward, who did not want to be a liar, would not repeat their wedding night—or even the night of his homecoming—again. And she knew that she would never feel like the young girl he had kissed in front of the elevator.

"I want it all," her husband was saying. "I want fame and fortune and you, John. I want to be happy."

The last word was smothered, something was happening between the two men. But now the thought of it didn't hurt. At least, it didn't hurt as much as it had.

When Edward continued, his voice was more subdued. "I want a clear conscience. Don't you see? I have to be honest with her. So she can make a new beginning."

No! You want to desert me and feel good about it. Then you will have a new beginning. I'll be alone with a sick mother, a brother who is worthless, and an opera house we can't keep. For a moment she thought she really could destroy him as Jonathan had said. But then she remembered Edward making up games when he helped her mop the floors. She remembered watching him on the stage when he acted. And then she remembered the canopy in front of the opera house with the Venable name on it.

Do not allow us to be disgraced, Mama had said.

Behind the closed door, Edward was saying, "I can trust Ophelia, I know I can."

If you were carrying Edward's child, I am sure he would never think of leaving you, Mama had said.

"Then, if you are determined to tell Ophelia, do it right away and be done with it," said Jonathan.

"I meant to," Edward said. "But now I think it would be wrong to say it and then just leave her. I'll wait until the tour is finished. Then I'll come back and tell her and stay with her as long as she needs me. I owe her that much."

Ophelia could see his face, the eagerness and sweetness in it, as he tried to find a way to make this horror right for her. That was when she began to cry. She turned from the bedroom door and ran down the hallway so the two men wouldn't hear her. She cried for herself and for Edward. Because she knew now what she had to do to both of them.

CHAPTER 38

Massonville 1897

Ophelia had no time to waste. The night after Edward and the company left Massonville for the second portion of the tour, she dressed herself with great care. She rouged her lips and cheeks, brushed her hair until it shone, piled it on her head in a pompadour—the style framed her face to perfection—and put on her most fetching dress. The billowing sleeves of her bodice accentuated her waist, which had been laced in until a man could span it with two hands, and a foam of lace at the bottom of her petti-coat peeked out rakishly from under her skirt. Satisfied that she had never looked better, she went downstairs to the restaurant to have supper with her mother.

When she reached the doorway, she faltered.

There is still time to pull back, said a voice inside her head. *You can go back upstairs and have your supper on a tray.*

But she couldn't pull back. She and Edward had been together as man and wife for only the one night when he first came home, and that was not enough. She walked into the restaurant, and joined her mother. As they sat at their table, she watched the hotel guests coming in for their evening meal, and thought about the possibilities.

She settled on a man who was as fair as Edward, although he was not nearly so handsome. He was a shoe salesman, she learned when she managed to share the elevator with him the next morning, and of course, he was lonely. The seduction was almost too easy. And he had a talent, her salesman did; he could play the mandolin. He accompanied himself on it when he sang to her, ever so quietly, in his room at night. She was grateful for that.

From the first, Ophelia didn't want her brother to know what she was doing. She wasn't sure why she felt that way, but keeping it from him wasn't difficult. She simply managed to be in her own bed each morning before Horatio returned home from his carousing. Mama was another matter.

If you were carrying Edward's child, I am sure he would never think of leaving you. Her mother had said those words. And then she had added, *There is always something we can do. We are never helpless.*

But Ophelia wondered if even the formidable Juliet Venable could imagine the lengths to which her daughter was going. She prepared herself to answer questions. But Mama never asked any. That was when Ophelia realized that her mother might not want to know what was going on, but she would not have to be told that the fair-haired salesman with a gift for singing must never again return to the opera house hotel.

The salesman moved on after five weeks. Ophelia could have wished for more time, but she told herself perhaps it was just as well. If she discovered that she had not been lucky in her gamble, she would still have time to try again with someone else.

Whether it was luck, or fate, or the power of prayer, she did not have to try again. She counted the weeks and told herself that the child she had conceived could have been Edward's. She almost believed it.

Jonathan did not return to Georgia with the rest of the company. After the close of the engagement in Trenton—which had been a triumph—he telegraphed to say that he would no longer be acting at the opera house. Presumably he had gone on to New York to prepare for Edward's arrival.

As for Edward, the man who got off the train and rode home with her in the opera house carriage was a different person from the one who had left her three and a half months earlier. He was too kind to be happy about what was coming, but there was a lightheartedness about him, as if a burden were about to be lifted from his shoulders. She watched him, and once again she wanted to cry. But this time she didn't.

However, when she and Edward were alone, she surprised herself by hesitating. She was going to trap him, but she would be trapping herself as well. Her shoe salesman might not have been the brilliant Edward Rain, but he had taught her things in the bedroom that she knew she would miss for the rest of her life. Because Ophelia Venable Rain of the Venable Opera House would have to be above reproach, so she would never again risk taking a lover. Somewhere in her mind she listened to a door slam shut for both Edward and herself. Then she informed her husband of her delicate condition.

At first, he wanted to deny it. Ophelia could see that every inch of his being wanted to shout that she was wrong, that this could not have happened to him. She watched him struggle to restrain himself, and was surprised at how much it hurt, even though she had known he would react that way. Her pain must have shown, because then he tried to smile. That was even harder to bear. However, her mother had not misjudged him. Edward did not leave.

Edward resumed his position as the leading man of the opera house, and every Sunday when he was in Massonville, he appeared in the church pew with his wife and mother-in-law. But he was changed. The old sweetness was gone, and in many ways he became the stereotype of the self-absorbed actor, his temper often short, his black moods feared by all around him. But none of it affected his work. Onstage he never stinted.

It was while he was on the road that Edward had his liaisons. When he returned home, the stage manager, whom Ophelia trusted for his discretion and loyalty, would mention a name, and the latest favorite would be dismissed. Edward never protested—after all, his "friendships" had to end somehow—and the entire situation was never discussed. Ophelia and Edward became what Edward had told Jonathan he did not want to become: liars. They lied to the rest of the world and to each other. But the Venable name still appeared in gold on the canopy over the entrance to the opera house.

Juliet did not live to see the birth of her grandchild. The baby was born three days after Juliet was discovered dead on the floor of her office. A ladder was found nearby, and the doctor speculated that she had been trying to climb up it when her weak heart had given out. She had been trying to reach her old Bible and her brother's dictionary—she had told Ophelia that she wanted the baby to have them. After Juliet's death, Ophelia wanted to throw away the old books, but she found she could not do it. She left them on the high shelf under the ceiling.

With Juliet gone, the entire weight of the restaurant, the hotel, and the opera house fell on Ophelia. Her brother's gaming grew worse without Mama to keep him in check, but unlike Juliet, Ophelia refused to pay his debts. Horatio left town in a rage, and whatever minimal assistance he might have been to her was lost. To add to her other woes, she was finding it extremely difficult to regain her figure after the baby's birth, which she must do if she were going to appear on the stage again. She never asked her husband to help her with her responsibilities. Once he would have done it without being asked, but now, it never occurred to him.

And what of the baby? She was a pretty little thing, born with a surprisingly full head of curly dark hair. When the time came to baptize her, in a moment of foolish hope, Ophelia proposed the name of Viola.

Edward's reaction was swift and cold. "No Shakespeare," he said. "Not for that one." That was when Ophelia realized that he had never touched the child. It was almost as if he suspected.

But how could he? And besides, she might be his.

Nevertheless, Ophelia was sufficiently frightened that she named her daughter Lilianne after her mother's mother, and she had the baby christened while Edward was performing a matinée.

Ophelia hired a nursemaid; she did not have the time or the energy to care for the baby herself. And, to be honest, there were many hours of her overly busy days when she nearly forgot her daughter's existence. But sometimes at night, she went into the nursery just to watch the little creature sleep. Ophelia would stroke the small round cheek that was as soft as peach skin. And there were nights when Lilianne, deep in sleep, would clutch Ophelia's finger in her tiny hand.

Edward tried not to be unkind to the child—there was just enough of his old sweetness left in him for that—but the little girl irritated him.

If he could just see how endearing she can be, Ophelia thought. *If he could just be a little happy about our life. We have a theater that is thriving; he is loved and acclaimed as an actor. We have so much to be grateful for. Why can't he forget the rest?*

But he couldn't forget how much Lilianne had cost him. It didn't help that the child had nothing of his look, and nothing of his quiet temperament.

But she could be his. She could.

When Lilianne was an infant, it was a simple matter to keep her out of Edward's way, but as she grew, she seemed to realize that the tall, scowling man over whom everyone made such a fuss was avoiding her. She was determined to claim his attention.

She was also fascinated by the theater, and would escape her caretakers to run backstage and watch Edward in rehearsals. His anger on such occasions often astonished the company. Ophelia would have Lilianne taken back to the family quarters, where the child could be heard weeping loudly. The next day she would try all over again to woo Edward. The pity of it was, she was a charming little girl: bright, high-spirited, and affectionate, and she was surrounded by adults who doted on her. But she craved the love of the one person who could not give it to her. There were days when Ophelia loathed Edward.

But then in the evening, Ophelia would stand at the back of the theater and watch him perform. She would be swept away by the brilliance of his Richard the Third, or his Cyrano. She would watch him switch effortlessly from the classics to modern works by Strindberg and Shaw, and she would fill with pride. And fear.

If he ever leaves the opera house . . .

So she indulged his moods, overlooked his temper, and never asked anything of him except that he act. She made sure he played every part he took a fancy to. When he grew weary of disguising the hokum in *The Prince of Zanzona,* she dropped the play, even though it was the most profitable piece in their repertoire. By that time, Ophelia had stopped acting in the serious works that were Edward's forte. Unable to reduce her weight, she restricted herself to playing Mrs. Wiggs in *Mrs. Wiggs of the Cabbage Patch,* Mrs. Malaprop, and other roles of the comedic line. It was for the best, she told herself; if she wasn't performing with Edward, she could focus all of her attention on staging productions in which he could shine.

And thanks to the money Edward earned at home and on tour, the opera house did not have to book vaudeville acts, religious lecturers, or circuses, as other big theaters around the country were forced to. In fact, Ophelia was even able to save for the lean times.

But in spite of all her efforts, she was never sure of Edward's intentions. Sometimes, she would think that she couldn't bear the uncertainty for another minute. *Let him go,* she would tell herself. *Let him do it.* But then she would remember his Cyrano. And she would overlook the dark mood, or the flare of temper, or the incidents of unkindness that seemed to be increasing.

But there came a time when she couldn't overlook his unhappiness anymore.

CHAPTER 39

Massonville 1907

The weeks after Edward came back from a tour were always difficult. He had heard the applause of new audiences in new towns, and for a while Massonville would seem unbearably small to him. And there was always the liaison that had to be ended.

His homecoming after his tenth year in Georgia was particularly bad. Edward's "friend" on the tour had been an actor who was many years his junior, and full of fire and ambition. Ophelia watched Edward mourn, and sensed that the youngster had been singing Jonathan Tyrell's old siren song of fame and fortune in New York. She also realized that this mood was serious. Although Edward was still handsome and at the peak of his theatrical power, he was at an age when old dreams come back to torment. And he was more infatuated than usual with the young actor.

However, Ophelia had weapons of her own. She planned a lavish reception to celebrate his tenth anniversary as the star of the opera house. Dignitaries from all over the state of Georgia attended, champagne toasts were drunk, and accolades were heaped upon him. The event was a reminder of all he had to lose. Then, while that reality was still sinking in, Ophelia engaged an actor for the upcoming season who had worked with the company before. In the years since he'd left them, Nicolas Hunter had not fared well. As Ophelia had hoped, he told chilling tales of the dearth of roles for a man of his—and Edward's—age in New York.

There had been a time when none of this would have swayed Edward, but ten years of pampering by Ophelia had made him soft—and afraid. Still, the siren song beckoned (reinforced, of course, by letters from New York, which Ophelia found in Edward's desk), and Edward was painfully torn.

It was at this juncture that Lilianne chose to surprise her parents with her theatrical debut. Later, Ophelia would learn from members of the company that the child had been inspired by the reception for her father, and had meant to please him. Everyone in the theater had known of the impending treat, but they had been sworn to secrecy. Over the years, Ophelia often asked herself if she would have stopped her daughter if she had known what the little girl was planning.

With true Venable panache, Lilianne had decided her show was not going to be a childish affair. She would perform in the greenroom at night after supper. Two stage carpenters were cajoled into setting up a small stage at the back end of the room, complete with a curtain. A spotlight was rigged up, and the wardrobe mistress fashioned a small robe out of a sheet for Lilianne. Chairs were carried into the greenroom so the audience—well-wishers from the acting company and stage crew—could watch in comfort. Two seats of honor had been reserved in the front row for her parents. Lilianne had chosen the program herself—it was to be an evening of songs and speeches by Shakespeare—and she had rehearsed in secrecy, so no one knew what to expect. On the great night, Nicolas Hunter lured Ophelia and Edward into the greenroom on a pretext that Ophelia could never remember later.

At the sight of Edward and Ophelia, the assembly broke into applause, and Nicolas indicated their seats with a flourish. Then he intoned in his hammiest voice, "For your delectation and delight, I give you a new star in the firmament! Ladies and Gentlemen, I present Miss Lilianne Rain!" Ophelia turned quickly to Edward, but his face was unreadable. Ophelia allowed herself to hope.

Maybe he will change toward her now. Maybe he will see her following in his footsteps and he will change.

Someone turned off the lights in the room, the spotlight was turned on, and Lilianne came out from behind her makeshift curtain.

The child was adorable. Her speeches had been chosen with a fine disregard for the gender or age of the character speaking, and there seemed to be no thematic connection between them, but her taste was excellent. Jaques, in his soliloquy from *As You Like It,* informed the audience that all the world was a stage, after which Rosalind from the same play bid them adieu in her epilogue. Viola promised to build a willow cabin at Olivia's gate in her speech from *Twelfth Night,* Titania's fairy Peaseblossom in *A Midsummer Night's Dream* was followed by the Boy in *Henry the V,* and in an oddly moving moment that made Ophelia gulp back tears, a ten-year-old Prospero from *The Tempest* told the house that his revels now were ended.

Mama would love this so. She would love my Lilianne.

After the spoken words came the songs. And oh, Ophelia's little girl was grand! Her voice was pure silver, and her ear was true. Ophelia had a brief memory of a gentle man singing in a darkened hotel room to a desperate seventeen-year-old girl, but she pushed it aside quickly. In front of her, Lilianne sang of lovers and lasses, sprites that flew on bat's backs, and the rain that raineth every day, with the joy of one who was born to be on a stage. She held her audience in the palm of her hand, until the final note was sung, and then she ducked behind her curtain for the last time. Everyone rose to their feet to applaud her. And it was not just kindness, Ophelia noted. This was a heartfelt tribute from those who recognized a peer.

Lilianne came out to make her bow, as Venables had done before her for three generations, and Ophelia understood for the first time in her life what people meant when they said they were bursting with pride. That might have been why, for once, she did not pay attention to Edward. She did not see that he was still sitting, staring at the stage in a daze. Or perhaps she didn't notice him because for once she did not want to think about him. She didn't want to know how it was affecting him to see the child, who had taken so much from him, display a talent that could be as worthy as his own. And Lilianne's talent was completely different from his. While Edward courted his public with his mind and his glasslike openness, Lilianne was all Venable showmanship and charm. In retrospect, Ophelia would wonder if everything would have turned out differently if Edward could have recognized something of himself in the child when she was on the stage that night. But he couldn't. Of course not.

Lilianne had seen the one person in her adoring audience who was not on his feet. She darted off her little stage and, in full view of everyone, ran to Edward. Ophelia saw Edward pull back, and she instinctively tried to restrain the child, but Lilianne shook her off.

"Did you like me?" she demanded of the man who, from the day she was born, had never shown her affection.

Please let him be kind, Ophelia prayed.

Edward managed a smile, and for a moment Ophelia thought the bad moment was behind them. But Lilianne's evil genius prompted her to speak again. "I'm good, aren't I?" she said. And in her voice there was an adult's challenge as well as a child's eagerness. "I'm as good as you."

Edward rose out of his chair and looked down at her. "There is one difference between acting and showing off," he said. "It is called talent. You do not have it. Please do not embarrass me in this way again." And he left.

People rallied around the child, and offered her all the usual palliatives.

"Your father is just tired, sweetheart," someone said.

"He's worried about the opening of the new season," another added.

"He didn't mean it," they all agreed.

But he had meant it, and Lilianne knew it. And there was nothing anyone could do to fix it.

After that debacle, Edward didn't return to the family quarters. Ophelia knew where he had gone. She put the now stony-eyed Lilianne to bed, and went out to the garden. Edward was sitting on a bench, facing away from her.

I am going to tell him what I think, Ophelia thought. *After all these years I am going to tell him.* She walked up behind him. He still had not turned. *I will never forgive you for what you did tonight!* She rehearsed the words in her mind, then drew in a breath to say them out loud. But she stopped. Because she could not blame him alone. What had happened was as much her responsibility as his. She started back toward the garden gate.

"Ophelia," Edward called out. When she turned to look at him, he was still facing away from her. "For the next tour, I think you should revive *The Prince of Zanzona.*"

"You hate that role."

"The tank towns I play have always loved it. It is cheap for you to produce and you do not have to pay a royalty for it. You will make a great deal of money with it."

And so, for the next twenty-one years, Edward Rain made a fortune for the Venable Opera House playing the old warhorse he despised.

When Lilianne ran away from home at the age of sixteen, Ophelia was not surprised. And she was not surprised when her daughter never returned to Massonville.

CHAPTER 40

Massonville 1935

The statue of Edward Rain stood revealed in all its glory. The audience applauded loudly, and probably with relief. Now they could move indoors to the relative cool of the restaurant, where they would be served lemonade, sweet tea, and the peach pecan pound cake for which the Venable Opera House was famous. Ophelia looked at her husband hunched over in the heat. Greeting the public would be too much for him today. She moved to him and said gently, "Wait until everyone has left the garden, then go back to the apartment. I'll make your excuses." He didn't say anything but she thought she saw him nod.

It had been seven years since Edward had walked out on the stage in a theater in San Antonio and forgotten his words, or, in theater slang, had "dried." The missing line was thrown to him by the prompter, and he made his way through the next speech, but he dried again. This time, no amount of prompting could help him; his mind had gone blank. He began to shake and sweat. The other actors on the stage tried to cover for him, but it was no use; the stage manager rang down the curtain. The next night it was worse; the sweating and shaking began in the wings before the play began, and when Edward made his entrance, he could not remember the scene well enough to ad lib his way through it. For the matinée the following day, they tried writing out his speeches and hiding the pages at strategic points on the set so he could read them. Edward collapsed as the curtain was rising. The tour was canceled, and they brought him home. The doctor diagnosed exhaustion, but Ophelia knew the real cause was playing a part he hated for so many years.

Edward was told to rest. He sat in the garden day after day, staring at the hedges and not speaking. It was over a year before he could concentrate enough to read a book. He never went back onstage.

However, the fortune he had made saved them. When the Crash came in 1929 and the banks started defaulting, not a penny of their money was lost, because Ophelia—who had not trusted any financial institutions after the panic of 1893—had locked Edward's earnings in her office safe. The Venable Opera House managed to keep its doors open throughout the Great Depression, when even theaters in New York were closing. Ophelia still had money left after the worst was over, and people started going back to the theater again.

And she had her niece. Five years after Lilianne left home, Horatio returned. He came back home because he was ill—it was the family weakness, heart disease—and he knew he did not have much time left. He brought with him his young daughter, Olivia. Dear, loyal Olivia, who, as she grew up, was totally devoted to her aunt Ophelia, the opera house, and the Venable legacy. And although Olivia did not have a drop of acting talent, Ophelia knew Olivia would keep Juliet's dream of a dynasty alive for another generation.

Now, as the sunshine beat down on the garden, Ophelia was feeling light-headed. She started to sway, and an arm caught her around her ample waist. "Are you all right, Aunt Ophelia?" Olivia murmured in her ear.

Ophelia nodded. "It's just the heat," she murmured back. "Get everyone inside, and I'll be along directly."

It was not just the heat. Ophelia managed to recover that day, and entertained her guests with Olivia at her side. But a month later she was dead of a stroke. Edward died two months after that. At his graveside, the minister said it was clear that Edward Rain could not bear to go on in this world without his beloved wife, and Olivia wept at the lovely sentiment. Her cousin, Lilianne, did not attend either funeral.

Part Four

CHAPTER 41

Massonville 2006

Susie watched her mom and Katie stare up at the statue of Edward Rain. Neither of them had said anything for a really long time, and Susie was about to point out that there was another statue in the garden that they hadn't seen yet, when Katie turned around.

"I can't let it go," she said in a kind of whispery voice.

Mom looked like someone had just told her all of her clients had fired her. "What?"

"Look at him." Katie pointed up at the statue. "He worked all those years to keep this theater alive. And now Mike Killian is going to tear it down. . . ."

"And you and I are going to get a nice piece of change."

"So many people cared about this place, Randa—"

"Those people have nothing to do with us!" Susie hoped Katie would realize that her mom's voice was getting all loud and high because she was afraid. "This theater has nothing to do with us!"

"Somebody thought it did. We can't let it all end."

"Watch me."

"I'll buy you out. I'll have enough money after I sell my co-op."

"Are you out of your mind? You can't sell your co-op. Where will you live?" Mom demanded.

"Here. I'm going to move to Georgia."

"You are out of your mind!"

"I'll live upstairs in the family quarters."

"You can't leave New York!" Mom was totally freaking now. "You can't live in that old dump! The wiring is shot! There was a dead squirrel in one of the chairs!"

"That's why God made exterminators and electricians."

"Your life is in New York. Your job, your agent, your boyfriend—"

"I hate my job. My agent wants me to retire and write a masterpiece. My boyfriend is a son of a bitch."

Katie was awesome, Susie decided. Her mother started walking really fast out of the garden. Katie tried to follow her.

"Randa, wait!" she shouted. "Will you slow down? I can't keep up with you." Susie could have told her not to try; Mom clocked major hours on her treadmill. "Where are you going?" Katie called out as Mom opened the gate and ran through it.

"She'll wait for us in front of the theater," Susie told Katie. "She won't let me walk back to the hotel without her. She's super-responsible."

"What the hell was that about?" Katie said.

"Mom doesn't want to like the opera house."

Katie turned around and looked back at the statue of Edward Rain. "It's not just the opera house. . . . It really is the stories." She was doing that thing adults did when they pretended to talk to a kid because they didn't want to look like they were talking to themselves. Susie nodded anyway, to keep her going. "Who left it to us?" Katie went on. "And why? Doesn't your mother want to know? I mean, forget Faulkner, didn't she ever read Nancy Drew?"

"You scared Mom."

"I scared *her*?"

"She thinks you'll get fired from your job because you'll lose your edge if you're not in New York, and no one will hire you ever again."

"Oh." Katie said, as if that was something she hadn't thought about.

"And you'll spend all your money on the opera house but it won't be enough to fix it because it's a black hole for cash and you'll wish you'd never come here but it will be too late, so you'll wind up all destroyed and broke like her father."

"I see." All of a sudden, Katie had stopped looking so strong.

"But that's just what my mom thinks," Susie said hastily.

"Right," Katie said. Her voice was kind of shaky.

"Mom is totally paranoid about not having money."

"Yeah." Katie started walking slowly toward the gate.

"I think what you're doing is awesome."

"Don't take this the wrong way, but I wish you were about twenty years older and that you'd balanced a checkbook a couple of times in your life."

"I know someone who's going to like it a lot that you're staying here," Susie said, trying to get them back on a positive note. "R.B.'s going to be really glad."

Katie wasn't listening. She was looking up at the back wall of the opera house. "You don't happen to know what they do when they point a building, do you? Because I think they did it once on my apartment building in New York and it cost over a million bucks."

"I bet R.B. could tell you who left us the opera house," Susie said desperately.

Katie started walking again. "He told us the grantor of the trust wanted to be anonymous."

"But don't you think he could find out?"

"He said that would go against the intention of the will. There's probably a rule about that in the lawyer handbook. They get disbarred, or shot, or something."

"You could ask him anyway. He really likes you." Susie hadn't thought about that until she'd said it, but R.B. and Katie would be cute together. Plus, with Katie getting kind of scared, it wouldn't be a bad idea for her to have another reason to stay in Massonville. "I think R.B.'s hot," Susie added, to push things along.

"You're talking about a man who wears a bow tie," Katie said. But she was smiling a little.

Her smile was probably why the next thing just came out of Susie's mouth without her wanting it to. "Well, you wear glasses. And that dress—" Susie stopped herself.

Her mother would have been totally destroyed because someone had said she wasn't perfect, but Katie just kind of sighed. "Bad, isn't it?"

"It's fine," Susie tried, but Katie was looking at her like she didn't believe it. "The color is kind of gross."

Katie sighed again. "I figured it would hide my hips."

Susie had to think about that for a couple of seconds. "The thing about R.B. is, I don't think he hides stuff. I think he wears those bow ties because he likes them. And that's cool." There were times when "cool" was the only word that worked.

Katie put her arm around Susie's shoulders. "You are a smart person," she said.

Her mom needed to get to know Katie better, Susie decided. Katie would be good for her. But when they caught up with her mother a few minutes later, she refused to say a word to Katie for the whole walk back to the hotel. Mom could get wired so easily.

Back at the hotel, Susie went online. She'd been trying to track down information about Mom's father, Richard Jennings. There were tons of genealogy websites, and she signed up for several of them, but she hadn't turned up anything. She'd finally convinced her mother to let her post some questions and a bio on a find-your-family website. But Mom wanted to supervise that because of all the bad stuff going on with the Internet. Susie sighed. That meant she was going to have to wait until Mom got over being freaked about Katie before they could check the responses.

•

CHAPTER 42

Massonville 2006

Katie had changed the gross-colored dress for a blue one with tiny straps that she almost hadn't bought because it had a waistline. She didn't want to see her hips in the mirror, but she thought her top probably looked okay. She'd already tried jamming her lenses into her eyes, and had come to the conclusion that life was too short. That meant that putting on makeup was out, since the last time she'd tried doing it without glasses on, she'd wound up with raccoon eyes. Instead, she settled for a quick swipe at her mouth with some gloss, and told herself to stop wishing she were a different person. Remembering she was having dinner with R.B. made her relax. There was something to be said for going out with a man you knew wasn't going to be better dressed than you were. Besides, Randa's spookily intuitive daughter had said that he liked her.

Being a quart low on girl instincts when it came to herself, Katie had decided to trust the kid. When she'd gotten back to the hotel, she'd called R.B. and asked if she could take him to dinner. He'd been pleased, although he'd said he'd be doing the taking out.

"Generations of Moultire men will whirl in their graves if I don't," he'd explained. She'd had a quick flashback to Jock pushing the check in her direction after every restaurant meal, and she decided not to knock the Moultire family's traditions.

Her purpose for the dinner was to try to convince R.B. to dig up whatever he could about their mysterious benefactor. And okay, she wanted to see his face when she told him she was going to be saving his beloved opera house. And then there was the great abs thing.

They met in the hotel lobby. He was wearing the seersucker jacket, but he'd ditched the tie. She'd planned to wait to tell him her big news over dinner, but when he came toward her, he looked so happy to see her that her brain went on defrost.

"I'm-going-to-keep-the-opera-house-I'll-sell-my-apartment-buy-Randaout-and-live-here," she heard herself announce like a soap opera ditz.

In a good soap scene, R.B. would have responded with mindless admiration, and a dawning realization that she might be The One. In a really bad script, he'd do Cliché Number Sixteen, also known as the Inappropriate Clinch in a Public Place. At the very least, the man should have been perky. And for a second he did flash a smile full of pure joy. Then it faded. "Oh, " he said.

It hadn't occurred to her that he would hurt her feelings. "Excuse me, Mr. Ya'll Come Down South and Get to Know Us," she said furiously. "Aren't you the boy who told me there are a jillion stories down here just waiting for me to tell them? Didn't you say I need this place?"

"Yes."

"Did you hear me say I'm saving your damn opera house?"

"Yes."

"So this is the part where you start telling me how brave and fabulous I am."

"Katie, have you really thought about this?"

Gallons of ice water were dumped over her head. "No," she said. "Because I can't think. I have to just do it. Please tell me that's okay."

"When I said all that . . . about the stories . . . I thought you'd stay for a couple of weeks . . . get to know us . . . see how it worked. . . . This is so fast . . . and . . ." He trailed off. "I want to know this will be good for you."

"Sorry. No guarantees." Then she did Daytime Drama Cliché Number One and burst into tears.

He held her. It didn't seem to bother him that there were a bunch of conventioneers wearing name tags staring at them.

"I'm scared shitless, but I want to do it," she told him after she'd gotten herself together.

"Okay," he said.

"I'm *going* to do it."

"I'll help you any way I can." She could have pointed out that she was a big girl and that she had to stand on her own feet, but it was just so nice having a man who wasn't her agent Teddy saying the word "help."

He took her to dinner at a pretty restaurant in the historic district and ordered champagne to celebrate. Afterward, they drove back to the opera house, and walked across the highway to the spot where wealthy steamboat passengers had once come ashore to see a play and spend a night in the hotel. There was a dock there now, which probably wasn't the original, but Katie didn't want to know that. Enough of it had rotted away to be atmospheric. She sat on a patch of grass in front of it, with her back to the river, and looked up at the opera house. In the moonlight, the rust stains on the façade didn't show.

"No matter what light there is, it glows," she said.

R.B. sat next to her. He'd taken off his jacket, and he was wearing a short-sleeved shirt, so with his bare arm brushing hers there was some nice skin-on-skin action going on. She wasn't sure, but she thought there might be a kiss in the air. However, she was a woman with a mission.

"Did you mean it when you said you wanted to help me?" she asked.

She could see he was a little thrown, which probably meant she'd been right about the kiss possibility. She'd just trashed the mood. Then he laughed, so maybe she hadn't, at least not permanently.

He pulled her to her feet. "If I'm going to tell you who left you the opera house, we're going to do it my way. That is why you wanted me to have supper with you—isn't it?" And before she could say no, it wasn't, no way, he added, "I started researching the chain of title right after we read the will."

Instead of instantly hitting him up for names and details, she heard herself ask, "Are you sure you should have done that? I don't want you getting into trouble. "

That surprised him. "Are you telling me you didn't ask me out tonight to pump me for information?"

Well, she had. But now, suddenly, the moonlight and champagne seemed to be kicking in. To say nothing of that near miss with Cliché Number Sixteen in the lobby.

"You work with your family. I wouldn't want them to be angry with you."

"Legally, I'm in the clear. Georgie'll probably throw a fit because it's not the most ethical thing I've ever done, and she's a real pain in the butt about that. Mama's always been a little ethically challenged, so she'll be fine, and Daddy . . ." He looked at Katie for a moment. "He'd tell me to go for it." He took her arm and led her across the highway to the opera house.

For the second time that day she stood in the garden behind the theater. Only, now the white light of the moon was shining down on the three statues. R.B. stopped in front of the one Katie hadn't had a chance to check out before Randa did her power walk out of the garden. Katie looked down at the date and name engraved at the base of the figure. OLIVIA VENABLE, it said in large block letters. Then, like an afterthought, SHANE was tacked on and stuck in parentheses at the end.

"Olivia was married to one Dellwood Shane," R.B. said. "Of course no one thought of her as anything except a Venable."

"I wonder what Dellwood thought about that."

"Not much, from what I've heard. It seems he wasn't the sharpest tool in the shed. And Olivia was a more liberal despot than the previous Venable women; at least she used his name on official documents."

He walked over to the opposite corner of the garden. Hidden behind the hedge was a fourth pedestal, with the date 1973 carved on it, but this one didn't have a stone figure.

"Olivia commissioned a statue for this plinth," R.B said. "But then for some reason that no one has ever figured out, she canceled it. She lost her son in 1973, which certainly would have explained it, but she stopped the work on the statue months before he died." He smiled at Katie. "That's just one of our little unsolved mysteries that I thought you might like." He had the look of a man who was handing out diamonds.

"Thank you."

He led her back to the statue of Olivia. "So here's the deal on your inheritance. Olivia walked away from the theater in 1973. The woman she
sold it to was named Tassie Rain."

"Rain?" Katie whipped around to look at Edward's statue. "But Edward
and Ophelia only had one daughter, and her name was Lilianne."

"You've been doing research on the family."

"I read the CliffsNotes. Randa's daughter downloaded a history of the
Venables from the Internet. I know there wasn't anything about a Tassie
Rain."

"She was Lilianne Rain's daughter—actually, Tassie was Lilianne's *adopted*
daughter. There's no record of Lilianne ever having had any biological
children."

"I don't remember reading a lot about Lilianne."

"She's another mystery. She left home when she was sixteen and never
came back. I guess Massonville wasn't glamorous enough for her. She went
into vaudeville—that much we do know. And at some point she adopted
Tassie. Tassie grew up and bought the Venable Opera House from Olivia.
When Tassie died last year, the theater went to you and Randa."

"Why?"

"That, I don't know."

"Is there someone who could talk to me about this Tassie?"

"No one in Massonville knew her."

"She owned the opera house for how many years?"

"Thirty-three. But she never hung around here. There was a caretaker
who looked after the place, and he was paid by the same Atlanta law firm
that contacted us. As far as I know, the only person in town who knew
Tassie Rain was Olivia."

Katie gazed up at the stone figure in front of them. Olivia Venable Shane
had been short and stocky, and her June Cleaver shirtwaist hadn't done
much for her. The skirt ballooned out over stubby little legs, which ended
in stubby little feet encased in high-heeled pumps. For some reason, those
feet were turned out in the stance favored by ballerinas and ducks. Pearls
adorned her neck, and she wore gloves. Her face was a square, punctuated
by a rather masculine-looking large nose, and her hair was swept back in an
unbecoming chignon. A little round hat perched on top of her head.

"Is she in costume?" Katie asked.

"Olivia wasn't an actress. Her main claim to fame was that she managed to hang on to the theater for thirty-eight years."

"That's why she rated a statue?"

"Her husband had it built in 1952 after she finally managed to produce an heir."

"Impressive. I think all Princess Di got was a ratty old tiara."

"The Venables were serious about their dynasty. And from what I've heard, Olivia was into it big-time. "

CHAPTER 43

Massonville 1952

Was there a spot on that teacup? Olivia held it up to the light. No, just a little bare place on the rim where the gilt had worn away. She put the cup on
the saucer, and went back to folding the fine old napkins so that the corners
with the embroidered *H* on them would be hidden.

"What's wrong with letting the darned *H* show, Doodlebug?" her husband Dell had asked when he'd found her sitting at the dining room table
with a diagram of the napkin fan she'd clipped from her favorite magazine,
and a pile of crumpled linen squares. It was impossible to explain to Dell
why using the napkins was an act of betrayal. The monogrammed *H* stood
for Honeycutt, the name of the family that had originally owned the opera
house. The Venables never spoke of them, and Olivia's aunt Ophelia had always managed to convey the impression that it had been Venable hands
that had built the theater. During her aunt's lifetime, the Honeycutt table
linens, their china, and their silver tea service—which Olivia had just spent
two days polishing—had been jammed into the back of a closet. Olivia had
discovered them there after Ophelia's death.

Olivia would gladly have used Venable linens and china if there had
been any, but her aunt Ophelia and her grandmother Juliet had been ac-

tresses who couldn't be bothered with domestic details. They had eaten in the hotel restaurant, and they had entertained there when it was necessary. It would never have occurred to Aunt Ophelia to invite a guest to have luncheon in her own dining room, as Olivia was doing on this day.

The napkin fans were done. Olivia put the diagram and the magazine article into the clothbound scrapbook she'd marked "Lilianne." The menu for this day's meal would be pasted in it as well, along with the recipes for the congealed shrimp salad, the little cheese rolls, and the peach pecan pound cake which had once been a specialty of the Venable Opera House restaurant. The restaurant was closed now—declining profits had forced Olivia to shut it down two years earlier—so she had made the dessert herself.

Olivia took the scrapbook into the bedroom. On the wall above her little writing desk was a shelf crammed with similar volumes. She wedged the new one in at the end of the row. These albums were her lifeline. Because she couldn't afford a full-time staff at the theater, she was the director, promoter, booker—and sometimes the handyman—as well as the producer and owner. She managed to wear all these different hats by organizing her thoughts in her scrapbooks. Her system bewildered Dell.

"Doodlebug, why are you putting a recipe for fried chicken in this book that has Tennessee Williams written on the front?" he'd asked her once. "Isn't he the man who wrote that play about the crippled girl with the glass animals and that old terror of a mother?"

She had served fried chicken to the president of the rotary club the night she'd convinced him to buy a hundred tickets for *The Glass Menagerie*. In her mind, the recipe and the playwright were inextricably entwined.

Convincing people to buy tickets for productions at the opera house wasn't easy. It hadn't been for years. By the late thirties, radio and the movies had dealt a major blow to live theater in America. The growing popularity of television a few years later all but finished it off. And Massonville had changed too. After World War II , the boys who had fought Hitler came home wanting brand-new houses with shiny appliances and big patios with barbeque pits. They left downtown Massonville with its mills and its rich history, and moved their families to the suburbs, where they stayed home most evenings watching Uncle Miltie and Lucy Ricardo. When they did go out for a night of entertainment, they didn't want to drive to an old theater near the docks.

As her audiences dwindled, Olivia was forced to spend the last of Uncle Edward's nest egg to pay her bills, and, after that was gone, there were times when Dell had to help her out with money from the household budget. Still, she managed to stay in business. She cut back her season from a year-round schedule to one that lasted only from June to September. During the winter, she rented out the lobby, the old restaurant, and the theater for parties and charitable events. Every once in a while, she'd allow a Broadway road company to rent the Venable Opera House. She could have done more of that kind of business, but the New York tours that were sent to small towns like Massonville were usually shoddy—Manhattan producers reasoned that the hicks would never know the difference—and Olivia refused any bookings that were not up to her standards.

"Who cares if it's not the best cast, Doodlebug?" Dell would say in despair. "They want to pay you!"

But the stage of the Venable Opera House was holy ground, where Uncle Edward had trod the boards and Aunt Ophelia had reigned. That was Olivia's legacy—her *glorious* Venable legacy, she'd told Dell solemnly. After Uncle Edward and Aunt Ophelia died, she had gone to the cemetery where they were buried side by side and had promised them that she would keep their theater safe for the family.

Aunt Ophelia and Uncle Edward had saved Olivia. Her father, Horatio, had been a gambler who had worked as little as possible and had lost every penny he'd made. Climbing out the window of a filthy boardinghouse to escape eviction was a way of life for Olivia when she was a child. She could dress herself in every article of clothing she owned in less than five minutes.

Her mother had died when she was three—probably of exhaustion— and for two years, Horatio himself was sick. He'd brought Olivia back home to Massonville and his masterful sister. Olivia, who had settled into a paradise of regular meals and clean sheets in her aunt's home, barely noticed it when her father died.

She'd kept the faith with Uncle Edward and Aunt Ophelia—in every aspect except one. Olivia couldn't act. When she was ten, her aunt took her into the theater to stand on the bare stage and recite a Shakespearean soliloquy of her choosing. It was a Venable rite of passage Olivia failed by panicking and throwing up. But the experience taught her to respect performers and the high-wire act they performed every night. As a result, good

actors always wanted to work at her opera house. Dell said she was hell on
wheels with actors who weren't good.

"God gives talent where He chooses," she told him. "If you're not
blessed, you find another way to make yourself useful. I did."

Olivia checked her watch. The time had come to unmold the shrimp salads,
and, using the little sterling silver form left behind by some Honeycutt wife,
to press the butter into daisy-shaped pats. But as she spread the butter, a
wave of guilt swept over her. Thinking about Dell always made her feel that
way.

*It shouldn't. I was always honest with him. Right from the night he pro-
posed.*

"Couldn't we sell that old barn of an opera house, Doodlebug?" Dell had
begged her that night. "The gosh darned theater never does anything but
lose money and be a heartache for you. And I don't care what you say, an
apartment just plain doesn't feel like a home. Not like a house with grass
and trees around it."

But she had told him that she had to live in the apartment in the opera
house. And she'd warned that she would always be a Venable and so would
her children.

Most people would have said she was out of her mind to risk losing him.
It was true that Dell was not a looker. Even when he proposed, back when
he was twenty-nine, he'd already started the beginning of a paunch, his
hairline was receding, and his eyes had a tendency to bulge. But Olivia
wasn't exactly Miss America herself. She was lucky to have a steady man
with a fine job—he was the manager of the Massonville branch of People's
Bank—wanting to marry her. After she'd spoken her mind, she had waited
for him to walk away. But he had married her instead, and for the next seventeen years he had lived in the apartment in the opera house when what
he'd really wanted was a backyard and a garage, and to be surrounded by
neighbors who talked about baseball, instead of actors who talked about
themselves.

The only change Dell had ever insisted on making in the Venable family
quarters was expanding the ancient bathroom and putting in a modern
shower. The huge new room cut into the foyer of the apartment, so now the
entrance, which had been quite elegant, was spoiled. And when you were

in the theater office, which was directly below it, you could hear everything that was going on in the bathroom. It had something to do with the way they had moved the old air vent. Olivia didn't understand exactly how it worked, but she was too embarrassed to use the office after that.

But that was the only thing Dell ever asked of me, Olivia thought. And suddenly she had to stop making her butter pats so she could wipe her eyes. Her Dell was not a knight in shining armor like Uncle Edward, who had saved the theater for Aunt Ophelia, and maybe her marriage wasn't the romantic story theirs had been, but she loved him.

There was only one way in which he had failed her, although maybe she was the one who had failed. After all the tests, the doctors still couldn't tell. She and Dell had never been able to have a baby. The specialist they had consulted had said there was nothing wrong with either of them, but nothing had happened, and now she was thirty-seven. Dell tried to make the best of it. "We have more time for each other, Doodlebug," he said.

But for Olivia, not having children was a catastrophe. She could accept her own disappointment, and even Dell's, but she was failing Aunt Ophelia and Uncle Edward. Because of her, the Venable line was going to die out; there would be no new generation to inherit the theater. And there was nothing she could do about it. For the first time in her life Olivia became depressed.

That was when she thought of her cousin Lilianne.

Over the years Olivia had heard rumors about Lilianne. People said Lilianne and her father had clashed and that he had been very harsh with her. It was hard for Olivia to believe that Uncle Edward had been wrong about anything, but she could see how he might not have been the easiest father. A child of his would have had to remember that, above all, he was a genius. As Ethel Barrymore Colt had said about her mother, Ethel Barrymore, "She was warm and wonderful, but let's face it, she didn't change our pants."

Lilianne had left home before Olivia had come to live at the opera house, and since Lilianne hadn't returned to Massonville, the two cousins had never met. However, Lilianne was a Venable, and her children, if she'd had any, could inherit the opera house.

The butter pats were chilling in the icebox along with the lemonade Olivia had made in case her guest didn't like sweet tea or Coca-Cola. Now it was time to ease the pound cake out of its pan. For some reason Olivia's heart started to race.

I've given little luncheons hundreds of times before. There's no need for me to be so nervous. But today there was so much at stake.

At first, Dell had balked at spending the money for a detective to find Lilianne, but Olivia had begged, and he never could refuse her anything.

"We'll make that cousin of yours live in this gosh darned theater," he'd joked. "See how she likes it."

It had taken the detective six months and a considerable portion of their savings to discover that Lilianne Rain was an entertainer—at least, she had been at one time. She'd traveled around the country in the twenties doing a vaudeville act called "Rain and Rain, the Sunshine Sisters."

"Thank heaven Aunt Ophelia isn't alive to hear it," Olivia had said to Dell. Aunt Ophelia had equated vaudevillians with performers of burlesque.

Exactly how many "sisters" there were in Lilianne's troupe, or what kind of act they had, the detective had not been able to determine. Nor had he been able to find any trace of Lilianne. However, after spending an additional five months searching, and a lot more of Dell and Olivia's hoard, he had finally tracked down a woman who had worked in the Sunshine Sisters act.

Olivia stepped back to give the luncheon table a final look. The Honeycutt china and silverware sparkled. The napkins, now without the monograms showing, were creamy white fans. The congealed salads were in the kitchen ready to be served, and the cake was sitting on its pedestal dish.

"If it were done when 'tis done, then 'twere well / It were done quickly," she murmured nervously.

She might not be actress enough to play Shakespeare, but she would always love the words.

Olivia took off her apron, smoothed back a few wisps of hair that had escaped from her French twist, and hurried out of the apartment. She walked down the grand staircase, let herself out of the theater, stood under the canopy that said THE VENABLE OPERA HOUSE in gold lettering, and waited for her lunch guest. The guest's name was Tassie Rain. According to the detective, she was Lilianne's adopted daughter.

CHAPTER 44

Massonville 1952

"So you want to know about Lilianne," Tassie Rain said. She was a tiny thing, and appealing in a brassy way, although you couldn't really say she was pretty. Her blue eyes were so round and big that she looked like she was always doing a comedian's double take, and her teeth pushed her mouth out in a constant pout. Olivia was sure that she and Tassie were about the same age, but Tassie's hair was bright blond—probably bottle blond—and it fell around her face in curls that were far too young for her. Her best features were a lovely figure and an endless supply of pep.

"Sorry to have to tell you, but Lilianne died in 1933," said Tassie.

It was a disappointment, but not the end of the world. "She must have been very young," Olivia said.

"She never even made it into her forties. Her heart just gave out."

"How old was she when she adopted you?"

"Oh, that wasn't ever legal, honey."

That was another disappointment—a much bigger one. But there was still hope for a child who was blood.

"The adoption was just done to dodge all those societies for the prevention of cruelty to children." Tassie shook her head and her mass of curls bounced. "Can you beat it?" she demanded. "Kids all over the country had jobs back then. Here in the South they worked in the mills until they dropped, and no one made a peep. But the nosey parkers had all kinds of rules for us because we were in show business."

"So you were in Lilianne's act," Olivia said.

"Yeah."

"The Sunshine Sisters?"

"Uh-huh. Then after the act ended, I went to Hollywood to be a movie star. With this mug and these choppers, can you believe it?" Tassie did an exaggerated grin that made her teeth stick way out.

She's the theater-y type, Olivia thought as the woman launched into a funny story about her days in Calfornia. "Theater-y" was Dell's word for actors who were always "on." They'd entertain you and charm you, and they seemed friendly, but they really didn't want you coming too close. Tassie Rain kept up her snappy patter so you wouldn't get to know her. However, she did seem genuinely interested in the opera house.

"I've heard so much about it," she'd said when Olivia had greeted her at the front door. "Lilianne talked about it all the time. I just had to see it for myself!" She'd backed up to get a better look at the façade. Her hard, blue eyes had softened. "Those were the days," she'd said. "Trouping around the country, doing split weeks, five shows a day—" She'd stopped herself, and had gone back to her bantering tone. "Hell, honey, don't let me get going on the good old days. I'll put us both to sleep."

Having identified her guest's nature, Olivia fixed an appreciative smile on her face and prepared to laugh at Tassie's jokes until she had an opportunity to bring the subject back to Lilianne. Dealing with actors was really very simple.

It took about forty minutes for Tassie to run dry. By that time, the salad and the biscuits had been consumed and Olivia had served the cake.

"If Lilianne never really adopted you, why do you use her name?" she asked.

"Oh, honey, I've had so many last names. After my last ex and I parted company, I said to myself, 'I'm going back to being Tassie Rain for the rest of my life.' " She paused, and for a second time her brittle little face softened. Once again, Olivia knew she was getting a glimpse of the real Tassie. "Lilianne was very good to me," she said softly.

"What was she like?"

"A real trouper."

"I never knew her, you see, and I was hoping you could tell me about her."

"Yeah. That's what your PI said when he called me," Tassie agreed. But she didn't offer anything more.

"I wanted to know if she was ever married or if she had a family."

Tassie laughed loudly. "Oh Lord, if you knew Lilianne, you'd know how funny that was. She wasn't the family kind."

This time the disappointment was so big, it felt like a physical blow. Olivia held on to the sides of her chair until her knuckles were white. *I spent all that money and time trying to find this little phony—and all she can say is that Lilianne wasn't the family kind? There's got to be more. I need more!*

"Did Lilianne ever have any children?" she demanded.

"She spent her life trouping around the vaudeville circuits. That doesn't leave a lot of time for a husband or babies. And she was practically a kid herself when she died."

"So . . . there weren't any children? There's no one?"

"No."

It's over. It can't be. But she just said it. There's no one.

"Are you okay?" she heard Tassie Rain ask.

She forced herself to focus. "I'm fine.

Uncle Edward, Aunt Ophelia, I'm sorry. It's over.

Then, as if God hadn't been mean enough, Tassie Rain said, "I've heard so much about this opera house—could I see it?"

Olivia showed Tassie around in a daze. They started in the dressing rooms and the greenroom and worked their way down to the stage. Tassie walked out onto it and looked out at the rows of seats. "It's beautiful," she said dreamily.

And it will end with me, Olivia thought. *When I die, it will be over.*

But it was when she took Tassie out to the garden to see the statues that she thought her heart would really break. Because she couldn't help looking at the corner of the garden that was directly across from her Uncle Edward's statue. There was a time when Olivia had planned to commission a statue of her aunt Ophelia to fill that corner. Then she would bring her children out here to look at the sculptures and teach them about their great legacy—

Suddenly, Olivia had to get out of the garden. She started to walk toward the gate, but her guest didn't follow her. Tassie was still staring up at Uncle Edward's statue. "So that's what the great Edward Rain looked like," she said grimly.

Olivia couldn't let Tassie's remark pass. On this day when everything was lost, she had to set the record straight. "I know my cousin was angry with Uncle Edward and Aunt Ophelia," she said. "But they really were great . . . and noble. . . . They gave up everything for this place. It's hard to keep it going. . . . You have no idea." To her horror she started to cry. "That's all any of us ever wanted. Just to keep the opera house going for the next generation. But now it's over." And it all spilled out of her; the struggle to pay the bills for one more season, the pretty little luncheons where she begged rich people to buy tickets to her plays; and good, sweet Dell, who never asked for anything but a new shower in the bathroom. She told the little stranger with brassy hair how she and Dell had done it all for the children who would inherit the theater and keep it going. The children she and Dell would never have.

Tassie moved to her, and the next thing Olivia knew, the woman she had written off as a theater-y phony was sitting beside her on a stone bench, mopping up her face with a handkerchief.

"It's okay, honey; you just let it come out," Tassie said as she put her arms around Olivia. "We all need a good cry sometimes."

After the sobs stopped, they stayed together on the bench, not saying anything, for a long time. Finally Tassie broke the silence. "Have you ever heard of Myrtis Garrison?" she asked.

The question came so out of left field that Olivia wasn't sure she'd heard it right. "I know about the Garrisons," she said, bewildered. "Everyone does." The Garrisons, who lived in a town not far from Massonville called Charles Valley, were one of the wealthiest and most influential families in the state. In the twenties the patriarch of the clan, Grady Garrison, had put Charles Valley on the map by creating the Garrison Gardens, which were known to horticulturalists and botanists around the world. Grady's son, Dalton—Mr. Dalt, as he was called—had just finished building a huge resort next to the gardens. The resort was already one of the biggest employers in Georgia; but it represented only a fraction of the family's wealth.

"I know the Garrisons do a lot of good works," Olivia fumbled, still wondering why the subject had come up. "But I don't understand . . ."

"Myrtis Garrison is Dalton's wife," Tassie said. "She's the one who does the good works. She has that big charity she runs, the Garrison Trust? They're in the newspapers all the time."

"Yes, but I still don't see—"

"They're always fixing up old buildings in the state that have what they call historic interest. I was thinking maybe the Garrison Trust would be willing to take over this place."

"Are you saying I should give away my opera house?"

"You're so worried about what's going to happen to it after you're gone. If the trust had it, you'd know it was going to be safe."

"I'm not dying just yet," Olivia said sharply.

"But it can take time to get that kind of thing set up. Why not look into it?"

Because the opera house belongs to the Venables—that's why. We are not a charity case.

"Olivia, you're going to have to leave it to someone," Tassie said gently. *And there won't be any more Venables after you.* Tassie didn't say that, but the words hung in the air.

"Wouldn't you rather pick a group like Myrtis Garrison's charitable trust instead of leaving it to be sold or torn down?" Tassie looked up at the back of the opera house. "It'd be just plain wrong to let anything happen to this place." Then she flashed her toothy grin. "It sure would have made one hell of a vaudeville theater."

In the months that followed, Olivia thought about Tassie's idea often. But she just couldn't make herself write a letter to the Garrison Trust.

"It feels like begging," she told Dell.

But Dell was all for the scheme. He even found out through his banking connections that there was a telephone number at the Garrison Trust where Miss Myrtis herself could be contacted two mornings a week.

"She goes to the offices there in Charles Valley and she answers the telephone like any secretary," Dell told Olivia. "It's because she doesn't want to
be like some rich snob who just throws her money around. I guess she
wants to know the little people."

Dell would never understand how Olivia's hackles rose at the idea of the
Venables being thought of as the little people. But she was going to have to
leave the theater to someone.

Olivia did what she always did when she felt a need to organize her
thoughts; she started collecting material for a notebook about Myrtis Garrison. It wasn't hard to find information—it seemed as if the newspapers
were always publishing stories about the woman who was called the First
Lady of Garrison Gardens. Olivia clipped the articles and put them in an
envelope in her desk drawer.

But she never actually made the notebook. *Next week,* she'd tell herself.
I'll do it next week. But she never did. Then came the morning when Dell
handed her a copy of the *Charles Valley Gazette*—she was never sure how
he'd gotten his hands on it—while she was drinking her coffee. There, on
the first page, was a picture of Miss Myrtis Garrison smiling in front of a
Victorian theater that looked like a less ornate version of the Venable Opera
House. In the article that accompanied the picture, Miss Myrtis was
quoted as saying, " 'Some of the most beautiful architecture of the last century went into our old theaters, which, tragically, are now being torn down.
Wherever it can, the Garrison Trust takes over these grand old gems and
gives them a new life.' "

Olivia looked up from the newspaper to see Dell watching her. "Olivia,"
he said. "All these years when you've been hanging on to this place because
you wanted to leave it to our children, I understood. But now there's no reason to keep on. All you're doing is eating your heart out here."

"I'll never give the opera house away while I'm alive," she said.

"You don't know what you'll do, Doodlebug. You might decide these people can do better by this old barn than you can."

He's right, said her brain.

Never! Said her heart.

"Just make a phone call and find out. That's all I'm asking," said her husband, who had almost never asked for anything.

She gave herself a deadline of two weeks. She noted it on the front of the envelope. *Telephone call to Miss Myrtis Garrison at the Garrison Trust,* she scrawled on the front of the envelope full of clippings, and she added the telephone number. As she wrote the hateful digits, they swam before her eyes. The mere idea of having to make that phone call had gotten her all dizzy, and she was mad at Dell for the rest of the day. She seemed to be getting angry a lot, she'd noticed, and sometimes she wanted to cry about nothing, which just wasn't like her. Dell said she'd feel better once she'd called Miss Myrtis—which really made her furious. Then she fainted. Over her protests, Dell called the doctor. And that was how they found out that at the age of thirty-seven she was going to have a baby.

Soon after they found out, Olivia rammed the envelope full of stories she hadn't wanted to collect into the back of the drawer in her writing desk. She wanted to throw it into the garbage, but that felt like she'd be tempting fate. She knew she was being superstitious, but the doctor kept warning her about the risks facing a first-time older mother. She told herself she'd burn the whole mess once she knew everything was going to be all right. But after her baby was born—a healthy normal boy she named after Shakespeare's Henry the Fifth—she forgot all about the newspaper articles.

Dell was beside himself with happiness—she hadn't realized all those years how much he'd wanted to be a father—and he arranged a surprise for her. On the day she came home from the hospital with Henry, Dell told Olivia to come with him into the garden.

"Close your eyes, Doodlebug," he commanded as he opened the garden gate and led her to the corner across from the statue of Uncle Edward. For a brief wonderful moment, Olivia let herself hope that Dell, who never listened when she talked about her family, had heard her say how much she wanted a statue of her aunt Ophelia placed in that corner. If it was there, that would be more joy than she could stand. But then he told her to open her eyes.

There was a statue in the corner. But the figure was not her aunt Ophelia. Instead, in the spot where that great woman should have been immortalized, Dell had placed her own unworthy self! He hadn't listened when she'd told him about the family history. He didn't realize that the garden was sacred, and the honor of having one's statue placed in it for posterity was reserved for the great ones—the actors. Not for her. Not for Olivia Venable, who couldn't act her way out of a wet paper sack. For a moment she wanted to smash Dell's stupid gift and have the pieces thrown into the river. Then she looked at him, standing next to her and beaming with pride.

"I know you always wanted another statue out here," he said. "If it was me, I'd rather have a new car, but to each his own." He reddened and all of a sudden his eyes were wet. "I just thought, now that we have Hank, you'll be able to show him this someday." He wiped his eyes on his sleeve. "How do you like yourself, Doodlebug?"

He'd given the sculptor a picture that had been taken of her the previous summer. She recognized it, because she remembered thinking she looked really hideous that day. The dress she was wearing was the ugliest one she owned, and she'd always hated the hat. But Dell still had that proud look on his face.

"It's beautiful," she said.

Olivia wrote to Tassie Rain to tell her the good news about her son, because Tassie had been so sympathetic. Tassie sent a beautiful baby blanket. Two years later, when Olivia gave birth to a daughter she named Desdemona, Tassie sent a little sweater with ruffles down the front. Olivia tucked a picture of the children into her thank-you note, and the two women who were so different began a correspondence. Sometimes they went for several months without communicating, sometimes they exchanged letters every week. Tassie's missives were brief, always asking for news about the opera house and Olivia's family. Olivia responded with reams of notepaper full of her triumphs and failures.

Poor Dell never did get to see his children grow up. When the boy he insisted on calling Hank was four years old, and the little girl he'd nicknamed Des was two, he died from stomach cancer. The doctor said he'd probably been sick for months, but, of course, Dell wasn't one to complain. After the funeral, Olivia discovered that there were no savings. Dell had been paying her bills at the opera house more often than she had realized. He hadn't complained about that either.

Already grief stricken, Olivia was now terrified. There was a small life insurance policy and Henry and Desdemona were eligible for social security. The three of them could have scraped by on those meager funds, but she couldn't open her theater that season. She wrote a letter to Tassie telling her about the predicament. She didn't even bother to try to lie to herself—over the years, she'd realized that Tassie was well-heeled, and she was hoping for a loan. Tassie sent the money a week later, but it wasn't a loan, it was a gift.

If you ever need help, don't be proud, Tassie wrote. *Ask me.*

But Olivia thought, *Tassie is my safety net. I won't ask her again unless I absolutely have to.*

And for seventeen years, no matter how bad things got, she didn't. Not until the very end.

CHAPTER 45

Massonville 2006

The garden seemed even quieter now than it had during the day when the sun was shining. Katie backed up so she could see all three of the statues. Her ancestors. Or maybe not.

"I have to go back to New York," she said to R.B. "I have to put my apartment on the market. I've never lived anywhere but in that apartment."

"Katie—"

"Don't tell me again that I can back out. Please? Because if I do, I'll never try anything. I'll be seventy years old living on the Upper West Side of Manhattan afraid to leave or— What are you doing?"

"Trying to kiss you."

He did it well. Okay, better than well. Much better. Being kissed by R.B. Moultire was like going through a six-point earthquake without the broken crockery. It was definitely an experience that left you needing to catch your breath. Which she didn't get a chance to do, because, after releasing her, he changed his mind and kissed her again. After which they both needed to catch their breath. So they just sort of stood there in the moonlight holding on to each other, which was also a very nice choice.

"I just wanted to say that you are brave," he said finally. "And . . . what was that other word you said when you told me you were keeping the opera house? Fantastic?"

"I don't remember. But I'll take fantastic."

Then he winked. It was a habit he could break, she told herself. People broke worse ones all the time—look at how many smokers quit. Then he began stroking her hair, and they went back to the holding-each-other-in-the-moonlight thing. If he never lost the winking habit, she thought dreamily, she could decide it was charming. There were options.

CHAPTER 46

Massonville 2006

Randa yanked her brush through the mass of curls that had replaced her once sleek hair, thanks to the Georgia humidity. She needed an appointment with her wizard of a hairdresser for a straightening treatment. She also needed to have her head examined.

"You could have told Katie you wouldn't do this breakfast without her," Susie said. She was sitting on the bed, watching Randa get ready.

After dropping her bombshell about moving to Georgia, Katie had mooned around for another twenty-four hours, most of it spent with R.B. He'd told her someone named Tassie Rain had left the opera house to them. It seemed that this woman was an adopted daughter of some member of the Venable family—a nugget that thrilled both Susie and Katie because, as Susie put it, "At least we know *something.*"

Then Katie had announced that she was flying north to wrap up her life in New York. When Randa had pointed out that they had a meeting scheduled with Mike Killian to discuss the sale of the opera house, Katie had smiled sweetly and said, "It'll be better if you break the news to him without me. I think he's into you." Before Randa could protest that insane statement, Katie had wondered off to pack.

So now Randa was going to have breakfast with the man. And she was going to look like an idiot. She tugged painfully at her hair. To make matters worse, Susie had labeled Katie and her lunacy "totally right-brained," a term of high praise that seemed to have replaced "cool" in the kid's vocabulary.

"Actually I'd rather go without Katie," Randa said between yanks. "She'd probably start babbling about finding the stories she's destined to tell, and I'd have to kill her." She began working on the other side of her head.

"I think you're glad she's going to keep the opera house from being torn down," Susie said. "I think that's why you're taking the meeting for her."

"I'm going because we made an appointment, and I believe in keeping my commitments."

Could I sound a little more boring?

"We owe Mr. Killian an explanation," she added.

Add prissy to boring. No wonder Susie thinks Katie's the right-brained one.

"Mom, you could have stopped this whole thing from happening. All you had to do was tell Katie she had to buy you out now, without selling her co-op first. You know she can't."

"I didn't need her to buy me out now. It might even be better for me tax-wise if I waited, and . . ."

Susie didn't exactly roll her eyes, but she came close. For the first time, Randa wondered at what age adolescence officially began.

"If I hadn't said Katie could wait to pay me, she'd have found some really stupid way to finance it," Randa added.

"Why would you care?"

Good question.

"I hate to watch anyone lose money."

"And you like Katie."

"I don't know her."

"You like what you know, Mom."

Two days ago her child would have been right. That was part of the reason why Randa was pulling the hair out of her head—literally. She *had* liked Katie. There had even been moments in the past three days when she'd thought what a pity it was that they lived on opposite coasts. But then Katie had started talking like the spoiled geniuses Randa had spent her career keeping out of bankruptcy court.

"Maybe Katie needs to be here to write," Susie offered.

"You don't need to be any specific place to write. We know people who do it from Los Angeles, for God's sake."

"I thought you liked Los Angeles."

"I live in Los Angeles; I have to like it. Ouch!" she added as she gave her hair a vicious tug.

"If you give me the brush, I could do that," Susie said.

"I'm fine, thanks."

It was a lie. But what had made her so upset—okay, furious—wasn't Katie or Mike Killian, or Susie, or the Venable Opera House. Ever since Katie had announced her nutball intentions, Randa had started dreaming about her father. She knew she was dreaming about him, even though she couldn't remember any of the details, because she woke up in the morning feeling sad and lonely, the way she had after he'd died.

Nothing she could do was going to make her hair lie flat. She grabbed a scarf and tied the mass of curls off her face. She was due to meet Mike Killian downstairs in the hotel coffee shop in fifteen minutes and no way was she going to be late.

"I like your hair," Susie said. "It's . . . kind of hot."

"I look like an unmade bed."

"That's what I meant," said her child, who was definitely growing up. "You go, Mom."

Originally, the get-together with Mike Killian was supposed to take place in his lawyer's office. But since Katie had decided to keep the opera house, and no one was going to need legal advice, Randa figured she might as well give Mike Killian the news on her own turf—relatively speaking. So she'd invited him to have breakfast with her at the hotel.

Although, she figured she probably could have saved herself the effort. Katie had told R.B. about her plans, and he had undoubtedly passed the news along to the rest of his family, one of whom would leak it to the Mayberry rumor mill. It was a sure bet that Mike Killian already knew what was up, Randa thought. The sure bet turned out to be a nonstarter.

"You're kidding," Mike said after they'd done the greeting ritual and ordered breakfast.

"No. Katie has decided she wants to keep the opera house."

"And you're going to let her?"

Why does everyone assume I'm her keeper?

"She's an adult," Randa informed him.

"She doesn't have the sense God gave a goose! Her kind never did."

"What 'kind' is that?"

He shot her a glance and then looked away. "You're a businesswoman; she's not. That's all I was saying."

I don't think so.

"You said 'her kind.' How do you even know what kind she is?" she asked.

"She's not exactly realistic—is she?"

That wasn't what you meant either.

Their waitress appeared. Mike had skipped the all-you-can-eat breakfast buffet and had opted for cereal and fresh fruit. She'd done the same, but neither of them was exactly digging in.

"So your friend really thinks she's going to save that old place," Mike said.

"She's not my friend—Okay, that came out wrong. It's not that I don't like her. I don't know her well enough not to like her—and that sounded wrong too. What I'm trying to say is—"

"You're connected to a stranger and no one can tell you how or why, and you're sick of the whole damn thing," he filled in. "You want to go back home where you belong, but this woman you don't know is messing up the works."

That was exactly the way she'd been feeling. But she didn't like the way it sounded.

"I may not agree with what Katie is doing, but she has the right to try."

"You don't believe that, Los Angeles. You know if this wasn't so stupid it would be funny."

She'd been telling Susie that for three days. But who the hell did he think he was?

"I don't hear you laughing," she said.

"You will when I buy that old rattrap. I'll have to wait until Miss Harder figures out whatever pie-in-the-sky she's got planned for it isn't going to work out. And that there's not a restaurant between here and Atlanta where she can find decent Thai fusion. But I'll get it."

The idea was making him way too happy. "What do you have against the opera house?"

"Me? Nothing."

"You're salivating at the thought of tearing it down. I've never seen anyone want to destroy something so much."

"That's crazy."

"My thought exactly."

He drew in a deep breath. "Okay, you want to hear it? That theater was closed down before I was born, but when I was growing up, all you ever heard around here was about how the Venable Opera House made Massonville so special. Why, back in the good old days it was written up in *The New York Times*! Bullshit snobs from all over the country had heard of us. I never could find anyone who'd gone to see any of the plays—but by God we were proud of it. Well, we had plenty to be proud of without it."

"So this is a populist move on your part."

"It's practical. The prime real estate that building sits on is going to waste. You may not like the condos I build, but people want to live in them. They're clean, and they're new, and don't kid yourself—most of your fellow Americans will pick that over charm any day of the week. I'm going to give people jobs. And when my condos are built, I'm going to sell them to taxpayers, which means there will be money for a whole lot of things like roads and sewers. That may not be as sexy as an old theater, but it will be a hell of a lot more help to the folks who actually live here."

He sat back, a man who had made his point. That was when Randa remembered a scene from her past—and she knew it was connected to the dream she'd been having. She was five years old and she was in her father's dressing room at the Shakespeare festival in Stratford, Connecticut, watching him get ready to go on as Rosencrantz in *Hamlet*. It was the only speaking part he had all season—the rest of the time he was doing walk-ons—but she saw how carefully and proudly he did his makeup and put on his costume. When he was finished, he turned to Randa and said, "*Hamlet* was written in 1601. Can you imagine that, baby, 1601!"

Mike was still leaning back in his chair, looking pleased with himself.

"Some things are worth saving," she said slowly.

I can't believe I'm doing this said a voice inside her head.

"If they're useful," Mike said.

"Define 'useful.' "

"Come on, Los Angeles, you're smarter than that. And saner."

"My father was an actor."

I really can't believe I'm doing this! said the voice.

"He wasn't successful, and he had too many problems to be a good father to me," Randa continued. "That was wrong."

Somebody shoot me, begged the voice.

But Randa kept on talking. "Wanting to be an actor, caring about it, that wasn't wrong. It wasn't practical, or smart; maybe it wasn't even sane. But how much that's practical and sane and smart hangs around for centuries?"

"Excuse me, what are we talking about?" Mike asked.

"Shakespeare wrote *Hamlet* four hundred years ago. Right now, somewhere on this planet, there's a bunch of actors trying to figure out if Hamlet had a thing for his mother, and just how much of a blowhard Polonius really was. Somewhere, in some language, someone is on a stage saying 'To be or not to be.' That play is still here." He was staring at her now. "My spreadsheets won't be around in four hundred years. No one will give a damn about how much money I saved for my clients, or how fabulous my new carpet is. They're not going to give a damn about how much profit you made with your condos. So you want to talk about what's really useful? I'll put my money on *Hamlet,* and the Sistine Chapel ceiling, and Beethoven's Fifth. That stuff has lasted for a reason."

Randa had been leaning so far forward she could have eaten the freshly sliced melon off his plate. She straightened up and waited for him to start laughing. Instead he looked at her for a moment, and she thought just maybe there was something a little gentle in his eyes. Then he poured some milk over his cereal and said, "So I guess this means you'll be moving to Massonville too."

"That's not what I said!"

"Yeah, it is, Los Angeles."

Oh. My. God.

CHAPTER 47

Massonville 2006

At first Susie thought it was her mother's hair that made her look kind of wild when she came into the hotel room. But then her mom said, "If we live here, if any kid gives you a hard time for even two minutes—you will tell me. Right?"

Susie felt herself go all funny inside. She and Jen had been texting for hours trying to come up with a way to blast her mother out of the Puke Carpet Palace, and they'd finally given up. Susie had accepted the fact that she was going to spend the next six years in a school where the teachers all had acting agents, or they were pitching a screenplay, and where all the girls wanted to be Paris Hilton. But now Mom was talking about the kids in Massonville.

"If anyone makes fun of your accent, or Greenpeace, or even suggests that you shouldn't read *Anna Karenina* or whatever the hell you want—"

"Mom, are we moving?"

"If you even start to feel like we've made a mistake, we're out of here. Nothing is written in stone, and—"

"Mommy, are we leaving L.A.?"

"You will always come first. Always. Remember that."

Susie threw her arms around her mother's neck. "I love you!" she shouted.

Her mother hugged her for a lot longer than she usually did, and then she did one of her all-business looks. "Start packing," she said. "We have a lot to do back in L.A."

Susie was heading out the door to her own room when she heard her mom's cell ring. Mom's voice sounded cold when she said hello, but then after a minute she sounded surprised and kind of weird. She snapped the cell phone shut and said in a strange voice to Susie, "I won't be having dinner with you tonight. The hotel has a babysitting service. I'll have them send up someone to stay in the room with you."

Susie decided it was no time to get into a fight about how much she didn't need a babysitter. "Why?"

"That was Michael Killian. He says there's someone he wants me to meet."

CHAPTER 48

Massonville 2006

Randa looked at her watch. It was five-fifty PM. Mike Killian had told her to be ready by six. She'd attempted to deal with her hair by washing it with the shampoo and conditioner she found in the hotel bathroom; now she smelled like a fruit salad, and she had ringlets. She'd run out of clean clothes, and since she wasn't about to trust any of her silk blouses to the hotel valet service, she'd raced down to the dress shop in the lobby and bought a lacy off-the-shoulder number with a tiered skirt that just cried out to be worn with the combs with fake gardenias on sale at the accessories counter. At least they would keep the ringlets out of her eyes.

When she went into Susie's room to kiss her good night, the babysitter, a girl from the local college, told Randa that she was as beautiful as Ashley Judd. Susie looked stunned. Blowing her kid's mind had its upside, Randa decided. It certainly was more fun than always being the predictable one.

She'd already blown Katie's mind earlier when she'd called to say Katie was going to be having roommates in the opera house. She'd made her announcement, then listened for several seconds while Katie swallowed large quantities of air.

"Why?" Katie had croaked when she could manage speech.

Randa had explained about her epiphany over breakfast with Mike.

"But you think I'm crazy for doing this. You said so. A lot."

"Yes."

"You said I'm gambling with my security."

"Yes."

"You live for security. 'Bottom Line' is your middle name."

"I would have said 'Risk Averse,' but that's close enough. Look, Katie, if you don't want a partner—"

"Are you kidding? Right now, I'd take on Attila the Hun as a partner—and that was so not what I meant to say."

"Okay."

"Just . . . tell me again why you're doing this. I mean aside from the *Hamlet*/Sistine Chapel thing, which I actually do get."

"You're probably my cousin or my niece four times removed, and I can't let you go down the tubes by yourself."

"So you're coming down them with me?"

"Yes."

There was a pause. "Thank you," Katie said, and hung up.

Yes indeed, blowing people's minds was fun. Even if images of hang gliding and bungee jumping were now running through Randa's brain.

When he picked her up, for a second Mike Killian seemed . . . not exactly blown away, but definitely surprised by her new look. Randa wondered if it was the good kind of surprised or the what-was-she-thinking kind. But then he took her arm and propelled her to his car without even saying "Hi," so she decided to hell with what he thought.

"Where are we going?" she asked.

"We'll be there in about fifteen minutes."

"That's not what I asked. Mind telling me who I'm going to meet?" There was no answer. "Okay, can you tell me why I'm going to meet this mystery person?"

"Los Angeles, don't push."

And that was all she could get out of him.

He drove through the city of Massonville, to what were clearly the newest suburbs. In the light of the setting sun Randa saw large houses sitting behind young trees that hadn't had a chance to do much growing. Mike turned into a gated community that looked a lot like Randa's neighborhood in Northridge. A security guard greeted him and waved them through.

"Let me guess, these McMansions are your handiwork," Randa said. His houses didn't deserve the nasty edge in her voice, but he did, after giving her the silent treatment for fifteen minutes.

"Uh-huh," Mike grunted, oblivious. What the hell was going on with him?

He drove on until he reached a cul-de-sac where he stopped in front of a modest one-story house—the smallest one she'd seen in the development. There was a big flower bed on one side of the front lawn and a vegetable garden on the other. The Silent One opened her car door, and she followed him up the walkway to the house. Something was cooking inside that smelled heavenly. The man who opened the door was a slightly grayer but equally spectacular version of Mike. He was in a wheelchair. And when he shifted slightly in the chair, it was clear that his left leg was a prosthesis.

"Randa, this is my father, Bill Killian. Pop, this is Randa Jennings." Mike had suddenly found his voice. Pop looked up and Randa found herself being checked out in a way that was not completely fatherly.

"Oh my," Bill Killian breathed appreciatively. "Please, do come in, Miss Randa."

His wheelchair was motorized and he zipped ahead, leading them into a well-worn living room with a fireplace on one wall and two large comfortable sofas placed conversation-pit-style around a coffee table. In a corner where it would have been hard to see from any part of the room sat a small, antique-looking television.

Bill Killian maneuvered himself to one side of the coffee table, which was covered with bowls and platters. Randa sniffed the air. Whatever was cooking, rosemary and garlic were involved.

"The lamb won't be ready for another half hour," Bill Killian said as he handed Randa a plate and a napkin. "Try my hummus; I make my own pita bread."

Suddenly Randa realized that she hadn't eaten since breakfast, and she helped herself liberally. Her host turned to his son. "Pretty as a picture, and she eats! My land, Michael." He held out a platter to Randa. "If you're fond

of spanakopita, Miss Randa, I pride myself on mine. And I have a nice little Italian red for you that I like with Middle Eastern food. Michael, don't
just sit there, give the girl some wine."

"Yes, sir," Mike said, and poured the wine. He was grinning too. Randa
hadn't seen him grin like that before. "Pop is a gourmet cook. He goes to Atlanta a couple of times a month for classes."

"I have to do something now that I'm retired," said his father. "You're
going to love those olives, Miss Randa. I marinate them in lemon juice and
a little hot pepper."

When he was satisfied that her plate was full enough, he wheeled himself next to an end table piled high with books and positioned himself under
a reading lamp. Clearly, this was his spot in the room. "Now, I do hope
Michael has told you that I can't help you personally. At least not directly,"
he said.

"He hasn't told me anything about why I'm here."

Bill groaned. "Lord, son, where are your manners?" He gave Randa an
apologetic smile. "You'll have to forgive him. The thing of it is, I've been uneasy about all of this—I mean, about telling you. I thought if you were going
to be leaving town anyway, maybe you didn't need to know all the history.
But then when you told Mike this morning that you wouldn't be selling . . .
Well, he said he had to do the right thing—"

"Pop, just tell her," Mike broke in.

Bill leaned forward in his chair. "He wanted to do it all along. He's a
good man, you know. Stubborn like his momma, and, Lord, can he carry a
grudge. But so did she, if she thought one of hers had been hurt. That
woman was like a tiger if anyone messed with Mike or me, and Mike is the
same—"

Now it was Mike's turn to groan. "Pop, Randa doesn't need to hear all
that. Tell her the story."

Bill sat back in his chair and seemed to collect this thoughts Finally he
said, "It was Elsie Harder I knew back in 1973."

"Elsie Harder?" Randa repeated.

"Yeah, Elsie Rose Harder—that was the girl's real name. But that summer she decided to call herself Rosalind."

CHAPTER 49

Massonville 2006

Randa put down her plate before she dropped it. She'd never believed that the hair could actually stand up on the back of a person's neck, but something was going on at the base of her skull.

"Rosalind Harder?" she said to Bill. "You knew Katie's mother?"

"Yes," he said.

"She was here in Massonville? And no one bothered to tell us?"

"I don't think there's anyone around here who would know but me." Randa watched Mike settle on the far end of a sofa. "Rosalind worked at the Venable Opera House," Bill went on. "It was a professional theater back in those days—a summer theater. I was told it was registered with the actors' union—I don't remember what it was called."

"Actors' Equity," Randa said.

"Of course you'd know that; you're in the business." So Mike had been talking about her. "The way I understood it," Bill continued, "if a youngster wanted to be an actor or actress back then, they had to be a member of the union. How they did that was, they worked as an apprentice at a professional theater."

"It's still that way," Randa told him. "But about Rosalind Harder . . . ?"

Bill nodded.

"The youngsters at the opera house did everything from making sets to cleaning the restrooms. But it was all behind the scenes, I guess you could say. So unless you were hanging around the theater, you'd never know Rosalind was there in 1973."

"But you were hanging around."

"The Venable kids were my friends."

Randa turned to Mike. "You knew about all this?"

"He didn't say anything because I didn't want him to," Bill cut in. "I've only told two people what I'm about to tell you. And I didn't let Mike in on it until a few days ago, when I heard that a girl with the last name of Harder had inherited the opera house." He paused. "I may have been wrong, not saying anything for all those years. But it wasn't my place—that's the way I saw it, anyhow." He moved his wheelchair to the coffee table and poured himself some wine. Randa decided that screaming with frustration wouldn't make the story go any faster. Out of the corner of her eye she caught Mike watching her.

"How much do you know about what happened here in the summer of '73?" Bill asked her.

"Just what my daughter has been able to research on the Internet and what R.B. Moultire has told Katie," she said. "The woman who owned the opera house back then was Olivia Venable. And she was the one who was planning to put that fourth statue in the garden . . . where the empty plinth is now. "

Bill nodded again. "But then something happened and she changed her mind."

"And a few months later, she lost her son." Randa picked up the thread. "After that she sold the theater. That's all I know. Oh, and according to my kid, there was another child in the family, a daughter."

"Her name was Desdemona," Bill said. "And the son's name was Hank. Well, it was Henry but everyone called him Hank. He was twenty that summer. I was eighteen, and so was Des—that was the nickname her father gave her before he died. If you called her Desdemona when she was little, she'd beat you up." He leaned back in his wheelchair, and chuckled softly. "Des always was a pistol. Later on, Hank used to have to finish her fights for her. He was the toughest tackle we had on the football team—not the biggest, but he could do damage. He told me once he had to be that way, because his mother put him in a lot of her plays, and there was always some guy who had to be taught that the acting stuff didn't mean what he thought it did. I was the quarterback on the team back then." Bill took a sip of his wine.

"That's not to say Hank minded working at the opera house. He loved the place. I was fascinated by it too. My folks were mill workers; I'd never met anyone like the actors who came to work for Miss Olivia. Those people had traveled all over; and they lived in New York City. That was heady stuff for me back then. And Des and Hank, and Miss Olivia, could hold their own with those big city people! They all used to quote Shakespeare for fun. They were special—"

"Pop, we don't need to hear about how great the Venables were," Mike broke in. His voice was harsh; he didn't like this part of the stroll down Memory Lane.

Bill turned to Randa. "Yes, you do," he said gently. "You really need to understand what it was those people managed to accomplish by keeping that theater going so long. And you need to understand what a tragedy it was when Miss Olivia sold it."

An image of her father dressed as Rosencrantz came into her mind. "I think I do," she said.

Bill Killian leaned back in his chair. "So, about 1973," he said. "Something was a little off for Hank that summer. Even before Rosalind came. I didn't see it at the time, but now that I look back . . ." He trailed off for a second, then pulled himself back. "Des and I had graduated high school that spring and we were both going to college—the first ones in our families to do it. I had a football scholarship, and Des got one for being smart. We were both going out of state too—me to Pennsylvania, Des to Massachusetts. People used to think we were sweet on each other because we spent so much time together, but it was never like that with us. We were just two kids who wanted to get out of Massonville, any way we could.

"Hank hadn't gone to college, and he started working full-time at the opera house right out of high school. The plan was, eventually he'd take over running it when his mama was ready to quit. But that summer, with Des and me leaving, I think for the first time he realized how much he'd tied himself down. He and Miss Olivia started crossing swords, which was probably bound to happen because they were so much alike. Normally Des could have smoothed things over between them—she was the glue that kept that family together. But all she was thinking about was college and getting away." Bill sighed. "I think the summer of 1973 was a real bitch for all of them."

"Do you know why Olivia Venable ditched the statue?" Randa asked.

"That's something I never did find out. Hank and Des knew, but neither of them would say, although I think Des came close to telling me once or twice. It had to have been something bad, that much I do know, because that fourth statue meant everything to Miss Olivia. I always thought it was something Des did that stopped her mother from putting the darned thing up."

CHAPTER 50

Massonville 1973

Des walked across the stage to the old trapdoor. She opened it, and began descending the rickety ladder—the original wooden one made in 1876—to the basement below the opera house. She climbed down the first three rungs, then reached up to close the trap over her head, before she continued down in the dark.

She didn't have to risk life and limb getting down to the lower regions of the opera house; on the side of the stage there was a perfectly good staircase that went to the basement. But she'd been going down this way since she and Hank were kids.

The air in the basement was damp, and it smelled old. Once, Des had tried to sweep the concrete floor—also original from 1876—but it had been a waste of time. The space seemed to breed dust. She turned on her flashlight so she wouldn't trip over the old elevator, a platform that had carried actors up to the stage level in the old days when plays featured witches and ghosts. The elevator and the trap were never used now, but no one had bothered to dismantle them. The stage had been modernized a couple of times over the years, but the basement hadn't been touched since the opera house was built. The smell was probably original too.

Des tolerated the smell because the basement was one of the few places in the opera house where she could escape from Ma and Hank and their only topic of conversation—keeping the theater afloat. Or, as Ma liked to put it, "carrying on our glorious legacy." As if that mattered, with everything else that was going on in the world.

The war in Vietnam had finally ended after protests, marches, black arm-bands, and four kids getting themselves shot at Kent State. The Supreme Court had voted that women had the right to have abortions; the Pill and the sexual revolution had changed the world forever; and the Beatles had written a song about Lucy in the Sky with Diamonds. There were new allegations coming out about Tricky Dickey and that burglary at the Watergate Hotel. The times, they really were a-changin', but her brother, who should have been in the big-ass middle of it with everyone else his age, spent his time helping Ma rent out the opera house for road shows in the winter, and running their summer theater after June. There were times when Des couldn't believe she was related to Hank.

She certainly didn't look like either Ma or Hank. Ma was short, and although Hank was muscular, he wasn't tall. They both shared the same curly black hair and strong masculine features, which looked lots better on Hank than they did on Ma. Des was tall and fair with a delicate chin and a small upturned nose. Boys thought she was cute until she started talking about politics. Her friend Bill Killian said she ran them off. She said it was a compliment when dumb rednecks didn't like her.

Des let her flashlight beam play around the walls of the basement. In the 1870s, the space had been used as a storage place for props. The goblets, masks, shields, and tea services had been all laid out on a long table placed against the right wall. Today, all the props and costumes were stored in a moth-proof room in the attic, but the ancient prop table was still in its original spot. Des kept a stack of her news magazines on it—she read them voraciously—and her stash of batteries for the flashlight. The magazines and the batteries were a bone of contention with Ma.

"They're so expensive, sugar," Ma would say in her sweet, tired voice. "Do you have to subscribe to three periodicals each month? We need a new cloak for Lady Bracknell in *The Importance of Being Earnest*."

It did no good for Des to point out that she had earned the money for the magazines and the flashlight batteries by working after school as a

cashier at Winn-Dixie. When Ma needed something for the theater, she assumed you'd be thrilled to help her, and if you weren't, she'd been known to
raid handbags and piggy banks. She was always shocked if you got mad.
That was why Des had put her earnings in the bank. The money she earned
was for college.

College was another bone of contention with Ma. "Theater people don't
need a formal education," she'd told Hank and Des. "When you're producing Shakespeare, you read about the Tudors, when it's Chekhov you study
the Russians—we learn what we need when we need it, and no school can
predict what that will be."

"I'm not a 'theater person,' Ma," Des had said once.

"You'll get over that, sugar," Ma had said, as if Des were five years old
and going through a phase.

But a college diploma was going to be Des's ticket to a new life. Furthermore, she was going to get that very important document in Massachusetts,
because she, Desdemona Venable, had won a scholarship to prestigious
Wellesley College. It was the first time a girl from her high school had even
gotten in to a Seven Sisters school, and the principal had wanted to hold a
congratulatory supper for her. Her mother couldn't have been less impressed.

Now Des sat in the lawn chair she'd dragged down to the basement. She
turned on her flashlight, pulled out the ham biscuit she'd grabbed from the
breakfast table, and opened her new copy of *Time*. She couldn't read long
this morning; she had to get to the Winn-Dixie early so she could ask her
manager for double shifts during the summer. Her Wellesley scholarship
covered only her tuition; she still had to pay for her own room, board, books,
and travel.

She could have had a job at the opera house for the summer, but if you
were one of Ma's kids, you got a paycheck when it was convenient. If it ever
was. "Don't we all have a roof over our heads and food on our table?" Ma
would say happily when you asked for your money. "Aren't we 'one for all
and all for one'?" Then she'd haul Des and Hank out into the garden to look
at the statues of Uncle Edward and the great Juliet Venable, who had
started the whole mess.

"Just think of the gift they gave us." Ma's face would glow with joy.
"Think how lucky we are to have our legacy!"

And Hank, the fool, would nod his head up and down like one of those little bobbing dolls you won for shooting tin rabbits at the county fair.

Des put down her magazine, and closed her eyes. There had been a time when Hank had been different. When they were little, they had agreed that they'd rather be eaten by snakes than grow up to be Venables and carry on their damn legacy. But then Ma snookered Hank into performing at the theater, and he turned out to be a good character actor. He never really had the dash to play leads, but if you needed a goofy sidekick or a stalwart best friend, Hank was your guy.

It wasn't until he turned sixteen, when Ma started "grooming" him to take over the old hellhole, that he really started to change his tune about being a Venable.

"If I want to be an actor, what's the point of doing commercial crap in New York or Los Angeles when I can have great parts right here at home?" he asked Des one steamy summer night.

It was evening and they'd escaped the heat of the apartment to sit on the front steps of the opera house. In the distance Des could see the river.

"If you act in commercial crap, at least it'll be your career," she said. "If you stay here, you'll be a part of the glorious legacy."

"Is that bad?"

"You've always said it was."

"Maybe I'm growing up. This theater is mine. When Ma turns it over to me, I'll be my own boss."

She tried another angle. "How are you going to act in the shows and run the theater? Even Ma couldn't do that, and she hates to sleep."

"I'll act in two plays each season."

"That's not a lot."

"But I'll get to pick the plays I act in." He drew in a breath. "It's the best of all worlds."

The words had come straight from their mother's mouth; Des could hear Ma saying them. And she knew there was no point in fighting with Hank anymore. Ma seemed so gentle and sweet, but she always managed to get what she wanted—from everyone except her daughter.

Des put the magazine aside reluctantly. One of Tricky Dickey's aides named John Dean was starting to spill the beans about the Watergate scandal, but she didn't have time to finish the article. How Hank and Ma could survive without even reading a newspaper, she'd never know. The funny part was, Ma had a reputation for being very "with it" politically. In fact, if you asked most people in Massonville, her mother was a champion for civil rights.

The story about Ma being a crusader for equality had started back in 1968 when a New York producer had called to book a play called *Jessie and Joe* into the opera house. It was a romantic comedy that had had a nice Broadway run because of the two charming leading actors who were now taking it out on the road. An Afro-American actress named Leonie Johnston was playing the part of Jessie; the rest of the cast, including the actor playing her love interest, Joe, was white.

"There's no smooching," the booking agent reassured Ma. "Just a lot of good old-fashioned sexual tension." Then he added, "But by the end, the audience knows what's going to happen."

Ma said yes without hesitating. People said she was brave or crazy, depending on where they were coming from. What they didn't know was, Ma agreed to take the play because she knew Leonie.

"You remember her, sugar," Ma said to Des. "She did small parts for us four summers ago. Leonie is very gifted."

And that was it. Because while Ma was vague about politics and she wasn't too clear on the names of any civil rights leaders except Martin Luther King, Jr.—who, she said, had a lovely speaking voice—Ma knew talent. And as far as she was concerned, if Leonie Johnston was talented, then Leonie would appear on the stage of the opera house. Ma never stopped to think about how people would react.

As it turned out, there was no negative reaction. Before the acting company left New York, its publicists sent out a story to the press. In it, Ma was described as "a crusader for human dignity," the Venable Opera House was "an old jewel where equal opportunity flourished," and Massonville was "an oasis of racial tolerance sitting in the heart of Dixie."

Several newspapers picked up the story, and then someone at the *Today* show heard about it. And before long, the mayor of Massonville was on television being interviewed by Hugh Downs. There were probably some people in Massonville who hated what Ma had done, but most of them enjoyed their hometown's moment in the sun. Then the mayor assured the fame of the Venable Opera House and the town by telling Mr. Downs and all of America about Ma's Kiddie Matinée.

The Kiddie Matinée was Ma's invention. Like most summer stock companies, the opera house had a program for apprentices. In most theaters, these kids did the dirty work and paid for the privilege. But Ma gave her apprentices the opportunity to work on the stage. The opera house closed every summer season with a play by Shakespeare. The apprentices were allowed to audition as understudies for the roles in this final production, and one special matinée was given in which they played the roles on the stage in front of an audience. After the mayor had bragged about this performance on the *Today* show, *The New York Times* sent a reviewer South to cover the kiddie matinée. The reviewer was so impressed that the newspaper continued to review the event every year afterward. Several other newspapers and magazines got into the act, and over time, dozens of articles were written about the apprentices. *Theater Monthly*, the only magazine Ma ever read, did a story about them every season.

Naturally all this attention made the theater glamorous. So, even though most of the mills in Massonville had closed and the town was struggling, the Venable Opera House built a new audience. In the summertime, buses full of eager playgoers who had read about the theater came in from all over. An entrepreneur who had refitted several old steamboats for tourists, and sent them up and down the Chattahoochee, even included a play at the Venable Opera House in his cruise package.

"*Jessie and Joe* was the goose that just keeps on laying golden eggs," Hank said long after the show had come and gone.

"I always knew Leonie Johnston would be a fine actress," Ma said.

There were footsteps on the stage above Des's head; Hank and Ma had finished breakfast and were starting a new workday. Des turned off her flashlight and ran for the side stairway, but she was too late. The trapdoor lifted and Ma's head appeared in the dark like a vision at Macbeth's banquet.

"Desdemona, sugar, I know you're down there," Ma called into the gloom. "Hank and I need you. And I don't want you using this trapdoor anymore; you'll break your neck," she added. Then she disappeared. Des turned on her flashlight and made her way up the stairs.

The stage floor was covered with pictures of young applicants for the summer apprentice program. There were snapshots, studio portraits, graduation pictures, and a few professional eight-by-ten glossies. Most of the professional photos came from the states surrounding New York City. Each picture was accompanied by an application form in which Ma had included three essay questions. They were the same every year: (1) Give a brief résumé of your theatrical experience—if any. (2) What do you hope to gain from a summer at the Venable Opera House? (3) What are your hopes for the future? Ma swore that the essays helped her pick the best candidates.

As far as Des could see, the apprentice pool was always the same. Most of the kids were conscientious little hopefuls who were never going to make it. There were usually a couple who had a chance, but as far as Des was concerned, all of them were as boring as whale shit.

"Desdemona, come over here," Ma commanded. She and Hank were sitting on the floor at the back of the stage. "Mind where you step, sugar."

Des picked her way carefully through the smiling faces until she reached her mother and her brother. There were twenty slots open for apprentices, and they'd narrowed down the field to forty possibilities. This was the point at which, every year, they began fighting. Why Hank bothered to get into it with Ma, was beyond Des, because he never won. But they were at it again. Ma had an application in her hand, and Hank was staring at what had to be the accompanying picture.

"What do you think, Des?" Hank held out the picture to Des.

That was the first time Des saw the girl who called herself Rosalind Harder.

CHAPTER 51

Massonville 1973

The thing that hit you immediately about Rosalind Harder was, she was born to be photographed. Her picture wasn't one of the professional efforts; from the looks of the awkward camera angle and the flat lighting, it had probably been a high school yearbook photo. But even so, those delicate features, high cheekbones, and deep-set eyes were worthy of a *Vogue* or *Harper's Bazaar* cover. The shot was black and white, but you could still see the way the highlights gleamed in her mass of long blond hair. Someone had made her sit sideways to the camera in the classic school picture pose, with her hands clasped in her lap, but Rosalind had managed to turn herself so that she was looking directly into the lens. She sat up on one hip with her back slightly arched and her shoulders thrown back; it was the kind of posture only a girl with total self-confidence could manage. She was a cheerleader, Des thought, or maybe she was captain of her school's pep club. Talking to her would give you a headache.

"Well? What do you think?" Hank repeated.

"She sure can smile."

"Don't you think she'd be a good choice? You can tell from her picture, she has presence."

"And knockers."

"Oh, for God's sake!" He reddened and threw a look at Ma to see if she'd heard.

Des clutched her heart and crossed her eyes. "Shall I compare her to a summer's day?" She paraphrased Shakespeare. "She art . . . is? . . . more lovely and more—"

"You're not funny," he growled. Hank knew his Shakespeare cold, and Des screwing around with the words was an old game that usually got him going. Not now. "If you're not going to be a help, get lost—will you?"

"Gladly."

But before Des could make her escape, Ma looked up from Rosalind's application. There were worry lines creasing Ma's face. "There's just something about this girl," Ma said. "She's so . . . unaware."

In a flash Hank was on the defensive. "She's young."

"She's nineteen. That's only a year younger than you are," Ma said reasonably.

"She says in her letter she lost both her parents and she's being raised by her grandmother. And she lives in a small town out in the middle of nowhere—"

"Actually, she's not too far from Birmingham in Alabama," his mother broke in.

"But it's not a sophisticated place. So maybe she's a little naïve—"

"Oh, she's not naïve. That's very clear." Ma turned to Des. "Her name is Elsie Rose. But she read about us—about the Venable family—in that *Theater Monthly* story, and . . . well, just listen to this." Ma adjusted her glasses and started reading the essay in her hand.

"My name is Elsie Rose. But I think that would look awful on a marquee. So when I read that everyone in your family is named after Shakespearean characters, I decided to call myself Rosalind."

Ma looked up from the essay. "She is nineteen years old and she's never had any professional acting experience or training, but she's already planning to have her name in lights?"

"Ma, she's just a kid." Hank turned to Des. "I think it's cute that she wants to copy us, don't you, Des?"

What Des thought was, she was smack in the middle of another one of their arguments and she didn't want to be there. But before she could weasel out of it, Ma waved the essay at Hank and said, "This thing gets worse." The worry lines were now trenches.

"*I know that the opera house is going to do* As You Like It *this summer,*" Ma read from the enterprising Miss Harder's letter. "*And I think that's an omen, now that I've changed my name to Rosalind. My gran and I believe in omens.*" Ma looked up again. "She hasn't even been accepted for our apprentice program, and she's casting herself in the leading role of our most important production."

"She's ambitious. She knows what she wants—" Hank started, but Ma cut him off.

"She's pushy," Ma said.

"Show me an actor who isn't."

There was something desperate in Hank's eyes. *This isn't just about a girl with a pretty face and no manners,* Des realized. *Hank needs to win one fight against Ma.* She looked over at her brother, who was staring again at the picture of Rosalind Harder. *And he needs a girlfriend.* She remembered the Hank who had once wanted to get out of Massonville. *He deserves a little fun in his life,* Des thought. *Why shouldn't he have a fling?*

"Ma," she said, "Hank's given up a lot to work with you at the opera house. He could have split right after high school—like I'm going to. What would you do then?"

Ma's eyes began to pond up. "Henry, I am grateful . . . ," she said in a shaky voice.

Tenderhearted Hank couldn't let her cry. "It's okay, Ma," he said.

But Des was made of sterner stuff. "You promised him he'd be in charge of the theater. You've been saying that for years."

"When he's ready," Ma sniffled.

"He's the same age you were when you took over. And he's not going to learn with you hanging over him. I think you should let him manage the apprentice program by himself."

Her mother was still teary; she really didn't want to give up control. But Hank was looking at Des as though she were his last hope. Suddenly she had an inspiration. "Besides," she said to her mother, "if Hank takes over with the apprentice program, you'll have more time to raise money for your statue."

It was a brilliant stroke. Ma was going to be sixty in less than two years, and the Massonville city council wanted to honor her. Her big dream was to put up a statue of her aunt Ophelia in the garden, and the council said they would pick up half of the cost. All Ma had to do was come up with the other half. The city fathers had made this offer before and had then changed their minds. The last time, the money for Aunt Ophelia's statue had gone to a municipal swimming pool.

This time Ma wasn't taking any chances. She'd already bought the plinth and had it installed in the garden, where it would be a guilt trip made of stone if the council even thought of reneging. But Ma wouldn't feel secure until her half of the funding was in place.

Ma stood up, and handed Rosalind Harder's application to Hank. "Henry," she said, "the apprentice program is yours to run as you see fit."

"I— You won't be sorry, Ma— thank you," Hank stammered.

"Your sister is the one you should thank. Now, if you children will excuse me . . ."

After she was gone, Hank got all mushy. "Des, I owe you—" he started, but she cut him off.

"You owe Great-Aunt Ophelia. Do you suppose Ma will have her sculpted as Mrs. Malaprop?"

Hank grinned. Thank goodness. When he was being intense, he could break her heart. "It was her signature role," he deadpanned.

"It's going to take a lot of marble."

"She wasn't small."

"She was a tank. And when you add the hoop skirt . . ." They were cracking up now. "Ma's going to have to buy a second plinth."

"Speaking of the one she's got, how the hell did she pay for it?"

"I don't think we want to know."

"I come from a line of terrifying females," Hank said.

"And don't you forget it."

The first thing Hank did in his new position as administrator of the apprentice program was accept Rosalind Harder's application. Ma had to bite her tongue when he told her, but she didn't say a word.

Rosalind Harder in person was spectacular—her eyes were turquoise-blue and her blond hair was so pale, it was almost like silver. Was that her real color? Des wondered. But after you'd looked at her for a while, you realized she wasn't quite as gorgeous as she'd appeared in her picture. That patrician little nose was a bit short, and the delicate mouth was thin. Nor was she as voluptuous as she had seemed. She was tall, probably 5'8", and she did have legs that seemed to start under her armpits, but she was kind of skinny.

Still, she had something. Every heterosexual man in the theater reacted to it.

"What the hell is the big appeal?" Des asked her friend Bill Killian. Bill was working at the theater that summer as the outdoor handyman, taking care of the grounds and doing repairs.

"Rosalind's . . . one of those girls," he said after thinking about it.

"That's all the eloquence you can muster? Aren't you going to be an English major in college?"

"It's hard to put into words. It's the old I'm-available-but vibe."

" 'But' what?"

"That's what every man wants to know. What would it take to have Rosalind Harder?"

"Speaking in a Biblical sense, of course."

"Sure. But it's more than that." He thought again for a while. "You want her to . . . lose it because of you. Fall for you hard."

There was a shine in his eyes that made Des twist inside. "Men are sick people."

"Hey, you're trying to figure out what makes her tick too."

She couldn't help it. Because no matter how much you wanted to, you couldn't ignore Rosalind Harder. Part of it was the way she put herself together. Most of the female apprentices favored an artsy, fresh-faced look, tying their hair back and living in scruffy blue jeans. Rosalind wore a full face of makeup every day, and her mane of hair fell glamorously to her shoulders. Pants were not her thing; she preferred dresses in feminine pastel colors, but when she had to wear work clothes, she went in for fitted bell-bottoms and crisp white shirts.

"Rosalind's a very complicated chick," Bill said.

Des thought about the way Rosalind carried herself, like a cheerleader strutting onto a football field. She thought about the big sunny smile that was bestowed equally on everyone, and she thought about Ma saying Rosalind was unaware. "No, I think she's very simple," Des said.

"Come again?"

"She's like a three-year-old. You know the way little kids are so bright and full of energy? It's because they don't doubt themselves. The rest of us are all screwed up: half the time we don't know what we want, and if we do figure it out, we're not sure we deserve it. Rosalind doesn't have thoughts like that. She knows what she wants and she goes after it. It's attractive because it's so simple."

Hank was thrilled with his protégé. "She has star quality," he said to Ma. "One day we'll be bragging that we had Rosalind Harder at our theater."

"But what about that voice, Henry?" Ma demanded.

Even Hank had to agree that Rosalind's voice was a problem. It was high and light and it had an oddly fake quality. It wasn't bad in everyday life, but Ma was thinking about the stage.

"The problem is, she's trying to get rid of her accent," Hank said. "She told me she spent a whole summer talking like Elizabeth Taylor."

Ma looked blank. "Why would anyone want to do that?"

Mercifully, Hank let it pass. "I showed her a couple of breathing exercises," he said. "That should help."

"It won't," Ma said flatly. "Her mind and her emotions aren't connected. She can't speak from her heart."

Later, she said to Des, "He's wasting his time with that girl."

"You promised you'd let him do it his way," Des said. "How is the fundraising going?"

"I have a luncheon on Saturday with the garden club. They may donate the proceeds from their crafts sale for Aunt Ophelia."

"Good for you."

Ma sighed. "I know I have to let Henry make his own mistakes, but it's hard to watch."

But Hank wouldn't believe he'd made a mistake. Not just because he was in love with Rosalind—although that was painfully obvious. With all that shiny charisma, it seemed like she *should* be a terrific actress.

"She's just inexperienced," he said to Ma and Des at supper one night. "She and her grandmother didn't have a lot of money, so she hasn't seen much live theater."

Ma started to say something, but she stopped when she felt Des's warning hand on her knee under the table.

"I'm going to coach her in a couple of roles," Hank informed them. Neither of them asked if one of those roles would be Rosalind in *As You Like It*. "She really wants to learn, " Hank went on. "I admire that. Most pretty girls think they can get by on their looks."

"She does seem to be a hard worker," Ma finally managed to say.

That was very true. Rosalind regularly volunteered for the worst shift— the all-night session known as doughnut crew because the kids working it were fed coffee and doughnuts to keep them going—so that she would have her days free to watch the professional company rehearse the next show. Sitting in on the rehearsals was a learning experience Ma offered her young thespians, but most of the overworked kids skipped it.

Except Rosalind. Every morning at eight, no matter how late she'd worked the night before, she had her private coaching session with Hank on the stage. Then, when the company came in at ten to rehearse, she was sitting in the house waiting for them. She always had a pad and pencil, and she took notes.

"And we're not talking about jotting down an occasional idea or two," Des reported to Bill. "I watched her for an hour yesterday, and I swear she never stopped writing. There she was, all dolled up in the middle of the morning—I mean, she wears false eyelashes—and she was scribbling away like she was taking dictation from God. It was hilarious."

"It sounds kind of sweet," said the boy who had always shared her sense of humor.

"All the director did yesterday was block Act Two. What does she think she's going to get out of that?"

"At least she's trying to get something."

As bad as Bill had gotten to be about defending Rosalind Harder, Hank was six times worse. The gossip around the theater was that they were sleeping together, and Des believed it. Whenever Hank took Rosalind's arm to help her off the stage, or opened a door for her, his adoration was written all over him. She'd picked up his habit of quoting Shakespeare, and every time she did it, he looked like he was going to burst into applause. Des knew he'd had girls before, although it wasn't something they'd talked about a lot, but he'd never been this crazy for any of them. The hard part for Des was, he was so happy. He was a big man in the little world of the opera house now that he was in charge of the apprentices. On top of that, he had won the prettiest girl there. The one everyone else wanted.

Thank you, Jesus, for the extra hours at Winn-Dixie, Des thought. It wasn't fun watching your only brother let the heat of his ass addle his brains.

Des was beginning to wish she'd never gone to bat for Hank with Ma. It wasn't bad enough that he couldn't talk about Rosalind without looking like a retarded spaniel; it was a foregone conclusion that he was going to let his angel play the lead in *As You Like It.* Des might laugh at the glorious legacy, but even she didn't want *The New York Times* to review a Kiddie Matinée at the Venable Opera House that starred Rosalind Harder.

"Rosalind playing Rosalind is going to be a disaster," Des told Bill.

"You've never even seen her act," he said.

"Ma says she doesn't have talent."

"Your mother hasn't seen her act either."

"She doesn't have to. Ma can tell about actors."

When Hank announced the cast list for the Kiddie Matinée of *As You Like It,* Rosalind's scream of joy could be heard halfway down the river. The announcement wasn't made until late on the day before the apprentices were supposed to have their first read-through of the play. Des figured Hank had waited so long because he was hoping it would be too late for Ma to say anything. He should have known better.

The first reading of any Venable house production was held in the theater. A row of chairs was set up across the stage for the cast to sit on. Their director—in this case, Hank—sat in the house to watch.

Ma waited until the reading was already under way. Then, with Des in tow, she snuck into the back of the theater and sat in the last row. Rosalind, who had seated herself in the center of the stage, was delivering a speech as they came in. At least, Des thought she was speaking. Her lips were definitely moving, but that light voice wasn't projecting. Ma frowned and they moved farther front. They had to move a second time before they could finally hear Hank's star. Hearing her didn't help.

It wasn't just the way she deadened Shakespeare's poetry with her ersatz Elizabeth Taylor accent. It wasn't the way she never directed her lines to anyone else onstage. Listening to Rosalind act was like sitting through a concert sung by someone who was tone deaf. She was singing in the key of E while everyone else was working in C.

She knew what her character was supposed to be feeling, and she tried to force herself to feel it. She made gestures; she arranged her face in expressions of happiness and grief. It was as if she were painting by the numbers.

The worst of it was, you couldn't stop watching her. The shiny charisma that never doubted itself was firmly in place. Glances from the other apprentices were tossed in Hank's direction, and Des thought he looked pale. But he was leaning forward in his seat, mouthing the words Rosalind was saying as if somehow he could play the scene for her. Meanwhile, Rosalind went on, blissfully doing whatever the hell it was she was doing to *As You Like It*. And Ma sat watching.

Thank God I'm getting away from here, Des thought.

Ma waited until Hank called for a five minute break. Then she called out "Henry, I want you!" and marched down the aisle to the stage. The members of the apprentice cast who had been wandering around, chatting and smoking, vanished. Only Rosalind waited for Ma to climb up onto the stage.

"Thank you for letting me have this opportunity, Miss Olivia—" she began, but Ma didn't let her finish.

"I'd like you to leave me alone with my son, Elsie Rose," she said.

Des watched as something in Ma's voice actually penetrated Rosalind's bubble of self-confidence. "I think I'll stay," she said.

"No, Rosalind." Hank said, and turned to Ma. "Go with the others."

Rosalind walked toward the stage door. Hank and Ma were too busy squaring off to notice that she never opened it.

"How could you, Henry?" Ma demanded. "How could you lead that child on?"

"It was a first read-through, Ma. She was nervous."

"She will never be able to play that part. You had no right to raise her hopes."

"She's improved since I started working with her."

"You can't work with what isn't there! You know she hasn't got the ability."

Des shot a quick look at Rosalind still standing near the stage door. Her eyes were black holes in a dead-white face.

Just a few more weeks and I'm in Massachusetts, Des thought.

"You're using our theater for your own personal ends, Henry," Ma went on. "You're infatuated with this girl and you're trying to buy her."

"I think she can play the part. And it's my choice."

"No. She will not appear in that role on my stage."

"You told me the apprentice program was mine."

"You can run the program, but you will change this piece of casting."

"Ma, don't do this to me."

"Don't you do this to the family! We have a reputation to maintain, Henry. We have a legacy."

And there it was. Ma had given her life for the dead Venables and the glorious legacy, and she couldn't understand that poor Hank was getting laid—probably better than he ever had been in his life—so none of that crap mattered to him right now.

I'm getting out of this loony bin, and I'm never coming back! But I can't leave them like this. I'm the one who went to bat for him, Des thought.

She was trying to come up with something to say that would make it right, when a voice from behind Ma piped up.

"You're wrong, Miss Olivia," said Rosalind. "I can play the part."

Ma whirled around, and Des waited for her to attack. But Ma's face softened. "No dear," she said gently. "You can't."

"I want to do it."

"And you deserve to. No one tries harder, or works more than you do. But talent is a gift, Elsie Rose. It's not fair, but some of us just weren't blessed."

"I'm nothing if I can't be an actress."

"You're pretty, you photograph beautifully, and you have a certain appeal. You'll find a way to have a career, if you want it so badly."

"But I want to be in *As You Like It*."

It was as if she couldn't understand the word "no." Des saw her mother consider trying to explain about talent again, but it was a lost cause. Ma copped out. "If we had chosen to do the *Taming of The Shrew*," Ma said. "It's a farce and Katharina is a much easier role. . . . Perhaps you could have handled that."

"I don't want to do what's easy!" For the first time, the voice that Ma had said was so disconnected from emotion was tight with pain. "I don't want to be pretty, or appealing! I want to be good!

Hank said, "Ma can't take the role away from you, Rosalind. I'm in charge—"

"No!" Rosalind cut him off. She walked over to Ma. "Please say you think I can do it."

"You can't. And I will not allow you to try," said Ma.

Rosalind wanted to scream, Des could feel it, but when she spoke next, her voice was quiet. "You'll be so sorry for this," she said, and she walked out. Hank ran after her.

Ma closed her eyes, and for a second she seemed to sag. Then she straightened up. "Go after your brother," she said to Des, "and tell him I'm canceling this morning's rehearsal. He'll have to hold new auditions tomorrow so he can recast."

"Ma, that's going to be humiliating. Let one of the other directors do it."

"Your brother wanted this responsibility. Now he has to live up to it."

Massachusetts, here I come, thought Des.

Hank didn't recast the part of Rosalind—he quit. For the first time since he'd appeared in *Cheaper by the Dozen,* at age eleven, her brother wasn't working at the opera house. He stayed in his room most of the time, but when Ma went out—she was gone almost every night now, speaking to civic groups that might be persuaded to cough up some money for her damn statue—Rosalind would sashay into the apartment, and Hank would whisk her off to his room. Des would turn up the record player and try not to hear the murmurs coming from behind her brother's locked door.

The murmurs didn't seem to be the fun kind. After about an hour Rosalind would stalk out in a fury, and several minutes later Hank would burst out of the apartment to find Bill and the guys from the maintenance crew. Des knew her brother had started drinking during these outings, something he'd never done before.

He can take care of himself, Des told herself.

But he'd never known how. And it was clear Rosalind was after something.

You'll be sorry, she'd said to Ma.

"I thought Rosalind would break up with Hank after she lost *As You Like It*," Des said to Bill, figuring he'd know what was going on.

"Guess not." Bill smiled the smile boys used when they weren't going to answer you.

"I don't think they're getting along very well," Des tried again. This time Bill shrugged. "Has Hank said anything to you?" she demanded.

"No."

"You lie like a rug."

"Leave it alone, Des."

"I just want to help him."

"Did it ever occur to you that the last thing that poor son of a bitch needs is more help from his sister and his mother? I swear, sometimes I think Rosalind is right."

"About what?"

"Ask your brother."

She didn't have to ask. That night she found out.

Ma was out of the apartment again, hitting up the Junior League, and Hank was in his room, which meant that Rosalind was on her way. So, instead of sitting in the living room with the record player blaring, Des made her way down the old spiral staircase to the office below the apartment. The office was never used anymore. Ma preferred to do her paperwork at the little writing desk in her bedroom.

As she reached the bottom step, Des was hit with an overpowering smell of mold. She turned on the light and saw wet patches on the ceiling and the wall behind the old bookshelves. The water damage was worst around the air vent, which was directly underneath the bathroom in the apartment. Her parents had redone it years ago, and now it seemed that the plumbing was leaking.

Des climbed up an old stepladder that was leaning against the wall, to see how bad the mess was. There were a couple of old books on the highest shelf that seemed to have gotten the brunt of the leakage. As she was taking them down, she heard the shower in the bathroom being turned on. She backed down the ladder, but she wasn't fast enough to avoid hearing giggles—male and female—coming through the vent.

Shit!

If she stayed in the office, there was no way she could avoid overhearing Hank and Rosalind. If she went back upstairs, she'd probably run into them coming out of the shower. Several potentially embarrassing scenes played out in her imagination, the worst of which featured her brother and his girlfriend buck naked.

I'll go kill some time down on the dock.

Des grabbed an ancient afghan someone had left draped over a chair, and, wrapping it around her shoulders, she tucked the old books under her arm and headed for the door to the lobby. The shower stopped and Rosalind's voice came through the air vent loud and clear.

"See how nice it can be to have a little privacy, honey bun," she cooed. "Without your mom and nosey old Des snooping around?"

If you want privacy, sleep with your boyfriend in your own room.

"Has your sister ever had a sex life of her own?"

You little bitch. Des moved closer to the vent.

"Don't knock Des." Hank belatedly came to her defense. "She tries to help."

"I'm just saying, isn't it nice when I can do this . . . ? And . . . this?" For the next few moments the only sounds coming through the vent were those of her brother alternately moaning and chuckling, which sent Des scurrying back to the door. But before she opened it, she heard Rosalind say, "This is why we've got to get out of here, Hank."

So that's it. Whatever squeamishness Des had felt about spying on her brother vanished. She moved to a spot directly under the vent.

The chuckling and moaning had ended. "Honey, we've been over this," her brother said wearily.

"I'm just thinking of you, darling." Rosalind's cooing had turned super sweet. "You're too good to stick around here for the rest of your life. I'll go to New York or Los Angeles with you—whichever one you want."

"I can't just walk away. The opera house is mine."

"Your mother will never give it to you. You saw what she did to you. She made you look like a fool in front of everyone."

"She didn't want it to be that way—"

"Hank, darling, when are you going to get mad?" There was exasperation in the voice now—Rosalind was hanging on to her temper by a thread. "When are you going to stand up for yourself?"

"I already have. I'm not working at the theater. I left Ma high and dry at the busiest part of the season."

"You should have left town!" The thread was close to snapping, Des could hear it. "What about what she did to me, Hank?"

"I know Ma hurt you. But I can't dump something that's been in my family for almost a hundred years. I want to build this place. I want it to be like the Guthrie or the Alley Theatre. . . . I have plans." Her brother was pleading now. "You and I could have a good life here."

Oh God, Hank. Don't.

"We'd have steady work. I talk to a lot of actors, honey, and they'd do anything for a regular job—like we could have here."

"Didn't you hear your mother tell me I was no good?"

"Ma won't be running things forever."

The thread holding back Rosalind's temper finally snapped. "So I'm supposed to wait until she drops dead?" she yelled. "Because that's the only way you're going to get your hands on this place." Hank tried to protest but she went on. "I'm supposed to live with your snotty sister laughing at me behind my back, and your mother saying I'm a no-talent, because someday you'll be in charge and I can act at the great Venable Opera House? Do you really think I'd set foot on that stage after what your mother said to me?"

"Rosalind—"

"I'm getting out of here, Hank. And if you don't come with me, you'll never see me again."

"I'll talk to Ma, I'll talk to Des."

Don't beg her!

"You're just upset, honey. Please don't leave!" her brother begged.

But there was the sound of a door being opened.

"Someday you should make your mother give you back your balls, Hank," said the classy Miss Harder.

Then the bathroom door slammed shut. A few minutes later the front door of the apartment slammed too.

Des waited for an hour. Rosalind didn't come back and Hank didn't go out. Figuring it was finally safe, Des went through the lobby and up the grand staircase to enter the apartment through the front door. The place was dark. At first she thought it was silent too, but then she heard a sound coming from her brother's room at the end of the hallway. She started toward it, then stopped. What she heard was her brother crying.

It wasn't until she was in her own bedroom that she realized she was still carrying the old books from the office. She put them on her nightstand and lay down on her bed. But the sound of Hank crying haunted her.

If only Ma had let Rosalind do the damn part. But Ma couldn't. *If only Hank would get away from the opera house and the goddamn legacy.* But Hank couldn't. *If only I hadn't talked Ma into letting him take over with the apprentices.* But she had. *Just a few more weeks and, Wellesley, here I come.* But for once that didn't help.

She picked up one of the ancient books—an old Bible. The water had soaked it pretty badly, which was a pity because it was a lovely thing with gilt on the edges of the pages, and a tooled leather cover. There was an inscription on the first page. The ancient ink had smeared, and the spidery handwriting was barely legible, but Des could make out the words "Maman" and "Juliet." Was it a gift to Juliet Venable from her mother? That would mean it was at least a hundred years old. Des closed it carefully and picked up the second book. This one was in worse shape than the Bible, but by holding it directly under the lamp she was able to read the faded title. "Walker's Critical Pronouncing Dictionary," it said.

The pages were stuck together. Des tried to pry them apart, but the binding was too soft from all the water. Not wanting to mangle an object that had survived for over a century, she was about to put it down, when something fell out of it. A letter.

It must have been wedged between the cover and the front page. There was no name or address on it, and the envelope looked as if it had never been opened. For a moment Des hesitated, reluctant to read unopened mail.

Get real. The person it was meant for is dead.

She peeled back the flap, and opened the letter.

The paper was brittle with age and yellow at the creases. But the handwriting was bold and quite easy to read. And it was a stunner. Des read it through twice to be sure she hadn't made a mistake. Then she began to laugh. Because according to the letter, the glorious Venable legacy was built on a secret that was far from glorious. A secret that had been hidden in an old book for a hundred years.

Des's sides hurt, and tears were running down her cheeks. *I've got to show Hank! This is what we beat our brains out for. This is what he gave up Rosalind for*—but she stopped laughing at that thought. She refolded the fragile sheet of paper and slipped it back into the envelope. Hank didn't need to see it. Not now. Eventually, when he stopped hurting, he'd get the joke—sick as it was. Ma would never get it. Des put the letter back in the old dictionary and stuck it with the Bible in her nightstand drawer. Ma must never see it.

CHAPTER 52

Massonville 1973

Rosalind waited two more days before she split. She took off late at night, and no one knew how she got to the train station. Her grandmother, when contacted, refused to say if she'd arrived home in Alabama. Rosalind didn't leave any kind of message behind for Hank, who flipped, of course. Unfortunately, Ma tried to make him feel better.

"She was right to go, Henry," she said. "She didn't belong here, and it was wise of her not to drag things out."

If there had been any hope of Hank accepting his loss, that speech ended it. He moved out of the family apartment and slept on the couch in the rec room at the Killians' place. Bill's mother called to tell Ma so she wouldn't worry, but for the first time in recorded history Olivia Venable was sick in bed. The flu was the official name of her ailment.

"Why is Henry doing this?" Ma asked over and over.

"He's in love with Rosalind," Des tried to explain.

"How can he be? She's insensitive and grasping and she doesn't have any talent."

Des thought about trying to answer, but she didn't know where to start.

"He needs to put all of this behind him," Ma said. "If Henry would just go back to work—"

"Ma, could we forget the damn theater for a minute? Bill says Hank got drunk last night and parked in their driveway to sleep it off. Your son is sleeping in his car!"

"That's why he should be here working. He needs to be useful."

Normally Des would have quit trying to fight and would have walked away. But now she knew the truth about their glorious legacy.

"Maybe he doesn't want to be useful," she said. "Maybe he doesn't want to give up everything for the goddamn opera house."

Ma started to cry. She'd never done that before.

I can never tell her about that letter.

When Des tracked Hank down, he looked whipped—and hungover.

"Don't you think Rosalind could have been happy here?" he asked wistfully.

Have you lost all your marbles?

"She's awfully ambitious," Des said.

"You don't think she loved me, do you? You think she just wanted that role. Everyone does."

"What do you care what people think?"

"If that was it, why did she stick around after Ma took the part away from her? She tried to get me to go to New York with her. Why did she do that?"

"Maybe she was afraid to go alone."

Or maybe she was trying to get back at Ma by taking you away.

As if he'd read her mind, Hank said, "She's not a bad person, Des."

There was a part of Des that felt like smacking him upside the head and telling him to grow up. Then she remembered him crying in his room. And she thought about all the sacrifices he'd made so cheerfully over the years.

He can't see Rosalind for what she is, because falling in love with her is the only thing he's ever done for himself.

"Why don't you get out of here, Hank?" Des demanded. "What the hell are you staying for?"

Because if it's the glorious legacy, sugar, have I got a story for you!

Hank read her mind again. "Don't laugh. It's the legacy. I'm not like you,

Des. Ma and me, we need the opera house, and the history. It's bigger than
we are. And we need something bigger than we are to make it all worth-
while. "

She wanted to scream because it was such a waste.

"I'm going to Alabama," Hank said a few days later.

"Why?"

"I need to know if she loves me. I'm going to try to make her come back."

Oh, Hank.

"When are you leaving?"

"I want to give Rosalind some time to cool off. And I've got to get myself
off of Mrs. Killian's sofa. She's about to throw me out, and Bill along with
me," he added, trying to smile. He was so sweet, her big brother.

*Three more weeks until I get out of here. Then I can stop watching him
throw his life away.*

But before that could happen, everything blew up.

CHAPTER 53

Massonville 1973

Ma was overjoyed to hear that Hank was coming home. On his first night back, she fussed over the supper as if it were one of her famous lunches, and she was careful not to say anything "helpful" about Rosalind.

In a week she'll be back to normal, Des thought. *God help poor Hank.*

Actually, things did roll along for just about a week. Hank went back to work at the opera house, filling in where he was needed, the way he always had. Ma didn't ask him to run the apprentice program again, and he didn't offer. In fact, Hank didn't seem to have much to say about anything. Des hated how quiet he was. She wished he'd go to Alabama and have it out with Rosalind. Maybe another dose of the little tramp would bring him to his senses. But Hank said he was still waiting for the right moment. Meanwhile, he'd started keeping beer in the fridge. Now he took a couple of bottles into his room with him when he came upstairs after the show. It wouldn't have been a big deal, but he'd never been a regular drinker before.

But it's not my problem.

Ma didn't notice that anything was wrong, which made Des furious.

After the hell Hank had been through, the least Ma could have done was pay attention.

However, there was something else bothering Ma these days. She spent a lot of time sitting at the kitchen table, going over long columns of figures and shaking her head.

Whatever it is, I don't want to know. In fourteen days I'll be on my way to Wellesley.

For the first time, Des really believed it was going to happen. There had always been a part of her that thought something would go wrong, but now she finally relaxed. She'd set aside some of her precious money for new clothes, and the prospect of actually going shopping was so thrilling, she had to talk about it with someone.

"I'll wait until I'm in Massachusetts to buy a winter coat," she babbled happily to her mother one morning after breakfast. "I won't know what to get until I see how cold it is. But I want to pick up a new sweater and a pair of shoes before I leave. "

"You still have plenty of time, don't you?" Ma asked from the sink, where she was rinsing off the dishes.

"I'm leaving in two weeks. I've told you, Ma."

"Of course you have, sugar. It's just with everything else on my mind . . ." She left the dishes in the sink, and moved to the table. "Please sit, Desdemona," she said. "I need to talk to you about something."

No! Whatever it is, no! But Des sat down.

Ma looked down at her hands to collect her thoughts. "I ordered the plinth for Aunt Ophelia's statue because I felt it would be a sign of good faith—for the city council."

You wanted to guilt-trip them into keeping their promise.

"I didn't have the money to pay for the plinth then," Ma went on. "I told them I'd have it by the end of the summer. But the sets for *As You Like It* were more expensive than I thought they'd be, and we had to repair the dock . . ."

Please don't let her say what I think she's going to say. Just this once let me be wrong about her.

"The stonecutter won't take the plinth back because it's already engraved, and I really don't want to return it, because I think that would send the wrong message to the city council."

Don't ask me for money. Don't.

"So, sugar, I need your help. I called the bank and I asked Mr. Roverton how much you had in that account of yours—"

"You did what?"

"I had to know if you have enough money."

"He told you?"

"Of course. He's one of the old-timers who remembers your father, and he's known me forever and he understands about the theater and the way my children and I always pull together in a crisis—"

"Ma, stop!"

"Now, just hear me out, sugar. Please?"

She's my mother. I can't throw this coffee cup at her.

Ma chose to take her silence as agreement. "I realize you have to pay for your room and board at that school."

"It's called Wellesley, Ma. I'm going to Wellesley College."

"But do you have to go there? We have a perfectly good school right here in Massonville."

"It's a community college! I got into a Seven Sisters school—one of the best in the country—and you want me to go to a community college?"

"I'm sure you can get a good education here. And it would be much cheaper—"

"No."

"Then you could wait and go next year. "

"No!"

"Sugar, this is no time to be selfish."

"I'm selfish? Me? What about you?"

"You know I have always put my family first—"

"As long as they're dead. What about Hank and me?"

"You and Henry always knew you were special."

"We were freaks! I wore clothes from the church thrift shop so you could buy a new curtain for the goddamn theater!"

"There's no need to be abusive—"

"Hank didn't own a car until last year. He was nineteen years old, and he had to bum rides from his friends! He couldn't afford to take a girl to his prom. We didn't have a television, and we never went to the movies."

"We had more valuable things to do with our money. I won't apologize for that. We are not ordinary people. We have . . ."

Don't let her say it.

"We have a legacy to uphold."

"You want to know about our fucking legacy? I'll show you!"

Des ran to her bedroom. She saw Hank come out of his room and follow her. She heard him ask what the hell she thought she was doing, but she couldn't stop. She grabbed the letter out of the old book and raced back to the kitchen. "Here, Ma!" she said. "I found this. It's a letter from Romeo Venable to his sister. You know who she was, Ma. She started the whole damn mess."

"Des, whatever you're doing, don't—" Hank started to say, but Des barreled over him.

"You know that pretty little story about how old Juliet got the opera house—the one where she bought it from the Honeycutt family after Lavinia Honeycutt had that tragic accident? Well, it wasn't quite like that, Ma."

Her mother's face was white. She was staring at the letter as though she couldn't look away. From somewhere behind her, Des heard Hank say, "That's enough." But it wasn't.

"James Honeycutt didn't want to sell the opera house, but Juliet had some dirt on him. He was the one who opened the trapdoor when Lavinia fell through it. He didn't mean to do it, but since he was plastered at the time, it wouldn't have looked real good. So Juliet kept his secret, but she made him sell. That's how we got our legacy, Ma. She blackmailed the poor bastard."

Ma was shaking her head slowly from side to side. "No," she said.

"And here's the real punch line. This is the part no one knew except her brother. Lavinia didn't die when she fell. Juliet went down to the basement to find her, and she was still alive." Des held up the letter. "Want me to read what her brother had to say?"

"Des, stop!" came from Hank.

"Okay. I'll give you the short version. Juliet Venable, the ancestor of us all, smothered that woman with a pillow from the prop table. It was Othello's pillow, which I think is a really lovely touch, don't you, Ma? Her brother was standing at the opening of the trapdoor and he saw her do it." She held the letter out to her mother. "Why don't you read it? There's a lot more in there about how he's leaving town because he never wants to look at her again—"

"Give it to me, Des," Hank cut in.

"No. I want her to read it."

"Give it to me now!"

Des handed it to him. For the next few moments the only sound in the kitchen was Hank ripping up the letter that had been hidden for a hundred years.

Ma was looking down at the table. Everything was quiet. Someone started to cry. For a moment Des couldn't figure out who it was. Then she wiped away her tears and got down on her knees so she could see her mother's face. "That's what you wanted me to give up Wellesley for, Ma," she wept. "That's what Hank is giving up his life for. That shit."

Hank made her go to bed. She assumed that he managed to get Ma to go to sleep too. But in the middle of the night, Des heard a noise in the garden. She ran to the darkened living room and looked out the window. Ma was in the garden in her nightgown bending over a fire. She was throwing something onto the flames. Something very familiar. Des turned and started to run to the front door of the apartment, but Hank was there, blocking her way.

"Go back to bed, Des," he said.

"Ma's down there burning her notebooks!" she said.

"Yes."

"I've got to stop her."

"No, you don't. You've done enough."

The next day Ma told the city council she didn't want the birthday celebration they were planning for her, and she'd changed her mind about the statue. Des went to Wellesley two weeks early and she didn't make any plans to come home for Thanksgiving. Somehow, after she left, Hank managed to pay for the plinth. He had the stagehands drag it to a corner of the garden where it was hidden by the hedge.

Part Five

CHAPTER 54

Massonville 2006

"Like I told you, I never did know what made Miss Olivia give up on her statue," Bill Killian said. "But after she did it, she never was the same. She turned the opera house over to Hank—all of it. Every time he tried to get her to help, she'd say she was too tired. It was like something had crushed her spirit.

"I went off to college. Des had already left. She wrote to me that she was worried about Hank. He'd wanted to run the opera house, but she said now his heart wasn't in it. He was still hung up on Rosalind, and Des thought if he could just see her again, and have her kick him in the teeth like before, maybe he'd get over her.

"But Hank was too busy to go anywhere that fall. It wasn't until I was home for Thanksgiving that he finally took off for Rosalind's house in Alabama.

"Rosalind wasn't there. And her grandma wouldn't tell Hank where she'd gone. He came back home worse off than he'd been when he left." Bill folded his napkin and put it beside his plate on the coffee table. For the first time since he'd started his saga, Randa had the feeling that he didn't want to say the part that was coming next.

"You've got to understand. Hank wasn't really a drinker," Bill said. "He was just unhappy and trying to make himself feel better. Sometimes he'd have a few at a honky-tonk he knew out on the highway. And one night I went with him." Bill paused again. Then he took the plunge. "When we got out of the bar, I knew Hank shouldn't be driving. I tried to stop him, but he got mad. I should have fought him for the car keys, but I felt guilty about him. So I got into the passenger's seat.

"The tree Hank ran into was on his side of the car. The highway patrol said they'd never seen a car get so smashed without being in a pileup. Hank died instantly. I broke both my legs—the left one was in four places—and my hip got messed up too. So, good-bye football scholarship. But to be honest, by the time I got out of the hospital I wasn't up for school—or much of anything.

"Miss Olivia sold the theater and went to live in an apartment outside Massonville. She stayed there until she got sick with heart trouble—that was about ten years later—and she died in the early eighties.

"After the accident, the doctors wanted to take my left leg, but I wouldn't let them. I had to use two canes and I hurt something awful, but I did get around, and I finally got myself a job at the post office. I was pissed off at the whole Venable family for what had happened to me, for a while, but then I met Mike's mother and she said she'd marry me. So it was hard for me to stay real mad about anything after that. Besides, Mary Alice—that was my wife—was mad enough for both of us. One night when my leg was hurting me real bad, she got into her car, drove over to the opera house, and shot out a window. It didn't do any real damage; the next day the caretaker just put in a new one, but I've got to admit it made me feel better." He laughed a little at the memory, and Mike joined in. They had both loved Mary Alice a lot.

"I finally let the docs amputate the leg and fix me up with a fake one. And I started using the tin lizzie here"—Bill patted the wheelchair—"so I wasn't in pain anymore. But Mary Alice never did forgive the Venables. She died five years ago—it was cancer—and right up to the end she was telling the nurses in the hospital that someone should tear down the opera house." He shook his head. "She was one fierce woman. The bad part was, Mike got to hear too much of all that."

"Mom didn't have to tell me the old theater needed to be torn down," his son grumbled.

"He's just like his mother—bullheaded." Bill smiled at Randa. "But if they love you—"

"Oh, for Pete's sake!" Mike cut in. His face was red under his tan.

"What happened to Des?" Randa asked.

"She stayed up north," Bill said. "She got a lot of degrees and wound up being an English professor—teaching Shakespeare, if you please."

"Did she ever get married?"

"She found herself a man who had three kids and didn't want any more. She wrote to me and said the good news was at least the goddamn glorious legacy wouldn't get passed on." He paused, then gave Randa a little smile. "Would you like some more wine?" he asked.

"Not if you want me to stay sober."

He's vamping for time again, Randa thought. *There's something else he doesn't want to say.* Then it clicked. "Why were you guilty about Hank?" she demanded. "You said that was why you got in the car with him."

Bill sighed. "He was unhappy, and I knew something that might have fixed that. But I didn't tell him."

"Rosalind was pregnant," Randa said.

Bill looked to Mike. "She's smart."

"Oh yes," said his son.

"Why didn't you tell Hank?" Randa asked.

"The night before Rosalind left Massonville, she came to my house to ask me to drive her to the bus station. That was when she told me. She didn't want Hank to know about the baby because he'd be hell-bent for election to keep her here, and she said she wasn't going to stay in some pissant little town where there was nothing for her—her words, not mine." He paused. "I guess the wonder is that, after Rosalind got successful, no one who was here that summer ever put it all together. I was the only one who knew, and I figured it was her secret, and she should be the one to tell it. Not me."

"So Katie is Hank Venable's daughter."

"Yeah."

"Her father wasn't killed in Vietnam."

"No, that happened right here in Massonville."

"And you never told anyone except Mike—and that was just a few days ago. "

"And I told Miss Olivia. When she was so sick at the end, I thought she had a right to know she had a grandbaby. She was in the hospital by then, and after I told her, she made me get her address book out of her purse and find a phone number. She wanted me to look up someone named Tassie— that's the name of a candy my mama used to like, so I've always remembered it. There wasn't any last name."

So that's how Tassie Rain knew about Katie. Olivia Venable told her.

"What about me?" Randa asked. "How do I fit in?"

"I don't know. I'm sorry."

So was Randa. She was surprised by how sorry she was.

Bill sniffed the air. "Lamb's done," he said. "Michael, take this pretty girl into the dining room."

Dinner was over. Bill had dusted off all offers of help with the cleanup, Randa had thanked him, and she and Mike were leaving. Bill saw them to the door. "I'm glad you're going to be keeping the opera house," he said. "I used to hate it, but now I think I'd miss the old place if it wasn't there."

At Randa's side, Mike shook his head.

"You really are a good son," Randa said as they were driving back to her hotel.

"What?"

"I kept wondering why you were so hot to tear down the opera house."

"It was good business."

"It was payback for Pop. The Venables took away your father's scholarship, so you were going to knock down their opera house. "

Mike swerved off the highway and stopped the car on the soft shoulder. He was staring straight ahead. . . . Okay, he was glaring.

I'm really making him angry. I should lay off.

Instead she said, "It didn't have to cost them all so much." And she realized she was talking to herself too. "They had choices. You don't have to cream your loved ones to get what you want."

"Pop didn't have a choice."

"Sure he did. And he knows it. That's why he's not angry anymore."

He was still staring ahead. His hands were gripping the steering wheel.
*After he throws me out of the car, I wonder if there's a way to call a cab from
out here.*

He turned to look at her. "I'm not sure how the hell I feel about you, Los
Angeles," he said.

She had to think about it for a while. "Back at you," she said.

He turned the key in the ignition and they drove back to the hotel in silence.

"It's the middle of the night, and I've been awake for four minutes." Katie's
voice on the phone was about an octave lower than normal. "So take it one
more time from the top. Slowly."

"Your father was named after Henry the Fifth," Randa said patiently,
"and your grandmother was the last statue out in the garden."

"I'm a Venable."

"Right."

"My mother, and this Henry person—"

"Most people called him Hank."

"Got it on during the summer of 1973, and I am the result. "

"That's it."

"There was no soldier who died tragically in Vietnam."

"No."

"I always knew there was something wrong with that story." There was a
pause. Then Katie said softly, "Poor Mother."

"It must have been hard, having to lie like that."

On the other end of the phone, Katie laughed. "Are you kidding? That
part was a piece of cake for Elsie Rose. But when Olivia said she didn't have
talent . . . That explains some things." She was quiet again.

"Katie? Are you still there?"

"Just processing. Trying to. It hasn't all sunk in yet—or would that be
sunken in? "

"It would probably help if you were awake."

"That too. When are you and Susie going back to L.A.?"

"We're flying out tomorrow afternoon to wind everything up. See you back in Georgia."

"Uh-huh," Katie said, and disconnected. Thirty seconds later, she called back.

"What about you?" she asked. "How do you fit into the dynasty?"

"Mike's father didn't know. There were a couple of Venable boys floating around who are still unaccounted for. Romeo Venable was one, and I think the other one was named Horatio."

"That could be hard to trace."

"Susie's been posting on a couple of websites that might help."

"If Susie's on the case, you've got it knocked. Night." For a second time the phone went dead.

But the marathon wasn't over. The next call was Randa's. "We're not going straight to L.A.," she told Katie fifteen minutes later. "Susie got an e-mail this evening and I just read it. This boy says his grandmother has been trying to find out about Richard Jennings for years. She's his sister. My aunt."

"You don't sound very excited."

"It's a long story. But I want to check this out. It's the only lead I've gotten. "

"Where are you going?"

"Louisville, Kentucky."

"Sounds very wholesome. Call me after you see your aunt."

CHAPTER 55

Louisville 2006

"Isn't the computer a marvel?" said the woman who greeted Randa and Susie at the door of her home. "I've been trying to get information about my brother for years. Then my grandson goes online, and here you are!" The house was on a wide, quiet street featuring deep front lawns, high hedges, and large trees. "Well heeled" was the phrase that came to mind—and not recently well heeled. This neighborhood had been established for some time.

The woman's name was Cressida. Aunt Cressida, although she'd asked Randa to please dispense with the "Aunt." She was somewhere in her fifties—tall, gray-haired, and with a full complement of laugh lines. She hugged like she really meant it, which was definitely not what Randa had been expecting.

So scratch the Evil Ice Queen image I've been carrying around for the past twenty years. But she still has some explaining to do for that night in Indiana.

Susie had already decided to like her. "So your name comes from the play *Troilus and Cressida*?" she asked.

"Gruesome, isn't it?" said Cressida. "You wouldn't believe what the other children did with it, when I was growing up."

"Try me," said Randa.

"Ah yes. You were hung with that idiotic woman/child from *The Tempest*. You'll have to blame my mother's people for that; torturing their children with Shakespearean names was a family tradition. Your father got off easily with Richard." There was the same lilt in her speech that Randa remembered from listening to her father. And she had a way of crinkling her nose when she smiled that Randa remembered too.

Okay, she seems nice. But there was still the prime rib dinner issue.

Cressida served them cookies and lemony iced tea. They sat at a table in a circular alcove at the back end of a large, bright kitchen. Floor-to-ceiling windows looked out over a pretty English garden. The chitchat phase of the visit passed quickly; Richard's death was touched on, and Susie's genius with the computer was praised. Finally the time had come to talk about the reason Randa and Susie had flown to Louisville.

Cressida began. "You want to know about Richard." She fixed her gaze on the garden outside. "It all started with our parents. My mother and father never should have married." It was clear she'd thought about this a lot. "Mother was artistic. She loved music, and museums, and the theater . . . especially the theater. That was her real passion. She read all of Shakespeare's plays to us when we were children, and she had a Shakespearean quote for every occasion. It used to annoy Father no end.

"My father wasn't a bad person; he was just a man of his day. He expected his wife to care for the children and run his home efficiently." Cressida laughed softly. "Mother never did anything efficiently in her life.

"Things deteriorated when she started spending her time at the community theater. If she'd limited her cultural interests to things Father could understand, like charity work for the symphony, I don't think he would have resented it. But she was acting in plays with an amateur drama group, and most of the people involved were long-haired Communists as far as he was concerned. He forced her to stop. That was when she really . . ." Cressida turned to Randa. "How much did Richard tell you about her?"

"Nothing," Randa said. "He wouldn't talk about any of you."

Cressida looked back at the garden. "Mother drank. I think she had always had a cocktail or two, even when she and Father were first married. But as she became more and more unhappy . . ." Cressida stopped again and looked at Susie. "Perhaps Susan would rather go into the family room and watch television? Or she can use my computer—"

"You can say anything in front of Susie. We talk about everything."

"Our family should have done more talking." Cressida's hands were clasped so tightly the knuckles were white. "When Richard was fifteen and I was thirteen, Mother committed suicide. Richard blamed Father for it. Richard and Mother were so much alike—and he adored her. I always understood how difficult it must have been for Father, being married to a woman like Mother, but as far as Richard was concerned, Father was a bully who drove her to her death." Cressida smiled sadly. "Sounds very Shakespearean, doesn't it? 'Full of sound and fury, / Signifying nothing.'

"Father remarried and Richard loathed his new wife. Richard met a girl—your mother—and Father loathed *her*. Then Richard announced that he was going to leave business school and become an actor. I never could decide if he did it as a way of slapping Father in the face, or if he was trying somehow to be loyal to Mother."

Randa remembered her father standing on an empty stage and saying there was no place like it in the world. "He did it because he loved it," she said.

"I'm glad to hear that," said Cressida. "Father cut Richard off, and Richard responded in true Elizabethan style by cutting all of us out of his life. I didn't know when he was married or when you were born. I never knew that his wife had died and he was raising you alone. I wish I had."

So do I, Randa thought, in spite of herself.

Cressida sat back in her chair. "I don't know what else I can tell you."

"We'd like to hear about your . . . our family," Susie said. "The history. Like, what part of the country they came from, and how long they've lived here."

"I believe the Jenningses moved to Louisville from the East Coast sometime in the late 1930s. The Honeycutts were originally from the south and they've been here since the 1870s."

Susie almost dropped her iced tea. Fortunately, Randa wasn't holding anything. "Your mother's maiden name was Honeycutt?" she asked carefully. "Not Venable?"

"No. I've never heard of any branch of the family called Venable. The Honeycutts owned an old opera house in the South, but they sold it sometime after the Civil War. That's how you and I got saddled with the names Cressida and Miranda. The company of actors who bought the theater named their children after Shakespearean characters. Cornelia Honeycutt, our ancestress and clearly a sadist, was so charmed by the idea that she took it over for her own family, and, God help us, we've been doing it ever since."

Randa's heart was beating hard now. "Was the opera house in Massonville, Georgia?" Randa asked.

"I'm not sure of the town," Cressida said. "But Georgia rings a bell. The one who would have known was Richard. He did a lot of research into Mother's family. I think he even went to see that old theater once."

CHAPTER 56

Massonville 1974

The hot sunshine seemed to bounce between the white front of the Venable Opera House and the surface of the river that ran in front of it. Honeysuckle grew along the sides of the sweeping drive up to the theater entrance, and Richard opened the car window so he could smell the scent as he drove. He'd left Louisville early the day before, but his car was old, and by the time he'd reached Georgia it was too late to see anything. So he'd stayed overnight in a motel outside the town called Massonville, which was where the opera house was.

Lois, the girl who was going to be his wife, had refused to come with him. They planned to be married as soon as they were in New York, and she had wanted to get there right away. She was afraid he was going to back out because she wasn't what his bitch of a stepmother called "our kind." What Lois didn't understand was, his stepmother's disapproval was one of the best reasons Richard could think of *to* get married. Besides, he didn't want to take on New York alone. Lois loved him and she believed in him and he needed that. But first, he wanted to see the old theater that was once owned by the Honeycutts—his mother's side of the family.

He stopped the car at the front entrance and got out. Above him was a

canopy with the words THE VENABLE OPERA HOUSE printed in gold lettering. He stepped back to see the front of the old theater with all its curlicues,
balconies, and rows of windows. The building was four stories high, which
seemed awfully tall, but he hadn't seen that many professional theaters.

He knocked on the front door but no one answered. There were several
large windows in the front, all covered with heavy curtains. Closer inspec-
tion revealed that they were locked from the inside. The theater was closed
up. He told himself he should just cut his losses and drive on to New York.
But then he thought about all the fighting with Lois about coming here, and
the long, bad drive in his junk heap of a car.

There has to be a door or a window I can break open, he thought. Then,
Are you crazy? People go to jail for that.

He'd brought his mother's flask with him—it was an old Honeycutt
artifact, and it had seemed right to take it on this journey. Richard usually
didn't drink until happy hour, but right now he needed to clear his head. He
took a quick swig. That was when he saw the curtain move in one of the big
windows. He was being watched! Visions from the movie *Deliverance*
rushed through his head.

Cool it. It was probably a breeze. But there was no wind blowing and the
curtain was behind a locked window.

Wondering what to do next, he looked around. There was a glint of
something shiny behind the hedge on the side of the theater. He began
walking toward it, and saw that it was the chrome bumper of a car. So someone really was in the theater. And whoever it was didn't want anyone to
know they were there.

That does it. I'm leaving.

He was opening his car door when a voice from behind him said, "You
do know you're trespassing, right?" He whirled around, half expecting a
banjo-playing chinless mutant. The tiny woman who was staring at him in
the sunshine looked to be around sixty, with died blond hair, prominent
teeth, and huge blue eyes.

"You're not going to pass out, are you? Or be sick?" the Lilliputian demanded.

"No," he managed. But he took another swig from the flask just to keep
the blood flowing.

"Good boy. Come inside." She gave a quick look up and down the empty highway. She really didn't want to be seen. "Let's go," she urged. Richard hesitated. She didn't seem deranged, but clearly, there was something wrong with her.

"I'm not going to hurt you!" she said. "Look at me, for heaven's sake. What could I do? Attack your ankles?"

"It's just . . . Do you have the owner's permission?"

"I am the owner, kiddo. I have the key to the front door." She held it up. "See?"

Richard stole a glance at the car behind the hedge.

"Yeah, you're right, I hid it. No one knows I'm here." He must have been looking doubtful, because she added, "I bought this place because a friend asked me to, but I don't intend to hang around. This is the first time I've been here and I've owned the theater for a year. If there are any problems, I want people to get in the habit of calling the caretaker instead of trying to find me. You understand?"

He didn't. In fact, what she'd just said didn't make any sense to him. But she seemed harmless—and she was offering him a chance to go inside the theater. He followed her to the front door. "I'm Richard," he offered.

"Tassie," she said as she fiddled with the old lock. "To what do I owe the pleasure of your company?"

"My people built this place."

She straightened up to stare at him. "You're a Honeycutt? Yeah, I know the name. Don't look so stunned, kiddo. The history of this theater is a matter of public record. The Honeycutts built it, the Venables hung on to it for ninety-five years, and now—there's me." She opened the door and ushered him into a lobby that was so ornate it made the outside of the building seem austere. "Welcome to the home of your forebears," she said. "Now tell me about yourself."

They sat on an old ottoman in the middle of the lobby and he told Tassie more than he had ever told anyone, including Lois. The tiny woman had a way of listening that seemed to loosen his tongue. Or maybe it was just that the whole situation seemed so unreal that there was no reason to hold back.

After he'd confided all his hopes and dreams, his new friend gave him a tour of the opera house. For two hours they went through the building and the grounds, until his mind was a whirl of chandeliers, sconces, marble mantelpieces, wainscoting, dressing rooms, hotel rooms, old statues, and a restaurant that looked like the set for Thornton Wilder's *The Matchmaker*.

When he thought he couldn't absorb any more, Tassie said, "I've saved the best for last," and led him out onto the stage.

He had never been on a professional stage before; his acting experience had been limited to college productions in the American Legion auditorium. Nothing had prepared him for this. In front of him were balconies, private boxes, and rows of seats as far as he could see. Under his feet was a wooden stage floor worn smooth by the actors who had worked on it for decades. And there was something else. . . . He sniffed the air.

"Yeah, it's that old backstage smell," said his companion. "Nothing like it in the whole damn world." She was watching him intently. "What do you think?"

"I'd like to kill the moron in my family who sold this place."

She laughed.

"I mean it," he told her. "Someday when I'm rich and famous, I'm going to come back here and buy this from you."

"I'll remember that, Richard," said Tassie.

She walked him to the front entrance of the theater. "So you're going to New York, to be a star on Broadway," she said. There was something sad in her eyes.

"You bet," he said.

She reached up to stroke his cheek. "Break a leg, kiddo." She opened the door for him. "But a word of advice?"

"Sure."

"Watch the sauce—it's done in more theater people than I can count."

CHAPTER 57

Louisville 2006

It was time to leave. Randa and Susie had told Cressida about the opera house and the Honeycutt connection, which had made Cressida cry a little.

"For Richard," she'd explained. "And Mother."

Randa had promised they would come back to Louisville for the next big family gathering. There was more catching up for them to do, they all agreed—years of it—but for the moment they were all talked out. Even Susie had had it. Besides, Randa and Susie had a plane to catch. Cressida walked them out to their rental car with advice about highway traffic and the best route to the airport, and kissed them both good-bye. But suddenly, Randa realized she couldn't leave. Not yet.

"Cressida, when I was a kid . . ."

Her mouth was dry. *Why is this so hard? It happened a million years ago.*

She stumbled on. "My father was on the road with a play . . ." She ran out of steam again.

"Yes," her aunt said carefully. "*Barefoot in the Park.* It was given in a dinner theater in Indianapolis. My family and I were supposed to see it."

Just let it go. It doesn't matter anymore.

"Why didn't you come?"

"We did, dear. We drove over to Indianapolis with both of the children. But Richard had given me the wrong date. We were a week late."

Oh God.

"I should have checked with the box office, but I was so excited to hear from him, you see." Cressida's eyes were starting to fill up again. "I should have known . . ."

I should have too. All those years, I should have known.

"We tried phoning the company in New York that produced the play to find out where you were going next. We thought we might catch you. But they said Richard wasn't working in the show anymore. They did have a home phone number for him, and we tried to call it . . ."

"But we had moved," Randa finished for her.

"I probably could have tried harder to find him, but I didn't want to seem like I was pressuring him, you know? I thought when he didn't call me, that maybe he was embarrassed because he'd made a mistake in the date. Or maybe it hadn't been a mistake, and he'd changed his mind about seeing me . . ." She trailed off.

"He hadn't," Randa said softly. "Really."

Her aunt looked at her for a long moment. "I'm sorry, Randa. It must have been so hard on you back then."

"Thank you for coming to the play," Randa said.

CHAPTER 58

New York City 2006

"Katie?"

Katie looked at the clock. "Randa, it's five in the morning," she mumbled.

"Sorry. Here's the thing, I'm a Honeycutt."

"Oh my God."

"I have cousins. And I gather there are many second cousins. Susie and I are going to meet them at Thanksgiving. I think everyone brings food, but I don't cook."

"No one will expect you to tote a casserole on an airplane. . . . So you and I aren't related."

"No. Susie was disappointed; she was hoping Romeo Venable had had a love child. I probably shouldn't have let her read *Anna Karenina*. Anyway, I just wanted you to know."

Katie felt herself smiling. "Okay."

"Katie?"

"Still here."

"I've been thinking about Des and Hank and their mother. It doesn't sound like hanging on to the opera house made any of them happy."

"Maybe that's our gig. To hang on to the old place and be happy."

"Does it bother you that we don't even know what we're going to do with it?"

"I figure it will come to us."

"From your mouth to God's ear," Randa said.

"Randa's a Honeycutt? I like that; it has symmetry," R.B. said when Katie phoned him from New York. They had slipped into the habit of calling each other twice a day.

"It's either symmetry or Tassie Rain had a sick sense of humor. You realize I'm the fifth generation of my family to get sucked into that opera house?"

"It is an old charmer."

"R.B., what the hell are we going to do with it?"

"What do you want to do?"

"If I didn't have to be an adult, I'd try to run it as a repertory theater."

"That would make the ghosts of your foremothers happy."

"Randa would never go for it."

"Mike, it's Randa Jennings."

"Where are you?"

"L.A. But I had an offer on my house today and Katie's closing on her co-op in a week. We'd like to start the repairs on the opera house by the end of the summer, but we don't know anyone in the construction business in Massonville. Could you give me a few names?"

"How about MK Construction?"

"You?"

"I do restoration work."

"You do realize we're discussing the old rattrap that's useless to everyone but a bunch of bullshit snobs?"

"Yeah. But my pop thinks you're cute. He wants to cook for you again."

"How's his Thai fusion?"

"He took a course last summer. How do you think I knew what it was?"

"I'll talk to Katie about MK Construction."

"I can tell you right now, the stage area is going to run you the most."

"We won't be using that stage."

"Sure you will. That's why you're moving here, Los Angeles."

CHAPTER 59

Massonville 2007

Susie folded the old afghan and spread it over the foot of her bed. She'd found it downstairs in the office under the family apartment, and Mom and Katie had said she could have it.

Susie, Katie, and Mom were all living in the apartment. Katie had been there first because her co-op had sold before the Puke Carpet Palace had. Before Mom had moved in, she'd been a little freaked about all three of them sharing the place, but the way it worked out, Katie spent almost all her free time with R.B., so they really didn't get in one another's way. Besides, when bad stuff happened, like the bathroom pipes bursting and messing up the old office downstairs, Katie could come up with something that made them all laugh. Even so, Susie was sure she'd be moving in with R.B. soon. He was always going, "If you'd let me make an honest woman of you, you could stop writing scripts for that soap opera and begin the great American novel." That was lame, since Katie had already started her novel, but she seemed to like hearing him say it anyway.

All of Mom's clients had quit when she told them she was leaving L.A., except the Lindsay Lohan clone, who'd said, "I totally couldn't fire you,

Randa. You're like my mother—only I never had to do an intervention for you." Since her sitcom had just been picked up for another season, Mom wasn't stressing about money for them to live on.

Susie smoothed a couple of wrinkles out of the afghan, and stepped back to admire it. Katie said it was probably a hundred years old, and it was kind of faded. But it was still beautiful.

It had taken Susie's mother and Katie almost a year to decide that they were going to try to have a theater company in the old opera house. Susie had always known that was what they should do, but still, it was awesome that they'd finally gotten it. And Susie knew they wouldn't have, if it hadn't been for the Fates. Susie was big on the Fates these days. She and her best friend at her new school, Ana Alicia, had gotten totally into Roman and Greek mythology, and the Fates were all over the stories. The Greeks called them the Moirai and the Romans called them the Parcae, but they were really the same thing. And if you looked at the old Norse legends, they had the Norns. So it seemed as if there were a lot of cultures that had believed there were goddesses who stepped in to make sure humans did what they were supposed to do. When she'd text-messaged Jen about it, she agreed that they should keep their minds open about the idea.

Ana Alicia, Jen, and Susie all agreed that the Fates thing was a good explanation for how Mom and Katie figured out what to do with the opera house. Because otherwise, when you thought about the way it happened, it was a little too weird.

Mom and Katie had been using the money they'd gotten from selling Katie's co-op and the Puke Carpet Palace to pay for fixing the opera house. The stage needed work, and they had decided to renovate it, even though they both kept saying that having a theater company would be too crazy. They were talking about making the opera house into a tourist attraction. Mom said maybe they could rent it out for weddings the way Olivia Venable used to do.

Then the Fates got going. First, R.B. handed them a list of philanthropic groups in Georgia that gave money to the arts. A couple of days later, Mom decided to clean out a funky little desk in her bedroom, and she found an old envelope with a bunch of newspaper clippings in it. They were all stories about some woman named Myrtis Garrison who used to go around fixing up old theaters in 1952.

"Isn't there a Myrtis Garrison on R.B.'s list?" Mom called out to Katie.

Katie started going over it. "Here's something called the Garrison Trust."

Mom showed her the newspaper articles and they found a phone number written on the envelope. When they checked it against the phone number for the Garrison Trust on R.B.'s list, they found an area code that hadn't existed back in 1952, but the rest of the number was the same.

"It looks like the Venables had some kind of history with this Myrtis Garrison," Mom said.

Katie was reading one of the articles. "If they did, the woman is in her eighties by now." She picked up the envelope and looked at the phone number. "We could call. What do we have to lose?"

Mom started dialing. "I'll probably get a voice mail." But then she stopped. "What do we want? What's our mission statement?"

"We're having the opera house placed on the registry of historic landmarks, and we're thinking of making it into an attraction for students and history buffs and—" Katie stopped. She and Mom looked at each other. Susie tried not to move so she wouldn't distract them and interfere with the Fates. Finally Katie pulled herself up very straight and said, "But that's not what we want to do with this place."

"No," Mom said. "It's not."

Mom dialed the phone number. She didn't get a voice mail; a woman answered. She said Mom couldn't talk to Myrtis Garrison because she'd died a long time ago, but the woman asked if she could help them. She said she was the one who ran the Garrison Trust now. Mom crossed her fingers and said she and Katie were exploring the possibility of establishing a not-for-profit regional theater. Mom made it sound official, like she knew what she was talking about, which was something she was very good at when she didn't have a clue. The trust woman said she'd like to see their figures and the business plan. Mom said they'd get the information to her in a week.

"We don't have figures, or a business plan," Katie said after Mom hung up. Katie looked kind of sick.

"By next week we will," Mom said. She loved pulling off stuff like that. "Besides, if this organization has fifteen cents to give anyone, I'll be stunned."

"R.B. said all the groups on the list were heavy hitters."

"The woman who has the deciding vote for this trust—we're talking the whole enchilada—answers her own phone, okay? She just told me they have only one lawyer on staff. She asked me to call her Laurel Selene. I don't think we're dealing with the Getty Foundation."

"Laurel Selene is a pistol," R.B. said when they told him about it later. "She does things her own way, and she's not fancy, but don't let that fool you. If she believes in something, she'll go to the wall for it. She's helped us with restoration projects all over the state. "

Mom and Katie spent about six months faxing and e-mailing and phoning back and forth with the woman named Laurel Selene. After the first week, Mom stopped saying how unbusinesslike the whole setup was, and started talking about how great it was to work with people who could actually get things done. Laurel Selene, Mom, and Katie finally came up with a plan that was so awesome Susie knew it must have come from the Fates.

The Garrison Trust already gave money to three state colleges in Georgia that had theater arts and music programs. Laurel Selene said they'd make the opera house a part of the school system. Mom and Katie would produce six professional plays a year, and the college kids would spend a semester at the opera house so they could get experience working at a real theater. Also, kids from a culinary school outside Atlanta would come in to work at the restaurant. They'd all live in the old hotel rooms in the opera house. That meant the schools would pay the opera house, and there would be a grant from the Garrison Trust too. They also had the inheritance Tassie Rain had left them.

It sounded like a lot of money to Susie, but when her mother ran the numbers, she said they'd still have to cut two shows. That was going to mess up everything because then they wouldn't have a fourth semester for the students and the schools would have to pull out. For a couple of weeks everyone was really down, but like R.B. said, when Laurel Selene wanted something, she made it happen. She found a rich lady to underwrite the last two productions. But the productions weren't going to be plays. For the last semester of the year, the kids coming to the opera house would be music students. The theater was going to produce two operas. When Ana Alicia heard about it, she said her dad really liked Plácido Domingo a lot. Jen said no matter what opera sounded like, Susie should be right-brained and open-minded.

The theater was back on track. But Mom and Katie still hadn't met Laurel face-to-face.

Laurel Selene had been thinking about that too. "I think it's time we all knew who we've been talking to," she said to Mom on the phone. "Can you come here to Charles Valley?"

CHAPTER 60

Charles Valley 2007

Laurel had told Mom and Katie she'd meet them at the house of a friend of hers. She called the friend Li'l Bit, which Susie loved because it was so Harper Lee. R.B. had volunteered to drive them there. "I've never been to Charles Valley," he'd said. "Usually when you work with Laurel Selene, she comes to wherever you are."

"The trip from Massonville to Charles Valley should take you about four hours," Laurel Selene had told Mom on the phone. "It's easy to find Li'l Bit's place. It's on a pie-shaped wedge of land in the middle of Highway 22 about twenty minutes outside of town. The house will be way back from the road and it'll kind of pop up from out of nowhere. Just make sure you don't miss it behind the magnolia trees."

It was a good thing she'd said that, because the house did appear from out of nowhere, and they would have missed it otherwise. R.B. turned up a gravel drive that had pine trees and flowers along the sides. The house was big and white with dark green shutters, and a wide porch that wrapped around it on three sides. On the porch were a swing, a large wooden chair that looked like it had been made for a guy, and a girly rocker made out of wicker that was all loopy and lacy, with a flowered cushion for a seat.

There were three women on the porch; one was sitting in the guy chair, one was on the swing, and the third was leaning against the porch railing. She had red hair pulled back in a ponytail and she was waving to them.

R.B. stopped the car, and as Susie, her mom, and Katie started walking toward the house, the red-haired woman came down the steps to greet them. She wasn't pretty exactly but Susie liked her looks. Her face was round, and she had round, brown eyes, and a mouth that was kind of round too. She was probably a few years older than Susie's mom, but she didn't have any makeup on, so she looked younger. She was wearing cowboy boots, a T-shirt, and jeans, and she was pregnant. "Hey," she said. "I'm Laurel Selene."

Everybody shook hands with Laurel Selene, and the two women on the porch stood up so she could introduce them. "This is Miss Li'l Bit." She gestured to the woman who had been sitting in the guy chair. Miss Li'l Bit was tall—not fat, but really big—and her gray hair was flying around her face. She was old enough to be Laurel Selene's grandmother, and she'd probably never been good-looking, even when she was a girl. She had kind eyes, Susie thought.

Miss L'il Bit stuck out her hand, and said, "How do you do?" Her voice was high and it sounded hooty.

Then the woman in the swing came over. She was as tiny as Miss Li'l Bit was big, and even older. But you could see that she must have been really pretty when she was young. She still was pretty in an old-lady way.

"This is Dr. Maggie," Laurel Selene said.

"Maggie, please," she said. Her voice was so low it kind of rumbled, which was strange coming from someone who was so small.

They went up onto the porch, and from inside the house, a dog started barking. "Petula, either go out or come in," said a man's voice. The door to the house opened and a guy wearing a doctor's coat over blue jeans came out carrying a chair. He was very cute.

"I don't need that," said Laurel Selene.

"Yeah, you do," he said. "You can't sit on the stoop anymore. By now you need a crane to haul you to your feet."

She gave him a dirty look, but she let him settle her in the chair. "This is my husband," she said. "Dr. Perry Douglass."

He told them to call him Perry, and they all did the introducing thing again. Then Perry said he guessed they needed more chairs, and R.B. said let him help get them, and Miss Li'l Bit's dog, Petula, who had to be a hundred years old, came outside and lay down near Susie's chair, which was awesome because then Susie could pet her. Miss Li'l Bit said they must want something cool to drink, and she brought out iced tea, lemonade, Cokes, and a glass of milk for Laurel Selene. Then she and Dr. Maggie started telling them about the Garrison Trust, which was connected to something called the Garrison Gardens and the Garrison Gardens resort.

"Garrison Gardens is one of the premier horticultural attractions in the United States," said Miss Li'L Bit with her high voice. "We have visitors from all over the world coming here to see our azaleas in the springtime. Of course it's strictly nonprofit."

"And then there's the resort." Maggie said in her low voice. "Which is strictly for-profit. Although a few years ago, it was not in good shape financially. And the gardens were doing poorly too. Laurel Selene turned all of that around when she took over."

"Laurel Selene has worked wonders," Miss L'il Bit hooted. She and Maggie talked as though they were finishing each other's thoughts. First you'd get the high voice, then the low one—it was like listening to a flute and cello.

"These people didn't come all this way to hear this," Laurel Selene broke in, but she didn't sound like she thought she could stop them.

"They are going to be working with you," said the high voice.

"They should know how clever you are, Dear One" added the low.

"Absolutely, Dear One," her husband said, grinning at her.

"You see, this is a rural community, and the people here depend on the Garrison enterprises for their livelihood. I'm afraid in the past those in charge have taken advantage of that fact," Maggie rumbled.

"But Laurel has proven that you don't have to exploit your employees to be successful," Li'l Bit said. Then she added, "Laurel Selene very much reminds one of dear Mrs. Roosevelt."

That made Laurel Selene's husband laugh, but Laurel Selene said, "If we're going to hand out bouquets, Randa and Katie should know L'il Bit is the one who will be underwriting the last two productions for the theater."

So Mom and Katie thanked her a lot and Miss Li'l Bit blushed bright red and said she'd always loved opera, and she wasn't doing all that much, and she didn't know why Laurel Selene had even bothered to mention it. And Mom and Katie talked about how glad they were that they had made that phone call to Laurel Selene at the Garrison Trust and how they almost hadn't done it, but they'd figured there had to be some reason why they found all those newspaper clippings about Myrtis Garrison.

Susie thought about telling them about the Fates, but decided they might not be quite right-brain enough.

R.B. asked if anyone knew if Miss Myrtis had donated money to the Venable Opera House in the old days. No one did know for sure, although Maggie remembered that Miss Myrtis had said once that the theater was America's greatest melting pot. Then Dr. Douglass had to get back to the clinic he ran with Dr. Maggie down by the old railroad station, and R.B. wanted to see it, so he went to follow in his car. After they were gone, Miss Li'l Bit asked if she could give anyone a refill on their drinks, and Laurel Selene looked at her glass of milk with a sigh and said, "I'd kill for a nice cold beer."

"Not for a while, Dear One" said the low voice.

"She's having twins," the high voice confided.

"Two girls."

"Tell them the names, Laurel Selene."

"Sara Jayne and Margaret," Laurel said. "Sara Jayne is for my mother and Margaret will be called Peggy." And Laurel Selene, Miss L'il Bit, and Dr. Maggie all turned to look at the wicker rocker that no one had sat in all afternoon.

CHAPTER 61

Massonville 2007

It was really late by the time they drove up to the opera house, but Mom said they could take Susie's new puppy for a walk in the garden before they went inside. The way the dog thing had happened was, Miss Li'l Bit had noticed Susie petting Petula, and she'd asked if Susie had a dog of her own. When Susie told her she didn't, Laurel Selene said they had one puppy left from a litter that had been born at the Peggy Garrison Shelter for Animals, if Susie would like it. Susie told herself she would understand if her Mom said no. Between moving from L.A. and living in the opera house and having a professional theater, Mom was already being more open-minded and right-brain than Susie ever thought she could be. A puppy might be too much for her. But Mom had said yes. Which was even more proof that the Fates were working—if Susie had needed it.

Katie, Susie, Mom, and the puppy walked through the gate into the garden. The newly cleaned statues of Juliet, Edward, and Olivia were white in the moonlight. The empty pedestal was visible now that Mom and Katie had removed all the brush from around it. "It'll be a nice picture for the school brochures," Mom had said. "You know, 'What is the mystery of the opera house garden?' " Mom was really into marketing the theater. Now she and Katie looked up at the statues.

"I bet they could tell a lot of stories," Katie said.

"Or we could make up our own," Mom said.

Katie nodded. The puppy pulled on his new leash. "Come on, King Lear," Susie said, and she ran with him through the garden in the moonlight.

Acknowledgments

For me, one of the happiest parts of the publishing process is the moment when I get to sit back and reflect on all the people who have given me so much during the time—the scary, funny, and totally rewarding time—that it takes me to write a book. I keep saying over and over again how lucky I am—and I have to say it again this time because it is so true. So thank you to Eric Simonoff, my amazing agent/friend, who is one of the biggest gifts I've ever gotten from the universe. Thank you to Gina Centrello, who allows me to continue doing this thing I love so much. Thanks to Laura Ford, who has been my friend and is now my editor, for stepping in and giving *Family Acts* such a thoughtful and amazing edit. Thanks to Libby McGuire—support like hers is rare and I am grateful from the heart. Thank you to the people who somehow manage to break through all the noise and distractions and get word of my books out there: Brian McLendon, Carol Schneider, Lisa Barnes, and Tom Perry. Thanks to Robbin Schiff for a brilliant cover, to Dana Blanchette for an equally beautiful interior design, to Dennis Ambrose for being so kind and patient, and to Bara MacNeill for a copyedit that saved me time and again from my own ignorance and dicey grasp of grammar. Thank you to Cecile Barendsma, who gets my books into the world.

Thank you to Gerry Waggett for the title we all love, as well as the research and hand-holding that get me through. Thank you to Cynthia Burkett for databases, references, recipe cards, research, and for being a sounding board of never-ending enthusiasm—but most of all for teaching me the unbelievable value of her kind of Rock of Gibraltar friendship. Thank you to Melissa Salmon, who gives me the present of her incredible talent every time we talk. Thanks to Charlie Masson, who is always there, and to Betsy Gilbert, who can always come up with a way to laugh. Thank you to Richard Simms, the genius blogger, and to Keven Haberl and Wil Perdue.

For information, education, wisdom, and advice, thank you to the following: Karen Lewis who handed me a library of treasures in a duffel bag, Rob Shaffer, consultant on kidspeak and thought; Marguerite Wood; Ruth Carpenter Pitts; Greg Miller; Sandra Okamoto; the Rev. Douglas Carpenter; the staff of the East Fishkill Library, especially Cindy Dubinsky and Carol Swierat.

For inspiration: thank you to my beloved godmother and aunt, Virginia Piccolo; Phyllis Piccolo; Mary Minnella; and Jessie O'Neil—may you all live forever. Please. Thank you to friends extraordinaire Barbara and Margaret Long, Ellie Quester, Kenya Shuchat, and Erin Clark. Special thanks to Kathy Patrick, the Pulpwood Queen—with her in my corner I can't go wrong. And of course, a huge thanks to the guys who are the glue of my life, my stepsons, Colin and Christopher Crews, and to the incomparable and gorgeous Annalisa.

And finally a hail and farewell to one of the first on my list of grand southern women who made me want to write, Margaret Garret, also known as Miss Little Sister.

ABOUT THE AUTHOR

LOUISE SHAFFER, the author of *The Three Miss Margarets* and *The Ladies of Garrison Gardens,* is a graduate of Yale School of Drama, has written for television, and has appeared on Broadway, in TV movies, and in daytime dramas, earning an Emmy for her work on *Ryan's Hope.* Shaffer and her husband live in the Lower Hudson Valley.

ABOUT THE TYPE

This book was set in Fairfield, the first typeface from the hand of the distinguished American artist and engraver Rudolph Ruzicka (1883–1978). Ruzicka was born in Bohemia and came to America in 1894. He set up his own shop, devoted to wood engraving and printing, in New York in 1913 after a varied career working as a wood engraver, in photoengraving and banknote printing plants, and as an art director and freelance artist. He designed and illustrated many books, and was the creator of a considerable list of individual prints—wood engravings, line engravings on copper, and aquatints.